DREAD AND BREAKFAST

Of my twelve novels, this one is my favorite. Wanted to share it with you.

Ron Ober

DREAD AND BREAKFAST

Don Otey

Copyright © 2005 by Don Otey.

Library of Congress Number: 2004099647
ISBN : Hardcover 1-4134-7315-6
        Softcover 1-4134-7314-8

All rights reserved. No part of this book may be reproduced or transmitted in any form or by any means, electronic or mechanical, including photocopying, recording, or by any information storage and retrieval system, without permission in writing from the copyright owner.

This is a work of fiction. Names, characters, places and incidents either are the product of the author's imagination or are used fictitiously, and any resemblance to any actual persons, living or dead, events, or locales is entirely coincidental.

This book was printed in the United States of America.

To order additional copies of this book, contact:
Xlibris Corporation
1-888-795-4274
www.Xlibris.com
Orders@Xlibris.com

26476

This story is dedicated to my darling Jo Ellen, my life's companion and the mother of our three beautiful children. It is also written for Don, Bob, and Debbie. I am immensely proud of all of them.

CHAPTER 1

"*B*rakes, Greg!"

The urgent voice jarred me awake, and I stomped on the brake pedal. Missed by inches adding a full size deer to my car hood. The buck bounded off into the trees as my car slid to a halt. I sat back and tried to calm my nerves.

Looked up at the rear view mirror. Nothing there but my gray eyes staring back wide with fright. The strange voice in my head was closer, plainer than ever, and I had no idea where it was coming from.

Oh, please, I pled silently, *don't let me go over the edge now. Not after all I've been through and survived. Two precious ladies are depending on me to keep it together. Can't let them down. Have to hang in and tough it out.*

My trip should have been a routine visit to my West Virginia clients. Maybe a chance to scare up some new business. But it was turning out to be a lot more than that. Hadn't had a good night's sleep all week. Weird thoughts pounded in my skull. Dad had spun off into his own world and it took him from us. Could it have been the same tormenter? Was I next?

No. Greg Bain was as sane as the next guy. *At least, that's what I wanted to believe.*

Then why did that haunting voice convince me to take a side trip? What was I doing on State Road 39 outside Richwood when I'd never been there in my life. Normally, the rugged beauty of the West Virginia hills would have taken my mind off my troubles—but not today. The weather outside was October, gray and cold, the sort of day when topping the next rise in the road could bring a whole new adventure in instant weather change—rain, sleet, snow, you name it.

Why had the voice chosen me to harass? The words were spoken in a calm, soft manner, almost a fatherly tone. But every time I started to think clearly, the voice returned and brought new doubts. It was the voice that had steered me onto the back road and nudged me on. Didn't have a clue why the urge to follow its advice was so compelling.

One thing was certain, though. If I dallied too long in the hills, I'd be in big trouble at home. Sarah had told me to be home by Friday night without fail. Couldn't disappoint my wife. Her exact words were *You need to be here, Greg, please. There's something important we have to discuss.* That was good enough for me. Sarah was the reason I was still alive after some difficult times. I owed her everything.

Well, no reason I shouldn't be home on schedule. Only Thursday morning with stops to make in Lewisburg and White Sulphur Springs. Then over to New Castle and down to Roanoke, back home to Sarah. Time to relax and enjoy the peace and quiet of the mountains that circled me. Even on a cold, dreary day, the West Virginia hills still seemed like home. Brought back wonderful memories of my college days not far up the road. Life was so simple then. All that mattered was being with Sarah, the girl who had captured my heart the very day we met. And playing basketball, of course. That was to be my career after graduation.

* * *

A fog came rolling in and chased the remaining sunlight into hiding. Suddenly I felt cold and alone. Spotted a diner up ahead. An old neon sign flickered on and off through the growing mid-day darkness. Richwood Diner. The voice returned, its words rustling in my ear.

Take a break, Greg. You'll be happy you stopped.

The gentle prompter was all the encouragement I needed to interrupt what had become a nerve—wracking drive. Not exactly a five-star restaurant, but I could hope for coffee that was strong and plentiful. Maybe someone could help me with directions to get me back on schedule, too.

Stared up at a sky that was rapidly worsening, turning a sickly murk-filled gray. Felt like a heavy, syrupy haze was clinging to my surroundings; a tangible sense of unrest, even foreboding, tugged at me. I shivered involuntarily, and hurried inside out of the suddenly chill air. Slid into a booth. A slightly plump waitress with a starched uniform and a wide smile swished over with her pad and pencil ready.

"What can I get for you, sweetie?" she managed between gnashes on her chewing gum.

"Coffee, please," I managed, my nerves still a bit edgy.

She stood there staring like she should know me, but that didn't seem possible since Richwood was new territory to me. Certainly wouldn't describe myself as eye-stopping handsome. Shade under six feet, short brown hair and gray eyes, 175 pounds. But her look was almost one of shock. Like to think I'm not that ugly, either! She could be a basketball fan. I still get that look sometimes from fans that saw me play up at Elkins College. After all, I was something of a flash back then.

"How 'bout somethin' with that java, sugar? Got some fresh meat loaf and mashed taters on the dinner menu."

Guess I was still distracted. Had to reset my internal clock. My wristwatch showed a few minutes after noon, and she was talking dinner? No matter how often I came to West Virginia, I never quite adjusted. Out here it's not lunch and dinner. After breakfast you have dinner and supper in that order. Right now it was time for *dinner at the diner.*

"Talked me into it," I answered. Amazing what a little encouragement will do. Her slump and slog morphed into a standup glide. She put a swing in her walk. Hmmm, maybe that was my good deed for the day.

I looked around the diner. Must be about a half dozen other patrons in booths and one weathered old gent sitting at a small table by the front door. Looked like he could be either a regular or maybe even the owner by the looks of the papers spread out in front of him. Checkered oil cloths on the tables and a heavy scent of grease and burned meat in the air. But considering the gloom that was gathering outside, the diner felt warm and homey.

"There you go, handsome." The toothy grin the waitress served with the coffee and meat loaf made me wonder if I had overdone the instant charm. She turned to go but I called out.

"Wait, miss. I could use some information. Is there a sporting goods store in town?"

"Sure, we got a little of everything in our little town, sugar." She made a series of hand motions. "Head on up Main Street this direction two blocks. Store's on the left. It's called Mountain Sports. Got any particular games in mind?" She arched her brow.

"Actually, I'm a sporting goods salesman. Thought I'd drop in and see the manager." From her expression I got the feeling she'd thrown out a leading question, and that wasn't the answer she wanted.

"Joe Dolan. That's his name. The manager, I mean. Tell him Wanda sent you over."

I almost came unglued. "Thanks, Wanda," I said, trying to stay calm. *She never knew she had just given me a very pleasant wakeup call.*

What a stroke of luck. Joe Dolan! I'd lost track of him over the years. Hadn't seen him since college when we paired up at guard on the Elkins College basketball team. The two of us had enjoyed a special comradeship and great success on the court. Owed Joe more than I could ever repay for keeping me motivated through the rough spots and talking me past the few losses we'd suffered as teammates. Maybe that strange voice bouncing around in my head was setting me up for something good this time.

CHAPTER 2

Ten minutes later, the meat loaf, mashed potatoes and gravy on my plate had disappeared. Think I inhaled them in my excitement. The quick meal and unexpected news that my old pal was in town already had the food grinding in my stomach. Maybe I should have asked for an antacid for dessert.

Hurried out onto the main street of Richwood in the direction Wanda had pointed. Spotted Mountain Sports up ahead and found a parking space. The downtown was almost deserted at midday. I looked up at the sky again and understood why. Angry looking clouds were churning in from the east, roiling and speeding low over the peaks. There was a hint of moisture spritzing on my bare head, and no doubt there was much more to come.

At least the glum day was going to bring me a special reward. I'd get a real kick out of the reunion about to take place beyond the green storefront with its windows full of sporting equipment. A reunion that had been delayed for entirely too long.

It was a nice enough looking store inside. Seemed to carry a good line of items for the standard high school and local sports. Also covered mountain biking, canoeing and skiing. With the motorcycle trails and white water rafters in the summer and the skiers in wintertime, Joe should be doing okay for himself if he hustled. And I'd never known anybody who would deny that Joe Dolan's middle name should have been Hustle. He was a bundle of energy on and off the court. Made me work hard to keep up with him.

"Can I help you, sir?" came the question from directly behind me. I'd know that voice anywhere. Wanted to see his expression when I turned around.

"Yeah, I want a big hug." I spun around and reached for the short, redheaded Joe.

"Poet! Is it really you?" He looked as if he'd seen a ghost. Then he hugged me and held on until I could hardly breathe.

Nobody had called me Poet since I stepped off the basketball court seven years ago. The name had a strange but pleasant ring. This red-headed shorty was the one who'd hung that nickname on me in the first place.

"Hot damn, Greg. Where you been so long, you peckerwood?" Joe had a way of lighting the room with his smile that always appeared to involve every muscle in his head. That hadn't changed.

"That's a story could take the rest of the day. I'd rather sell you some sporting goods."

Dolan chuckled. "No, you're confused. See, that's *my* line."

"Not today, friend. You are looking at the sure enough bona fide representative of First Sports of Charlotte, North Carolina. I'm here to brighten your day and make all your wishes come true."

"Same old Poet. Reelin' out a line a mile long and ten feet wide." Joe showed me to the back of the store and called out, "Take over on the floor, Jake. I'll be in the office." A slender young man gave him the high sign.

Joe's office walls were lined with pictures from our basketball days. I pointed to one of them, two young men in basketball uniforms; a skinny, brown-haired youngster with the face of an innocent kid and a shorter redhead.

"Were we ever that young?" I asked. "Looks like we just stumbled in off the hay wagon."

"Hey, buddy, we were young but we were slick," Joe said. Then he looked me over carefully, and his expression changed. "Tried to reach you every way I knew how, Greg, but never heard from you after the ah . . . the . . ."

"Accident. I know, Joe. Got your messages. Just didn't feel like talking to anybody for a long time, especially friends who could have helped. That was my stupid period. But it's all behind me now. I finally realized that not being able to play pro ball wasn't the end of the world."

"I don't want to open any old wounds, pal, but can you talk about it now?"

"Like I said, that's a part of my life that's long gone. I'm a new man. Sarah saw to that."

"Sarah? Sarah Cooper?" Joe broke out in a broad grin.

"The one and only. She's been my wife for four years. Best thing that ever happened to me, pal."

"You know I always said she was meant for you, Greg. We had such great times together when we were wild and craaazy college kids."

"Well, she was a real godsend. I went through some bad times after the accident but she stuck with me through it all and kept me going."

"Your mom told me you'd be okay. Complications?"

"Mostly the ones I made for myself, Joe. Did a pretty good job of screwing myself up for about two years after they pulled me out of that ditch. Still, though, I was the lucky one. My teammate Billy didn't make it."

"What actually happened? I've wondered so often about that accident and the way it wrecked your career. We were all pumped to see you take on the big time and show them how the game is played."

"Biggest thing ever happened in Elkins, pal, having one of their boys go that high in the NBA draft. My head was spinning. The signing bonus was our nest egg to buy a place for Sarah and me. We had our plans set for a spring wedding after my rookie season was over. Planned to look you up to ask you and Julie to stand up for us. Then I made a crappy decision."

Dolan lit a cigarette, and he offered me one. I shook my head.

"Man, everybody back home was with you when you headed to the big league, Greg. We were crushed when we heard about the wreck."

"The transition to the pros really wasn't as tough as I thought it may be. After all, we didn't exactly compete against the Carolinas and Michigans of the world at Elkins. Have to admit we did hold our own against some pretty good Division II teams. I was fitting in well with the Hornets. At six feet I felt like a sapling in a forest full of tall oaks, but my speed gave me a big edge. Think I could have been a starter before long. Then I crawled into the car with Billy Turner after he'd had too much to drink. Last thing I remember was sailing off Interstate 77 somewhere south of Charlotte, rolling into a rocky creek bed and blacking out."

"Damn, Poet. I heard your shooting hand took the brunt of the crash. What a rotten break for the purest shooter I ever saw." He fumbled with some papers on the desk. He avoided looking directly at me, but his words reminded me how much mutual respect the two of us had shared both on and off the court.

I absent-mindedly flexed the fingers of my damaged right hand that would never again be a hundred percent. "Yeah, but Billy didn't make it out of that streambed. Sure, I spent some agonizing days in that hospital, but I was still alive. Then, it became obvious I wasn't going to get full use of my hand back. Thought about how close I came to buying it myself. Spun off somewhere into my own little world. My career was shot, and I went into a terrible funk of self-pity."

"Hey, I don't need to know any more. This has to be painful for you to talk about."

"No, I want you to know, Joe. Hell, you and I go back a long way. We fought the hardwood wars together. Shared splinters and ankle sprains. I've needed to spill my guts to somebody for years, and it's time I let it out now."

"Then I'm listening, buddy. Lay it on me," Joe said and scooted his chair closer.

"Well, I was in the hospital in Charlotte for five weeks bound and determined to sort it all out on my own. Like a pig head I refused the advice and help Mom and Sarah wanted to give me. Even ignored my instinct to talk it out with old friends like you. Then the drinking started."

Joe grimaced. "Oh, no. You were always the sober one. I remember being falling down drunk more than once when you got me home in one piece. Probably prevented me from getting my butt kicked in a lot of bars when I was too wasted to back down."

"I know, and if I had insisted on driving Billy home that night, none of this would have happened. I didn't use my brain, and that mistake was really working me over. Knew he was too blotto to drive. Couldn't help blaming myself for the accident. Of all the dumb ways to react, I hit the bottle myself. Practically crawled inside a whole procession of bottles for the better part of two years. Rationalized that I was using it to ease the pain. Sarah never gave up on me, but she reamed my ass regularly about what I was doing to our future. I could have lost her if she hadn't been too stubborn to give up on me."

"Had no idea what you were going through, Greg. Wish I'd been there to help."

"Nobody could get to me. Rolled up in my own little cocoon and refused to listen. Might have drowned myself in booze and self-pity if it hadn't been for Sarah. She was on my case really hard one day, and I raised my hand to hit her. When I saw the shocked look in her eyes, it damn near broke my heart. Joe, I would have cut off my shooting arm at the elbow to erase her look of frightened disbelief from my memory. Totally disassembled on the spot. Begged her to forgive me. From that moment I started to turn my life around. We were married a few months later. Joe, you're looking at a happy man."

Just then the soft, prompting voice stole back into my head.

A man with an adventure ahead, the voice whispered.

I grasped my head with both hands and shook it hard.

"You okay, Greg?" Joe jumped to his feet when he saw my obvious discomfort. "Can I get you something?"

"No, I'm okay, Joe. Get these little twinges. Holdover from the car wreck, I guess. They go away as quick as they come on. Where were we?" He stared at me, but apparently accepted my less than honest explanation.

Joe sat down and went on. "You look a lot like the old Poet to me, pal. It's great to see you again. Now that the bad times are over, let's look ahead. We were a pretty tight foursome—you, me, Sarah and Julie—back in the good old days. Let's make plans to get a new start on an old friendship."

He was so right. We had made new acquaintances and casual friends in the Roanoke area, but nobody we had shared good times and bad with like the Dolans. Both of the girls were distance runners in high school. They could put us to shame in the endurance department. I swear the weekend chases they led us on up and down the West Virginia hills were more strenuous than anything coach put us through on the basketball court. We always felt they derived some form of sadistic pleasure from running us two jocks into the ground.

Joe and Julie were married before their last year at school, and seeing how happy they were together made Sarah and me even more anxious to get settled down. We served as their maid of honor and best man. The four of us were inseparable. The long runs ceased, though, when Julie reached mid-term with her pregnancy. She almost made it to graduation before their son Jason was born. We'd joked about having to carry our well-rounded friend out before the ceremony was over, but she outsmarted us. As soon as exams were finished, she went into labor and delivered a beautiful baby boy.

I changed the subject. "How's my godson, Joe? Bet Jason's growing like a reed." We loved little Jason almost as if he had been ours.

"He's heard all my stories about the legendary Poet Bain. He's seven now." Joe reached for a framed photo on his desk. Held it out to me. A handsome little redhead with the same sparkle in his eyes as his dad.

We had vowed to stay in touch with the Dolans when we went our separate ways. Sarah kept her promise but I drifted away from them even before I went into my alcoholic doldrums. Once Sarah mentioned that our friends were talking about moving out west somewhere for a job Joe had been offered. Had the best intentions of calling Joe and catching up, but I was already totally immersed in training with the Hornets. Then I let them get away. By the time I emerged from my fog and we had set a wedding date, the link was broken. All our efforts to locate the Dolans failed.

Well, that was all behind us now. I wanted to rekindle the close bond we'd had. It would be one more checkpoint on my way back to sanity. Roanoke and Richwood certainly weren't that far apart. I'd let Sarah know about this stroke of luck, and we'd plan a get together as soon as possible.

Joe must have been reading my mind. "Let me have your home telephone number, Greg, and I'll put Julie in touch with Sarah. Somewhere along the way we lost your Mom's number. Just got sloppy about checking on the best pals we ever knew. The girls always made all our plans for us. Don't see any reason to change that now. Julie's gonna love it when I tell her you're here."

"We'll make it happen, Joe. Now about your sporting goods needs . . ."

"Right on, pal. I have the bulk of the school business and the youth and adult league sales in Nicholas, Greenbrier and Pocahontas Counties. Always looking for new, improved items for my clients. We also get a lot of the mountain bike crowd in the spring and summer and the skiers in the winter. Even do some fall out business with the Gauley River whitewater rafters. My prices are good compared to the touristy places around Snowshoe and such."

Our equipment line was of great interest to Joe. He immediately jumped on several of the uniform items. Liked our ability to custom design uniforms and deliver them rapidly. This could be a very profitable stop for me from a sales standpoint. Much more important was how much good it had done me personally to be able to unload to a trusted friend. For the first time in weeks I was beginning to feel normal again.

"Can't tell you how much it's done for my morale seeing you again, Joe. Of course, you always did have a way of picking me up."

"Stay over, Greg. Let me call Julie and have her whip up something special for dinner. We'll kick back and relive our exploits. Jason can bend your ear. He's sure that since his godfather was a pro, he's destined for the NBA, too."

"Wish I could stay. I'm on sort of a tight schedule, and Sarah's expecting me home tomorrow. Still have customers to see down the road."

"Sure you want to brave that scary weather out there? Looks like we could be in for a real cloudburst."

"Not much choice, Joe. Have to meet my customers. Give Julie and Jason my love."

"Just promise me you won't be a stranger. In fact, I was thinking—how would you feel about dropping by to give a clinic or two for the local kids?"

"I'm over this way often, so we can work out something. My shooting arm isn't what it once was, but maybe I can give the kids some pointers on technique."

"Hell, Poet, these kids will be thrilled just to get the chance to stand on the same court with you. You're a legend in these hills. Expect a lot of them have your picture nailed on their walls."

We finished putting together a merchandise order for the store. I looked at my watch. It was after five o'clock. Had to get down the road if I hoped to meet my schedule. Home by tomorrow night was one target I couldn't miss.

"Joe, it's time for me to move along. Great seeing you again. I have your initial order, and I'll be back through in, say, three weeks to see what else you need."

"The sooner the better, Greg. Sure made my day, pal. Hell, you made my whole year! Plan to spend the night next time. Julie would love to see you, and Jason would be heartbroken if I didn't bring you around."

"Got yourself a deal. Now, how do I get across to Interstate 64? I plan to spend the night in Lewisburg and meet an early appointment there tomorrow."

"Head on down State 39 to Mill Point. You'll hit US 219. Just go south to 64."

"Then I'm off. See you soon, Joe."

"Count on it. Be careful, man. That storm could hit most any time now. If I were you, I'd scoot down the road right smartly. It's nearly thirty miles to 219. These sudden drenchers can be nasty up here in the Yew Mountains."

"I'm on my way."

The wind had picked up. There was thunder in the distance, but it was getting closer. Knew from experience that getting caught on a West Virginia mountain road in a driving rainstorm wasn't on my list of favorite things to do. More than once I'd had to pull off and sit out a downpour. The first big raindrops started hitting the windshield. I needed to get to Lewisburg in time to find a motel for the night. Then I didn't care how hard the rain poured.

The low voice came back to me again.

Drive between the raindrops. Keep it in the road.

CHAPTER 3

Okay, I admit being out in those mountains was a little quirky. The annoying voice had shoved me in that direction and put me behind schedule. I was flying high, though, after seeing my pal Joe. Brought back great memories of the days before real life caught up with me. That short visit had also reminded me this was no time to reflect on what might have been. I was lucky to be alive and able to make a better future for Sarah and me. If I got the coaching job at Tech, we'd be in tall clover. Either way my life with Sarah was great. I had to move beyond this self-pity crap and get on with life.

What started as a soft patter of raindrops began a staccato rhythm against the windshield. I notched up the wipers, and sat a bit straighter in my seat. The angry black sky belched a jagged streak of lightning, and it let loose a torrent.

Hold your head up. Pay attention, Bain, I scolded. *Save the daydreaming for later.* The rain was pelting the car, and I thought I saw signs of sleet. Put the wipers on full tilt, but I could barely see the road ahead.

Joe's parting shot about a nasty rainstorm was the understatement of the year. I'd only gone a mile or so outside Richwood when the skies literally opened up. The water was coming down by the barrel full. White line in the middle of the curving road was out there somewhere, but I was damned if I knew where. Weather never spooked me before Charlotte; however, a recurring nightmare of a wet road and a long hospital stay had me rattled. It was getting very dicey. Knew I could navigate the curves, but who else may be out in the storm coming to meet me on the twisting road? The rain was pounding down so fast there were washes swirling across the highway. When a flash of lightning lit up a bank ahead, I swore there was mud sliding down the hillside onto the road.

Worst of all, the voice was back, urgently scolding in my ear.

Look at the speedometer, Greg. You're going way too fast. You have plenty of time to get where you're going tonight. Plenty.

Looked down at my speed and backed off the gas. Then I noticed that the needle on the fuel gauge was below the quarter-tank mark. Laughed out loud; it was a nervous, edgy laugh.

"Got yourself in a fix, huh, Greg? Where's your head? Run out of gas out here and you'd better hope this thing floats. Could be all downhill in a big metal boat." Had to admit how jittery the storm had made me. I never talk out loud to myself, but I suddenly felt very alone. There was no choice now but to plod on ahead and hope for the best.

Focused my eyes on the middle of the road just in time to see a car emerge from the rain and hurtle toward me. He'd commandeered part of my side of the pavement. Oh, no! Swerving probably saved my neck, but braking was a bad idea. The car went into a skid, and I fought the wheel with both hands. Had to get that baby back toward the centerline. Looked to my right. No railing on that side. A flash lit the sky momentarily, and it drew my eyes to a sheer drop off the right shoulder. Tops of evergreens over there far below the road. I was almost resigned to my fate, but I refused to give up. Fought as hard as I could to stay on the road. For long moments the car seemed to float, and I was sure it would roll and slam me around. My heart was *already* doing flip-flops, and my teeth were clenched, ready for the impact that was coming.

The tires stuttered and skidded as if they had a mind of their own. Just as I was about to curl up in a ball and await my destiny, the wheels finally gripped the pavement. Thump! The car settled back onto all four wheels and shimmied to a stop. I sat there trembling all over. My car was probably sitting smack in the middle of the road, but I didn't give a hoot at this point. Just wanted to stay right there with the loud rain driving against the roof and get my heart rate back to normal.

Pay attention, Greg! Slow down. There's important business ahead. Try to keep yourself alive.

Like I really needed the voice. I was shaking so hard my teeth were clanking. Hadn't wet my pants since I was a tow-headed youngster. I must have come very close before the car stopped. There was no place to pull over, so I just had to keep creeping along looking for a break, shelter, anything to get off the road. Slowly inched ahead, scanning both sides of the highway for exits or even wide shoulders. If I could escape the tedium of driving in this downpour with the merciless rain pounding away at my brain, I'd gladly pull off the blacktop and sit out the storm for as long as it took.

Caught a glimpse of something up ahead reflecting off my headlights. There to one side of the highway was what appeared to be a small metal sign that read 'Plenty' marking a paved road. Nothing more, only the single word.

Now the hammering rain had me talking out loud again.

"Well, Greg, old boy, looks like you don't have much choice. It's either Plenty, whatever that is, or an uncertain fate on a flooded highway. Haul this thing off the road."

The worst that could happen was I'd be stranded in some whistle stop community for a few hours while the storm passed. That beat the prospect of sliding off the road and lying undiscovered at the bottom of some dark hollow—or even worse. A transformer on the telephone line overhead popped, and it sent out a shower of cascading sparks. The visual jolt sealed my decision. I tentatively turned onto the side road, carefully guarding against dropping a wheel into a ditch.

At least the road to 'Plenty' was paved and two cars wide. I drove at a crawl; crept toward whatever relief may lie down this hasty detour. Must have gone more than a mile off Route 39 before I rounded a bend, and saw a single point of light winking through the sheets of rain.

I could barely make out the form of a run down old building. Lightning flashed often and close by and lit up the surroundings. The sign fronting the roadside swung wildly in the wind, but I could see the faded words Ace Oil. There was a dim glow from inside the structure. Thank heaven, an open gas station with human beings who may be able to help me on my way. Anyway, the old saw 'any port in a storm' couldn't be more appropriate than at this moment in my turbulent, up and down life.

The car front bucked against the fast flowing water as I turned onto the dirt and gravel storefront area. Held on and fought the steering wheel. The trick now was to avoid washing into a chug hole after coming this far. I needed to get under the welcome shelter of that overhang and out of the thundering rain. Two ancient gas pumps stood defiantly against the storm. Made me wonder if this was a working station or just a peeling clapboard relic of times gone by. Occurred to me that if the gales continued, this old antique of a building may just float away before I could get inside. Couldn't be sure it wasn't a mirage created by my frantic brain, anyway. Thought I could see someone inside, and there was a sign over the entrance that read Harmon's Gas and Grocery.

Brought my water-logged vehicle to a stop beside one of the pumps. The rain pelted the overhang with a tinny sound, but at least it was no longer punishing the car's roof and my aching head. What a relief it was to shut off that droning engine and slump back in the seat. Finally a break in the monotony and a few moments of relative quiet. The rain had been so loud and persistent on the roof and windows of the car that I was sure it had managed to pierce my skull. A terrific headache was coming on. If nothing else, I hoped to rest briefly at this remote spot, get a headache powder, and fill up the gas tank for the journey home. That is, if those rusty old pumps still worked.

The store windows were covered with poster ads for chewing tobacco and soft drinks. Somebody inside peered out for an instant, but I didn't see any movement toward the door. He returned to whatever he was doing. Well, that suited me just fine. I'd sit right here, and we'd ignore each other.

Began to believe I was glued to that seat, anyway. Now that there was time to take notice, realized I was sweating profusely. My clothes were soaked through even though I hadn't been out of the car. Ol' Greg Bain had been reduced to one scared puppy by the storm and the near collision. My head throbbed and my arms and legs trembled; I was a total mess. After a concentrated effort, made my legs move and relaxed my death grip on the steering wheel. An escape from the front seat was possible after all.

"Oboy, Greg. You took a huge bite out of the bad luck weenie this time, didn't you?" I mumbled. Then I prompted, "Keep moving forward. Everything will be all right."

But I hadn't counted on stepping out into muddy water up to my ankle.

"Damn. Sure is a good day gone sour," I grumbled and dashed for the door.

The rickety steps leading up into the gas station groaned underfoot. Judging by the elevated entrance, this probably wasn't the first time the water had been high in the parking lot. A snatch of melody from long ago ran through my head.

'River, get away from my door. Don't want you 'round here any more.'

The man behind the counter *could* move after all. He stirred and stuck a finger as a bookmark into the paperback he was reading. Slowly separated himself from his chair, leaned over the counter and faced me. He looked to be in his fifties, rumpled clothes and a stubble of a beard. His bulging cheek almost certainly harbored a big chaw of tobacco.

"Kinda wet out, huh?" His laugh was more like a high-pitched cackle.

"Yeah, thought for a while I might drown out there, end up having my body recovered somewhere downstream. With that rain blasting my eardrums, I had to find a dry spot to even think. Get these downpours often?"

The storekeeper answered with a shrug. He folded back a corner of his dog-eared paperback and dropped it on the counter. Turned his attention to me and asked, "Whatcha lookin' fer, mister?"

I scanned all around me. His place apparently provided a poor excuse for a filling station and general store of sorts. From the looks of the goods on the dusty shelves, it wasn't a place I'd want to do any food shopping, though. Looked like the fat back and turnip greens kind of grocery that was typical years ago in small hill country towns. Reflected that Plenty must have managed to miss out on both the chain store and major gas brand trends. Found myself looking for the salt fish bar, tobacco plug cutter and crank kerosene pump. Had the feeling he was waiting for me to order five pounds of dried brown beans, a slab of pork, a bag of biscuit flour. Probably had a charge sheet as long as my arm, and he likely owned a piece of everybody in the community until their blue welfare checks came in. The store even had its own resident black and gray cat skulking around. Unfortunately, the animal seemed to have the run of the house. Not a pleasant thought for a food outlet.

"Said whatcha need?" the man repeated.

The best I could manage to answer his question was, "Uhhh . . . I hurt all over."

"'Pears you could use some warmin' up, friend. The coffee kittle stays on all time. Could be a might strong, but it'll warm your innards."

"I'd drink battery acid if it would thaw out my insides and stop my shaking. Need a Goody's powder, too, for this hammering headache. Give me three or four more for later, too."

"Got some right at hand. And here's a cup for some blue john if you're so inclined." He held out a stained, chipped mug in his leathery hand, and pointed toward the back of the store. There was a pot-belly stove back there with a rickety looking pipe that reached up through the ceiling.

Blue john. There's an expression I hadn't heard in quite a while. Some of the hill folks boil their coffee on top of a stove in a tall pot, and they let it slowly roil throughout the day. The result is something they've dubbed blue john. It is without a doubt the strongest caffeine jolt I've ever experienced. *Look out head, look out stomach*, I thought. This would either cure my headache or kill me where I stood.

"I'm Harmon, stranger. Harmon Grace." The storekeeper came out from behind the counter waving a hand for me to follow. "You sure as hell picked a bad time to be on the road. Got to be either a salesman or somebody that's big time lost. Maybe both." He cackled.

"All of the above", I said. "Greg Bain, Harmon. Sort of fell into some bad timing. I travel out here selling sporting goods. Storm came on so fast it caught me off guard. I should know by now how quickly these mountain drenchers come on. No way would I drive in this stuff given a choice."

There was a tall painted metal pot perched atop the stove. He poured me a cup of the thick, dark brew, and I took a sip with the headache powder. Harmon asked, "Where you bound for, Greg?"

I gasped out loud as the coffee hit bottom. Harmon's lips curled up in a little smile. "Is it done yet?" He hooked a thumb in his suspenders and chuckled.

"Well, I *was* trying to make it over to 219 and down to Lewisburg, but that looks pretty iffy right now. Lucky I'm not floating in the nearest river by now."

"Yeah, that would be the Cranberry. She gets to flowin pretty swift all right when a thunder bumper like this one comes along."

"How long do these downpours usually last, Harmon?"

"Ain't no tellin. These gully washers hit mighty sudden. Sometimes they go on for hours an sometimes they're over quick like. Tell you one thing, Greg. I sure wouldn't be out there in the mountains tonight on a bet."

"Let's say this one's going to be a long storm. Where might I find a place to stay tonight?" I was asking hopefully, but anticipated a totally disappointing answer. And from the looks of the store, Harmon's Gas and Grocery wouldn't make much of a shelter, either. Probably leaked like the bottom of a rotten bucket.

"Plenty ain't exactly uptown, mister. We got this store and a couple of shops that sells knick-knacks and bib overhauls. Got a little café, a post office and a smatterin' o' houses. Plenty never did amount to much of a town in my time here but it's quiet and peaceful. Well, usually . . ."

"So there's nowhere I can find a room for the night?" I didn't like how this predicament was developing. Hated to think I was about to rent space by the pot belly for the duration of the storm.

"Oh, yeah. We got one o' them, too. Called the Plenty Comfy Bed 'n Breakfast."

I waited impatiently for more information, but Harmon had suddenly stopped talking. He had even interrupted the constant chewing motion with his jaws. Stood looking me up and down, rubbing his stubble as if toying with a thought that wouldn't quite form.

"Did you say Greg Bain? We may be backwater down here, but we know our basketball. Played up to Elkins while back, didn't you?"

"That I did, Harmon. Had my moments. Right now I'm a sporting goods salesman scratching for a living. Just chose the wrong road with a gale coming. You were saying about the B&B?"

"The—oh—the Comfy. It's about half a mile up the road. Easy to find—big ol house on the hill just through the village. Biggest damn house in these parts, so you're not likely to miss it. They got some rooms up there they rent out. I hear tell it's not bad at all. Got to be a damn sight drier than what you just came through."

"Right now I wouldn't be hard to please, Harmon. Looking for a hot shower. A decent meal, and a warm, dry bed. Anything beyond that would be gravy."

"Myrtle and Carl Roop run the place. Good folks, but a bit odd sometimes. Pretty much keep to theirselves. If you hurry on up there, you should make it in time for supper. Myrtle does set a fine table."

"Thanks. Now if I can trouble you to fill my gas tank, I'll be on my way."

"Still purty wet 'n windy outside. If you don't mind, can you drop by in the mornin for your gas? Right now I don't even have the spunk to brave that storm to go next door to my own house else I woulda already closed for the day. Be open by eight in the morning, though. Word of advice—you don't wanna miss Myrtle's country breakfast before you set out."

Not much choice, I thought. *Soon be rocking on empty, and he probably had the only gas within miles of this place.* "Sounds good to me," I answered reluctantly. "See you then."

So it was back out into the teeth of the storm. I'd be safe enough from the rain until I reached the B&B. But I expected to take a soaking while I retrieved my bag from the trunk and made a mad dash for the front porch stairs.

Once again the soft voice stole in and prompted me.

Now you're on track, Greg. Just follow your instincts.

"Leave me alone, damn it. Get away from me. Let me think!"

"What's that, Greg? What'd you say?"

"Nothing, Harmon. Just mumbling to myself."

Hum after me, boy—Can't-get-you-out-of-my-mind.

CHAPTER 4

My first glimpse of the huge house on the hill set me back. The massive structure literally imposed itself over the small village of Plenty through the rainy gloom. I could make out a gravel road turning off and winding steeply toward the house. A split rail fence guarded the road entrance, which was flanked by a mailbox on a severely leaning wooden pole. The sign in what appeared to be a hand carved mounting announced proudly in painted white letters 'Plenty Comfy Bed and Breakfast. Come Be At Home'.

I carefully turned off the pavement through the rush of water across the entrance. Accelerated to negotiate the steep climb. The closer I drew to the structure on the hill's crest the more impressive it grew. In fact, it was so massive it was foreboding. A wide porch surrounded two sides of the house. There must be twenty rocking chairs lined up along its length. High gables and upper floors surrounded by verandahs made the house seem oddly out of place perched above the modest homes in the village, as if it was a reminder of Victorian elegance long past. I could imagine the town squire living in that mansion many years ago keeping watch over the activities of the common folk in the town below.

Although it was obviously the worse for wear in its current state, the Comfy must have been dazzling in its first incarnation. Strange, though, even though this mansion was much larger, all I could think of with the storm roaring around me on all sides was the old house overlooking the Bates Motel. Half expected to see the image of Mother Bates sitting in her rocker by an upstairs window.

Come on, Greg, I cautioned, *it's bad enough without reaching for morbid thoughts like that. It's a place to dry off and lie down. Relax and follow your instincts like the voice said.*

I inched the car up as close as I could get it to the front staircase. There was ample light on the big porch and at the huge double door entrance. With luck this would be a quick dash. Regretted not having set my suitcase on the back seat so I wouldn't have to dig in the trunk for it. But it was get soaked now or drenched later. If I could only reach my coat on the back seat and get into it, maybe that cold October rain wouldn't deal me too much punishment.

Jammed on my hat, scrunched down under the coat's collar and dug out my suitcase. Sloshed to the stairs and almost fell up them in my haste. Straightened up to meet soft brown eyes and a kindly face that fairly glowed with a welcoming smile.

"Well, Lord have mercy, son. Come in out of that gale." A gray-haired, motherly looking lady had stepped out onto the porch, and she motioned for me to hurry inside.

"I hope you have a room—Mrs. Roop, is it?"

"We always have a room," she said, and she urged me into the expansive front hallway. "Fact is, we only have a few guests tonight, and you're in time for supper. Come along."

I felt guilty tracking in water when I noted the puddle forming at my feet. Looked at her with apology, but she waved off my unspoken words.

"Don't you fret, son. It'll all mop up. Get in here by the fireplace and warm yourself."

I stopped long enough to place my suitcase on the throw rug and step out of my water soaked shoes. Glanced over at the corner near the front door. Saw a tall, lighted curio cabinet containing some odd looking objects. Probably antiques or family treasures. Followed her to the parlor where a roaring hearth fire warmed the room.

"I'm Myrtle Roop." She extended her hand.

"Greg Bain, ma'am."

She reached for both of my hands, and rubbed them rapidly in hers as we stood before the fireplace. For an instant, I flashed back to my childhood with Mom warming me after a cold day outdoors on my sled.

Myrtle saw something in my eyes; she let go of me.

"Sorry, Greg. I did that on instinct. You looked like you were chilled to the bone."

"Quite all right, Mrs. Roop. Made me remember when another brown-eyed lady used to warm me up like that when I came in out of the winter chill."

She grinned, and her eyes had a twinkle about them. "You just stand right there, and I'll bring you something to chase the chill away."

I did a visual sweep of the massive parlor with its glowing hearth and ceiling to floor drapes. With some amusement, I reflected that we must have played basketball in some small town gymnasiums in high school that were not much larger than this room. The rose velvet of the curtains was well worn, but their line and edging were lovingly placed. A group of four overstuffed armchairs clustered invitingly near the cheery fireplace. Across the gleaming hardwood floor stood a huge red velvet sofa and two matching chairs. Off to one side was a grand piano that had to be a genuine antique. I walked over to take a closer look at the magnificent instrument.

Mrs. Roop returned to the parlor; she saw me admiring the piano. "That's Carl's prize possession, Greg. He can't play a lick, but I think he loves that old piano more than me." She offered me a steaming mug.

"It's a lovely grand, Mrs. Roop. May I play it?"

"If you're going to stay here, you have to learn to call me Myrtle, son. Everybody else does. I'd love to hear you play. But first, you need to drink this."

"What is it, Myrtle? Smells like hot cider with cinnamon."

"It's that and a little something special. You're not a teetotaller, are you?"

"No, I take a drink now and then."

Actually, I thought, *I need to steer clear of anything alcoholic considering my history. But maybe a light one wouldn't hurt. May stop my chattering teeth.*

"Good, 'cause Carl makes some of the smoothest moonshine in these parts. There's just a taste of it in there."

I took a long draught of the warming liquid. The glow spread all the way to my fingertips. Carefully cradled the mug on a lace coaster, and sat down at the piano to try some runs. Played one of the few light classical pieces I knew, and marveled at the tone of the music from the old grand. The nameplate bore the name Boesdorfer. That was a famous old line that was highly prized.

"I've rarely heard such a fine instrument, Myrtle, and it seems to be in perfect tune. How do you manage way out here to keep it . . ."

"Oh, I play some, too. Guess you could say I'm blessed with perfect pitch. My daddy owned this piano before me, and he used to let me help him tune it." She sat down. Her fingers floated over the keys.

"I think you're wrong, Myrtle. I believe Carl loves the grand because you keep it looking so beautiful and play it so well for him."

"Speak of the . . . this is my husband Carl. Carl, meet Greg Bain, who's going to be with us for . . . how long *are* you staying, Greg?"

"Just tonight if the rain lets up. Have appointments in Lewisburg tomorrow." Carl Roop offered a well-calloused hand and a strong handshake. Carl was a big, thick man. Not fat, just big and bulky. I could read a life of hard physical labor in his stocky build. But the dark eyes were friendly, and the smile looked genuine.

"Pleasure, Greg," he said.

"Nearly washed away out there on the state road today. Then another car tried to run me down. Sure glad to find this place."

"Well, maybe we can make this a time for you to remember," Myrtle offered. "I'm having pork roast for supper and my special recipe apple pie for dessert. There are only a few guests, so we'd love some company here in the parlor after supper. Can't let that nasty old storm take all the fun out of the day."

"That's an invitation I'll be happy to accept, Myrtle. Need to have a hot shower and get into some dry clothes before we eat, though. Look forward to getting to know you, Carl."

He nodded. "Likewise, Greg. Myrtle serves up some first rate eats. We like to start supper promptly at seven o'clock. Come along with me. I'll get you registered and settled in."

I followed Carl toward the front desk. Stopped to pick up my shoes on the way. They had been wiped down and stood at the parlor entrance. I looked all around in puzzlement, but Carl merely whispered, "Must be those little fairies again," with a grin and a chuckle.

The rooms for guests were up a long, winding staircase on the upper floors. We rounded the second floor landing and kept climbing. I found myself wondering why, if there were only a few registered guests, my room was on the third floor. I dutifully trudged along behind Carl as he placed my bag in the room then he handed me a big brass key on a ring with a tag that said 'Comfy.'

"It's a beautiful room, Carl. But so large for one person."

"Myrtle gave me her little wink and head nod so I knew she wanted you to stay up here. We call this the Blue Room for obvious reasons. It's our best one, but she doesn't often use it. This one and ours are the only two that have their own private bathrooms. That should be a plus on a chilly October night."

"Now I see what your sign out front means, Carl. You folks really do know how to make a fellow feel at home."

"Just be sure to stay on Myrtle's good side. Be at supper by seven."

"You can set your watch by me. Can't wait to taste her cooking if it's anything like her hospitality."

I set about getting back to normal after a trying afternoon. Stripped off my rain soaked clothes, and left them in the bathroom to dry out. Turned on the shower. The hot water settled me down; it gradually warmed my body. May yet salvage a restful evening after my hectic trip out of Richwood.

Felt refreshed as I toweled off and walked into the bedroom. Stood nude in front of the antique mirror. *Not bad for a has-been athlete,* I thought. Still had a hungry look in those steely gray eyes, and my strong legs could carry me on the basketball court. Except for the damaged arm, I'd still be in the big time playing pro ball. A moment of indiscretion sure had played hell with my bright future. But after the accident and those long weeks in the hospital, I was lucky to escape with no more than a busted wing and loss of mobility in my right hand. Fortunately, I had Sarah to help me over some very rough times and get me started again.

Once Sarah worked her tough love magic and jarred me out of my alcoholic lethargy, I got back to staying in condition. She goaded me into running with her again after a two-year layoff. Our weekends were filled with jogs up Catawba Mountain and Twelve O'Clock Knob, biking over Bent Mountain and along the Blue Ridge Parkway. My hand was still impaired, but I knew my legs would have carried me over, under and around most of the pros I faced. Unfortunately, there would never be an opportunity to test that conviction.

Noises from the hall jarred me out of my daydream. Couldn't remember whether I'd thrown the door latch. Sure didn't want someone walking in on me in the buff. Before I could dash over to check the door, there was a soft rap, and the knob turned ever so slightly. Dove in the opposite direction and pushed the bathroom door nearly shut. A sharper rap was followed by an unfamiliar feminine voice.

"Are you in there, Mr. Bain?" While I was debating whether to answer, she entered the room, and I quickly retreated. Held the bathroom door open a crack to watch a small woman with waist length raven hair place extra pillows on the bed and fluff them. She stood with her back to me and hummed softly as she worked.

I was intrigued by her graceful movements. Wanted to see her face; but this was no time to make my presence known, clad as I was in only a hastily wrapped bath towel. If she came toward the bathroom, I'd have to warn her away. Better she be startled than embarrassed at my near nudity. She turned halfway in my direction, walked to the chest of drawers and stood on her toes to place an extra pillow on its top. Her remarkable beauty was riveting. I estimated she must be somewhere in her early or mid-twenties. The childlike innocence of her lovely, youthful face made it difficult to determine her exact age. There was an aura about her, too, an attraction I felt strongly but couldn't quite explain.

The girl scanned the room briefly, but if she sensed my presence she gave no indication. She turned back to the bed. Mumbled something under her breath that I couldn't make out, and she patted a pillow one more time. Then she silently slipped into the hallway. I sighed heavily. Wondered if it was merely relief or something more.

* * *

The hot shower had worked wonders on both my headache and my outlook. I almost bounded down the long flights of stairs to the dining room. If my fate was to be waylaid in Plenty on my backwoods trek, this seemed to be as good a place as any to sleep over. The Roops were delightful people, and the appearance of the lovely little nymph in my room had added a tantalizing twist to my stay.

"You look like a new man, Gregory," Myrtle said. "It is Gregory, isn't it?" She came from the kitchen to find that Carl had already seated me for the meal.

"Yes, that's my proper name, Mrs . . . uh, Myrtle. Almost no one has called me that, though, since I was twelve years old. Announced to my family one day that I was all grown up and wanted to be called Greg. My parents could hardly contain their amusement, now that I think back on it. But after that, only my little sister Beth addressed me as 'Greg-o-ry' when she wanted to get my goat."

Myrtle snickered. "Then Greg it is! Have some of my lentil soup and homemade rolls. I'll get your roast pork dished up in just a jiffy."

I wanted to ask her about the young woman, but didn't know how to broach the subject. Perhaps the girl would show herself later in the evening so I could meet her. Couldn't get her out of my mind.

The Comfy dining room was warm and homey. Must have been ten tables with gingham tablecloths. Bright covers with bowed ties on the chair backs and gingham curtains with tiebacks at the windows. Myrtle's cooking was indeed first rate. Pleasant aromas wafted from the kitchen, and the food that followed fulfilled my fondest hopes for a meal on the road. Felt more like one of Sarah's home cooked meals prepared especially for me. I lingered over my pie and coffee, thoroughly enjoying the feeling of contentment and a full stomach. There was no pretense about the cooking at the Comfy. It was honest country food in the best tradition, and I totally absorbed myself in Myrtle's tasty dishes. Couples sat at three other tables. They all appeared to be equally delighted with supper.

One of the other men boarders looked over at me and asked, "First time at the Comfy?"

"Sure is. I'm impressed," I mumbled as I dispatched the last of the delicious warm apple pie.

"Myrtle knows how to set a table, all right. My wife and I never miss coming over to stay at least one night every time we bike up here. Just finished the final bikers' rally of the year up on the trails. Our reward is to spend our last night with Myrtle Roop's hospitality and scrumptious supper."

"I'm surprised she doesn't have more boarders than this. The Comfy is a real find for tourists."

He lowered his voice and responded, "Oh, she should keep the place full. Homiest place and best value for miles around. But those of us that know about the Comfy are a little selfish. We don't spread it around. Keeps it nice and quiet for us."

* * *

I stayed in the dining room sipping coffee, listening to the howling wind and steady rain, feeling fortunate to be inside. Myrtle asked, "Would you be more comfortable in the parlor, Greg? I can bring you and Carl more coffee in there. He's anxious to bend your ear. You know, get some news from the outside world." Then she leaned down and whispered, "Play him something on the Boesdorfer."

"Okay, I'll fill in until the real musician arrives," I teased.

She blushed and chided, "Such blarney as I never heard."

Carl was sitting in the parlor in front of the fire in one of the inviting armchairs, his feet propped up on an ottoman, snoozing away. I didn't have the heart to disturb him. Took a seat, picked up the Pocahontas Times newspaper and began reading. The news was mostly about the summer season that had come to a close Labor Day when the river rafters and mountain motorcyclists had left the area. A few hardy souls had come around for a late fall bike rally on the trails. Sounded like a stretch to me, volunteering to be buffeted by those chill October winds. If they rode today, they got a wet surprise as well.

The Times related how in a few weeks the snows, natural and machine made, would bring the skiers to the mountaintop resorts not far away. I supposed the Comfy managed to take some of the overflow of tourists during all seasons. But it was far enough away from the real centers of activity to likely make it a choice of last refuge for most tourists. The others didn't know what an experience they were missing.

Myrtle came into the parlor after a few minutes with a china coffee service. She looked at Carl and shook her head. When she had poured me a steaming cup of fresh coffee, she bent over to peck Carl on the cheek.

"Wha—Myrtle?" He stirred and cleared his throat.

"Yes, old man. You have company. Reckon we can keep you up awhile?"

She sat down in one of the big chairs, and a large white cat suddenly appeared. Myrtle beckoned to the cat, and it jumped into her lap. I did a double take when the animal looked up and surveyed me with eyes as soft and brown as Myrtle's! Funny, I thought all cats had green eyes.

"This is my precious Greta. She goes wherever I go, except for the dining room. That's strictly off limits to you, isn't it, girl?" The cat seemed to comprehend her words, purred and licked her hand.

"Never saw a brown-eyed cat, Myrtle."

"Carl found her when she was a kitten. Said he took one look at those eyes and knew she was meant for me."

Carl sat up and rubbed his cheeks.

"Sorry I was snoozing when you came in, Greg. Myrtle's roast pork does that to me. Every time she cooks it I stuff and then go out like a light."

Myrtle looked at him and shook her head.

"Wish I could rest that easily," I told him." I'd consider it a blessing. Been catching up on the local news in the Times." I laid down the newspaper to settle in for a chat with my hosts.

"Not much happening around here anymore that interests me," Carl said. "Lucky if we get through a season without some crazy tourist running over somebody or breaking his own fool neck on the bike trails or the ski slopes. We're tucked back in the hollow here, though, so they have to go out of their way to bring trouble to town."

Myrtle frowned at him. "Now, Carl. Don't go getting on your high horse about the tourists again. After all, we do get some of them over here, and we've met some nice folks. Haven't heard you complain about the money they spend here, either."

"Just wish we had the good old days back, Myrtle, when we were left alone to mind our own business." Carl yawned then continued. "All we had to worry about then was the damn old witches."

I sat up straight. "Witches? Here, Mr. Roop?"

"Ask Myrtle. She's the household authority on witchery and such."

Myrtle suddenly took on a whole different look. There was near fright in her eyes. She said, "Maybe we shouldn't be alarming Greg with old wives' tales."

"No. I'm captivated by the folklore of the mountains," I replied. "In fact, I'm trying to be a writer. Always on the lookout for new story material."

"Well," Myrtle began, "it's said the Yew Mountains hereabouts were once full of witches, good *and* bad ones. In fact, one of the most powerful and evil of them all was a Shawnee Indian woman that lived in an old shack up behind us, near the top of the next ridge, the place we call Pennick's Knob. When my Daddy was living, I heard him say the old woman's daughter had put an evil spell on this house. She was sweet on Daddy, but he spurned her in favor of my Mamma. The Indian girl told him that if she couldn't have Ezra Charlton, nobody else ever would, either. He forbade her to step foot on the place again."

"That's fascinating, Myrtle. I really didn't know witches were part of the local history. Of course, this county is new territory to me. Went to college in Elkins, but never made it down here to Pocahontas County before today."

"Yes, old Blood Sky Hawk was apparently some terrible hag. Her daughter, Moni, went to school with Daddy down the valley. The women were still living up there on the ridge when I was a little girl, but Daddy was careful that I never met up with the old woman. I did see her daughter in town a few times, though. Have to say she was genuinely beautiful."

Myrtle walked out into the entry hall to the corner curio cabinet and brought back a strange looking object I had noticed when I first entered the house. The device was roughly ten inches tall, and it somewhat resembled a totem at its center with carved human and animal faces on a lacquered pole. Protruding in all directions from the pole were bits and pieces of what looked like feathers, garlic, dried flowers and other things I couldn't identify.

"I was puzzled when I saw that item, Myrtle. Does it have something to do with the witches?"

"This is a kind of protector a lot of people around here used to keep in their homes because of witches like Blood Sky and Moni Hawk. It's called a scoot-booger. Wards off boogers—you know, evil spirits."

"But surely you don't believe you're still in danger from the old witch after so long?"

"Maybe not her. She'd be more than a hundred years old by now if she hadn't come to an untimely end."

"What do you mean untimely?" I was hooked, literally on the edge of my seat.

"That's the beginning of a long, sad story. A lot of unexplained things have happened around Plenty and on this farm over the past fifty years."

Her voice dropped. She started to gather up the empty cups. It was plain to me that she was uneasy about continuing this line of conversation. By now she had piqued my interest, and I had to hear more.

"Please go on, Myrtle. You seem to have strong feelings about the protection that charm gives."

"Sometimes strange things happen in this house, Greg. We hear noises we can't figure out, and things turn up missing for no good reason. Greta hears things we can only guess at and whines." She stroked the furry white ball in her lap and Greta purred. "I just feel safer with the scoot-booger right there by the door. Now that's enough about witches for tonight. You don't need to get in a stew before bedtime. Need a good night's sleep after your scary experience out in the storm."

"Well, tonight I'll be too deep in sleep to hear anything, strange or otherwise," I told her.

"I pray you have a good night's rest, son. The Blue Room has the most comfortable bed in the house. We'll hope it's a quiet, dry night for you. But as long as I live here, it's a lead pipe cinch the scoot-booger will stay right there at the front door under that light to discourage any evil spirits from entering the Comfy."

Carl finally spoke up. "What did I tell you, Greg. She knows all the stories. She's been looking over her shoulder ever since I've known her. I'd be the last one, though, to say this place isn't a strange old house. Why, one time . . ."

"Carl! That's enough," she scolded. "Our guest won't sleep at all tonight."

"Oh, I can fix that." Carl grinned and shifted in his chair. "A little sample of my shine will relax him. He'll rest like an innocent baby."

"Not tonight, Carl." Alarms were sounding in my head, telling me I was playing with fire. It was time I remembered my promise to Sarah and to myself as well. No more booze.

He cast a disappointed look at me.

"Had a large problem with alcohol not too long ago, Carl, but I've put it behind me. Can't take a chance."

Myrtle looked a bit shocked. "I'm sorry I put temptation in your way earlier, Greg."

"Don't give it a second thought," I reassured her. "It did stop my teeth from clanking and warm me up. Just don't want to push my luck."

Carl spoke up. "Won't make that mistake again."

I turned toward him and said, "Myrtle tells me you're the recognized prime distiller around here."

He shook his head. "Mind you, I don't take much myself, just for medicinal purposes and for relaxing. Helps me when this old back of mine starts acting up, getting stiff on me. I do enjoy running off a bit now and then for my close friends. Keep a little stock on hand in the root cellar."

Carl reached down beside his chair. Produced a mason jar half full of a liquid so clear that I thought he might be pulling my leg. It looked more like spring water. Then he stashed it away out of sight.

Myrtle, Carl and I sat late into the night in the parlor with the fire keeping us warm as toast while the cold wind blew outside, and the rain promised no letup. Carl sipped his moonshine. We talked about how things used to be in simpler times when Carl tended to the crops, the sawmill and the cattle. Then he got down in his back when a falling tree sideswiped him with a limb that nearly crushed him. They had to close the saw mill and open the bed and breakfast to keep their heads above water. There would be no charity for the Roops; they were bound and determined to make their own way.

Several times I tried to steer the conversation back to the subject of the Yew Mountain witches. Myrtle wouldn't take the bait. Every time I probed she changed the subject. Finally I gave up. Decided she was too smart for me to coax back to a topic she obviously didn't feel comfortable discussing. So I moved on.

"Do your families live around here?" I asked.

It was immediately apparent I had said the wrong thing. Myrtle visibly slumped, took on a far away look then rose from her chair. Greta squealed and jumped to the floor. They both stalked out of the room. Her reaction completely flustered me. I looked at Carl in helpless guilt.

"I'm sorry, I didn't mean to upset her, Carl."

"You couldn't know, Greg. Myrtle's had more than her fair share of tragedy in her family. Had a little sister she adored. Marietta's gone now, and we don't talk about her. Then she lost both of her parents while she was still a very young girl. Her grandparents raised her right here in this house till we were married. She's a strong woman, but family is a touchy subject with her."

"Please tell her I apologize. I really didn't mean to pry."

Carl went to the hearth and took one of the fireplace tools from its stand. He poked and stirred the logs then turned to face me.

"I'm sure there was no offense taken. She just goes off into her own world now and again."

"It's time for me to go upstairs now, anyway. I thoroughly enjoyed supper and our visit this evening. Almost hope the rain doesn't go away so I can stay longer. You're wonderful people."

"Thank you, Greg. Sleep well. Oh, and don't take my witch stories to heart. It's just a way to reflect on the past and remember the good things, too. Plenty hasn't been so bad to us after all."

I made the climb to the third floor noticeably slower this time. The events of the day were finally catching up with me. The effects of that one toddy Myrtle had offered in the parlor hadn't worn off yet. Convinced me that after all this time I still couldn't take a chance, must not back slide or I would be right back to my old ways. Beneath its deceiving smoothness, Carl's product concealed a powerful afterglow. In fact, I wondered now if Carl hadn't taken a few tastes after supper and conveniently blamed his snooze on too much roast pork. That drink and the storm had drained me of energy. Very drowsy. A full stomach and the flickering flames on the hearth made me want to curl up right there in the parlor for the night. Forced my legs to move, said my good nights and made the way to my room.

The Blue Room was a large, intriguing chamber. I could well imagine that it may have served in other days as the master bedroom of this huge house. Drapes of blue velvet hung in scalloped elegance with tasseled tiebacks. They graced tall windows at one end and at the outer wall of the room that suggested airy openness in warm weather and the evening moonlight for its occupants. The ornate wall covering was a cream background with Dresden figures of people, carriages with sleek thoroughbreds so realistic they seemed to be in motion. A private bath was off to one end of the room, and there was a substantial alcove with a dresser, chest and desk made of cherry wood. The center of the gleaming wood floor was covered with a sculptured carpet the shade of cornflowers. Against the wall nearest the door stood a massive, high four-poster bed with perhaps the most inviting thick, azure colored comforter I had ever seen. It was definitely a room made for luxurious rest.

With the tiring events of the day and a warming drowsiness washing over me, it was all I could do to keep my eyes open long enough to get out of my clothes. I snuggled down between the sheets under the big, fluffy comforter and concentrated on getting to sleep. However, in spite of my fatigue, I lay there running a jumble of thoughts through my mind. Tossed and turned, reflecting on my impressions of the Comfy and its owners, the strangely beautiful young girl, my wild experience on the flooded road.

As I peacefully slipped away in the warmth of the big bed, the voice returned.

Be careful, Greg. Things are not what they seem.

CHAPTER 5

The day had been, in Myrtle's words, a time to remember. A recurring voice in my head kept moving me toward the town of Plenty. The unexpected reunion with my old pal Joe Dolan did me a world of good. Then I almost bought the big one out there on that flooded highway. Literally rescued by the turnoff to Plenty. Who would have thought that in this deserted looking stretch of country there would be a place like the Comfy? The warm hospitality and wonderful folks took my mind off the raging storm.

Already, though, there was an uncanny atmosphere of familiarity all around me. Had I been here sometime during my childhood but just didn't recall the visit? Why did I feel like I should remember the Roops and their huge old mansion? Can't remember ever feeling so warm and positive toward people this quickly.

Quit it, Bain, I kept telling myself. *Your writer's imagination is running away with you again.*

I had filled my college years with courses to train myself for a literary career and earned an English degree. If basketball hadn't come along as an alternative, I may at that very moment be sitting behind some newspaper copy desk. Better yet, I could be in a cluttered den writing my latest best seller. No matter how important the sport became in my life, there was always another ultimate goal for me. Some day I would spend my time crafting words trying to make my mark in print.

With Sarah's patience and her encouragement I knew the time would arrive when it would all come together and let me fulfill my ambition to write seriously. Truth was, she was probably a more skillful word weaver than I would ever be. But she shared the dream of my own success because she knew how much I wanted it. And there would be an expert critic and editor right in my own home to keep me on track.

Dad had encouraged me since grade school to tune my athletic skills. He worked with me with unbelievable patience through long drill sessions. Taught me the finer points of the dribble and passing. We studied offenses and defenses with x's and o's until I saw them in my dreams. And the shooting—he was an absolute stickler on shooting technique. Dad taught me how to alter the path and arc of the ball for every conceivable type or size of opponent. He drilled me endlessly on every facet and angle of shooting precision. Many times when I sent the ball in a looping arc over the fingertips of a much taller opponent, I pointed toward heaven and said silently *"That's one for you, Dad."* My adversary would register disbelief when he missed the block and heard a swishing sound behind him.

"Your Dad could have been a first class college player," Mom had told me. "He was bound to do his duty instead. We were married right after high school then he joined the Army a year later and went off to Vietnam. You were born before he came home."

I never saw him play competitively so I couldn't say how talented Dad may have been, but his technique and desire would certainly have made him a prime college prospect in my eyes. Maybe he was reliving that possibility through me. It was clearly a labor of love for him.

Dad's words rang in my ears as plainly as if he stood in the room.

"Shake and bake. Hustle, Greg. Get it on."

"Can I take a break now, Dad?" I would say. *"This is hard work."*

"Just a few more minutes, son. Have to build your endurance. Staying power and skill are your edge over the tall players. Just hang in and grit your teeth."

I found myself smiling with satisfaction now as I dwelled on my college days and how Dad had been able to see the outcome of all those long years of effort. He shared every victory with me, and he was always near to say just the right words when we came up short. There were many nights when he had no business on the road, slogging through snow and ice to make the journey from Roanoke over to Elkins or to some other West Virginia college town to watch me play. I knew that somehow he would be there in the stands for every game. When the pro scouts came to visit, he was even more excited than I was, though he would never let on. As always, it had to be my decision, and he avoided influencing me as best he could. Nobody could have been prouder than Dad when he and Mom traveled to the NBA draft with me and watched me hoist my new Charlotte Hornets jersey.

I could reflect back on those pleasant memories now without the regret I had once felt at having my career snatched away from me. Dad's dreams had been fulfilled, and I had enjoyed so many wonderful moments.

It gave me considerable comfort to know that I had done everything within my control to succeed, but my pro career wasn't meant to be. Now maybe my writing would flourish as I had always hoped.

The nickname Poet began as a prompt from my teammate Joe Dolan.

"Quote that dummy in the blue shirt a line from one of your poems," Joe had called out during a game one night. "That oughta confuse him, poet."

My opponent turned his head toward Joe, and I drove around him for a dunk.

Joe tagged the defender and said, "Quick for a poet, too, ain't he?"

A local sportswriter near the scorekeeper picked up on Joe's comment, He started referring to me as Poet Bain. Some of my early writing efforts had already been published in the school paper and in small magazines. Was there really a future out there with my name written on a novel?

My future for the moment was with the precious person back in Roanoke who I would return to in the morning. Not only was Sarah encouraging me to pursue my love of writing—she was even working at it herself. She always could turn a phrase, and the editors were beginning to realize her talents. Could that be what she meant about our having *something important to discuss* when I made it home? Maybe she'd scored a hit with some of her witty works so we could celebrate her success.

I would know soon enough. Had to get some sleep now. The day had been a tiring experience, both mentally and physically, and I needed to rest. My headache was finally gone, but I felt an extraordinary haze swirling around me. Seemed to be a pungent fragrance nearby. I was too tired to look for the source. It was hard to think clearly as I began to float away. Ah, peaceful sleep.

That wasn't going to last.

* * *

This would turn out to be a long, disturbing night in the Blue Room.

I half awoke and tried to clear my groggy head. Still lying secure under the covers. A pronounced chill filled the room. Fought to keep my eyes open and looked around, my eyes straining to see into each corner of the Blue Room. Everything seemed to be just as before until my search reached the far wall. The drapes were flapping briskly, and a gale of cold air rushed through the open windows.

Then I heard the sound. A low, wailing chant was coming from somewhere, perhaps outside or maybe within this very room. A high-pitched chant in a female voice. The same cadence repeated over and over; it wasn't *sweet dreams, baby.* Sounded like the Indian chants of the Shawnee women at mountain festivals I'd gone to.

The chant droned on. My first impulse was to cover my ears and ignore the ghostly sounds. Cold air continued to wash over me in waves, and I saw that the massive center-opening windows were swung fully outward. Knew I had to make it across the room to close them.

I felt for the lamp switch on the night table. My fumbling fingers brought only a dull click. The electric clock, one of Myrtle's few concessions to modern convenience in her furnishings, remained dark. Oh, great, now the storm had knocked out the power. Could be freezing in here soon.

Those windows were closed when I turned in. There was no doubt in my mind. The thought added an extra chill along my spine as I reluctantly struggled out from under the warm covers. Hurried across the room; shivered as the cold cut through me, and the blowing rain stung my face. Felt like the temperature outside had dropped. Those were pellets of sleet attacking my cheeks and stinging my ears when I reached the windows.

Incessantly, the rhythmic chant grew in intensity, and the pitch of the wail screeched against my eardrums. The sound seemed to be coming from outside. If I could shut it out and give my throbbing head some relief, that warm bed and slumber time awaited me. Shivered and chattered thinking this would have been a good night to be wearing wool pajamas—if I had owned pajamas of *any* kind.

The heavy swing-out windows fought my efforts to pull them closed. Had to tug and lean to force them toward me to secure the latch. As soon as the windows were shut, the chanting abruptly stopped. The ringing in my head went away, and I felt a moment of peaceful silence. For a few seconds at least I felt like I could even tolerate the chill that had found its way down into my very marrow.

Before I could sprint to the bed, lightning lit the room for a flickering moment. When I looked down at the window ledge, a dark red wetness lay in a puddle on the sash. The crimson stain oozed down the wall and began to collect on the wood floor. I reached out to touch the flow, but found nothing but water and bits of sleet crystals on my fingers. It had been so real that I checked twice, three times in the recurring flashes that played against the windows. The room was entirely too cold for me to stand there quaking in my shorts. Finally I was satisfied that my eyes were playing tricks on me.

"Where are you when I need you, voice?" I spluttered aloud, and shuddered as I sought the refuge of that big blue comforter. But I was alone in the frigid room.

"What's happening to me? You're filling my mind with ghosts." I plunged deeper down into bed.

The empty silence was finally broken by the placid voice encircling me with its soothing tones.

Patience, Greg. Let your fate unfold.

I curled up tightly under the covers; tried to calm my nerves. Lay there and trembled with the shock of the cold wetness from the blowing icy mist until my body temperature began gradually to return to normal. *Well,* I thought, *at least the Blue Room is dry, and the storm has to end.* That was encouraging, although outside the night was still black and angry.

In spite of my best efforts to shut out all thought and get back to sleep, my head filled to overflowing with tangled bits about witches and mudslides, strange voices in my head and cats with brown eyes. I had to shake those confusing thoughts and get on with the serious business of giving my exhausted body some genuine rest. This was no way to save up for what I had in mind when I made it home to my honey.

* * *

Sometime during the night I stirred and felt a chill again. This time, it was as if a cold wind had whipped through the room and passed. Half conscious, I tried to focus my eyes and remember my surroundings. Was I awake or dreaming, I wondered. Scanned the room back and forth. A dark form in a long robe shimmered into sight beside the four-poster, and I blinked through sleepy eyes to make out what I seemed to be seeing.

"Who's there?" I cringed in puzzled fright, actually clutching the covers as if they would shield me from this unknown peril.

Decided perhaps it would be best for me if the figure didn't reply at all! My demons were getting real now and entirely too close.

A tense silence followed. The form lifted a flickering candle higher, and a face floated in its light. I swallowed hard. Tried to decide whether to run, hide beneath the comforter, or merely melt before this specter reached out to touch me. "What do you want? Go away," I croaked.

Then I looked closer at the glowing face framed in long raven locks. The feeling of relief was overwhelming. My visitor was the young girl I had seen in my room before supper. She finally spoke to me very softly.

"I'm sorry if I alarmed you. Ma Roop asked me to go around and check on all the guests. The lights are out, so I brought you a candle and some matches." She lit a long white taper with her own, and set it in a shallow dish on the nightstand.

My lips wouldn't move. Just wanted to lie very still and enjoy the thought that I wasn't under assault from unreal forces after all. Finally, after a pronounced silence, I managed, "Thanks. I may need them. It's black as a well bottom in here." Reached out to take the matches. Found her fingers satiny smooth and warm in the chill room.

I hoped my extreme tone of relief hadn't been obvious to her. In fact, the shock of her standing over me had suddenly reminded me that I could use a quick trip to the 'necessary' before I seriously wet my drawers.

"Ma says there's a fresh fire stoked in the fireplace if it gets too cold for you up here," she said sweetly, and beamed as she reached out to adjust the glowing candle.

The candle cast a soft light through the room, and I marveled again at the striking beauty of the mysterious young woman. Now that she no longer presented a threat, I wanted to know more about this intriguing creature Myrtle had sent to attend to me. It was an awkward moment, but maybe I could at least learn her name.

"Thanks, miss—uh—I'm Greg. What do I call you?"

But she merely smiled, her full lips parting over gleaming white teeth, and spun on her heels. A moment later she was gone.

CHAPTER 6

Morning dawned cold and clear. The room was flooded with light. My clock was back on, and the lamp was glowing though not needed. Forgot to switch it off. What an improvement the bright room was over the stupefying episodes of the night. Maybe the storm had played itself out so I could be on my way today.

Myrtle had cleverly selected the clock to fit the room décor. It looked like a small antique mantel clock that had a small digital readout and also incorporated a radio. Both the hands and numbers showed it was five AM, and a preset alarm set the radio blaring. A somewhat static laden voice was presiding over the country music, delivering local news snippets. I learned from 'Jerry Bob' that the time was actually eight o'clock, so the power had been off for quite a while sometime during the wee hours of the morning. That meant I had overslept and had to get cracking, as Mom would say, to make my appointments. Guess Myrtle's fabled country breakfast would have to remain a treat to be savored at another time.

There were traces of that strange fragrance from last night. I instinctively reached into the pillowcase to explore the slight lump I had felt under my head. Extracted a small silk pouch. A sniff confirmed my suspicion that it was the source of the heady smell.

Was this some sort of sachet the Comfy used to lull its guests to sleep? I'd have to ask Myrtle about it before I left. Tossed the packet onto the dresser beside my wallet and other pocket items.

I was about to hurry to the bathroom and speed through my morning routine. Then good old boy Jerry Bob advised there were road conditions to report after last night's heavy rain.

"Hoo, boy, did she pour! Looked like a cow whizzin' off a flat rock. The bridge comin' out of town east side of Richwood is under water, and there's a mudslide over the road near the Cranberry River. So, if you're plannin' to drive anywhere between Richwood and 219 today, folks, I got two words of advice for you—fergit it! Good news is, the storm does appear to be past us, and the streams should go down in a few hours. Then the road crews can clear out the mud and debris. Should be clear sailin' by sometime this evening. So just sit tight, boys and girls, and give a listen to your old buddy. If your phone's still working, call in your requests."

Yes, I had a request for this phony, but he didn't want to hear it. Cut short Jerry Bob's annoying patter with one twist of a knob. Plopped back down on the edge of the bed and exhaled. His report had literally taken the air out of me before the day even started. It was too late to call Sarah. She would already be at school with her class of high school students. We have an unwritten pact that I never call her at work unless there is an emergency. The appointments for today were off, and I'd have to let the customers know. Then the top priority for the day would be to catch Sarah as soon as she returned home this afternoon. Had to break the news that whatever she had planned for this evening would have to wait through no choice of mine. That was going to be very hard for me to do and not at all pleasant for her to hear. But at the moment I seemed to be trapped, cut off from the outside world, and I wasn't going home, or anywhere else, for another day.

I stumbled to the shower and stood under the spray to finish waking. Put my head under the water and tried to drive out some bewildering visions from the dark hours. Pondered the meaning of the things I had experienced and wondered if they had been real or only made up in my mind. The brief encounter with the young woman had been real enough. The candle and matches by the bed seemed to confirm she had been there. But what about the eerie chant and the bloody windowsill? And was it my imagination that I had been somehow swept away by a dizzying lightheadedness not once but three times during the long darkness in the Blue Room?

Needed to make myself presentable, clean up my act, shave away a day's dark beard stubble. The old mirror over the bathroom sink was large but not well lit. Had to squint a bit trying to search out the worst of my beard. Then something caught my attention for a fleeting moment, and I turned around to see who or what was watching me. There was no one there, only an unnatural feeling deep down in my bones. Guess the baffling night had unnerved me more than I realized.

I returned to the task at hand until a slip of the hand brought a sharp, "Damn it," and a stinging chin. Bled like a stuck hog. Wondered how a small miscue could produce such an inordinate amount of blood. Back in the old days of the straight razor they had devices called styptic pencils. Those aids generally stemmed such oozing. This time, though, it looked like I was gushing the red stuff. Think I could have pasted a whole roll of tissue paper on that cut without stopping the bleeding. I finally pressed a cold cloth firmly against my wound and stood for several minutes while the hemorrhaging dwindled and stopped.

The cloth was soaked so I wrung it out under the faucet. As the bright red ran free in the sink bowl and disappeared, all I could think was *what is this, blood on the windowsill, blood in the sink? Is somebody trying to send me a message?*

The calm, measured voice came sneaking back into the recesses of my brain.

Blood is thicker than water, son. Family is everything.

The voice had called me son. Was it possible that I had been receiving subtle directions from Dad all this time? The voice wasn't right, but then what did I know about how voices from the other side may sound to humans? The thought made me a lot less apprehensive, though, about the visits the voice was paying me.

* * *

"There's my little sleepy head. What a fine morning this is." Myrtle was in the kitchen.

"Guess I bunked in a little longer than I meant to this morning, Myrtle. I was so looking forward to your legendary breakfast, and I seem to have missed it. Couldn't pry myself out of bed until now."

"You just tell me what you want, Greg, and I'll scare it up. Anything at all."

"*Would* like some toast and maybe a scrambled egg."

"Find a seat anywhere, and I'll have it right out to you." She took a closer look and frowned. "You okay, Greg? Looks like a major boo boo on your chin."

"Carelessness, Myrtle. Maybe I was too anxious to make up lost time. It'll be all right."

She shooed me to a dining room table and poured my coffee. I slowly sipped at my morning brew; thought again about what I needed to take care of today. Reset the appointments. Call Sarah before nine. Gas up at Harmon's. Screw my head back on straight.

In a matter of minutes Myrtle brought me eggs, toast, cereal and a bowl of fruit.

"Got to get a good meal in you before you go charging out into that cold air." She sat down and obviously wanted to talk.

"I won't be going anywhere this morning, I'm afraid. There are road problems both east and west of here, so it looks like my destination for the day is Plenty."

She beamed and said, "Then we'll have more time to visit. That's good."

"Maybe you can give me some more of the local color."

An idea was beginning to form way back in the deepest folds of my brain. Maybe there was a story here that could be the beginning of my first attempt at a novel. Witches and curses. An ancient manor and simple folk of the hills. Why not? Plenty had been only an unlikely refuge under difficult circumstances, but it could be the inspiration I needed to buckle down and write seriously.

"Did my stories keep you awake? Is that why you slept in so long?" Myrtle asked.

Just like my Mom. Never could keep anything from her.

"No," I lied. "That's a great bed, and I snoozed away."

"Well, I didn't," Myrtle replied. "It was a long, cold night. Just hope you didn't take a chill up there in the Blue Room. Must have been three or four hours without power."

"Three according to my clock," I replied.

"Well, it was too long for me. Carl and I finally got up and went down to the parlor. Kept warm by the fireplace till the lights came back on. You must have been freezing."

"How could I be cold under the world's comfiest cover? It's a lovely room and a bed fit for a monarch. By the way, Myrtle, I found this in my room."

I produced the small pouch, and she took it from me with some hesitation.

"Strange," was her initial reaction.

"Is that your special sachet to promote pleasant dreams? The fragrance went to my head."

"Never saw it before. Where did it come from?"

"It was lying in my room." For reasons unclear to me at the time, I didn't tell her that it was concealed inside my pillowcase.

She frowned and called out, "Tabetha! Come in here, honey."

The beautiful little vision I had glimpsed from the bathroom and viewed in the still of the night came silently gliding into the dining room. She was even more stunning in the morning light than I had realized in our earlier encounters. She stood maybe five feet six and had raven hair falling to her waist. Even with her head tilted downward to avoid direct eye contact with me, I could see that her features were finely chiseled. Her skin was the shade of coffee with cream. Her eyes, or what I could see of them, were deepest brown, approaching black and had long lashes. The plain, unbelted dress she was wearing didn't begin to conceal the alluring curves of her body.

"Tabetha, this is Greg Bain. He found this packet in the Blue Room. Do you know where it came from?"

The woman child looked up. Her eyes were endlessly deep. She looked from Myrtle back to me with a quizzical expression. Her look was one of pure innocence.

"No, ma'am. I didn't see it there." She stole a quick glance at me then lowered her head once more.

"Okay. Would you bring us some apple juice? Have to get some vitamins in this fine young man. Nobody goes hungry at the Comfy." I watched her slip away into the kitchen, her long hair flowing behind.

Tabetha returned with tall, frosty glasses of juice. She set them down, nodded in my direction and left as silently as she had entered. Had a definite aura about her that projected a mixture of mystery and innocence, and I didn't know which to believe. There had to be a story behind her being here at the Comfy. I made a mental note to pursue that as a topic of later conversation with Myrtle.

When I snapped out of my temporary trance, Myrtle had untied the pouch's drawstring and emptied out what appeared to be an assortment of dried flowers and herbs. She stirred them with her forefinger; studied her findings carefully. A knowing smile crept across her face.

"Sure beats me how this could have gotten in your room, Greg. I'd say that someone who's stayed up there has a secret admirer. Can't remember when we last used the Blue Room. Anyway, I see a willow leaf, a juniper sprig, pear seeds, and there's the scent of vanilla. All of those things are believed by some to have powers to attract and win one's love and attention."

"Powerful medicine, huh?" I said in a skeptical tone.

"Best not scoff at things beyond our understanding, son. Who knows what drives the unexplained directions our lives take at times?" Then she searched the bag's contents further and laughed out loud.

"What prompted that?"

"There are also juniper berries and hawthorn in the mixture. That means that the spell spinner not only wanted to attract love, it was a man she was seeking. She wanted him potent and fertile in the bargain. Sure you don't have a secret admirer out to get you?"

"Wow! Maybe I ought to take that thing home, hide it under my pillow and tell my wife her spell worked."

Myrtle blushed outright. When she recovered, she admonished, "A lot of folks I know would say you're toying with powerful forces when you make light of the powers that plants and herbs can play in spell casting. Be careful what you say."

"I'm sorry, it was a perfect opening. There's a great deal you could teach me about the lore of the mountain folk, the Indians, the herbalists. I'm genuinely interested in learning about these things. Could be great background for some writing I'm mulling over. I promise, I'll take it more seriously."

She shook her head and accentuated it with a hand wave. "That's enough for now about the odd and unusual, Greg. Time you enjoyed the sunny day outside. Have you taken time to see what a wonderful, brisk morning it is after that awful downpour and sleet storm?"

"Normally I would have taken an early jog, Myrtle, but I spent a good part of my morning looking at the backs of my eyelids, so I didn't think there was time," I admitted sheepishly.

"Maybe you should take a nice long walk instead to work off your breakfast."

"That's a great idea. I'll do that."

"Be sure, now, to wear a warm coat, because it's still pretty nippy. The ground is probably frozen in places, too, so watch your step."

"Yes, *Mom*. I'll even take my mittens."

"Bit of a smart aleck, too, aren't you?" She waggled her finger at me.

Before I ventured out I wanted to contact the store managers who expected to see me today. Went into the parlor and picked up the phone. No dial tone. Guess the storm took out the telephone system, too. Walked outside with my cell phone and found the 'no service' warning on the screen. Now I really was cut off from contact with anyone beyond these tall hills. Gave up and went to my room to pull on my spandex jogger and my running shoes.

Time for me to challenge the frosty outdoors.

CHAPTER 7

The morning was glorious. Who would have pictured a crisp, sunny day like this after the all night gloom I had endured? This was the way I remembered my fall days on campus at Elkins when the sheer invigoration of the sunlight and fresh, clean air made my blood flow and my spirits soar. It was mornings like this when Sarah and I would rendezvous at our agreed meeting spot to walk hand in hand to early morning classes.

Trees along the ridges on three sides of Plenty were still tinged with flecks of ice from the late night sleet. Under a frozen sheen the bright fall colors of red, orange and gold leaves showed through. A thin coating of ice rimmed the puddles of standing water in the lane, and brown grass crunched beneath my steps. On balance it was a day to be savored with a freshness about it that cried out to be inhaled.

I stepped down from the front porch and turned toward the rear of the house wondering what lay between the Comfy and the woods beyond. From what Carl had said last night, a place called Pennick's Knob was in that direction. I walked along the narrow dirt lane past a now abandoned barn and silo. The lane was bordered by a rail fence that must have once corralled the farm's cattle. My stroll took me down a gentle slope toward a small stone structure dug back into the hillside. Farther down the path were a stream, a still pond and a winding trail leading up toward the high ridge.

My curiosity got the best of me. I veered off the path to climb the hillock toward the stone front enclosure. From what little I knew of such things, my conclusion was this must be a springhouse or root cellar of some sort. That turned out to be a good guess, because I stepped down onto the cobble-stone surface to find a fresh water spring trickling from a pipe stuck into a grassy wall. A padlocked door stood next to the pipe. There was a shiny, somewhat battered long-handled ladle hanging by a string on a peg at eye level. I toyed with the ladle and wanted to taste the water but held back. Where I lived we were very careful about trusting open water with so many pollutants in the atmosphere.

Just as I was about to talk myself away from the springhouse, a hand touched my shoulder, and I almost created my own new spring.

"Go ahead, son," a shrill, squeaky voice told me.

Startled, I wheeled around, forgetting the low overhead. The roughhewn planks overhead stood their ground, and my skull felt like it had been severely compressed. When the pinwheels of color finally went away, my blurred eyes settled on an old man hunched over in front of me. He had been nowhere around that I could see when I stepped down onto the stones and yet, in the blink of an eye, there he was.

"Didn't mean to give you a start, youngun." He grinned and showed a mouth full of rotting teeth and sickly brown gums better left concealed.

"Oh, that's okay, sir. My head should regain its shape in a few days."

"Whacked her purty good, huh?" His high-pitched laugh reminded me of Harmon Grace's although it was considerably weaker. "I said go ahead. Take a good swig. It's the sweetest water in West bygod Virginny."

I took the ladle from its peg and held it under the pipe. Collected a generous mouthful and raised it to my lips. He was telling the truth. It was like I imagined Carl's moonshine would taste straight—pure and clear, clean and wonderful—but without the afterglow.

"On a scale of ten, I'd give it an eleven, sir."

The old man's face lit at that. "Well, bless my soul, a young man with manners. Age sure don't git respect the way it used to."

He stood before me in a flannel shirt and khaki pants, his unkempt white hair rippling in the breeze that funneled through the springhouse entrance. His beard was scruffy and tobacco-stained, but his eyes were clear and penetrating. Seemed to be sizing me up for some reason.

"I'm staying up at the Comfy for a couple nights, sir. Name's Greg Bain."

"I already know who you are. News don't pass around here lest it passes through me. You're that basketball player from up the road got caught out in the big blow last evenin. My name's Dillard Westerly, and I'm right proud to make your acquaintance, boy."

The gnarled old hand he offered was more a collection of liver spots than it was a hand, and his fingers were drawn and arthritic. His palm was clammy to the touch. He smiled again, and I wished he hadn't bothered when a stream of tobacco juice dribbled down his chin.

"Not a basketball player any more, sir. Just a traveling salesman trying to make a living running the mountain roads, Mr. Westerly."

"What do you think of the Comfy, Greg? And you can call me Wes like all the rest of the town folk do."

"I'll bet it was some place in its heyday, Wes. It's beyond big; it's a massive old house. The Roops are first class people in my book."

"Myrtle and Carl's okay and doin better than most would with as many disappointments and setbacks as they've had. Didn't keer too much for her folks, though. Them Charltons had more money than Midas and run a piece of just about everythin in the whole valley. Myrtle's a good girl, though, and she's got herself a honest, hard workin man."

I thought to myself that there must be an interesting story behind a family with that much influence over a community.

Neither one of the Roops seemed to have a pretentious bone in their bodies, so the family's money certainly hadn't gone to their heads.

"They've done everything possible to make me feel at home . . . Wes."

I was still having a hard time calling someone that much my elder by his first name.

"You know about the curse on the Comfy?" He looked me over almost as if he was deciding whether I was entitled to share some dark, delicious secret.

"No, but I'd like to know. By the way, isn't it a little cold for you out here this morning?"

Our introduction had been so oddly sudden that I was only now beginning to take complete stock of this visitor. He must be pushing eighty years old yet he stood there jacketless on an October day that was on the wrong side of crisp. The chill air didn't seem to concern him in the least.

Wes shrugged. "Don't bother me none, boy. Used to chase bad guys and whisky drinkin injuns round these hills in the worst kind o' weather and never missed a day o' work."

"What *was* your work, Wes?"

"Well, back when Plenty was in full swing with coal minin nearby and the sawmill goin strong right here on this farm, I was the town's sheriff. Fact is, I had that job for more years than I keer to think about. Now the only law they got is the sorry force down to the county seat." He turned his head and spat tobacco juice at a little bird that had stopped nearby to drink from a pool of water.

"Then the town wasn't always this small?"

"Lord, no, boy. We had near five hun'erd people here at one time. Had enough stores that people didn't have to leave town to do their shoppin fer necessities. What with the declines in minin and millin and the strange goins on, the heart just sorta went outta Plenty after awhile, and most of the people drifted away."

"What do you mean strange goings on, Wes? Does this have anything to do with the witches I've been hearing about at the Comfy?"

"Has ever'thin to do with witches fer as I can see. All started with that infernal Blood Sky Hawk up to Pennick's Knob fifty years back."

"I heard a little about her. Maybe you can fill in the details. Sounds like a story, and I'm a writer."

"Nobody knows more of the history of Pocahontas County than I do, son, and I don't mind tellin it if you have the time to listen. But I'd leave it be, keep it to myself if I was you. You don't wanta get people from the outside excited or stir up no evil spirits."

"I'd be grateful if you'd tell me what you know about the Hawk woman. Was she really a witch?"

"Not a doubt in my mind. Old hag was as evil as they come. Them as knowed her before I did said she was a lovely child just like her daughter Moni. The older she got the uglier all that evil made her. Injuns around here clean disowned her and run her off from the tribe, so she set up in a rundown cabin up near the Knob. I seen her more times than I keer to remember. Mind you, she was only in her fifties when the fire took her away, but I can tell you she was one horrible lookin old gal. The evil in that witch's insides had eat her beauty clear away and left nothin but pure ugly."

"Is the story true about the spell on the Comfy? And what did you mean about a fire?"

"Hold on there, son! Let me tell it in my own good time. First of all, there was Moni, her daughter. A real looker, that one was. 'Course, she was still young, so the evil hadn't took a firm hold to her yet, I reckon. Fact, I carry a picture of her, mostly to remind me how beauty can be deceivin."

He extracted a worn old wallet from his back pocket and flipped it open to a faded picture of a pretty young woman. From what I could see in the faint photo, Moni had indeed been lovely in a striking way. Something about her seemed familiar.

"Go on, Wes. This was the girl who chased after Myrtle's dad?"

"She's the one. Deviled Ezra Charlton, and swore she'd have him one way or another. Put a hex on the Comfy and everybody that lived there. Boy, she was your classic poor loser."

He rared back and laughed that high, shrill giggle. Then he looked me squarely in the eyes.

"Worse, she had a witch for a momma."

The matter of fact way he made the statement did nothing to diminish its impact. I could feel the gloom descending around me again, even on this golden sunny day. Why should I feel so personally involved with his story when I had met the Comfy's residents less than twenty-four hours ago?

Wes continued in his drawling monotone.

"Well sir, the evil deeds started to happen a few years later when Ezra's second born was snatched up in broad daylight and spirited away. Her and her sister Myrtle was playin in the yard when a storm come up. Their mama, Lizbeth Charlton, went out to fetch them in the house, but Marietta, the two-year old, was gone. I was told Myrtle was sittin there almost in a trance. When 'Lizbeth asked her where her sister was, she seemed confused and said the wind took Marietta away."

Maybe it was only the cold air whistling around the springhouse. I felt a chill pass through me that was as deep as the one I had experienced in the Blue Room last night.

"Please go on, Wes." I was riveted by his words.

"Next thing I was scootin out here to check on a missin child report. It was gettin to be cold outside—bout this time of year, matter of fact. We knowed the child would be in danger in the woods from the cold and the wild critters. Had to move fast."

"And did you find her?"

"There you go hurryin me agin."

"Sorry, Wes. I'll be quiet and listen." Drew my fingers across my mouth in a zipping motion.

"That's better." He spat again, and this time the poor little bird gave up and moved on. "Well, I headed back down the hill and got me together a search party. We combed these hills and hollers from one end to the other; found nary a sign of the child 'til we started up the ridge toward Pennick's Knob. 'Bout halfway up, one of the men picked up a little gold chain and locket. I knowed it from first sight. The two Charlton girls had identical lockets on gold chains around their necks. The lockets had tiny pictures of both girls. It was common practice back then to have a Shawnee medicine man bless such objects to show that their wearers was soul mates for life. Never held much to their heathen beliefs myself."

My look at that moment must have been one of rapt astonishment. Wes curled up his lips in a sadistic smile. Either he was feeding me one of the largest loads of horse manure ever shoveled to an outsider or he just delighted in holding me spellbound. If his story was true, it had needed telling for a long, long time. Either way, I was totally hooked, and he knew he had me captured.

Wes leaned back against the stone wall of the springhouse dugout. "There was nothin to do but climb on up that ridge and check it out. The afternoon sun was sinkin, and we had to make some progress before night fell. I could feel the men's energy pick up now that they thought they was onto somethin. So on up towards the Knob we clambered, even as a storm was about to catch up with us. We had to find that child before the cold winds came."

I was hanging on his every word now, so absorbed that I didn't realize that we were no longer alone.

"What's going on here, you two?" Myrtle poked her head under the low roof to look in on us.

"Greg, you'll catch your death out here listening to Wes spin his fancy yarns."

"Aw, Myrtle, just givin the boy a bit o' local history. No harm done."

"I doubt that, given your penchant for tall tales." She stepped down onto the stone floor, and pulled a key from her apron pocket. "Anyway, I need some things out of the root cellar, so I'll have to ask you to step aside and let me get to it."

Wes gave me a look that said, *Oh, well, maybe another time.* I felt let down over the untimely interruption, but my history lesson was definitely over for now.

"Let me help you, Myrtle," I said when she turned the key and tugged at the door. The old man, with great effort, navigated the three steps back to ground level.

"Thanks, Wes. Can we continue later?" I asked.

"Just look me up, Greg," he said over his shoulder, already shuffling away. "I'll be down on Main Street somewhere. We can pick up where we left off."

"I hope that old codger hasn't filled your head with nonsense, Greg. He's a little on the peculiar side sometimes." She put one finger aside her left ear. Made small circles and grinned.

We took several jars of canned goods from the root cellar, and lugged them back to the house. I hadn't finished my intended route on this morning's walk, so I resolved to continue my inspection of the grounds this afternoon. Maybe the chill would be off by then. May even get up the energy to make this round a light jog and get back on my conditioning routine.

Meanwhile, my head was spinning with Wes's words.

CHAPTER 8

While Myrtle attended to preparing the mid-day meal, I retreated to the front porch and a big, comfortable rocker. I had brought along my laptop with several files of draft storylines. But this would be the day to start a new project. My fingers couldn't move fast enough recording my experiences from last night and this morning. To a casual observer it would have presented an odd scene. There on the porch of that ancient house, sitting in an antique rocker, was a man pounding away on a laptop computer, an icon of modern technology.

Must have worked for a couple hours, totally absorbed in the story that was beginning to form in my mind. Took a break to rest my fingers and dwell on my impressions of the village, its people and its legends. Set the computer on the floor and inhaled the fresh air. Looked down at the quiet little village. The morning chill was beginning to leave as sunlight streamed onto the porch. Sort of a drowsy feeling to the mid-morning quiet. The trees no longer glistened with their veil of ice. Once again they showed the colors of leaves that would soon be a late fall memory. People were beginning to move about on the streets of Plenty. I stretched and yawned. Sat back to take in the peaceful scene, and felt my eyes growing heavy.

Moments later, without even knowing when, I quietly slipped off to sleep.

Saw myself pulling into our driveway in the Roanoke Valley. Left the car behind and walked to the door, almost running in my haste to see her. Then, suddenly, she was there with her arms outstretched, welcoming me home.

"I could hardly wait for you to be here, honey." Sarah cooed.

"Hi, Twinkle Toes." She had once tried ballet and earned that nickname from me.

"Come inside and listen to what happened to me. This calls for a huge celebration."

Now I'll find out about her big secret, I thought. Then I'm going to pick up this gorgeous hunk of woman, carry her upstairs and . . .

That wasn't going to happen right away, because the scene, without warning, faded from view. I was somewhere totally different, trying to wish myself back to Sarah's side. This scene was ugly.

The excruciating nightmares and hallucinations were back from my two lost years not so long ago. All sorts of weird images danced in my head. "Leave me be" I called out, but they circled and taunted me. Wild animals on all sides, half-human demons snarling and pointing. Specters darting and taunting me. Horrid, flaming eyes, gleaming teeth. I was running as hard as I could and lost ground with every stride. My lungs were bursting. Leg cramps tore at me. Doubled over in pain and stopped running, ready to fight or surrender to the designs of my tormentors.

But just as quickly as the creatures had appeared they were gone.

I stood in the middle of a cavernous gymnasium with a basketball, pounding it slowly against the boards, listening to the hollow, ringing echo. Dribbled the ball on the hardwood until it transformed into a severed, bloody head leaving a trail of red as it ricocheted off icy cobblestones. My legs ached from exertion. Dad shouted from the sideline, "If it hurts a little, you'll appreciate it when it stops. Hustle, son. That's my boy."

The goal was straight ahead. I could make it now. Drive and shoot. Then a six-legged tiger floated past, extended all its limbs and roared at me, baring menacing molars, clawing frantically at me. "Huh, can't scare me, you ugly old pussy cat. Here I come". I charged the furry creature head on then feinted to my right. It took the fake, and I deftly spun and went left around its outstretched talons. I was flying toward the basket, hanging in mid air with the ball high above my head. Old Greg was so far up it was like taking a snapshot of the rim from rarified air. With the ball firmly in both hands I swept downward to slam it home. But I was looking straight into the mouth of the biggest copperhead snake in this or any other world. Its forked tongue was extended, and the serpent was poised to sink its fangs into my hand.

"Wake up, son. Come out of it. It's just a bad dream." The words came drifting to me from some distant land, and I felt a hand on my shoulder shaking me frantically.

"Sounded like a whole army of banshees were after you out here," Carl said. "That nightmare must have been a real four-alarm doozy."

He was standing over me with a look of concern. I was saying something even I didn't understand as my short journey to the gates of Hades ended. It had been too real, too like those other times when I thought I was sinking into my last alcoholic stupor; when it was clear I had to be dreaming. Didn't know how to get back from that other world. Another of those times when I was certain reality would slip out of my reach forever, and I would slowly drown in a large bottle of whatever was near at hand at the moment.

"Carl, you look so good I could kiss you. Thank God you woke me up in time." I reached for him.

The big man drew back and said, "Strange talk, Greg. I'm just glad you didn't fall off the porch the way you were thrashing around, screaming about tigers and demons."

"I'm okay now, Carl. Just give me a minute to wake up." I stretched and stood carefully.

"Came out to tell you dinner'll be on the table in fifteen minutes. Missus says come along, she's got some specialties for you to enjoy."

"Seems like I just finished breakfast, Carl. Don't know where I'd put anything right now." I held what felt like a too round belly with both hands and feigned a belch.

"Not the right answer, son. When you're at Myrtle's house you eat when she calls. Wouldn't want her put out at you, now would you? She's keen on seeing your reaction to what she's cooked up."

"I see your point. I'll be right along and bring my best appetite."

Three meals a day at the Comfy would soon have me thinking I was back in my childhood with Mom and Gram Adams stuffing my fat little cheeks. Went inside to douse my face with cold water and come awake.

* * *

Couldn't do justice to her cooking but relished everything I sampled. This lady would put most of the big hotel chefs to shame with her subtle twists and flavorings. Every dish was an experience. Don't know how she managed it and still made money for the B&B.

"Myrtle, let me ask you about that delicious salad—the crunchy little chunks that tasted nutty but didn't look like anything I've ever seen."

"Oh, you mean the chinquapins. Most of the native chestnut trees around here were killed by the blight a long time ago. A sort of chestnut we call chinquapin grows on a bush, though. The nuts are good for eating right off the bush or for roasting like the ones in the salad."

The word chinquapin rang a bell, but I couldn't put my finger on where I'd heard it. Perhaps it would come to me later. "Well, I have to say you are one talented cook, Chef Roop. There's a big, round guy inside me that keeps knocking on my ribs trying to get out. If I stay here long, you're bound to release him."

"Wait 'til you see what I've planned for supper. Do you like gooseberries?"

"Can't say I've ever met a gooseberry, Myrtle."

"Then don't miss supper. I'll show you a whole new taste." I slid my chair back; patted a very full middle. Come rain, snow, frogs or pestilence, I would have to set my clock for early, early in the morning and get in a longer jog or I was going to burst wide open.

"Say, Greg. How do you feel about a little walk to burn off some of those calories?" Carl must have seen I was in a bit of discomfort.

"You read my mind. Where are we going?"

"I want to show you something. It's a bit of a climb, though. Think you're up to it?"

"Anything short of spikes and pull ropes I can handle. Don't like hanging out in midair."

"Nothing like that. Just want to walk you up to Pennick's Knob and show you a view of the farm from up there, and we can talk some more about the old witch if you want."

Well, I wanted to do that and more. This was my chance to pump Carl for all the facts I could gather for building my story about Plenty. There was a book somewhere in this tale. After my horrifying nightmares in broad daylight, it was high time I concentrated on something, anything that would focus my attention and drive those visions away.

CHAPTER 9

As we headed down the lane in back of the Comfy, I told Carl about my encounter with Dillard Westerly. He raised his eyebrows and smirked.

"Had to happen. Wes probably heard there was a new pair of ears in town to listen to him go on about the old days. Old codger been filling your head with wild tales, Greg?"

"Is he as big a liar as Myrtle seems to think he is? I found him fascinating. Are you saying he makes it up?"

"Oh, I wouldn't say Wes makes up his accounts. He just tends to stretch the facts a bit. That old man represents a lot of history. He was in a position for years to know the particulars of most everything that happened around here. Had police records on everybody in the valley and half the county for one violation or another. Lots of local folks suspected he used that information to his own advantage come election time. Served a lot of terms as the sheriff."

"He was telling me about the Hawk woman who lived up the ridge and about Myrtle's sister that was lost."

Carl frowned.

"I suspect most of it was true enough. Bet old Wes dressed it up, though."

"Now I understand why Myrtle was so upset when I mentioned family, Carl. What a terrible way to lose a sister she loved."

"They never found Marietta, and the missus grieves to this day about her loss," Carl replied. "She won't give up hope, though, that Marietta is still out there somewhere and they'll be reunited. Myrtle still wears her sister's locket on a chain around her neck along with her own. Has pictures of her and Marietta in it."

That part matches with Wes's story, anyway, I thought.

"And Blood Sky Hawk? Wes painted a pretty gruesome picture of the old witch."

"Wouldn't have to bend the truth much on that count, Greg. Don't remember her, but from what I've been told, she was about as evil as they come and wretchedly ugly to boot. Blood Sky's been a sorry legend in these parts for over half a century. A real plague on our valley in her time."

He wrinkled his brow and made a sour face. Turned away and went silent.

"Don't stop now. I want to hear all about her, Carl."

He waved me off with one hand and said, "Time enough for that later. Wait 'til we get up on the Knob. You'll understand all you'd ever want to know about old Blood Sky."

Pointing off to the left of the footpath, Carl abruptly changed the subject.

"Over there is a nice little swimming pond that's never used anymore. Had a drowning there about forty years back—Maxine Pride, a girl who'd been a schoolmate of Myrtle's folks. Nobody's wanted to venture out on the pond since that happened."

"What's that charred building on the other side of the lane, Carl?"

"The sawmill. We took a lot of timber off this land, and had a right busy mill for years. After that big old limb whacked me square in the back, I couldn't do much bending or lifting. Still got a mighty stiff back on bad days. Then we lost our best worker, Warren Brainerd. Wild animal mangled him up in the woods. Had to shut down the mill for lack of somebody to watch over the other workers and keep them moving. It sat empty for over ten years before a couple of drunken old fools managed to burn it down. That and the drowning at the pond were part of what built the idea in the locals' minds that the Charlton farm was hexed."

"But Myrtle said her father started that rumor when the witch's daughter pronounced some sort of curse on him and this place. Thought it had to do with revenge by a jilted woman."

"Oh, that was only the beginning. Every time there was an untoward incident anywhere on the property after that the curse story grew bigger. And there have been plenty of incidents to fuel the legend. You'd never convince some folks that things happened up here only because the farm covered so much of the local land. Had lots of places on it where accidents could naturally happen. People kept seeing witches and curses in everything that went on within miles around this big old farm."

We walked for a long time in complete silence, and I took in the pristine beauty of the surrounding hills. Within a fifty mile radius were the Gauley River water excursions, the Snowshoe Lodge ski slopes, numerous motorcycle trails, even the huge government observatory and telescope at Green Bank. Large numbers of people from the outside frequented the area, and they obviously brought with them tales of places beyond the quiet little valley. It was surprising that this end of the county was relatively unaffected by all of the civilization just beyond the nearby ridges. It was truly a peaceful refuge from the hurry and bustle, and I found it hard to believe anything sinister could be lurking in its pastoral scene. Plenty would make the perfect setting for me when—if—I ever became a serious writer as I dreamed.

But what about last night? What did it all mean—the open windows, the bloody windowsill, the pouch of talismans that seemed to weave some spell over me?

* * *

After an exhausting climb, during which I had to ask Carl, many years my senior, to stop several times for me to catch my breath, we emerged into a clearing. The opening was well concealed from below by tall trees, even when the hardwoods had lost most of their foliage this high up on the ridge. Towering pines guarded it from view and served to shelter it from prying eyes. A dark area in the center of the clearing contained the remnants of an old fire. I deduced that a small cabin had once stood in that meadow before it burned to the ground. Its ashes had been cooled in the winter snows and scattered by the fierce mountain winds.

I knew what this place was, and Carl could see that I knew. An aura of gloom and gathering shadows hung over the heap of burned timbers and tangled tin. As we walked slowly toward the blackened spot, I glanced to my left and saw Carl's lips moving. I'd been so taken by the sudden change of scene that all sound had escaped my notice. He had been speaking to me all along.

" . . . and then they came upon this clearing and the old hag's cabin," Carl went on, thinking I had heard every word he was saying. "There was candlelight in the windows and a fire on the hearth. The men in the search party knew this was no ordinary home. They didn't know what to expect from the witch, so they had their guns at the ready. Or at least that's what Wes told me way back when I was much younger. Understand he was the only one who ever talked about being up here the night of the fire."

"So the witch was in the cabin?" I asked.

"Blood Sky was there all right with her daughter, Moni. I'm told the men knocked but got no answer, so Wes kicked in the door. The two women were huddled up in a corner, and the old witch was mumbling under her breath. Then somebody asked her where they were hiding the child. Wes said old Blood Sky shrieked something like, '*You defile my house. A curse on all of you and on all your offspring!*' Then she went back to mumbling again and shaking her hands at them."

Merely repeating the witch's venomous words made Carl shudder. He cast a wary eye around the meadow. I could almost feel the witch somewhere out there watching us.

"There wasn't much to search in that one room cabin," Carl continued. "The sheriff's party turned everything inside out and found no child. So Wes called them off, and they continued on their search through the woods. Told me he could hear talk among the men that they still believed the witch was behind the kidnapping but there was nothing more he could do."

"But I thought the cabin was burned with the women inside."

"Oh, it burned down, that's for sure. A lot of folks thought some of the boys in the search party might have sneaked back up here that night and set off the fire. There was no proof, so the sheriff couldn't bring anybody in."

"Who exactly did people suspect of setting the fire?"

"Well, Wes had deputized several men. Let's see, there was Morton Feeley and Jason Hatchett. Warren Brainerd was with them although he never spoke of that night in all the time he worked for us. Bert Grace, Harmon's dad, was in the party. Most likely others Wes never mentioned. The subject of the fire just sort of died a natural death after awhile, Wes said, and nobody was ever brought to justice for putting the torch to that cabin."

"Did the women die in the fire? Blood Sky and Moni, I mean."

"That's the strange part. No bodies were found in the ashes after the fire cooled. There was only old Blood Sky Hawk, most of her flesh burned clean off, laying out there in front of the cabin, face up in a young snow. Wes described it to me one time, and I damn near puked listening to him. To this day, no one has a clue where her daughter Moni went that night or why she wasn't in the cabin when it went up in flames."

"Was there ever a trail to the little girl? To Marietta?"

"Wes says he called in the state police and tracking dogs. Had an all out search by lawmen and locals that covered the whole valley and surrounding ridges. After seven days and nights the search was finally called off. The feeling was that Myrtle's sister had either died in the cold, maybe in one of the slew of caves on the slopes, or that she'd been set upon by wild animals."

There was that eerie sensation again that I was being watched. Out there in the darkness beyond the tree line there were eyes staring directly at me—not at Carl, just me. They were accusing eyes that bore in relentlessly, assaulting me from all directions.

I wanted to say, "Look, I'm an outsider. Don't blame *me* for what happened here."

The silence was broken when Carl tugged at my sleeve and said, "Over there beyond those pine trees a piece is where I keep my still. It's the safest place in the county. Nobody wants to get near this spot after what happened up here. Run off a bit of moonshine once in a great while when the supply gets low. Nothing commercial, you understand, just for me and my closest friends. Clear as glass and smooth as a baby's bottom."

Somehow I knew this wouldn't be the last time I would stand in this place that others feared and loathed. I couldn't know just yet what an impact that next experience would have on my life.

CHAPTER 10

Before we left the ridge, Carl led me up the trail to the top of Pennick's Knob, and we stood surveying the valley below. In the brilliant afternoon sun I could see the bowl of hills that protected the village of Plenty. We climbed out onto a rock ledge that jutted over the valley hundreds of feet beneath us. Prominently perched above the town was what had once been the thriving Charlton farm. Even from a vantage point that distant from the village, the Comfy was impressive. The big house dominated the scene attended by out buildings, rolling fields and overgrown pastures. What a shame, I thought, that all this had gone to seed. Carl was pointing out the original boundaries of the property marked by the beds of streams and tree lines.

"There must have been thousands of acres on the Charlton place, Carl. I wonder if that girl Moni was after Ezra for himself or just wanted his land."

"Oh, I'm sure it was some of both. Word is he would have made a fine catch for any young lady with or without the land thrown in. His folks had built a nice fortune to pass on to Ezra along with four thousand acres of prime farm land. Story is he was apparently a right charming young man in his own right. Wish I'd had a chance to know him."

"Is all the land still part of your property?" I asked.

He shook his head. "No, we've sold off some sizable parcels to developers that come in here with big ideas and more money than they have sense. Everybody wants a piece of the tourist action. They never seem to get around to developing any of their far-fetched schemes. It did help keep us in spending money through hard times, though. We still have over twenty seven hundred acres. Guess we'll hang on as long as there's food in the larder and a glimmer of hope in Myrtle's eyes that her sister is coming home some day."

The visit to the Knob had given me a much better idea of what the valley looked like. I could see where many more houses had stood. Now there were only open foundations and fallen structures, rusted bits of tin roofs and crumbled brick chimneys. That visual statement added an exclamation point to the proclamation of a town's slow, agonizing death. A curtain of melancholy hung over what was left of the once proud community of Plenty. There was little doubt its remaining residents were only marking time.

Straggled back down the ridge behind Carl wishing I could do something positive for the unfortunate people left behind by progress, resorts and interstate highways. Deep down I knew that the time for action had come and gone long before I arrived in Plenty.

As we passed quickly through the site of the cabin fire on our way down the trail, I shivered in the brisk autumn breeze. The wind was playing tricks on me, whistling, moaning its way through the tall pines that circled that mournful place, rattling the crumbling leaves of oaks and maples soon to be bare. The recurring voice came silently and took up residence inside my head. Curiously, this time the tone was reminiscent of a softly crooned lullaby.

Hush my babies, don't you cry. All your troubles soon be over.

On the trek back down to the Comfy we both kept our silence. Carl was either talked out or merely tired of dredging up unpleasant memories. For my part, I was too busy processing all the confusing facts people had been throwing at me since I dropped into their lives. Or maybe 'dropped' wasn't the right word for my presence in Plenty. Perhaps it was planned that the road to the village would appear to me at the height of my frustration. The jarring events of last night could be leading to some new crisis in my life. Or it may be only my overactive imagination causing me to lose touch with reality, what with all the talk of witches, curses, love spells and mysterious town tragedies.

As we walked the sometimes not clearly marked footpath down the ridge, it occurred to me that a fellow could get himself badly lost between Pennick's Knob and the Comfy. With dense woods on both sides and the path's ups and downs, curves and sways, the way back could be a difficult task to navigate. Luckily I had the area's best guide, given that Carl no doubt had trekked the ridge many times in all seasons. Sometimes the vertical drop was so severe I found myself straining to keep from breaking into a half-falling, half-running gait to stay on my feet. The wet, slick leaves underfoot didn't help, either. So much for missing my morning jog. This was an even better workout, a real leg stretcher.

Did some serious thinking between stumbles and trots. At this point I was torn between two strong forces. My logical side cried out to race to my car, point it away from the Comfy and get the hell out of here as fast as possible. But my inquisitive nature, something deeper and more persuasive, kept repeating that Greg Bain was no longer simply an observer here. I had become an active part of the troubling sequence of events that had occurred in Plenty. It was as if the burden had been placed squarely upon me to solve a longstanding riddle, and I was struggling with how to even begin.

* * *

Myrtle was as cheery as ever and bustling about the kitchen with her supper chores when we returned. Tabetha moved in her silent, abstract way. She listened to Myrtle and followed her every instruction. Carl and I took up seats on two tall kitchen stools and drank down some much needed hot coffee. The kitchen was warm, beyond warm from the heat of two ovens baking supper treats. Pleasant aromas filled the air promising an interesting supper meal. Myrtle had propped the kitchen door open to help cool the room.

I marveled at Tabetha's graceful movements. She swirled silently about as if on the tips of her toes; gliding, never lurching, making her steps seem effortless, even choreographed. Cautioned myself that I was entirely too caught up in this mysterious and lovely young woman. She caught my eye for an instant then walked between me and the strong sunlight filtering in through the open kitchen door. I nearly fell off my seat. The thin cotton dress was almost transparent in the strong backlight, and the form of her body was instantly outlined. Beneath that simple dress Tabetha was clearly quite bare. Either she was unaware she was standing in the light or decided to treat me to an extended view. She stopped and remained motionless, her back arched, legs slightly apart, while my eyes devoured the sight of her. All the while she looked directly at me without expression. Then Myrtle called to her.

"Honey, come over here and help me get this bowl down." The girl went to help her. I could swear there was the hint of a mischievous smile on her lips as she turned away from my stare.

I fidgeted on my stool and shook my head. Forget it, Greg. You're fantasizing.

There was no denying that whatever I had glimpsed—or thought I had seen—had moved me, more than a happily married man should find himself stirred. Just being in the same room with Tabetha was beginning to affect me. Had to exercise better hormone control.

Myrtle interrupted my distraction. "Hope you fellows had a nice hike and worked up a healthy appetite," she said. "I imagine Carl walked your poor legs off, Greg. Tabby and I have been in here just creating up a storm while you two went exploring."

A particularly pleasant, sweet scent issued from one of the ovens. I fancied another delectable dessert, chock full of ingredients I'd never heard of, much less eaten, being readied to delight our palates. Myrtle seemed to take particular delight in tantalizing with new flavors and surprises from her magic recipes. Seemed both of these ladies knew how to tease a man's senses in their own special ways.

"You're going to spoil us, Myrtle, with your cooking."

"Hush up, now, and get out of my kitchen. You gents go on out of here and solve the world's problems. We girls will concentrate on keeping our little part of the world fed."

I glanced at my watch and saw that we had been on the ridge for quite a while. The time had flown without notice, and it was nearly four o'clock. A twinge of guilt hit me. Carl had me so absorbed up on the ridge I was about to forget my most important chore of the day—calling Sarah. She would be arriving at the house in a few minutes from school, and I needed to break the news that I couldn't make our 'tryst' this evening. We were both going to be disappointed, and I was dreading the sound of her letdown. No choice. It had to be done. Besides, right now I needed to hear her voice, let down or otherwise, to feel a touch of the real world.

I bowed to the busy cooks and headed for the parlor. My attempts to reach my customers to reschedule appointments had met with only frustration earlier today. Then Carl advised me that those 'little cell things' didn't work around here. So I wrote off my cellular phone until I emerged from the Yew Mountains and instead opted for another try at the quaint brass phone in the parlor. It looked like, my Dad would have laughed, something out of a French cathouse with its ornate handset and out of fashion dial. Under the circumstances it would serve the purpose.

Things were looking up. There was a dial tone, and the call to Sarah actually went through.

"Hi, sugar. How was your day at school?" I asked.

"Where are you, wise guy? I expected you to be home by now."

"Funny thing happened to me on my way back to civilization. There was this monumental storm, and the roads in both directions were washed out."

"Are you all right, Greg?" I kicked myself for being so dramatic and causing her undue concern.

"Oh, yes. Wasn't gobbled up by any chug holes. Just had to get off the road before I had to swim. Found a place to get in out of the rain, but the roads have been closed all day. So I'm stuck here for another night."

There was a long, tense pause. I swallowed hard, anticipating her letdown. Instead, Sarah spoke in quiet, measured tones. Her disappointment hung palpably in the distance between us while she was trying her best to conceal it. God, I felt like a cad, and it wasn't even my fault I was corralled in this remote place.

"I was so looking forward to this evening, Greg, for more reasons than you can imagine. But I understand. Can't have you out on the roads in that kind of weather. We'll have to wait one more night."

"I'm so sorry, Sarah. If there was any way I could have gotten home, you know I would have."

"Rain check, then, poet man. Keep me in your heart. I'll always be here for you."

The short hairs on the back of my neck bristled, and my heart skipped a beat. We didn't make it a practice to be melodramatic with each other. Our bond was easy going and playful most of the time. She did lay some harsh words on me when I had the drinking problem. That was to be expected and certainly deserved. This sudden turn in her mood alarmed me.

"Are you okay, Sarah? I mean, really all right?"

"Sure. Why wouldn't I be? Just wanted to tell you that I miss you, and I can hardly wait for you to be here." Now I really was apprehensive. She had used those exact words in my dream when I was in the porch rocker visualizing my homecoming. I'd never known her to keep anything important from me before, so I had to believe she was being forthright.

"I'm truly sorry, baby. This delay was unavoidable. Some good may have come of it, though. A story fell into my lap that may be my first chance for a complete novel."

"Then your time hasn't been wasted. I'm here when the hills turn you loose. By the way, just where are you calling me from?"

"Right now I'm sitting in the parlor of the most unusual bed and breakfast you could ever imagine. It's in a village called Plenty off West Virginia 39 in Pocahontas County. First time I've ever been in the county."

"Plenny?" she repeated quizzically.

"Plenty—as in a whole bunch. You know these West Virginians are imaginative when they name a town—Job, Nubbin, Pickle Street. We have another one to add to our list."

She giggled. Back at school the subject of West Virginia town names had been a long-standing inside joke between us. I had once remarked that if we could just find a couple of places called Ecstacy and Bliss we'd have the perfect locations for our honeymoon and our full-time residence. Her reply had been that Peaceful and Quiet would be just fine with her.

"And you're at a B&B?"

"They call it the Plenty Comfy—no pretense in that name, huh?"

"I won't ask how you could be so far off your normal route. You can tell me later."

"Wish I knew, honey. It just seemed to happen." *She didn't need to know just yet about the voice that sent me here. At least not until I worked it out in my own mind.*

"But I did stop in to see an old friend of yours, Sarah. Quite by accident. Joe Dolan has a store in Richwood, back up the road a few miles. He sends his and Julie's love."

Her voice instantly brightened at hearing their names. "Julie and Joe? Oh, Greg. That's wonderful!"

"Now that we know where they are, I want to come back to see them. Maybe even bring you by on the same trip to meet the great folks that run the Comfy."

"Oh, I'd love to see Joe and Julie again. Let's make it soon."

"Can you tell me why tonight was special for you, Twinkle Toes? Even if I can't be there, can you still share your secret with me?"

She hesitated. "No, honey. This is something best kept until we can talk about it face to face. I really do understand, Greg. Your delay couldn't be avoided. I'll always be here for you."

That feeling crept up my neck once more. Now I wanted to keep her on the phone for as long as possible, to listen and savor her voice. I wanted to talk about anything and everything.

She could tell me about her day with the teenagers she worked so hard to teach language skills, fill me in on her latest project—she always had something new in progress—read me stock reports or recipes; hell, I didn't care as long as it was her voice on that phone.

"Have you seen Mom this week?" I asked.

"Of course I have. We spent last night at her place working on one of her quilts. She's fine."

After we lost Dad, Sarah and I thought it was important that we be near Mom. She was still a vibrant, active lady in her early fifties, but James and Ruth Bain were always such a devoted couple that we worried about her when he was no longer there for her. I found a position with the FirstSports company covering a territory in western Virginia and eastern West Virginia. The Roanoke County school board was happy to have Sarah join them as an English teacher, and we moved to Salem a few miles from Mom. The two most important people in my life had become close friends, which was reason enough to convince me that I never wanted to leave my old home area again.

"I want to tell Mom about my experiences in Plenty. She'd enjoy hearing about the folks I've met. They're what she always referred to as the salt of the earth, hill folks with an uncommon amount of good sense and wisdom."

Whoa, Greg, leave out the witch part. Sarah didn't need that to worry about. I'd relate it all to her in good time, very slowly and with care.

On and on we chatted, and the mood of concern and foreboding completely left me as I tuned in to her sweet voice. I could sit here forever and listen and shut out the rest of the world. We *would* come back here together, and I would see that, for all the local tale spinners, the Comfy was only a very warm and hospitable old house with a strong feeling of home. Or did I only *need* to be convinced of that?

"Guess I'd better let you go and get ready for supper, Sarah. I'll be home by the time you're off work tomorrow. Love you, honey."

"You take care and hurry back to me," she said. "Love you."

Then she was gone, and I sat all alone in the parlor. Much more contented than I had felt since I first stepped across the Comfy's threshold and stood like a wet puppy making a puddle on Myrtle's rug.

I looked up to see that Tabetha had come into the room, and wondered how long she had been standing in the doorway. She had an enigmatic quality, the ability to lurk about soundlessly then choose the instant at which she would make her presence known. This habit both irritated and intrigued me. As reluctant as I was to admit it, she also had attracted my attention because she was such an enchantingly beautiful young woman.

She held a silver tray with a teapot and cup and a plate of cookies.

"Tea time, Mr. Bain." I was beginning to think she had been struck mute, but seemed to remember she had spoken to me last night, however briefly.

"Thank you, Tabetha." High tea was a fine tradition I frankly had not anticipated sharing at the Comfy. The Roops obviously had more class than I had perceived.

"That's a lovely name—Tabetha. Can't recall meeting anyone by that name."

She smiled and told me, "My mother called me Tabki, Mr. Bain."

"I prefer Tabetha. Would you call me Greg, please? I'm really not that much older than you, and it would make me more comfortable."

"Mr. Greg Bain, Ma Roop says there's sheet music in the piano bench if you want to play the grand."

Well, at least she got the Greg part out, but she still addressed me like an elder.

Took a sip of my tea and turned to ask her if I could play something she liked. She had already made her retreat from the parlor. By now my curiosity was aroused, and I very much wanted to engage her in further conversation. She had referred to Myrtle as Ma although I knew she couldn't be the Roops' own child.

There was no resemblance whatsoever to either Carl or Myrtle in the young woman's exotic features. So I speculated about her background and how she happened to be here as virtually a member of the family.

Myrtle had offered no explanation and perhaps I had no right to know; that didn't keep me from wondering.

CHAPTER 11

Talking to Sarah had gone a long way toward calming my strained nerves. Felt better about being here for the few more hours it would take to work my way home. That didn't keep me from wanting to stay awake for as much of that time as possible. I didn't want to find myself trapped in another frightmare running from six-armed tigers or marauding copperheads. Spent a long time at the Boesdorfer picking my way around the keyboard on some of the old standards that were tucked away in the bench's collection of sheet music.

Heard footsteps and turned as Myrtle entered the parlor. "You don't give yourself enough credit, Greg. I see a love of music and a natural musical ability in you. How long did you take lessons?"

"Never had a formal lesson in my life, I'm afraid. My Mom taught me what I know and nurtured my love of music. She said she could tell what sort of day I'd had by listening to the old upright when I came home. If I was frustrated about something, I usually took it out on the keyboard. Made cheerful music if it was a good day."

"I like the way your eyes light up when you talk about your Mom, Greg. She must be a fine lady. Wish I could meet her."

"Her name is Ruth. Lives over near Roanoke, and we see her almost every day. She's my rock."

"When you say we, I take it there's also another someone special."

"My wife, Sarah. We've been married for four years. I'm twice blessed with those two looking out for me."

"And your father?"

"He died several years ago. Spent a tour in Vietnam, and never was quite the same afterward. There was never a more dedicated family man than my dad. He taught me everything I know about the game of basketball, too, and whatever success I had playing ball I owe to him."

"Can I bother you to let me look in the bench for something, Greg? Want to see if a certain piece of sheet music is still in there. It was my daddy's favorite." I stood aside, and she rummaged about in the bench.

"Well, bless my soul! It's right here, and so is a key I didn't know was in here." She turned a small brass key over and over between her thumb and forefinger.

"Maybe it's the key to lock the keyboard cover," I ventured.

"No, it's not big enough for that." A smile slowly crept across her face.

"I think I know what it fits."

She wheeled and walked over to the cherry wood secretary standing in the corner, and tried the key in a brass keyhole. She jiggled it and turned it first one way then another until it gave and rotated. The secretary front resisted then yielded to her determined tugs. It swung down to reveal a writing surface. Myrtle let out a squeal of delight when she saw it open. She turned toward me, and her smile lit the room.

"This compartment has been closed since I was a little girl. I had no idea where the key might be. We couldn't figure out how to get in without ruining the secretary. It was Daddy's pride. He said to me one time that everybody should have their own secret place, and this was his very own special storehouse for keepsakes."

I had the distinct feeling that she had opened a personal treasure trove, and I should leave her alone to discover what wonderful things lay inside that secretary. I rose to leave the parlor.

"I'll be down for supper in a while, Myrtle. Hope you find some great memories."

"Please stay, Greg. This will be even better if I can share it with somebody right now while I'm excited. Carl went down to Harmon's for some pipe tobacco, so it has to be you. Please?"

"You know I couldn't refuse you, Myrtle. Just didn't want to seem nosy."

She held up a bit of red and white cloth tied into a bow. I heard her swallow hard, and watched her wipe a tear from her cheek.

"Look at this! It's a hair ribbon that used to be a favorite of mine. Daddy pinned it up in the center of all the pigeonholes." Her eyes were misty, and she sniffed as her fingers caressed the little bow.

Myrtle searched through the many small spaces where bills and notes lay, scanned through the letters and the scraps of paper, touched the pencils and pens as though she hoped she could establish a connection with the hands that had held them long ago. Then her hand wandered to a large yellow square of heavy stock. She took a closer look. Then she lovingly clasped it to her breast. Tears rolled down her cheeks, and she stared out the window, her mind no longer in this room. She was instead years away.

I touched her shoulder and asked, "Is everything okay?"

She held up the paper for me to see. A caricature of a man drawn in crayon. He had brown eyes. The entire surface of each eye was colored. The eyes weren't pupil and white, just a pair of big brown orbs atop a wide smile. Over his head was a little gold circle that a second look confirmed was a sort of halo. In block letters of blue above the halo was written "My Gardin Anjel." Below the picture was a penciled verse.

"It's what I called my Daddy—my guardian angel. He was such a kind and gentle man, and he loved us both so much—Marietta and me. I was his Punkin, and little sis was his Sweet

Tater. When I gave him this card, he picked me up and hugged me and bawled his eyes out. That was just after Mamma passed on; I was six years old. Before another year had gone by, I lost my Daddy, too. Granny and Grampa Charlton loved me and cared for me, but it was never the same again."

I could feel my heart in my throat. It was akin to losing a dear family member of my own, and I certainly could relate to her loss. "Can I get you something, Mrs. Roop?"

"I told you, my name is Punkin—I mean Myrtle." She giggled over her slip of the tongue, and we both laughed until her tears were gone.

She went back to her treasure hunt, and lifted a small cloth-covered book from its recess. After a brief peek inside, she closed the cover, caressed its surface with her palm and clutched the book to her heart. Looked at me with an expression of anticipation and wonder.

"It's Daddy's diary."

Then she tucked the book back into its pigeonhole, closed the secretary and turned the key. "I want to savor every word," she said, and spun about to go to the kitchen.

I collapsed into a big overstuffed armchair, and sat alone in the quiet parlor. The fire on the hearth was not yet set for the evening, but my mind's eye saw dancing flames as surely as if they were roaring already. Smoky images passed by and hovered for but a fleeting moment, then were each in turn gone before I could relate them. I felt emotionally spent by the rapidly moving events in which I was now becoming a link between others, a common thread in the extraordinary happenings involving the people of Plenty.

To my total surprise, the cat Greta joined me in the chair. She jumped squarely into my lap, and cuddled up next to my stomach, rubbing back and forth, purring. I hadn't seen her acknowledge anyone else but Myrtle. Something must have told her that I could be trusted. She looked up once with those big, brown eyes, then settled and went fast asleep as I slowly stroked her fluffy white fur.

Then I slipped away without warning for a long while in front of that cold hearth. The earlier nap on the porch had done nothing to curb my fatigue. If anything, it had made me feel even more strung out. My body badly needed some rest, and I didn't have to prompt it to give in to the moment. Greta remained motionless in my lap. We must have presented a strange sight snoozing soundly in the middle of the afternoon.

Carl's face hovered above me, an amused look lighting his face, and I became dimly aware that he was calling my name and touching my arm.

"You sure like your mid-day naps, Greg." He looked at the white ball comfortably perched in my lap. "Looks like you made a friend, too."

I had totally conked out, and Greta was still snoozing away. I was encouraged to note that there had been no ghastly visions this time. No supernatural embodiments or nerve-jangling surprises had disturbed my rest. As far as I could tell, I had finally slept like a baby, and was refreshed beyond my fondest hopes. The night ahead no longer held the threat of terror.

"You might want to get yourself ready for supper," Carl said

I looked at the time. Almost seven, so Greta and I must have had a good long slumber. I eased her to the floor, stood up and stretched.

"Thanks, Carl. *Could* use a little freshening up after our long hike this afternoon."

Shooed Greta from the parlor, and climbed slowly toward my room. Freshened up and put on my one remaining clean shirt before heading for the dining room. Even slipped on the tweed blazer I kept handy for emergencies. I just felt like going the extra measure, sort of in celebration of both the new and calmer me and of Myrtle's exciting discoveries. Anything more, including a tie, would have been rather presumptuous.

The dining room was a bustle of activity. There were at least nine or ten small tables in the expansive room, and most of them were occupied. I speculated that Myrtle and Tabetha must be very busy in the kitchen about now. Asked a gent at the next table, "Is this a normal crowd for Friday night?"

"Friday and Saturday are the two days each week Myrtle makes an exception to her rule. Every other night she insists on her boarders having their complete privacy; serves no meals to other than the bed and breakfast trade. On the weekend, she opens the dining room to the public, and the local folks come from all around to share her cooking magic. I wouldn't be surprised if there was already a whole new shift of people waiting in the parlor to share Myrtle's magic now that the roads were reopened this afternoon."

"Glad I came down early. She said she had a special surprise dessert, and I wouldn't want to miss out on it."

"Don't know what she's planning. I'll wager it'll be nothing short of wonderful, though" the man said.

Tabetha appeared and poured my water, She set down an inviting salad of fruits and greens and a basket of rolls. The sweet aroma of bread fresh from the oven set my taste buds singing. I nodded my approval to the girl, and started another adventure in Ma Roop's culinary arts. The captivating young woman managed the hint of a smile before hurrying away.

For the second night in a row, I sinfully stuffed myself, but still waited with great anticipation for the last course to arrive. Myrtle delivered the surprise in person—a large wedge of warm, fragrant pie topped with a dollop of whipped cream. She stood grinning her approval of her handiwork, and eagerly anticipated my reaction.

"Gooseberry pie for my special new friend," she announced. She added, "Bon appetit, mon cherie," in perfect dialect. She was a constant source of wonderment, this sweet Myrtle.

I sank my teeth into the tart berries, and remembered that two of the jars we had carried back from the springhouse this morning were filled with what I assumed to be some sort of fruit I had never before seen. So this dessert had been created from her special berry stash in the root cellar.

"An experience, Myrtle—a whole new taste sensation."

"Thought you'd approve," she said and hurried back to the kitchen.

Then it hit me, and I sat with my fork suspended in midstroke. *Chinky pins and gooseberry pie.* That's why the term chinquapin had sounded so familiar. My sister Beth used to enlist me to help turn the jump rope when she was short one holder. She and her playmates used to sing little rhymes as they did their routines with the rope. There was one that went "Chinky pin, something, gooseberry pie."

* * *

When the guests retired to their rooms and the locals departed, I went downstairs to find the Roops waiting in the parlor. The house was quiet. I wanted some quality time with them before I had to leave. After breakfast I would make a quick stop at Harmon's, gas up and hurry on. Should be able to meet my delayed appointments in Lewisburg by mid-morning. Then I would be humming over Catawba Mountain back to my Sarah.

"Reckoned you were so full of gooseberry pie you'd already turned in, Greg." Carl gave me his snort of a laugh and offered the mason jar. "What you need is a little taste of the local mist for digestion." I waved off his offer.

Myrtle fixed him with a stare that could have turned him to stone, and he quickly realized what he'd done.

"Sorry, Greg. I wasn't thinking."

I smiled and said, "Enjoy, Carl. Just count me out." Then I picked up the conversation.

"Our venture up to the Knob pretty well did me in. You're a hardy man the way you took that ridge in stride; it was a workout for me."

"Comes from years of experience, son. Used to tell Myrtle I should have a mule to carry me up that trail. Reckon any mule I ever saw, though, would balk at the climb."

"I'm grateful to you for the tour and the background, Carl. I do believe there's a story here that needs telling."

"Might be good for Plenty to get it all in the open and out of our system," Carl said. "Whatever you need, you let me know. I'll help any way I can." He looked over at Myrtle as if to say *Hope that's okay with you.*

She caught the inference behind his look and volunteered, "Me, too, Greg. I've kept it bottled up way too long, and I trust you to do justice to our legend."

"Then you'll be seeing me again—and soon. I'd love to bring Sarah over and stay awhile. We both have some vacation coming, and I can arrange my schedule with my clients to give me a little breathing room."

Myrtle told me, "I've started to read this." She held up the small cloth diary.

"I know those thoughts are very personal between you and your father, but I would appreciate sharing whatever you choose to tell me, Myrtle."

"There's a lot for me to tell, and I'd like for you to read it later. Think you should look up Dillard Westerly again, too. I josh him about telling tall tales, but he knows an awful lot about this county."

"So I'll be sure and see old Wes when I come back. May even want to do some scouring through old newspaper accounts and library records. Where is the nearest library, Myrtle?"

"For Pocahontas County that would be down at the county seat in Marlinton."

"One other source I want to explore is someone who knows the culture and customs of the local Indian population. A source that could furnish insight into Blood Sky's background."

"I may be able to help with both the library and the Shawnee contact. Let me think about it," she replied.

We continued our banter late into the evening, There was no more talk of the legend or witches' curses. That issue had been put aside for now. They wanted to talk about here and now and good times yet to come. I think Carl drank enough moonshine for both of us, and he finally drifted away into la-la land. Myrtle told me how she would teach Sarah to make her apple pie and start a quilt when we returned while I ran my errands. She would save the Blue Room for us and 'do it up' just so, she promised.

Once, Myrtle briefly went out of the room to ask Tabetha to make us some cocoa before bedtime. When she came back, she was astonished to see that Greta had settled into the chair with me.

"You should be honored. In all my days I never saw that cat take to anybody but me. Always said it was because she was such a good judge of character. Well, she sure has warmed up to you."

"Oh, Greta and I shared a cat nap right here earlier, so I guess she's accepted me."

She knows you're the one whispered the voice just when I had begun to think it had left me.

CHAPTER 12

I lay in the bed and mulled over my plans for coming back to Plenty. My mind drifted back to the days just after the beginning of my rookie NBA season. Stayed in touch with my folks and with Sarah regularly as the Hornets darted around the country on road trips. Being away from them for such long periods was a real test. The loneliness made me work even harder to concentrate on the game rather than missing the three of them. Until the season was over, we would have little chance to get together, so I had to be content with hearing their voices on the telephone.

Mom worried about my getting to Roanoke for Christmas. Dad wanted to know everything about what was happening to me, and I knew he was soaking up every scrap of news he could find on how our games were going. Sarah just wanted to be with me and know that I was okay. She impatiently looked forward to our wedding day when she could leave her teaching job in Wytheville and join me down in Charlotte.

Then Mom called to tell me Dad had experienced one of his setbacks. That was her term for the episodes he had gone through periodically as he flashed back to some painful memories of Vietnam. Could never get him to talk about those feelings, although

I had always thought we were as close as a father and son could be. He waved off my probes, and indicated there were some things better left alone.

This time Mom sounded genuinely concerned for his mental health. He had apparently drifted farther away from her than ever before. She feared he would be permanently traumatized by this episode. I tried to talk to him, but he was evasive as always. He only wanted to discuss my progress as a 'big timer'. All the time we were talking there was an overpowering premonition that I should get on a plane and fly to Roanoke if I ever wanted to see my Dad alive again. Don't know how the idea came to me; it was like a steady beat in time with my pulse saying *'go to him, go to him. GO TO HIM.'*

The coach wasn't happy. I explained it was a family emergency, and I had to have some time off. He reluctantly agreed to four days away if I would fly on my own to meet the team in Cleveland on Tuesday. Made a reservation to Roanoke for early the next morning. Dad needed me, and I couldn't let him down.

The call came in the middle of the night. Beth was on the other end of the line, so I knew immediately something was wrong. We genuinely cared for each other, but my little sister and I were never known to routinely stay in touch. Perhaps we thought we'd maintain contact by osmosis since we both checked in on our parents regularly. Her illogical call deep into the night and her tone of voice were both alarming.

"It's Dad, Greg." My heart raced. "He was killed tonight."

"How? When, Beth?" I was overcome with grief, so much in shock I couldn't even vent my emotions. There was just an empty sensation of a loss that could never be reversed.

"He was having one of his setbacks; walked directly into the path of a truck. Mom screamed at him to stop, but he never let on that he even heard her warning."

Couldn't speak. Couldn't even think. This wasn't happening.

"Greg? Are you there?"

"I was already booked to fly down there in the morning, Beth. Mom had told me she was worried. I'll be at the house by ten." All

I could do then was hang up the phone and feel more alone than I had ever felt in my life.

In a terrible moment of tragedy, my Dad had been snatched away from me. Why it came to mind now so vividly as I lay in the darkness of the Blue Room, I can't say. But I later speculated that it had something to do with my lingering doubts about my own mental well being with a strange voice repeatedly prompting me. Frightening stories of witches and tragic deaths were fresh in my mind, and I wondered if my sanity was steadily slipping away.

For whatever reason, the memory unsettled me. Tossed and turned in a frantic effort to lose myself in sleep. Had to bring myself back and think about the present. Tomorrow was going to be a busy day on the road, and I surely didn't need another near miss due to inattention. Finally, after what seemed hours, I slipped away into a deep sleep.

This was not to be the restful time I had hoped. A dim awareness seeped into my brain, and an eerie sound throbbed its rhythm at my temples. Flat, thumping sounds like a single drum beating started as a slow, faint vibration and steadily grew.

I squeezed my eyelids tightly shut, and clamped my hands to both sides of my head. Whatever this latest harassment may be, I didn't want to see it, wanted nothing to do with it. My mind was made up. Wouldn't play the game. Whoever these demons were, they would have to pack up their bag of tricks and slink away. Old Greg was taking his ball and going home.

No matter what I did, the drum was there, and it was getting louder and more insistent. The beat increased in cadence and urgency until it was tattooing my ears at a level near pain. Tentatively opened one eye, hoping this was all just a mistake. Remembered the Goody's powder lying on the dresser, and tried to convince myself that a pounding headache could be countered by one of those magic remedies—my own personal scoot-booger. My eyes began to adjust to the light in the Blue Room. I saw that last night's storm had left in its wake a bright moonlit evening. The light streamed in the windows, and sent a soft glow through the entire room. Cast a long stationary shadow toward where I was lying.

Then the shadow began to move, an almost imperceptive movement at first, then more pronounced until it began gliding toward the big double windows. I glued my gaze to the apparition and followed its progress. As if standing on a slowly revolving wheel, the dark figure turned to face me. There were no distinct features, no eyes looked back at me, but I was certain that a person—real or otherworldly—was staring me down as surely as my proper name was Greg-o-ry Bain. And the advantage was his—hers—its.

"Who are you? What do you want of me?" I asked, trying to keep my voice from cracking. No answer.

"Please! Tell me why you're here."

Without so much as a nod or a word, the vision turned slowly away as deliberately as it had faced in my direction, stood before the windows and seemed to float gently toward them. The windows swung open as if on cue. A strong gust of wind blew past the bed and ripped the covers from my suddenly clammy limbs. This was too real to be a dream. I was an active part of this scene, and there was no escaping it now.

A warm and comfortable repose had been transformed into a shivering fright. The bed was now ice cold, and I imagined myself stretched out on a marble slab, exposed to the frigid night air. The cold soaked through every pore, worked its way deep down into my veins, making my blood slow and my heart flutter. Gathered all my strength to bolt upright off the icy bed. The apparition seemed to be perched on the windowsill, looking out into the moon-filled night. The drums reached an ear-splitting intensity, and that same eerie chant I had heard last night built once more.

"Stop. Please stop," I called out, and tried to close the distance between myself and the ghostly figure.

As I lunged forward toward the apparition, a chorus of drums and the sing-song chanting punished me with their cacophony. My legs went from stinging cold to a complete loss of feeling, and they gave way under my weight and left me in a heap halfway across the room. I lay there trying to regain my composure, trying to stand on feet that weren't responding.

"Wait! Let me see who you are. Let me touch you," I pleaded. I strained to hear a reply; the phantom made no sign that it heard. As if stepping through an open doorway, the figure moved forward, and it dropped from view into the moonlit night. The drums and the chant reached their crescendo. Then they abruptly ceased. I was alone in the freezing air staring intently at—an empty room.

The feeling slowly returned to my feet. I tested my legs, first standing carefully and then making my way back to the bed as if sleepwalking. Picked up the emergency light I had brought in and set on my table after last night's power outage. The light had a large battery pack that cast a strong beam to the ground. The yard three stories beneath my window sloped away to a shallow creek bed. I slowly cast the beam in all directions; saw absolutely no sign of a body or anything else out of the ordinary. Was my mind playing cruel tricks again?

For the second night I was experiencing a strange ritual of torment in the Blue Room. Why were these ghostly visions appearing to me? What could I do to shut them out? I thrashed about in the bed helplessly for the rest of the night, and sleep came for only fitful and brief periods. The most welcome sight of the tortuous night was the sun making its way into the room as dawn broke. If I didn't make a break from this place today, my mind was going to continue to conjure up horrific sights until my sanity abandoned me completely. This had to be the day I made it away from Plenty and home to my sweet Sarah.

CHAPTER 13

The radio blared in my ear.

"Good morning, all you fine mountain people! It's old Jerry Bob back at the wheel steering you good old boys and girls through another fine West Virginia morning. Bit on the chilly side out there, so bundle up. She's in the mid-thirties and breezy but clear. Best of all, the roads are open, and it's clear sailin' for all you travelers and commuters."

At least I was starting the day with a bit of good news. If I could just shake the remnants of last night's experience and sink a tooth into a hot breakfast, I could be on my way. Three quick stops then home. There would be lots of time later to think about the implications of what had happened in the Blue Room during the night. Had to get a handle on whether I manufactured those visions in my troubled mind. Maybe my sanity really was in jeopardy, and the voice in my head was my warning.

The room was much chillier than I had expected. Even with the big blue comforter shielding me, my head was uncomfortably cold. I lifted myself on one elbow to peer across the room. Wished I hadn't. The double windows that were securely latched before I turned in were standing wide open. That made me carefully play back the moments after I watched—or dreamed I saw—the figure drop out of view. Tried to remember what had happened next. Okay, I had retrieved the emergency light and scanned the ground below then . . . returned to bed without bothering to close the windows. Reacted like I'd been dealt a blow to the ribs and sank back onto the pillow. Damn! Could my midnight vision have been real, not just imagined?

"Yes sir," Jerry Bob's grating voice barked, "all you early risers on the hunting trail get your warm duds on, put the gun on the rack and tie that blue tick coon hound in the back of the pickup. Put your ugly butts and your pocket warmers on those tree stands. It's time for Mr. Stag to tuck his tail and run."

That was enough of Jerry Bob and his down home chatter. I reached over and turned the dial. He was probably a street boy from Philadelphia or New York, anyway, affecting his phony version of hill chatter for the locals. Most of them probably had him pegged. Guess they could put up with his making an ass of himself as long as he played their favorite country songs. A little soothing music without his patter was what I needed.

Walked over to the windows; took one more look down at the yard and creek bed. Nothing there. Latched them shut and shook my head, as an involuntary shiver passed through me.

My packing was a breeze, since I only had to stuff dirties into my bag. This trip was in overtime status, and I was seriously strapped for clean clothes. Seems I had made a good initial impression with the Roops, though, and I didn't want to ruin it by showing up all ruffled for breakfast. Myrtle's tender care and a good meal would surely lift my spirits and settle my seriously jangled nerves. I found my least rumpled shirt and pants, laid them out, hurried through my shower and shave and started downstairs.

First I needed to catch Sarah before she left for school so I could reconfirm that I'd be there by this afternoon. I could have a few moments of privacy on the phone in the parlor. Picked up the brass handset, and there was no dial tone. It was dead as a rock. Oh, great! The roads are clear, and now the phone system is down again. No need to try the cell phone. Knew that wouldn't work until I cleared the hills. Had to wait to talk to her or maybe just check in with Mom once I was east of the mountains.

"Bright eyed and bushy tailed today, aren't you?" Myrtle was busy scurrying around the kitchen serving her guests their country style start. "Sit down. I'll have your food right out to you."

She was so cheery this morning. I almost resented anyone being that high, especially when I still felt strung out from the disturbing night. But no one could be miffed at Myrtle for long; she was such a kind soul. When the breakfast rush was over, and most of the guests had left the dining room, she came over to sit with me.

"I must say, your reputation for making the best country breakfast in these parts is well earned. I could learn to start every day this way. I already have to do penance with about a week of extra jogging to take care of two suppers and all the other food you fed me yesterday."

"Wish you didn't have to leave us so soon, Greg. Carl and I have both taken to you. I think you already guessed that. Do you really have to go today?"

"Have a lady waiting for me who would be very upset if I was another day late, Myrtle. I promise you that Sarah and I will both be back. She has to meet you folks so she can feel as much at home at the Comfy as I have."

"On second thought, you look a little peaked around the gills, son. Didn't sleep well?"

"As a matter of fact, I don't think I slept at all. It was a long night."

"Bed not comfortable? Room too cold? I'm sorry."

"No, nothing that was your fault or the Comfy's. I just had too much going through my mind to rest."

"You need one of these," she said.

She turned to a decoration hanging in one of the dining room windows. Attached over a nail by a leather loop was a wooden hoop with intricate fiber webbing woven throughout its center and two feathers on its perimeter. Three leather thongs dangled downward from the hoop, and at the end of each thong hung two more feathers.

I took a long look at the object, and tried to remember where I had seen anything like it. Knew right away that it had something to do with Indian superstition—exactly what I couldn't say.

"It's called a dream catcher. The local Shawnee believe having one near will bring good sleep undisturbed by bad dreams. The hoop catches and filters dreams, and allows only the good ones to float down to the sleeper. It traps bad dreams, and they die at the first light of dawn."

"Sounds like I could have used that last night. Some pretty crazy visions were floating all around me."

"When you come back I'll have your own personal dream catcher for you to hang on the bed post to protect your sleep. I believe a dream catcher is more powerful when it's been blessed by a true medicine man, so yours will be as strong as we can make it."

"Enough about me, Myrtle. What did you learn from the diary?" My question brought a serious, almost somber expression to her cheery face. Couldn't tell whether her reading had displeased or disturbed her.

"That book is the most mesmerizing reading I've ever seen, Greg. My Daddy put his innermost thoughts down in the little diary. I couldn't stop reading once I started."

"You know I'm totally swept away by the story of your father, but I won't pry unless there's something you want to tell me. It's entirely up to you, dear Myrtle."

"Oh, I want to share it, only it'll take time. Can't part with the book just yet, not even for a day. So you'll have to make good on your promise, and come back up here to read it. And please bring Sarah and your Mom, too."

"You can count on that, Myrtle. I want to pursue the legend that's built up around the Comfy, and I need to learn as much as possible about this place. My book is already coming together in my head."

"I told you I could help with the library," she said. "Called a girlfriend of mine that works over at the county library in Marlinton. Velma's also the closest thing we have to a historian around here.

She said she would do some spadework before you came by to be ready for you."

"That's great. Do you have any idea who I can see in the Indian community about their legends and superstitions? I really need to get a handle on Blood Sky and her daughter, particularly their Shawnee background."

"A wonderful man worked for my Daddy then for Carl here at the farm until he was killed by a wild animal near Pennick's Knob. His name was Warren Brainerd, and his nephew still lives nearby. I'll ask the boy who he considers the wisest elder in their circle."

Suddenly her face lit up, and she snapped her fingers. "Wait! I know. Daddy had a friend just down the road by the name of Chief John. He's a shaman, a Shawnee medicine man. I'll look him up and have him bless your dream catcher before you return. Then I'll ask if you can come see him."

"Well, as much as I hate to go, Myrtle, I should be on my way home. Thank you so much for all you've done, and I *will* be back. It's a promise."

Brought my suitcase and laptop downstairs, paid Myrtle for my stay and paused briefly to say goodbye to Carl. Myrtle swept me up in a hearty hug that left me breathless but glowing. As I turned to exit I caught a fleeting glimpse of Tabetha lurking at the end of the foyer with her unfathomable stare.

CHAPTER 14

First a stop at Harmon's Gas and Grocery for a fill-up. Last thing I needed was to be stranded on my way out of the Yew Mountains. Besides, I wanted to prime Harmon Grace for a follow-up visit when I came back to Plenty. Wes said I should see him, and old Wes was the acknowledged authority on what went on in the valley.

Harmon was in his normal posture, tipped back in his chair, reading material in hand. Had a cup on the counter, so I guessed he was punishing his stomach with some high-test blue john. The old black and gray cat wandered around the store foraging—for what, mice or morsels of foodstuffs? Harmon barely took notice when I entered his store until I spoke to him.

"Finally getting ready to leave," I said.

He slowly tipped his chair forward. Tore himself away from the paperback. Harmon made the routine act of standing up look like an Olympic event in slow motion.

"Well, here's that feller pert near drowned the other night. How you doin' today, mister basketball?"

"Much better, I have to admit. Myrtle's care and attention and some fine meals took care of that."

"Enjoyed your stay at the Comfy, didja?" He gave me a brief replay of his squeaky cackle.

"The Roops are fine folks, Harmon. Know how to make an outsider feel at home."

"They're salt of the earth, Greg." That expression sounded familiar.

"Wish I could stay longer. I have business to attend to, and family is waiting for me over in Roanoke."

"You ain't too far from home after all, are you? Just a flatlander, heh, heh."

"Need to fill up my tank and shuttle off, but I fully intend to be back for another visit."

As he coaxed the old pump and chewed incessantly on something—maybe tobacco, maybe just his cud—I broached the other objective of my brief visit. "Dillard Westerly tells me that next to him, you probably keep track of what goes on around here better than anybody. Like I said, I plan to come back. Could use some time with you then to talk about Plenty and the local people. It would be very helpful. Can I count on that?"

"Hell, I ain't going nowhere, and the business don't overpower me as you can plainly see. That old fart Wes might be surprised how much I know about things around here including things about the sheriff and his shady dealings."

"I expect to be back through Plenty in a couple of weeks at most. Like to sit down and have a long conversation with you, Mr. Grace."

"No, see, Mr. Grace was my Daddy. I'm just plain old Harmon. What you got in mind? As the old sayin goes, you writing a book?"

"Actually, that's exactly what I plan to do. I believe you could add some valuable background for what I'm putting together. I want to write about the Charlton place, the witch's curse and all the tragedies that have occurred up there over the past fifty years. Try to take away the mystery that's hanging over Plenty."

"You talk about old Blood Sky Hawk and all the other loonies running around up in the hills, I can tell you a thing or two. Cost my Daddy his life. Surely did. Weird place, the Comfy. You real sure you want to open that can of nasty night crawlers, boy?"

"Absolutely convinced, friend. It may be the best way to cleanse this neighborhood of a bad reputation and get some people and business back in here. If I can show a logical explanation for the things that have happened, maybe folks from outside Plenty won't treat it like a forbidden place. You wouldn't argue with an increase in customers, would you?"

"That'd suit me just fine. You drop in anytime, Greg. We'll chew the fat about whatever you like. Get my old wood stove stoked up. We'll spin yarns as long as you want." He took my money and shook my hand. "See you real soon, neighbor."

"You bet. Hold that thought, Harmon. I'll be back."

Before I pulled away from the station, I planned ahead to call Mom as soon as I was beyond the mountains. At least she would know I was on my way home. Might be able to get the word to Sarah quicker than I could. Hurried out to State 39 and turned east. Then the voice spoke to me.

Joe Dolan is a good old boy. You two should talk more often.

The day was only beginning, and the voice was back in my head again. I tried to shake it off.

That did prompt an idea, though. *Why didn't I try reaching Joe on my cell phone?* There was a chance it would work in the other direction between here and his store in Richwood once I was out of the bowl of hills surrounding Plenty. I could ask him to relay my message to Mom for Sarah. She would be tickled to hear from him. At least the voice interceding in my life may bring a positive result this time. I dialed the store number and Joe answered.

"Joe, it's Greg. I wonder . . ." He cut me short; nearly shouted in my ear.

"Thank God, Greg! I don't know what possessed you to call, but it's a blessing. Apparently the phone lines are all out down that way. Your mom located me somehow, and she just called here with an urgent message. I was about ready to tear out of here to find you. Sarah took ill, and the doctor doesn't know what's wrong. They've rushed her to Roanoke Memorial Hospital for tests."

His news took a few seconds to soak in. Then my heart and my mind both went into fast forward.

"You're a life saver, buddy. I'll go straight there. Leaving Plenty right now. Call Mom for me. Tell her I'll be at the hospital as soon as possible."

The drive down State 39 could have been an improvement by light years over my experience of two nights ago. Except for the fact that the road was still curvy and demanded my full attention, it would have been a pleasant drive toward Mill Point and the junction with US 219 without driving into the teeth of a pounding storm. Now Mom's news had turned that prospect upside down, and it presented me with a new urgency. With me plunging ahead around bends and the possibility of line huggers bringing head-on hazards, I was on the edge of my seat. Sarah was in good hands, but I needed to be there. An overpowering wave of fear took hold of me. Sarah's problem was no routine upset. This was something far more serious.

As soon as I was east of the mountain peaks, I tried Mom's home number and drew only her answering machine. Well, it was time to see if the cell phone we bought her for emergencies was turned on. Punched in the number on speed dial while negotiating turns in the road. Several rings later Mom answered rather tentatively.

"It's Greg, Mom. What's going on with Sarah? Can you update me?"

"The doctor is totally stumped. Sarah's vital signs are good, but she's not improving."

"What do you mean, not improving?"

"Greg, honey, about half an hour ago she slipped into a coma after the tests showed almost normal readings. It's something the doc has never seen before. He's staying right here until we find the problem."

"Guess Joe Dolan got through to you by now. I couldn't reach you from back in Plenty."

"Yes. When he called he said you were on your way. Sarah told me how excited she was about you finding Joe and Julie out there.

The number where you were staying wasn't answering, so I searched until I located Joe. Thank God. Sarah went into her coma soon after that."

"Oh, no! And here I am on country roads hours from home. Damn my sorry hide! Why couldn't I be there when she needs me? She never let me down when I needed her so desperately."

"Now I don't want to hear you talk like that, Greg. You couldn't change what happened to her. Please be careful, and don't do anything foolish. Sarah and I need for you to be safe."

"I will, Mom. Watch over her. I'll be there soon."

I disconnected, and felt another kick of adrenaline surge through my system. There weren't any shortcuts now; I just had to keep boring ahead at breakneck speed. Then the soft voice whispered in the back of my brain.

She'll always be there for you.

How did the voice know the exact words Sarah had spoken to me in my dream?

I reached the intersection at Mill Point, and prompted a near collision with a logging truck in my haste to turn and speed down 219. My car phone was hands-off, so I could use it without stopping if I could locate some telephone numbers. Occupied my mind for a few hectic miles by calling my clients to tell them I had an emergency. Told them I would have to get back to them later. There was no way I was stopping anywhere with my darling in a crisis.

Miraculously, I made it through the back roads and small towns without crossing a patrol car and landing in jail. Have no doubt that a dozen local lawmen could have pulled me in for excessive speed if they'd chosen to chase me. I was sparing no horses in my headlong flight to Sarah's side. Despite Mom's reassuring words about Sarah's normal readings, something in my brain insisted I hurry. I was convinced she was in great danger.

This was such a helpless feeling. Sarah needed me, and I was on the road again. Had to make a drastic change soon; needed to spend more time with her. My efforts at finding a new job had been all dead ends so far. It should have been long enough by now to get some feedback on my chances for the assistant coach's job at Tech.

Tried hard to take Mom's advice and moderate my speed. I wouldn't be any good to Sarah lying in a hospital or morgue somewhere between West Virginia and Roanoke.

Kept repeating to myself, *Just take it a step at a time, Greg. She needs you there in one piece.*

Never could listen to my conscience. Every time I slowed, a picture of Sarah flashed before my eyes, and I sped up again. The thought of her lying in that hospital ripped me apart. Kept checking the mileage as I careened around curves. There were probably motorists behind me reporting to their local constables about a maniac on the loose.

Plenty and dreams, mysterious voices and head games, even speed limits and lawmen were of absolutely no importance to me now. All that mattered was to see Sarah and coax her awake.

CHAPTER 15

Finding the hospital was no problem. It was those last agonizing moments before I reached Sarah's room that had me in a near panic. What if her condition had gone down hill, and I didn't even know it yet?

I sprinted through the parking lot at full speed. Passersby looked at me like I was some sort of lunatic. I ignored them, tore past and bounded down the sidewalk like a man possessed. Reached the front desk out of breath and gasping to get my question out.

"My wife was brought in this morning," I panted. "Her name is Sarah Bain. Can you tell me where she is?"

The receptionist was, I'm sure, very efficient. However, it seemed like she and everyone else was moving in slow motion. She gave me Sarah's room number, and pointed the way to the elevators. I raced down the hall; attacked the elevator doors as they attempted to close.

Mom was sitting by the bed with a look of deep concern. Sarah appeared to be sleeping peacefully but with no movement at all. I nearly broke down when I saw the monitors attached to her. Their rhythmic beeps in the otherwise silent room unnerved me.

"She's doing fine, son. All her signs are still good. She just can't seem to shake out of this coma." Mom reached out, and put her arms around me to console me.

"I'm sure she knows you're here, Mom. That has to be a great comfort to her." I went to the bed, bent over and kissed my wife gently. There was no response. She did feel normal to the touch, and her steady breathing was even and strong.

"I'll stay right here with you, sweetheart, until you wake up. Nothing could pry me away."

She showed no sign of recognition, no movement, not even a fluttering eyelid or a twitching finger. It was like someone had reached into my chest and ripped out my heart. I wanted so desperately to go back a few days and call off my trip, to be there by her side from the first instant she took sick and needed me close. But I couldn't change any of that now, so I would simply sit here and refuse to budge until she came back to me.

"You visit. I'll be nearby." Mom kissed my cheek, and she quietly left the room.

The news of Sarah's illness had come down hard on me from the outset. Now that I had seen her it struck me with sudden, sickening force that lying in that bed in front of me was my whole life. Any aspirations I had, any plans or schemes for the future, were of no value whatsoever if I didn't have her to share them with me. If necessary, I would move heaven and earth to see that she was back with me, whole and healthy, no matter how long it may take.

She lay there so still and beautiful. I took her hand in mine, and held onto her for dear life. As many bad times as there had been not long ago, all of them my own fault, I only wanted to remember the good times in our lives at this agonizing moment. Closed my eyes and pictured my favorite memories.

I saw Sarah running barefoot through the tall grass at the edge of a stream, her brown hair swept against her face and shoulders. She eluded my grasp and headed for the water. Laughed and taunted me. "I always could run your scrawny butt into the ground, Mr. Round Ball." That made me more determined to catch the lovely nymph and make her say 'uncle'.

Then I was close behind her, almost catching her small waist with my outstretched hand before she stepped off into the gurgling stream. She turned toward me, and her lilting laughter caressed me with its music. I caught her arm and tugged at her. Down into the creek we tumbled. Both of us landed solidly on our backsides, fully clothed and soaked to our hips in the cool water. I drew her close to me, and brushed the brown locks back from her face. We shared a long kiss, then I whispered "I love you, you sexy wench." We stood, our lips still joined, ignoring our thoroughly soaked clothing. Streamed creek water from our garments as we retreated to a grassy knoll a few feet from the bank. A waiting picnic basket was forgotten in favor of more exciting delights.

After all she and I had come through together it just couldn't turn against us now. We had too much time and love invested in a relationship I wanted to enjoy for every day I had remaining on earth. I simply refused to believe my Sarah could be snatched from me so abruptly without so much as letting me say goodbye to her. Then I silently admonished myself for even thinking of the word goodbye because I wouldn't accept that outcome.

An odd chill crept into my being, and the feeling sent a dull ache all the way into my bones. I had the eerie sensation that my unanticipated visit to the community of Plenty and her sudden illness were connected in some abstract way. In some twisted fashion I could be responsible for bringing on her coma by an action or omission I couldn't yet pinpoint.

The voice joined me while I agonized over this thought.

Follow your heart and all will be well.

For once, I didn't resent the voice's intrusion upon my thoughts. I was beginning, in fact, to feel more comfortable with its mutterings when I sincerely wanted to believe what it was telling me.

Don't know how long I sat with her small hand pressed between my palms. I sank so deeply into thought that I drifted away into much-needed sleep. Stirred only when someone touched me on the back.

"Are you all right, Tater?" Mom asked. For an instant I was that little towheaded child with Mom rousting me on a cold morning to prepare for school. Even shivered with the prospect of sallying forth into the bitter winter winds with only Mom's hot oatmeal and cocoa to fortify me. "Greg, are you okay?"

I shook off the sleepy haze and looked up at her. "Oh, sure, Mom. Just didn't get a lot of sleep last night, and I must have dropped off for a minute." Then I checked to be sure the sleeping beauty with her hand in mine was still breathing normally. She was beautiful and still, so still.

"Maybe you can give me the answer to something that's been worrying me for the past two days, Mom. Sarah told me we had something very important to discuss as soon as I was back home. It sounded as if she had a special homecoming planned before that storm completely changed my timetable. It's been gnawing at me ever since."

"I would guess she was saving some highly valued bit of news for you and you alone. You'll know as soon as she wakes up, I'm sure. Couldn't say what it may be, though."

Her answer fell short, and I wasn't certain why. Mom and Sarah had grown so close that they often confided in each other things they wouldn't tell even me. It was hard to believe my wife had anything important happen in her life that she would conceal from Mom. There was a definite hint of evasiveness in her reply, but I knew she wouldn't keep anything from me that would have the least chance of harming either Sarah or me. Decided not to pursue the subject for the time being. When she was ready Sarah would tell me herself.

"Mom, you have to be worn out. I'm sure you've been up since Sarah first called and told you she was ill. Why don't you go home and sleep. I'll call if there's any change here."

She really did look at this point like she was struggling to keep her eyes open.

"If you're too tired to drive, we'll call a cab. We can always leave your car parked here, and I'll come for you later."

"No, I'll manage fine, son. I'll leave in a little while. It's only a short drive."

"Please, Mom. I'd feel better if you took a break."

"Well, maybe for awhile. Just be sure you call if there's any change at all in her condition. You get some rest, too. Pull up another chair and put your feet up. The important thing is that you're here for her now."

As I had done without question for all of my thirty years, I took Mom's advice, positioned another chair facing me, kicked off my shoes and got comfortable. I was soon in the arms of Morpheus.

* * *

In my sleep I was back at the Comfy taking stock of all I'd learned during my stay. Myrtle was filling my head with the details of her father's diary while she stuffed my stomach with assorted delights from her fragrant kitchen. Then we were in the parlor. Carl sat by mutely observing and steadily draining his jar of crystal clear relaxer. Myrtle stroked her beloved Greta in her lap. I listened while she related how her Daddy had pined away after his Sweet Tater and his Lizbeth and slowly drifted away from her. She told me about all of the incidents that had built the story surrounding the Comfy to legendary proportions. Try as I may, though, I couldn't quite make out just what events she meant. There was a little old librarian and an Indian medicine man, people I hadn't yet met. Already, both of them were taking shape in my mind's eye.

Drew a mental picture of a kindly old gentleman as Myrtle's father, Ezra Charlton. Then it struck me that I had formed him all wrong in my imagination. He couldn't have been more than twenty-six or twenty-seven when he died. Maybe she had a picture of him somewhere that would add to my background story for the book.

Wes and Harmon were bending my ear with their tall tales about the witch's curse and their voices blended into a totally indistinguishable blur of words. Tried to say 'one at a time, please'. They both kept droning on and on.

Then I was standing alone in front of a small cabin high up on a ridge, and it was still smoking as a thousand eyes kept vigil, watching me suspiciously from behind tall trees. There were dark figures of men congregating near the cabin. I could see them clearly except that their faces seemed to be hidden from me. A smoldering heap roughly the size and shape of a human form lay between the men and the cabin. I puzzled over the hazy images that flashed by in rapid succession.

I was holding one arm extended full length in front of me with some object grasped tightly in my hand. As I stared intently and strained to focus my eyes on the object, it turned into the scoot-booger from the hall curio cabinet. Seemed I was using it as my talisman against the presence of evil, my protection against bad spirits in this tragic place on the ridge.

When I awoke from my nap my first feeling was to be thankful that it had contained no horrible fantasy as could have been expected by now. Instead, my thoughts had somehow coalesced into an introspective probing of the bits and pieces of information collected in my time at the Plenty Comfy. Although the pieces didn't yet fit together in a coherent fashion, I knew a return trip to Plenty would change that. In fact, getting back to the Comfy was the only way my mind would ever be at rest. Maybe if I heeded the call and did the bidding of that persistent voice in my head, I could rid myself of both the legend and the voice.

Doctor Jameson came from behind and spoke to me. "Having a little snooze, Greg?" I noticed Mom had apparently never left; she sat quietly by watching over Sarah and me while I slept.

"Ah, hi, doc. Trying to unwind after a fast trip." I was so glad he was attending to Sarah. Doc Jameson had been our family doctor all my life, and there was no one whose medical judgment I valued more highly.

"How's our girl doing? Let me see." He checked the monitors and tested her reflexes. Muttered something about being at a loss, then he shook his head. That bothered me greatly.

"What can you tell me so far, doc?" I asked.

"Well, first and most important is the fact that all of her readings look completely within the normal range. She is in no immediate danger, but I can't for the life of me identify her underlying problem. Medically, it just doesn't stand to reason that she would lapse into a coma with the strong vital signs she exhibits."

"Are there more tests you can do? Is there medicine that will help?"

"I'm looking at all possibilities, Greg. Also contacted a couple of specialists who should be here later this week to consult with me. They may have some of the answers we need."

"Whatever it takes, doc. You know best. I just want her back from this other place she's in."

"And you can be confident that she'll get the best care possible. In the meantime, your being here is the strongest medicine she could have. Just keep talking to her."

"Are you sure there isn't something more you're not telling me? She hinted to me yesterday that something had happened she wanted to discuss with me, and it's been tearing me up inside wondering what it could be."

His face changed expression. He glanced at Mom then turned away and fiddled with one of the knobs on a monitor. When he returned his attention to me, Doc Jameson was as expressionless as before. "I'm genuinely stumped, Greg. We'll keep at this puzzle till we figure it out. In the meantime, patience is our byword."

"I can take it, doc. If the tests have shown any possibility of a serious condition, I need to know and face it with her. Let me handle my share of the burden."

"Now don't let your fears cloud your judgment. This is no time to let your concern for her make your imagination run away with you. If there was anything seriously wrong, I'd tell you. Haven't I always been honest with you, Greg?"

"I know, and I'm sorry if I sounded skeptical. It's just that she means everything to me."

"Trust me, son. You've known me since I delivered you into this world. Give it some time."

I nodded, and turned back to Sarah as he left the room. When I glanced out into the hall, he and Mom were talking and he shrugged. Doc turned, saw that I was watching and quickly moved on. Try as I might I couldn't shake the impression that they were keeping something vital from me.

CHAPTER 16

For the next five days I sat by Sarah's side and talked to her. Relived with her all the wonderful experiences only the two of us could share. Never before had I had a one-sided conversation with my wife. On second thought, maybe there was one time. When I asked her to marry me, it seemed like hours before she gave her answer, although she would probably say her reply took more like a matter of seconds.

Ever since I first met this wonderful woman she had been the ideal verbal foil for me. Our conversations could be, and normally were, both stimulating and thought proving. Serious practitioner of the English language that my mate was, there were times when I was more like the student being tutored by a strict teacher. Even then I realized her coaching added to my word skills, and she could help me grow as a writer when the proper time came. She was a tough and devoted debater on issues that ranged the full spectrum from abbreviations to zucchini, abacus to zoology. I had always considered her a formidable conversationalist.

That's why it seemed so queer now to be going on and on to her about every subject that popped into my head. At first I actually paused to wait for her comebacks; then, realizing I had to carry the discourse for now, I resumed my droning. The nurses must have thought I was a bit over the edge with some of the things I was telling her when they made their rounds, but they always managed a knowing smile for me.

I relived the past ten years over and over with her, carefully avoiding those two terrible lost years clawing my way out of a black hole when she was constantly offering me a pull rope to safety. Even as endearing as her devotion was during those tough months, I couldn't bear to dwell on that dark time now. Much more comforting and reassuring were the private times we savored with only the two of us interacting. Those were times when the rest of the world was shut outside our sphere of perception and we saw only each other.

In those memories we were together at an isolated table in a dark restaurant. We shared the Hawaiian sunset on a cliff overlooking the ocean. Walked together in a crisp, clear Colorado morning with new fallen snow crunching under our boots, and cuddled by a warm fireplace as the wind howled outside our cabin door.

When I remembered our most intimate moments, I leaned closer and whispered, virtually crooned, the memories into her ear. I was carrying her across the threshold of our first house bought with part of my bonus money and equipped with every modern convenience for the girl who would be the center of my life. All of the tangible effects in that home were of no consequence to either of us at that instant. I looked down at her, and she smiled her silent assent. The groom carried his bride directly from front door to staircase to bedroom, and we consecrated our new home properly.

The days ran together. Hour upon hour I talked to my sleeping beauty. Talked until my mouth was dry, found a cup of coffee to gulp down and started anew. Mom brought me food and comfort items, and she spelled me each day so I could retreat to the house long enough to clean up and return to my vigil. How many times I retraced the same memory paths with the silent Sarah was hard to say. It didn't matter. This is exactly where I wanted to be, and all she had to do was listen and fight her way awake. I wouldn't budge until she did.

Somewhere during my watch my sister Beth came down from northern Virginia to check on us. I was so absorbed I thought it was Mom when she stole up behind me and put her arms around me.

"Don't you have a hug for your poor little kid sister, big brother?"

I stood and gathered her up in my arms. "Beth! I'm so glad you came. Just reminded Sarah how she and I actually skipped rope together when we were fully grown to see if we could still do it. Told her how you used to tease me that boys couldn't keep up skipping like girls."

"You did pretty well for a boy, I must say. Enlisted you enough times as a rope turner when nobody else was handy, and you were usually a good sport about it."

"I was okay until you would get miffed at me for turning too fast and would yell 'Greg-o-ry' at me. You knew I couldn't stand for anybody to call me by that name." We shared a healthy howl remembering our childhood rivalries.

"But you always knew you were my favorite brother, didn't you?"

"Hell, girl, I was your *only* brother. That didn't give you much to pick from, did it? Now answer a question for me, sis."

"I'll try."

"There was a skip rope ditty that went chinquapins, something, gooseberry something. Do you remember that one?"

"Let me see." She closed her eyes and concentrated. "Now I remember. It was:

Chinky-pins, crabapples,
Gooseberry pie,
Jump up, jump up,
Reach for the sky."

"That's the one. Where did you learn that rhyme, Beth?"

"Oh, maybe from one of my playmates. Or maybe Mom taught it to me. I really don't remember. Why do you ask now?"

"No particular reason. Just came to mind. So, tell me, how are Gramps and Gram Adams? I suppose you still get around to visiting them often?"

"Every chance I get. We were talking about you the other day, and they were saying it's been way too long since you and Sarah took time off and came up to Leesburg to see them. You used to get such a kick out of riding their horses and helping Gramps on his vet rounds with the animals. Now that he's retired he has lots of time to spend with the horses. I know he'd love to share that time with you."

Mom's parents had lived in the Roanoke valley all their lives until Gramps went to northern Virginia to a more lucrative veterinarian practice. They had bought a beautiful farm in horse country, and he eventually retired from looking after farm animals and pets. I really would love to see him and Gram.

"I know we're way overdue for a visit, Beth, and I'm downright ashamed of myself. Maybe when Sarah pulls out of this baffling coma, we'll find some time to take a break and set our heads straight. The farm would be a good place to do that."

"See that you remember that when the chance comes, Greg. They really do want to see you, and you know they're getting on in years. Don't wait too long." Beth always did have a way of making me feel guilty. This time she made a valid point. I would accept the hit.

"Sis, I have a big favor to ask of you. Can you stay over a couple days and be here with Mom and Sarah?"

"I think I can manage that. Some particular reason?"

"Sarah and I went up to Blacksburg about a month ago so I could interview for a position as an assistant basketball coach at Tech. I need to go back tomorrow for a follow-up visit. Feel like one of us should be here with the two of them until we get Sarah back on her feet. You know Mom would never admit she's beyond exhausted. Having you here to help would be such a great comfort to her."

I thought about my pending visit to Tech. The university had an unexpected coaching vacancy. I had submitted a blind application some months back hoping to eventually find my way onto the coaching staff. That application was still in their candidates' stack; they narrowed their list of candidates, and the prospects still included me. They liked my record as a Division II player at Elkins and shared the NBA's high opinion of my playing ability. However, what really attracted the head coach's attention, as he himself told me, was the intensity with which I had always been a student of the game. Dad had instilled in me a true love of basketball. Apparently it showed through in my performance in high school and college. They believed that would carry over to the players I would help coach.

My feeling after our visit to the Blacksburg campus was that both Sarah and I had made a good impression on the staff. They'd called and asked that we return for a second visit, and that appointment was now just a day away. I'd have to explain that Sarah was ill and couldn't be there. We couldn't miss this opportunity. Could be golden for both of us. They'd have me actively involved with the game I love, and Sarah could continue her teaching job for the time being. With the breaks faculty usually get, we may even be able to work out her finishing her doctorate and finding a position on the college staff. The beauty is we could still live where we were and commute up the mountain within an hour each day. Hopefully, there could be a big decision to make on my own soon even if she didn't wake up right away. This was just too important to pass up.

"You go ahead," Beth said. "Sounds like the perfect job for you. I'll help Mom watch after Sarah. And good luck, Greg."

"Knew I could count on you, sis. Mom's about worn out. It'll do wonders for her to have you here."

I was so absorbed in my excitement about the potential new job I hadn't noticed that Doctor Jameson had entered the room on his daily rounds.

"Still here, Greg? Have you even been away from that spot at all today? Well, I see another one of my kids is here, too."

Beth stood and shook the hand that had delivered her as well. "I hope our special girl here is doing better, Doc," she told him.

"She's more than holding her own, Beth. We just can't get her to open those pretty brown eyes for us. Greg's been working on that day and night. It's only a matter of time."

Doc brought us up to date and reassured both of us that Sarah was continuing to show no adverse signs from being in her coma. In fact, her condition resembled a deep and peaceful sleep, and her readings were perfectly normal. There was no medical reason he could find that she shouldn't be able to awaken at any instant and be fine and ready to go home. I found myself peering deeply into those kindly eyes hoping he wasn't giving us the watered down version of her condition.

Don't hold back on me now, Doc, I thought. *Not after all these years.*

Mom came into the room and gave Sarah, Beth and me kisses all around then turned to the doctor.

"I told both of them," he said, "that she's doing great if we could only get her to wake up. In her present condition she could go straight home with you if she wasn't sleeping. We've kept her fed and she's strong."

"Then help me convince Greg that he needs a change of pace, doctor," Mom pleaded.

"My advice would be that he go about his normal routine and let us look after the patient," Doc Jameson said. "In her subconscious she has to know by now how long he's been standing guard over her, and she would know that he needs a break. Seems to me you should go back to work, Greg, and I'll do the worrying for both of us."

Mom agreed. "That's exactly what I've been trying to tell him, doctor. I'm here, and Sarah won't want for anything. We can stay in touch daily. Greg can get back here in a matter of a few hours at most."

"But I'd be out on the road for days," I protested. "How much good would I be constantly thinking about her lying here?"

Doctor Jameson assumed a stern tone. "Greg, I think it's best you do what your mother says and regain some order in your life. Sarah will come around in her own good time, and your mom will be right here watching over her. Now go on and try to get back to normal as far as that's possible. It's what's best for both of you now."

I was fighting the idea of being away from her for more than brief periods until she was awake. But they both made perfectly good sense. It was time to try to get back to making a living for us. I had to quit dwelling on her problem every waking moment, if that was possible. There was still that nagging notion ricocheting around in my skull that the answers to all of the current dilemmas in my life, even her puzzling coma, were back up there somewhere in the Yew Mountains. Maybe that was illogical, but somehow it made sense to me. My brief encounter with the folks in Plenty had made a lasting impression on me, and the timing of Sarah's problem coincided with all the stress I had been going through in the mountains. Could the key to her recovery be there in Plenty, not here? Far fetched? Maybe. It was real enough in my mind.

"Okay, I'll agree. But you can expect to hear from me every morning and evening while I'm on the road, Mom."

"I'll keep you read into everything that goes on here at the hospital, son. Just ring me anytime. You know where I'll be."

So I would continue on from Blacksburg and try to catch up with my missed appointments. And a return to Plenty would definitely be on my schedule. The sooner I put the riddle of Plenty behind me, the better I could concentrate on seeing Sarah through this crisis. A soft whisper came to validate my decision.

She'll always be here for you the voice repeated, and I knew what I had to do.

CHAPTER 17

Reluctantly I left Sarah's side. Gave a long explanation to my silently sleeping darling about why I had to be away. Wanted to believe I saw the tiniest of smiles play across her lips. I quickly admitted to myself, though, that was because I wanted so badly to think she understood and agreed.

Sarah listened silently to my careful accounting of where I would be and what I'd be doing every day. As if she would simply pick up a phone and tell me to come home when she was ready, I mapped out for her the busy schedule for my entire road trip. First, there was my visit to the campus to talk to Coach Carter then the weekend to do some digging for information in Plenty. On Monday morning, if all remained the same here at home, I'd venture farther up the road to Elkins, Buchannon, Clarksburg and Weston and come back the faster route by Interstate to Wytheville and Roanoke; take a full workweek to complete the necessary customer stops. I assured her that all of this was subject to immediate change if I had news from Mom that there had been a change in her condition. I would plan to be at the Comfy for three nights over the weekend to make a real start on working out the riddle that was going to launch my book.

My days would include frequent checks by telephone with Mom at the hospital. I would pray to hear that Sarah was awake asking for me so I could hurry back to her. If she wasn't ready to wake up yet, then I'd plod on and bury myself in the work at hand and try to keep happy thoughts for her. Wanted to be two places at once, but told her I knew this compromise was best for both of us.

* * *

I arrived on the Tech campus mid-morning and went directly to see the coach.

"We were expecting your lovely wife to come along on this return visit," Coach Carter told me. "She made quite a hit on your first trip up here, Greg."

"I know, Coach. She was looking forward to coming back. She's ill and just couldn't make it today. Sarah's as pumped up about this opening as I am. She'd like a chance to finish her doctorate work in education right here if it all works out."

"Well, I've got to tell you, Greg, you're on our short list. We need to make a decision very soon with the new season just around the corner. Are you prepared to come on board within two weeks or less of notification if you're selected?"

"All I owe the company is a proper notice. The flexibility of my work makes just about anything possible. There's nothing I want more than to be directly involved again with the sport I love."

We talked recruiting, player development, training drills and how I felt about player discipline. Sensed that the coach and I had much in common in our approach to coaching. What I didn't know before now was that they had already been watching me. For the past two seasons, I'd been helping a local high school coach on a volunteer basis, and one of the Tech recruiters had taken notice of my work with the players.

It was a solidly encouraging interview, but I didn't want to get myself too hyped up about my chances. This was a major university, and they could pick and choose from a lot of people with more experience.

"I want you to know, Greg, we're all impressed with your credentials and your style. We know you have coaching skills plus the ability to teach your knowledge of the game to the youngsters."

"Being a part of your staff and the university would be a thrill, coach, and you'd have my full energies."

"The board is scheduled to meet and make the final decision. I have a large vote in that," Carter said. "You'll have an answer within two weeks or less. Maybe you'll get the chance to make good on that promise. We're facing a tough season."

Before leaving the campus to head toward the West Virginia mountains, I stood mid-court in the cavernous Cassell Coliseum. At heart I was still a small town boy accustomed to playing in high school combination gymnasium/auditoriums with splintering floors and stages that caught me broadside when I was blocked into them. This was the unbelievable big time. Most of the college floors I had played on couldn't approach this facility. The coliseum was better than some of the professional venues the Hornets had visited. Looked far up into the upper seats; imagined ten thousand plus screaming fans packed inside this gorgeous house watching my players perform. It was a mind blower. I was ready to get started, anxious to put the guys through their drills, excited about the game nights to follow.

Called Joe Dolan on the way over to Plenty, and he immediately asked for an update on Sarah. When I told him how perplexed the doctor was, he made a request.

"Julie wants to know if it would be all right for her to drive down and see Sarah at the hospital. You know how close they were in school. We used to say they were joined at the thigh, hip and brain."

"It's not a pretty sight watching her sleep her life away like that, Joe. Is Julie sure she wants to see her in that condition?"

"Beats sitting here worrying about her, she says. Might do some good for both of them, who knows? I can't imagine two people thinking more alike than that pair."

"Tell her I'd be grateful if she would pay Sarah a visit. Nothing I'd like better than to see them together. Give me a date and time she plans to be there so I can alert Mom and Julie can stay at our house."

"Julie suggested Tuesday the 21st. She can take three days that week and make a nice long visit. Said she could get down to Roanoke by the middle of the day and go straight to the hospital. Stay until mid-day Thursday."

I gave Joe all the necessary information for Julie to find Mom and directions to locate the hospital. This would be great for Sarah. I was convinced by now that she could feel our presence, and she just couldn't get through to us. Maybe her closest ever girl friend could coax a reaction from her. At this point I was ready to try anything with the slightest chance of breaking her coma.

"Tell Julie I love her for this. Expect to be on the road for awhile, but I hope to see her and Jason on my next swing out this way."

"You hang in there, Poet. We both know you have a strong woman, and there's no way she'll let this thing whip her. Sarah has everybody pulling for her. She'll come through it just fine."

We said goodbye. Hoped I would have better news for him the next time we spoke.

CHAPTER 18

My return to the Plenty Comfy was more like a homecoming. Myrtle and Carl greeted me in the style of a prodigal son. But then the Roops had treated me in a special way from the second I first stepped across their threshold. The connection we'd made seemed to be even stronger than I had thought.

Myrtle bundled me up inside her arms. Carl pumped my hand, and asked if I was ready for another climb up the mountain. They both reminded me that there was a roaring fire on the parlor hearth and a big easy chair waiting for me. Carl wanted to hear all about what was happening in the 'big city'.

"Tabetha, come in here and take Mr. Bain's bags," Myrtle sang out. "I'll get him some hot cocoa."

The baffling young woman appeared in her usual fashion as if materializing from thin air. She approached so silently that her footsteps were soundless on the gleaming hardwood floor of the foyer. Cast a shy smile in my direction, ducked her head and picked up my bag and laptop.

"Hi, Tabetha. Good to see you again," I offered. She nodded ever so slightly.

Every time we were in the same room I felt a compelling urge to look into Tabetha's eyes and try to guess what was going on in that pretty head. She refused to give me the chance, always carefully avoiding looking directly at me. There had been only that one fleeting instance in the kitchen when she knew full well I was admiring her form and had stared straight into my eyes. What I had glimpsed in that moment was playfulness, invitation, a delicious promise that quickly became a warning of trouble ahead. Or was I merely making it all up?

"Blue Room," Myrtle instructed.

"How's Sarah, Greg?" She took my hand and patted it while she waited for my answer.

"Not a lot of change. Her vital signs are good; she just can't wake up. We keep hoping. I'm poised to head home if there's a change, either for the better or worse. Mom's watching her, and our doctor is doing everything he can."

She smiled encouragement, and led me toward the kitchen. "I've been busy making arrangements for you to see some people. How long did you tell me you'll be here this time?"

"Three nights. Only wish I could have brought Sarah with me. I'm convinced she'll be out of her puzzling coma soon. She just has to be, Myrtle. Leaving her right now was possibly the toughest thing I've ever had to do. Mom and the doctor insisted it was for our own good to get on with life."

"Your mother has the number here at the Comfy?"

I nodded. "Said she'd call instantly if anything changes either way."

"Good. Then let's think about things we can do something about. We'll leave Sarah to the care of your mother, the doctor and the good Lord."

Tabetha had disappeared. Myrtle and I talked about her Halloween preparations, and after a few minutes the girl came back to the kitchen carrying a big flowered bag and kissed Myrtle. She was bundled up against the cold. Appeared ready to travel.

"Happy dreams, Ma Roop," the girl said.

"Be safe, Tabby. We'll miss you." As Tabetha stepped out the kitchen door, Myrtle turned and explained, "She's going off to visit some friends for the next couple of nights. Miss her like crazy when she's not around. Couldn't love her more if she was my own."

"Has she been here for a long time, Myrtle? I notice she calls you Ma. Carl seems to be very protective of her, too."

"Little slip of a thing showed up at the kitchen door one morning more than six years ago. She said she was a good worker and housekeeper. Wanted to know if we could use her help."

"Just like that? She appeared from nowhere?"

"Sure did. Something about her told me to take a chance. Had a look, a childlike innocence I couldn't resist. Happy I listened to my instincts because she's been a joy to have in the house. Does whatever I tell her and learns fast. Carl has a soft spot for her, too; he treats her like his own daughter."

"Is she from around here, from the Yew Mountains I mean?"

"Really don't know for sure, Greg. She's never wanted to talk about her past or her family. That's fine with Carl and me. We can accept her for herself."

"So has she lived at the Comfy all that time?"

"Well, almost. I noticed she was walking to work. Didn't like the idea of her being out alone all times of day and night. Wouldn't say how far she was walking to get to work, just that she was fine trekking here every day. We asked her to pick a room rent free, and told her she could stay full time with us. She finally agreed."

"That is one beautiful young woman, Myrtle, but she's awfully distant—at least to me."

"Oh, she's just shy, Greg. It's part of what makes the sweet child so lovable."

I wondered if either one of us knew all we should about the 'sweet child.' I was uneasy every time Tabetha entered a room. The way she seemed to watch me made me more than a little uncomfortable.

We sat silently for a long while in the kitchen sipping our cocoa. Finally I said, "Tell me, Myrtle, what are you learning from Ezra's diary?"

"It tells the most absorbing story, Greg. I've read and reread it, and I still get a thrill every time I think about it being a record in my Daddy's very own handwriting. Carl can tell you I've cried like a baby more than once, though, because it has very personal meaning to me. Reliving those happy days all over again with my Mamma and Daddy and my little sister Marietta has been wonderful."

"Will I have a chance to see what he wrote?"

"You'll have the entire book tonight. I would never let it leave the house. Wouldn't entrust it to anyone else, but for you I'll gladly make an exception. Want you to read it for yourself so you can give me your impressions."

"I consider that an honor, Myrtle. Then maybe we can compare our reactions, and you can tell me where I've misread. This is going to be a very interesting evening for me!"

"Let me say before you start to read that there are some pretty dark passages in that little book. The first part tells about the time from when Daddy dated my Mamma through when he was aware that Moni Hawk had designs on him. Picks up soon after he and Mamma were married, and tells how happy they were. There's a long period after that when he made no entries until I was born. The later pages tell how much he cared for Mamma, Sweet Tater and me, and they show the terrible agony he went through after losing all of his family except for me. The very last entry was made on the day he . . ." She broke down and couldn't continue. Her shoulders heaved with deep sobs.

"Don't put yourself through this for me, please," I begged her.

"Just need a minute to get a hold." She dried her cheeks, reached for the cocoa and poured refills.

"Are you sure you're up to discussing this? I can wait."

"Have to get it out sooner or later, and you're almost like a son to me, Greg. I can't explain it, but from the first time I ever laid eyes on you, I've had a special feeling about you."

My silent reaction was *So I haven't been imagining the feeling that's grown between us. She's sensed it, too. It's almost like that dash for refuge from the thunderstorm was an unexpected return to my roots.*

She continued, "Anyway, the diary tells about how much my Daddy adored the girl that would some day be his wife. It was plain that never changed, clear to anybody that ever saw them together. Then he talks about how he ran across his classmate Moni Hawk up on Pennick's Knob one day, and she asked him to meet her there again. She told him about her mother Blood Sky who got her name from the blood red sky that blazed on the night she was born. It's not clear how the old woman ended up living in the cabin up there on the ridge or exactly who was Moni's daddy, though."

By now I could tell that the diary was the very key I needed to start assembling the puzzle and writing my book. I resolved to resist any temptation Carl may send my way to share his moonshine, keep a clear head to read through the night if necessary to absorb the entire book of Ezra Charlton's reminiscences.

Myrtle went on. "Moni explained to Daddy that her Shawnee name, Moni M'weowe, meant Silver Wolf. She told him of her knowledge of herbal medicine and potions, spell casting and dark arts learned from her mother. Said that Blood Sky had been accused of being a bad witch. Her own Shawnee people didn't understand her powerful magic. The teens in the school Moni, Daddy and Mamma attended teased and taunted Moni about being the offspring of a witch. She hated their treatment. Moni professed her deep and undying love for my Daddy. Said she wanted to belong to him for life. The curse on our place began when he turned her down."

I was hanging on every spellbinding word. Myrtle was opening up a whole new world to me. Could have sat there for hours and listened; however, she looked over at the wall clock and stopped abruptly.

"Have to start fixing supper now," she said. "Can we continue in the parlor tonight? Should be quiet there. If not, we'll sneak away somewhere. I'm just itching to have you read the diary and talk about it with me. I'll tell you everything I can remember about those times."

CHAPTER 19

After dinner, Myrtle, Carl and I retreated to the parlor for another three-person tete-a-tete. The Comfy was almost empty on this night. The other guests had either driven over to Richwood for the 'night life'—occurred to me that at best that probably amounted to a movie and a soda shop stop—or had settled down for the night in their rooms. I welcomed the relative seclusion and a chance to talk with the Roops. Wanted to hear everything Myrtle had to tell me about the diary. There was a glow from the fireplace, and the lamps cast a dim light through the big room. I was beginning to feel at home in this big mansion with these two wonderful people.

Carl asked, "Are you going to work this boy over with more ghost stories, Myrtle?"

"No, every word of this is the truth straight out of Daddy's diary. Now hush up, and you might learn a thing or two, old man." He smiled a grin that said 'got her riled up, didn't I'. Then Carl raised his ever-present mason jar, poured a shot into a small glass, and proceeded with his nightly entertainment. Don't know how he could manage that powerful stuff on a regular basis.

"She has my full attention, Carl. I don't want to miss a thing she says. The last time I was here, either that love pouch was doing a job on me or Tabetha was slipping me mickeys in my cocoa. Every time I climbed the stairs it was like I had been drugged. Couldn't wait for my head to meet the pillow."

He answered with a grin and a chortle, took a sip and sat back in his chair.

Myrtle said, "Don't think I've ever told even Carl the whole story about how Marietta was taken from us. It's time I shared it with somebody, so I'll tell you both now."

Yes, finally, I thought. No more of Wes's tall tales or guessing. Myrtle was clearly the only person who could tell me about the kidnapping as an eyewitness.

"Marietta was my very own darling—my soul mate. Mamma used to say I didn't need a doll baby, I looked after little sister like she was a china doll. We did everything together even though I was five and she was only a baby three years younger than me. Never entertained the thought that she wouldn't be near me for the rest of my life. Then came that terrible October day."

Carl stood and stirred the coals in the fireplace. The room was aglow with the hearth's warmth, and its shimmering shadows played across Myrtle's face as she continued.

"It was a long time ago, but the memory is stamped forever in my mind. I can see it like it happened yesterday. Mamma let us out the kitchen door into the side yard to play after breakfast. She told me to keep an eye on Sweet Tater while she finished getting dinner started. It was sunny but cold out, so we were both bundled up. She said first sign we were either one getting chilled, I was to gather up Marietta and scoot on in the house. We had our tea set, and were enjoying our very own tea party. Then Marietta told me she wanted to 'jump up.' That's what she called jump rope. She saw my girlfriends and me do our routines, and sister wanted so much to be like us.

I took our rope, and tied one end down low on the maple tree so I could turn it for her. Marietta tried so hard with her short little legs, hopping on first one foot then the other. All at once a strong wind came up. It knocked me down and tumbled me over. When I stood up and looked around, I was almost down to the creek, and Marietta was nowhere to be seen. I ran around in circles looking for her. Then I screamed loud as I could for Mamma to come quick."

Wes had mentioned something about a wind when the girl was snatched away. At least he had that much straight.

"Mamma asked me where Marietta was, and all I could say was that the wind took her. I didn't know how else to explain it. We searched all around the yard, and Daddy scoured from here to the springhouse and down to the road in front of the house. There was just no sign of the baby. That's when Daddy called the sheriff, and he went with them in the search party."

"There was no one else near when Marietta disappeared? You heard no unusual sounds?"

"There was just that strong, cold wind that cut me to the bone. So sudden and powerful it sent me tumbling head over heels toward the creek bed. My little sister was there with me one second, and she was gone the next."

"Do you remember any of what happened after that—the search for Marietta and everything, I mean.?"

"Only what I've pieced together over the years. People tried to tell me about it when I was older. I've heard so many versions that it's hard now to sort out where my memories leave off and other people's stories begin. You've heard Wes—I swear, that man makes up his tales as he goes along. Daddy must have suspected that Moni Hawk was carrying out her revenge on him by taking away one of his girls. I think the sheriff believed that, too, but neither one had any real proof. The only clear recollection I have after her disappearance was clinging to Mamma, being terribly afraid someone would come and whisk me away. Daddy put down in his diary his impressions of what went on during the search. They looked for Marietta through the whole valley and in all the nearby woods and streams. Checked caves up on the ridge and low spots in the hollows that might hide a little girl from view. But they had no luck at all other than finding one of these." She raised the lockets dangling from her neck.

"Yes, Wes told me about finding the locket on the ridge footpath," I said. "Except for that, there was no solid clue, no other lead to where Marietta may have gone?"

"Nothing other than the chain and locket they found on the trail. Wes told me years later that seemed to convince some of the men that Blood Sky and her daughter were responsible for taking my sister away. Daddy gave the locket to me, and it will stay right here on this chain with my own for as long as it takes for my Sweet Tater to come back home."

She caressed the tiny silver hearts with her fingertips.

Myrtle rose and left the room for several minutes. Carl finally broke his silence.

"You ought to feel special, Greg. She's never talked about this with anybody as far as I know. It's like you opened the floodgates, and she wants to spill it all out. Best thing could happen—get off her chest what's been bottled up for fifty long years." I noticed that he was so enthralled by what he was hearing that neither the glass nor the mason jar were in sight.

Myrtle brought back a fresh pot of coffee. Her eyes were noticeably redder than before. Don't think the coffee pot was the only reason for her trip to the kitchen. When she had poured us another bracer and settled with her coffee and Greta, she continued.

"We all grieved so over the loss of Marietta. Mamma tried to hold up. It was clearly more than she could bear. I remember her sad eyes and how she would hug me close to her and sing to me. She watched Daddy and me pining after sister. It was like she didn't know how to cope with all the sadness."

Myrtle fussed with the coffee server as if she needed to keep her hands occupied while she spilled out all her closely guarded secrets. I had prompted what had to be painful memories.

"They tell me there was a terrible flu epidemic in the valley the next year," she said. "In my heart I always felt that Mamma died of grief, but they told me she was weak and sickly and then the flu bug hit her. Mamma was taken that winter, and Daddy sank even lower into his grieving. You saw the card I made for him. He looked at it and did something I had never seen my Daddy do. He bawled like a baby."

Myrtle choked to a stop for a long moment. She stared across the room, and sighed heavily before going on with her story. For a long interval, I think she sensed only two people in that room, and neither of them was Carl or me.

"Ezra Charlton was a strong, proud man. He was stern but loving with us girls. Never raised his voice that I can recall, but we knew in an instant what we were to do when he spoke. I loved my Daddy, and I never felt as close to him as I did after Mamma passed on. There were just the two of us in this big old house. Even then, though, he filled the house with his love for me. We would sit for hours and talk. He talked to me more like a grownup than a child of six. Told me how much he loved me, and said how he missed my dear Mamma and sister. Daddy would look into the fireplace and seem to be a million miles away. Then in a heartbeat he'd be back with me, laughing about some silly thing the two of us or the whole family had shared."

This had to be agonizing for Myrtle, but I couldn't let her stop now. I could almost see the pages of my book writing themselves as she spoke. Felt selfish about pushing. I rationalized, though, that Carl was right—repeating the story would be therapeutic for her.

Carl was riveted to his seat, hanging on her every word. Any moonshine he'd sipped tonight was wasted because he looked cold sober at the moment.

"Late at night," Myrtle said, "I can recall many times hearing Daddy crying in his room. He had moved down from the Blue Room, which was always my parents' bedroom, to sleep next door to me on the second floor, Said that way he'd be close in case I needed anything at all. I felt my heart break a little each time I heard that strong man cry. None of us will ever know the pain and agony he went through in those final months."

Again she faltered and tried to speak, but her voice had deserted her. She reached into the little gingham purse that sat on the table by her chair, and took out the small book. She offered it to me without a word.

I rose and took the diary; bent to kiss her cheek. Bless her heart, she had laid bare her soul to someone who was practically a stranger. It made me feel somehow oddly connected to this whole five-decade legend.

"I'll treasure every word. Thank you, Myrtle."

She eventually regained her composure, and went out to the curio cabinet. Returned and offered me a webbed hoop with feathers.

"I promised you this dream catcher would be waiting for your return. The Shawnee medicine man you'll be seeing later made it, and he gave it his blessing. His name is Chief John. He was a dear friend to my Daddy, a wise and kind man in Daddy's words. With his personal blessing the dream catcher will give you peaceful nights and pleasant dreams. Hang it on the bedpost nearest your head for sound rest tonight."

That would be invaluable as the evening wore on. A long night lay ahead of me in the Blue Room with the diary and the Plenty legend. Once I collapsed in the bed I'd need all the peaceful slumber I could manage.

I clutched the diary and stared into the fireplace. A quiet voice rose from the flames; it drifted softly to me.

The night is just beginning, and so is your adventure.

CHAPTER 20

Well past ten o'clock. I climbed the long stairs to the Blue Room, wide awake and anxious. The anticipation of seeing the first person accounts written by Ezra Charlton so long ago surged through me like an electric current. Excitement powered my footsteps, and I cradled the little cloth bound book like a newfound treasure.

Myrtle's comment about her father moving down to the second floor told me why the Blue Room was seldom used. It had once been the master bedroom as I suspected. Why had she chosen to let me sleep there? But then who knew why the Roops had made me feel so special from the moment I arrived in this house. Realizing I was sleeping in the room once shared by Myrtle's parents made me feel a part of the Comfy's history. I took a seat at the cherry desk in the alcove. My hands actually trembled as I opened her father's diary.

Ezra had started keeping his record well over fifty years ago. His initial entry told how he had found the girl he wanted for always, and he wanted to tell of his happiness. Elizabeth Goins attended with him the small local school that served all the children in the valley. They had known each other since first grade, but he never really discovered his feelings for her until they were in their high school years. Ezra had watched her blossom, and now he realized how special she had always been to him. From that moment on, Lizbeth, as he called her, became the one who must share his life. She was constantly on his mind. He couldn't wait for opportunities to spend time with her.

Lizbeth at last gained permission from her father to have Ezra come calling, and he wrote in the diary about his nervous anticipation over time alone with her. That first date, however, took place on her front porch with both parents watching his every move. Little happened beyond, as Ezra put it, a lot of wear on the porch swing and nervously answering Mister Goins' questions. Didn't seem to matter Ezra was from the richest family in the valley. What mattered to Mr. Goins was whether this young man was worthy of his daughter's time and attention. As downright nerve-wracking as that first experience was, Ezra made it clear that it couldn't curb his enthusiasm. He captured moments from his return visits to Lizbeth, and wrote how she had completely stolen his heart.

Ezra's written words swept me away. His descriptions and their depth of feeling made the events seem real. More than that, the words became personal to me. He wrote of meeting with his classmate Moni Hawk on Pennick's Knob and developing a close friendship with her. They returned again and again to the Knob. She became someone he could trust with his innermost thoughts. He confided in her how Lizbeth was to be his future.

He had the uncanny ability to record the precise words that were spoken; that drew me into the scene with them. As I read on I ceased to be an observer. I *became* Ezra Charlton living his experiences. My transformation into the mind of Ezra had become complete by the time I read his account of the encounters with Moni. His words transported me into that long ago world. Ezra wrote of that first meeting on the Knob:

Moni had an attraction I couldn't explain. She was the most mysterious, yet one of the prettiest, of the girls in my school. No one really knew her, and she didn't encourage close ties with anyone. When she showed a desire to be my friend, I never felt threatened because I assumed she must realize how completely Lizbeth owned my heart.

Moni stood at the hilltop with me and talked about the beauty of the valley below us. She said she was happy we could share these moments. Then she held out her arms and twirled before me to show off her dress. She looked beautiful in her russet colored dress of fringed leather with a bright orange belt cinching her small waist. The sheen of her coal black hair glistened and framed the stark whiteness of the ever-present wolf's tooth necklace at her throat. She stood on her toes in Shawnee moccasins; danced to some silent music in her head. Then Moni told me she was wearing her fall colors just for me. Her tone had turned abruptly serious. I stared at her and struggled uncomfortably for words to answer.

"I love this valley, Moni," I told her. "It will always be my home."

She seemed to sense my uneasiness, so she reassured me.

"Ezra, you know you are my closest friend," she said. "I cherish our visits to this quiet spot. Please say we can always come to the ridge to spend time together, that it will be our private place. Here we will share our secrets and our dreams, things we would tell no other."

"But your mother, Moni . . . what does she think of your meeting a white boy like this?" I asked.

Moni answered that her mother knew that I was special to her.

"But she is a fiercely proud Shawnee and a . . .", I began. I stopped short of the word I was about to use for fear of offending both Moni and her mother.

"I know the stories you've heard about my mother, Ezra," she told me. "She is a strong medicine woman. People misunderstand her, even our own Shawnee. The have called her a witch. Her full name is Ps'qui Menquotwe. It means Blood Sky in honor of the red heavens that flamed on the night she was born. From the beginning the tribe knew she was destined for power among our people. You have heard the others at school tease me about my mother. They, too, call her a witch. It is not true. She is a wise woman who wishes them no harm."

"Yes, I've heard their taunts, Moni, and watched your pain. Even my Shawnee friend Warren Brainerd has been unkind to you," I told her. "He and I have argued about this. Warren says I don't understand the red man's ways."

Ezra continued to make entries about their visits on the Knob. *I grew to value her special friendship,* Ezra wrote. *I sensed her need to be accepted, and shared the anger at her shoddy treatment by our classmates. She sadly admitted to me that her mother had been cast out by the Indian community. Blood Sky went to live near Pennick's Knob long before Moni was born. Moni told me her mother gave her the Shawnee name Moni M'weowe, which in their language meant Silver Wolf. We shared laughter and good times. I was happy to have a friend who would listen to the things that were important to me.*

Then came the diary's troubled account of how Ezra and the girl had met high atop the Knob on a blustery fall day. The leaves had turned, and all around them the hills were painted in the yellow, orange and flame hues of autumn. Once again his words made me a part of that scene as surely as if I had been standing with them. Ezra continued:

We walked out onto the rocky ledge, and I looked down at the valley. I marveled anew at the beauty of the hills and streams laid out before me. Moni breathed a lengthy sigh, and I felt her warm breath playing on the back of my neck.

"All this will be mine some day, Moni," Ezra wrote. *"I can't believe my good fortune."*

"Yes, your own kingdom to share with the right woman, Ezra," she answered. *Her tone made me nervous.*

"This is where Lizbeth and I will raise our family and grow old together. And I will always treasure your friendship, dear Moni."

She stole up behind me. I felt her arms slide around me. She pressed her lips to my ear and whispered.

"It is Moni the Silver Wolf who loves you, Ezra Charlton. With all my heart I want to be yours."

My pulse quickened as I turned to face her. "But I love Lizbeth. We are to be married soon."

"No. That cannot be, my proud stallion. I want to be yours now and for all of my life. Love me, take me now, my dear Ezra, here in our own special place." *Her deep, dark eyes filled with a raw passion that excited me.*

She implored, and her words were suspended in the crisp air, forming something between a plea and a command. Moni was relentless, determined to have her way. Her long, nimble fingers fluttered over my skin, ripped at my shirt, and her lips urgently searched. I thrust her away from me and stood on the ledge, confused, unsure; turned my back to her and stumbled over my own words.

"I can't be untrue to Lizbeth. Please understand. I can't . . ."

She circled around to face me, her back to the rock's steep edge. Her eyes suddenly were hot with anger, a look I had never seen in them. I feared for what she may do next. She faltered, and I grasped her arms to bring her back from the dangerous drop at her heels. She misunderstood my action and pressed closely against me.

"You will need no other, my Ezra. The moment is right for us. I am yours."

"No, Moni. Please. I'm committed to Lizbeth."

Moni stiffened. "I will not allow it," *she spat.* "Your soul belongs to me and me alone. What we share is more than mere friendship, It is ordained by the spirits, blessed by these ancient hills." *She pressed even closer.*

"No. Accept the truth! I am your friend, nothing more. I don't feel for you the way I love Lizbeth."

Moni looked up, glared at me, and her eyes began to glow. The afternoon sun could be deceiving me, but I would swear they took on the color of raw, burning coals that bore in on me and seared my skin. An intense rage came over her, a fit of anger and hate I would not have imagined possible in my gentle friend.

"If I cannot have you, Ezra Charlton, then you will never belong to another." *Moni raised her arm and pointed her forefinger at me, made a circular motion with her hand, a strange, ritual-like pattern.* "I revile you and swear a curse on your house and all that descend from you."

I shuddered at the sheer hatred that dripped from her words, Ezra penned.

"I forbid you to ever again step foot on our farm, Moni. You are no longer my friend."

She wailed, and the sound of her cry echoed through the hills and tore at my heart. My decision was made. I walked away from her, and never after that day did I return to Pennick's Knob.

* * *

I closed the diary and sat back, emotionally exhausted by the impact of the little book's words. A somber mood of foreboding flooded over me, and a pronounced chill filled the room. I rose from my chair to close the windows against the night air. Peered into the distance, and caught movement below on the trail past the springhouse. A small figure with a bag in hand passed from view around the bend in the road then reappeared on the footpath leading up toward the ridge. From this distance there was no way to be certain. The moonlight lingered on the dark figure long enough to provide what I regarded as recognition. Tabetha was headed up the trail toward Pennick's Knob.

The sight unnerved me. Why would a defenseless young woman hazard a trip on that dangerous road at this hour? Those woods could be full of bear, wildcat, all kinds of nighttime creatures. Carl had made no mention of anyone living up on the Knob. If Moni had left for a weekend visit, who could she possibly be seeing in those deserted woods?

Before I could allow my train of thought to be permanently broken by this queer sighting, I returned to the desk and picked up the diary. Took in a deep breath and resumed my reading.

Ezra wrote about the births of his two precious daughters, Myrtle and Marietta. The first girl he gave her grandmother Charlton's name, Myrtle, although Ezra admitted to rarely calling her anything other than Punkin. Three years later Lizbeth presented him with a second child. They named the baby Marietta after her maternal grandparents' town of origin, Marietta, Ohio. Ezra awarded her his own pet nickname—Sweet Tater. He adored the girls, and he delighted in basking in the love they returned many times over to him. He wrote that his two little darlings had a special attachment, and they would always have each other no matter how cold or unforgiving the world became. Ezra longed for a son in his own image, but his girls were his delights.

I stretched and yawned. Clearly this was going to be a long session of compelling reading. Carefully, I made my way down the stairs as quietly as I could, and set about preparing a pot of hot water for tea to brace me for the challenge. Snatched the pot from the burner the instant it started whistling so I wouldn't disturb anyone. Poured a cup and dropped in a tea bag.

There was a noise behind me. I whirled around toward the sound. Myrtle stood at the kitchen door in her long robe and fuzzy slippers.

"Didn't mean to wake you, Myrtle. Must have made more noise than I thought."

"No, I just felt restless. Carl was snoring away. Came down to get some warm milk." She paused and fixed me with an intense stare. "What do you think of Daddy's diary?"

"I have a long way to go; every page is an emotional adventure."

Myrtle took the pot from my hands and refilled it. Took down a silver tea pot. "You'll need more than that cup to get you through the diary, Greg."

"Thanks, Myrtle. I can't put it aside now until I've finished."

"Some of what Daddy wrote troubles me terribly. When you finish we need to have a long sit down."

"It's evident how deeply he cared for his family, Myrtle. I just finished reading about his two little girls."

"What follows," she said, "is a lot darker. It's downright disturbing. I want you to read it all first, Greg, and draw your own conclusions."

We sat in silence while she slowly sipped her warm milk, and I sampled the tea that would keep me going until the little book was finished. Then I wished her a pleasant night, took my tea pot and cup and climbed the long stairs to continue reading.

The night was drawing on, and it had been well beyond twenty-four hours since I last closed my eyes. But my chore was no longer just riveting reading; it had become a compulsion. I was determined I wouldn't stop until every word in that book had been revealed to me. At this juncture I simply no longer controlled what every fiber of my being knew had to be done. I must delve to the bottom of this dark family saga. It held me in its grasp as surely as if I were an integral part of what was preordained to happen next.

* * *

Before I shut my eyes in the Blue Room, I resolved, my first reading of the book would be complete. Plunged forward, drinking in Ezra's words on each neatly scribed leaf, impatient to hear what lay ahead. Well into the book Ezra's tone altered abruptly. There was a note of increasing mental agony. The change came when he first recounted the day of Marietta's disappearance. The facts as Myrtle had remembered them were essentially the same, although his account added new details.

Ezra wrote about the first frantic minutes after learning Marietta was missing:

The first place I looked for my baby was along the creek bed. Myrtle's topsy-turvy tumble had sent her near the edge of the slope down to the stream. I searched along the banks and found impressions in the soft ground near the water that could be footprints. They led away from the creek into the meadow. The tall grass in the pasture beyond toward the springhouse was trampled here and there. There were no signs of disturbance past that point.

I didn't know what else to do. Ran back to the house and called the sheriff for help. Wes brought a search party of local men. He assured me that we would find Marietta in time. Three of the best trackers in the valley—Mort Feeley, Jason Hatchett and Bert Grace—were with him. He said we'd call on some of 'them danged injun guides', too, if we needed them.

I joined the posse and we searched in a widening circle away from the house. Wes finally called for help from around the county then from the state police. One of the men found Marietta's locket as we climbed the trail that first night up toward the Knob.

"Has to be that damned old witch and her daughter done this foul deed.," Bert Grace bellowed. He fingered the rifle he was clutching.

Bert's words struck terror in my heart, Ezra wrote, *as I remembered Moni's curse on my house and all that descended from me. I privately told Sheriff Westerly what Moni had screamed at me, and I asked him to not repeat it to anyone else.*

Wes told me he 'Knowed all along it had to be that ugly old Blood Sky hag and her snooty, teasin' little bitch of a daughter.' Why he would describe Moni in those words puzzled me.

We entered Blood Sky's pitiful little cabin, Ezra continued, *and found the two women huddled in a corner, trembling but defiant.*

"Have you seen my baby?" I asked them.

Blood Sky screamed, "You have no right to invade my home. Leave us alone."

When I looked into Moni's eyes, they belied her guilt. I knew she had to be behind this horrendous act. Her curse rang in my ears as if minutes rather than years had passed since she pronounced it . . . 'a curse on you and all that descend from you'.

"How could you do this to me," Moni? I asked. "We were friends. Marietta is an innocent child."

She stared at me with cold hate in her eyes, but she said nothing.

We searched every inch of that small cabin, and found no sign my Marietta had been there. The men upset the table and chairs, turned out drawers of clothes in an old chest, ripped a mirror off the wall and dashed it to the floor. I felt ashamed to be a party to such destruction. Wes and his posse left her home in a shambles to press the search throughout the surrounding hills. They were determined and dedicated, but after many days the trackers gave up on finding my Sweet Tater alive. I was heartsick.

It just didn't seem right that a little girl could wander beyond the reach of a dedicated band of men that arrived on the scene so soon. I questioned who set fire to the cabin later that evening. Wouldn't have put it past some of my companions on Dillard Westerly's detail. In fact,

I never trusted Wes himself. The most agonizing part of thinking about the fire was the possibility that we hadn't been thorough enough at the cabin. My own child may have perished in those flames. The thought gnawed at me that I could have been in part accountable for Marietta's death.

From that point on Ezra's diary contained no cheery notes, no accounts of happy days, just a relentless pouring out of the pain of someone who grieved. That is, none but a single entry. It described his unbridled joy over the gift of a birthday card from his precious Punkin that showed him as her 'Gardin Anjel'.

I pushed ahead as my eyes grew heavy, and fought off sleep as best I could. Determined to complete a first reading of the diary's revelations before the night had passed. Each page bore the mark of Ezra's despondency more plainly than the preceding leaf. The story became ever more desperate as Ezra watched his dear Lizbeth falter and succumb to influenza. Only Punkin remained to console him and give him respite, however briefly, from his sorrow. Every passing day seemed to become more unbearable, and the diary entries were more desperate.

Ezra told of his torment and the unexplained sounds that deviled him:

I sought but never found the origins of noises that came first in the night then recurred at all times of day until my head was filled to bursting with their unceasing invasions. There were bumps and thuds in the night, animal howls and screeches during full light of day. The steady drumbeats and the unearthly screams from out of nowhere, the rushing water that never quite arrived, the wind that wailed but never rustled the leaves.

Ezra was a man going mad under the onslaught of torment without pause. The last entry in his diary was dated October 31st,

Halloween Day. Myrtle had told me that was the same day her Daddy was taken from her, but she had never said how he died.

In his words, written in a hand that was becoming more a scrawl in those final days, he was *closer than ever before to putting an end to my misery. Some day my Punkin will understand I could not bear to have her see me this way. The Blue Room is beckoning to me, and I fear I can resist no longer.*

As I closed the book after its sudden conclusion, a great weariness came over me. I was mentally drained by the tale that had drawn me in so totally that the anguish was now my own, and Ezra Charlton was merely the scribe documenting my own torment.

One tiny blessing was accorded me on that dark evening. I collapsed into the big, warm bed and slept the slumber of a clear conscience, though, as the days went on, I wasn't sure of even my own innocence in this saga.

As I drifted away into a deep sleep until dawn, that soft voice returned to me and hummed the chorus of a familiar old hymn.

Farther along we'll know all about it . . . farther along we'll understand why.

CHAPTER 21

Today would be an important day in my search for the truth about the legend of Plenty. I began early with a brisk jog. The morning air nipped at my nose and cooled my lungs. Jogged toward the village and ran past Harmon's store before turning around. Since I hadn't exercised like this in nearly three weeks, two miles was quite enough for my first venture out. There was a definite spring in my step. Felt like a million dollars after my shower and shave. When I alighted refreshed at the foot of the staircase whistling a tune, Myrtle met me with her usual cheery good morning.

"I see you're a religious man."

"Why do you say that?"

"The hymn you're whistling. Farther along..."

"Oh, it just came to mind for some reason. Mom did raise us to be God-fearing, church-going kids, though."

"She sounds like I would have pictured her with a fine son like you. Now get in here and let me warm your tummy with some of the lightest flapjacks you ever buttered down. Even have maple syrup tapped over in Highland County, Virginia at the fall maple festival. That's about as rib sticking a breakfast as you're going to find. Add Carl's homemade sausage and some fresh eggs, and you'll be ready to tackle the world."

"Or at least be ready to do battle with my trusty laptop. Myrtle, I have a lot of writing to do today. The diary was as exciting as you advertised and more. Must have read until two or three o'clock this morning. If I can manage to get as much into my writing as Ezra did, my literary career should be a success."

I followed her to the dining room where she positioned me by a window filled with warm sunlight. She was gone only briefly, and she returned with coffee and juice.

"You'll have to settle for me today. Tabetha won't be back from her visit till Sunday."

"Did you say she went up to Pennick's Knob to see someone?"

"Don't know where you got that idea, Greg. Far as I know, not a single soul has lived up there for years."

Then, I thought, *either I saw a mirage last night or something isn't quite right here.* I needed to ponder that.

When I had polished off a hearty breakfast a la Myrtle Roop, I sat back and debated whether it was possible to move. Myrtle had apparently observed my progress without hovering because her reentry was perfectly timed.

"So tell me what you thought of the diary."

"Myrtle, I don't remember anything written that moved me as completely as Ezra's words in that wonderful little book. I have to tell you I'm beyond being just an observer. Feel like an essential part of the story myself. Rejoiced and suffered right along with your Daddy. Why it hits me with such a personal impact I can't begin to explain, but there is absolutely no way I can turn back now. The story has to be told; the mystery of the curse has to be solved. I'm convinced it's up to me to do both."

"Something I can answer for you? I'm ready." She settled in.

"More questions than I can begin to ask. That's going to take us a long time to cover. I do wonder about two things that were unclear in the book."

"Oh? Try me."

"Did Ezra ever tell you about the sounds he heard, how they hounded him day and night?"

"Until I read it in that diary, Greg, I never knew the depth of his torment. He never mentioned the sounds to me or asked if I heard them. Daddy was a private man. Never shared his pain with anyone. I don't think Mamma even knew when he was feeling bad or troubled. He just went about his business pretending nothing was wrong."

"He never mentioned the unexplained sounds even though they seemed to be stealing his sanity?"

"Not a word. I just marked up his anguish to the loss of a daughter and a wife who were very dear to him. As far as I know, those strange noises were his own private burden."

"Now my second question. I realize this is painful, Myrtle. Can you tell me how your father died? There was a final reference to being drawn to the Blue Room."

"No one ever explained that to me, Greg. They told a seven-year-old child her Daddy had been taken away. I decided it had to be his broken heart, and I never asked for more."

Something in her voice told me that not only did Myrtle not know the exact circumstances of her father's death; she chose not to know. Perhaps Wes or Harmon could fill in the details, and I could decide later what to do with that delicate information. The last transgression I wanted to commit was to cause this fine woman any greater pain than she had already endured.

"I have a request, Myrtle, that I want you to consider very carefully. If you say no, I'll cease my probes now rather than bring any discomfort to someone I've grown to genuinely care about."

"Whatever do you mean?"

"My personal desire is to run the legend to ground to find logical explanations for everything that's happened here. You don't need to have this cloud hanging over you, the Comfy, the whole community of Plenty. But that could bring unwelcome publicity and reopen old wounds. If you tell me to stop now I will."

"Greg, I've always felt deep down that the whole story needed to be told. Sure, I have misgivings, but I'm ready to take whatever comes along. I'm already feeling better about the whole affair now that I've been able to share the load and talk it out with you."

"I'm glad you feel that way. My heart tells me I have to follow this to its conclusion. My next stop is to find Wes to continue our conversation. That old man knows a lot more than he's telling."

* * *

Wes wasn't hard to find down on Main Street. Everyone in Plenty knew the former sheriff. He wasn't one who circulated quietly wherever he went. I found him holding forth at the little Coffee Cup Café, which appeared to be the unofficial meeting place for all the old codgers of Plenty. Anyone in town had but to step through the front door of that place to know Wes was holding court spinning his yarns.

"Well, lookee here who I see. Come back to have old Wes set you straight about the goins on in these here parts, boy?" He slid across the bench seat, and made room for me to sit. Then he thrust out that worn old arthritic hand for a limp greeting. I nodded to the assemblage of listeners, and dutifully took my place beside him.

"Yes, I'm back for a short visit to the Comfy with a lot of unanswered questions." That brought an assortment of reactions from the gathered geezers that ranged from mild interest to rolled eyes.

"How's your head, son? Got any ringin in your ears from a lopsided noggin?"

He had stumped me. Then I realized what he meant. "Oh, the collision with the springhouse roof. No, the double vision only lasted a week or so."

Wes looked concerned for an instant until I pointed a finger at him and made a raspberry sound.

"Got a sense o' humor, too, dontcha?" I could see Wes wasn't accustomed to being on the receiving end of a jibe.

"Thought I might ask for some time one on one to continue our earlier conversation, sheriff."

"Almost sounds good to hear somebody call me that again after all these years. Also brings back a lot of bad memories of dirty deeds and criminals I chased down and put away in my time in office. Probably caught more bad guys than that whole fancy county police force they got down to Marlinton these days."

Right away I realized that unless I got Wes away from his cronies quickly he would be off on another long winded dissertation about the bad old days. Then I'd never get my time alone with him.

"Can you break away? Answer some questions for me, Wes?"

"What you got in mind, boy? I might be coaxed into talkin private like if they was a big fat dinner in the bargain. Got any pull with the cook up to the Comfy?"

"Sounds like the perfect solution to me, sir."

He flashed that smile with his rotting old mouth and said to his companions, "See there. I told you this young feller had a proper upbringin. Ain't nobody other than him called me sir in many a moon. That includes all you geezers. Come to think of it, most that did before was lookin for a break from the local lawman not knowin what a hard ass I was."

His weak, phlegmatic cackle was echoed by a couple of the men at the table.

"We could go up there and have our talk in the parlor then put away one of the finest dinner spreads this side of Paris. Sound okay to you, Wes? I'll drive you up there."

"You just lead the way, son. I'm yours till the food settles. Then I'll be about my Main Street rounds." I guess doing that made him feel he was still a part of the daily scene in what was probably the only town he had ever called home. I calculated that making the rounds on Main Street wouldn't take a great deal of time for anyone, even a bull shooter like old Wes.

* * *

I knew as soon as we appeared at the Comfy that Myrtle wasn't overjoyed to see Wes in her home. But I was also satisfied that she appreciated the importance of my drawing him out. Needed his take on the events in Plenty for the past fifty years. He knew facts that could fill in gaps in the Plenty story nobody else could explain. He had even made a large concession to propriety by tossing his chaw and wiping his tobacco stained mouth on a dirty handkerchief before we started our ride from Main Street. That was probably about as formal as Wes ever got.

Despite her apparent dislike for the dean of Plenty's old farts, Myrtle put up a good front and played the perfect hostess as usual. She made sure we were comfortable at a small table in the corner of the kitchen, and brought us warm cider with oatmeal cookies to hold us until the dinner meal was ready. Probably wasn't anxious for Wes to mingle with the guests in the dining room, and I certainly understood. Thanked her for both of us, and launched into my discussion with my guest.

Told the sheriff, "I'm trying to piece together all that's happened here in the valley that involves the Charltons and the Comfy. You're obviously the most knowledgeable person in the community on the history of Plenty."

He drew himself up until I feared for his poor backbone. It couldn't have been that straight for ages. With his chest thrown forward as far as the old man could manage, he proudly proclaimed, "I know more about this damn place and these honery people than anybody that ever drawed a breath in Pocahontas County."

Well, I thought, *now that we have the testimonial out of the way, maybe we can get down to cases*.

"There are some things that puzzle me, Wes. I thought with your first hand knowledge you could set me right."

"Do my best. Fire away."

"First, tell me your feelings about Blood Sky Hawk and her daughter Moni. Were they really as evil as some have told me?"

"That old woman was evil clean to the core, son. I wouldn'ta put nothin past her. Heaven help anybody made an enemy of that hag 'cause they was in for hard times. Seems to me it was a pure blessing that took her away before she could wreak more havoc on the good folks of this valley. We had a lot of unsolved mysteries that always seemed to point toward her. Just couldn't pin nothin on her."

Myrtle hovered in the kitchen trying to hear what Wes was saying while pretending to be busy. She interrupted our conversation long enough to serve our dinner. He dove into his plate like he hadn't eaten for days, and began to forage his way through the meal. Other than the slurping sound as he dispatched her beef noodle soup and his loud chewing of everything else, which I did my best to tune out, there was time and solitude enough for me to begin to roll some heavy thoughts around. Finally I got his attention and asked him a question.

"You said unsolved mysteries. What kinds of mysteries, Wes?"

"For instance, had a feller shoo her off his property one day. Next thing he knew four of his cattle was spittin up blood 'til they died. Vet never could figger out what caused it."

"That could have been a coincidence, right?"

"How 'bout Sid Parsons? Called her a dirty old hag one day. Poor old fool dropped dead of a heart attack 'fore the sun set. And the Williams woman that couldn't pay her for some herb medicine that cured her baby's whoopin cough. Baby turned worse overnight, choked and died next mornin. I could go on all day with tales like that, every one of 'em recorded on the books."

Wes snatched up the last hot roll from the bread basket, and he slathered on enough butter for three rolls. He gnawed away as I mulled over what I'd heard.

One fact was becoming crystal clear to me. Once the locals had hung the label witch on Blood Sky, she seemed to be automatically blamed for every mishap that took place in the valley. There was, of course, the strong chance that she may actually be responsible for some of the events. However, I could tell that her detractors were ready to heap blame on her at every turn.

"What about her daughter? What do you know about Moni, Wes?"

He settled back with a toothpick and issued a hearty belch.

"Showed you her picture. She was a right purty lil thing run around like she had the only twist on Main Street."

"Would you show me her photo again, Wes?"

He reached into his pocket to take out the worn wallet. Laid the fading picture on the small table in front of me. Moni was wearing an unusual necklace in the photo.

"What's that at her neck, Wes?" I pointed.

He didn't even look at the picture. Answered from memory. "Oh, some kind o' animal teeth. One of them silly Injun superstitions." I flashed back to the diary and Ezra's words about her ever present wolf's tooth necklace.

"She was a beautiful woman, sheriff."

"Yeah, and she was mighty stuck up to be the low born bastard child of a dastardly old witch woman and a halfwit Shawnee boy."

"Then you knew Moni's father?"

"Such as he was. Yeah, I knowed him. Blood Sky had long since been banished by her fellow Shawnee when she decided to take a mate from among them. Put a spell on a 16 year old Injun, and lured him to live with her up on the ridge. Used that boy to sire Moni then did away with him when he was no longer of any use to her."

"How do you know that?"

"I looked into the matter when he was found at the bottom of the cliff below the Knob. My theory is that dang old Blood Sky drove him crazy, deviled him till he jumped off the rock ledge to get away from her. Never seen a body with that many broken bones."

"Couldn't it have been an accident?"

"Not in *my* book. Just wish I coulda made a case that she had a hand in Carter Hawk jumping off that cliff. Hell, the old gal mighta pushed him herself. Me, I always figgered he took the plunge to escape from her houndin him."

"But you haven't told me about Moni."

"Not much to tell. As I said, she was a stuck up little bitch thought she was too good for any white man. I knowed she'd come to no good end. Hope somewhere along the way it caught up to her. Deserved to burn in hell, that one did. She tried to snare Ezra Charlton in her net, but he wiggled away. Not that I was ever any great fan of them money huggin Charltons lookin down their noses at us common folk."

Talk about bitter! This old man was carrying around a load of venom and ill will large enough for all the residents of the valley. Was there anybody he *did* like?

Myrtle brought us dessert. Our small table in the kitchen had spared her the embarrassment of exposing Wes to her other guests. She looked relieved that his lack of table manners hadn't encroached upon her dining room. I mulled over what Wes had said as we dispatched the peach cobbler. Needed to encourage him to tell me more while he was talkative. Maybe I could coax more time out of him after our meal was over.

When we continued our talk, I pressed for more details about the kidnapping and the recurring tragic events on the Charlton property since then. Wes, however, was full and content, and he just wanted to curl up somewhere for a siesta. When he started toward the parlor, it was time for action. If I didn't get him outdoors into the fresh air soon, our session would be over.

"Don't sit down, Wes. I have some important questions to ask you. Will you take a walk with me down toward the pond and the old saw mill?"

He clearly would have preferred less strenuous after-dinner activity, but he shrugged and rather grudgingly collected his bones together to follow me. We turned down the lane with a brisk breeze in our faces.

"What's so danged important it couldn't wait, Bain? It's downright chilly out here." He hugged his shoulders and feigned a shiver.

He certainly didn't mind standing coatless on an even colder morning at the springhouse when he'd had the stage and was dazzling me with stories of Plenty in the old days. Well, it was my turn, and he'd have to play the game by my rules this time.

"Thought maybe it would help me to see the scene of the accidents and have you repeat what you said the other day. I can't seem to make a clear connection between a drowning, a fatal fire, and Harmon's dad dying at the burned out mill."

"Told you that was all the work of that damn ol' Blood Sky and her daughter, boy. What else could you possibly need to know?"

"Humor me, Wes. Let's stop by the pond first." He stuck a new chaw in his mouth and grumbled.

We veered off the lane, and took an overgrown footpath to the water's edge. A stream flowed from the ridge to feed a pond with a surface as clear and calm as a sheet of glass.

"Carl said the girl that drowned here was a schoolmate of Ezra and Elizabeth Charlton. Was she down here swimming alone?"

"Near as we could tell, she was all by her lonesome. Maxine Pride, that was her name. Damnedest thing, though. Ever'body agreed she was about the best swimmer in the whole valley. Musta took a cramp or something. Hell, wouldn't many besides her even brave that cold water pond in late October. Water's over ten feet deep out there in some places, and there's only that old wood platform in the middle to cling to."

I looked out across the calm surface of the pond, and wondered how a strong swimmer could fail to reach either shore or at least the weather beaten platform that stood maybe fifty feet away.

"No sign of foul play, I take it. No evidence someone else may have been here with her?"

Wes looked away, and he caught his breath before answering. "Hadda been, I'da said so, now wouldn't I? Just one of them senseless accidents. Now let's us get back up to the Comfy and warm up. Then you can run me back down to Main Street."

"Not just yet, Wes. Walk over to the saw mill with me."

"You're beginning to get on my nerves, youngun. Don't know what you're trying to prove."

"Give me just a couple more minutes if you would, sheriff. You know how these things came about better than any other living soul." That brought a smile to his lips.

The old mill sat abandoned, much as it had been left after the fire I imagined. Heap of blackened timbers, a window frame with the glass panes smashed, lumps of burned tarpaper. A rusty shovel was lying on the ground. I picked it up and poked at the ruins.

"Didn't it seem a little odd to you that the men who died here chose this spot to play cards? They could have met any number of places that were warmer and more comfortable. And why only the two men? Hardly sounds like a typical poker session to me."

"So now you're gonna tell me my business, huh? When'd you get to be a policeman?"

"Just using logic, Wes. Look at this wheel where Bert Grace died. What could have possessed him to be at the old mill years after his friends died? What is it you're not saying that could tie those accidents together?"

Westerly stared at me, his mouth wide open as if he was about to speak, then dropped his eyes. "Nothing here more'n I already said. Give it up, boy. Told you the witch's curse was responsible."

I poked the rubble with the old shovel again, and an unpleasant surprise reared its ugly head. Something moved, and before I could react, a large brown copperhead slithered toward me. Then another and another.

"Judas priest, you stirred up a nest of them devils!" Wes jumped back and stumbled toward the lane.

I stood my ground, chopping at the snakes with the old shovel, but they had me outnumbered. This was no time to stand and fight with an angry swarm of poisonous fangs. Tossed the shovel into their midst and hightailed it.

When we were a safe distance away up the path, I turned to a shaken Wes, who was panting and wheezing with the effort of his escape. Asked him, "You okay, sheriff?" Reached out to support him but he knocked my arm away.

"Don't need to be helped. Ain't no critter in these hills mean enough to get the best of me. I've tangled with wildcats and vipers, wolf and bear, and whipped em all."

"Well," I said, "that's not the only den of snakes we're dealing with here. There's more going on than you're saying, and I intend to get to the bottom of it."

He looked away from me.

I was more convinced than ever that Wes was holding back something that had convinced him the witches were involved. Why after all these years would he refuse to reveal it? He had to hold the key to the puzzle of the Plenty legend, and I wouldn't 'give it up,' as he said, until the riddle was solved.

The voice joined our conversation with a whispered warning in my head.

Nothing succeeds like dogged determination, boy. You've sunk your teeth into it. Clamp down and hold on tight.

CHAPTER 22

I took Wes back down to Main Street to join his cronies. He didn't miss a beat; saw one of his buddies outside the diner, and launched right into another of his tall tales. It was as if our discussion had never taken place. This old reprobate had one thick hide, but I wasn't through with him—not by a long sight.

Spent most of the afternoon on the Comfy's front porch. Set about documenting what the diary and my conversations with Myrtle and Wes had supplied me so far. For the first time since my 'Poet' days in college, I was genuinely absorbed in crafting words. This task, though, was more than I had bargained for. My emotions poured out onto the screen along with the words. I was living this tale and had gone from storyteller to participant. The events were happening to *me* on a very personal scale. The full spectrum of responses coursed through me from the joy of family through the terror of a violently uttered curse to the deep despondency of hopelessness and resignation. In an eerie and frightening way the diary's words were my words, and the experiences belonged to me. I was ensnared in a trap of my own making.

As immersed as I was in my work, one priority stood above all others. I had been calling Mom at the hospital twice a day since leaving Roanoke. Yes, we had an agreement that she would contact me immediately if there was anything she needed to tell me. It somehow made me feel closer to my sweet Sarah hearing Mom's voice on the phone. My brain was by now in total overload, and my fingers ached from the frantic pounding they had been giving the keyboard. Time to pause before supper and make a connection, however fleeting, with home. Folded into the deep comfort of one of Myrtle's big parlor chairs, found my calling card and lifted the brass handset.

"Guess who."

Mom replied, "Sitting here reading to Sarah, Greg. I believe she can hear me, and I know how she loves to read the classics. Just finished telling her you'd be calling soon."

"Have you seen any response, Mom? Any movement?"

"Nothing specific yet. Like you, I imagine at times that she moves or flutters her eyes, but I know it's mostly wishful thinking on my part. Doc Jameson is still encouraging. He says to tell you to think positive. We're all doing the best we know how, and we're letting nature take its course."

I know Mom wanted to be encouraging, but Sarah's coma was a heavy weight pressing down on all of us. My life would remain suspended until she awoke.

"Mom, I'm scared. Every day she lies there in that bed I feel her slipping a little farther away from me. I need to know she's going to be all right because she means the world to me."

"Don't you talk yourself into getting down, son. I have faith that she's being watched over. You must believe, too, that things will turn out for the best."

"You know what she's done for me, and how much I owe her."

"And she knows how devoted you are. Just give it time, Greg." She paused to let that sink in then asked, "How is your stay at the ... Comfy, is it?"

"So far it's been more productive than I could ever have imagined. Well into laying out my book about Plenty. Keeps me from constantly dwelling on my concern for Sarah. I'll be here at the Comfy tonight and tomorrow night then start my customer visits. I'll call you every day."

"Just let me take care of our girl while you go about your business. You'll be home soon enough."

"I'll check in at every stop so you're never out of touch with me. Love you, Mom."

"Take care, son. We both love you very much."

Before she could hang up, I made a decision I'd been pondering.

"Wait, Mom. I need to ask you a question. Can you tell me how Dad's setbacks came on? How he acted when they took hold?"

The myriad of intense emotions I had experienced since returning to the Comfy had rekindled my concern that my mental state may be worsening. There was still that nagging doubt eating at the base of my brain telling me I was entirely too close to the fine line between rational and over the edge. If I could find a clue, a link to my Dad's problems, maybe I could fight my slide in a more coherent manner. So far I was ad libbing my response to what could be a total mental breakdown. Mom was silent for an uncomfortably long time. Then she seemed to force herself to talk about those disturbing times.

"At first your Dad wouldn't talk about what was causing him to wake up in the middle of the night in a cold sweat mumbling words I couldn't understand. He did finally let me inside his nightmares once he felt he couldn't cope with them on his own."

"Was he just mumbling or actually saying words you didn't recognize?"

"No, the words were clear, and sometimes he almost shouted them. None of the language was familiar to me. I caught bits and pieces, and when I told him some of the things he had been saying, there was fright in his eyes. He told me the words I tried to repeat sounded like Vietnamese."

"So he was having flashbacks to something that happened in Southeast Asia?"

"I was never able to give back to him enough of what he had shouted out to make it clear what his words meant. Something in his expression told me, though, that he was very aware of the memories that had caused his outbursts."

"Did he ever mention hearing recurring voices in his head? A voice talking directly to him?"

This was my greatest concern; that the pattern was continuing with me and would only worsen.

"He said that in his dreams there was a Vietnamese woman hurling insults at him and dirty, ragged little street children tugging at him begging for money and candy. That's about as much as I could get. Didn't mention any voices other than theirs."

"Thanks. I needed to know that more than you can imagine."

"What's wrong, son? Why are you asking me these things?"

"I'm fine, Mom. Really am. Dad's been on my mind a lot lately, and I had to know."

"You're sure that's all?"

"Yes, Mom. I'll call you some time in the morning." Felt ashamed of myself for shading the truth with her. But I was also aware that I'd never been able to mislead Mom. She was probably still fretting over what could have prompted my pointed questions.

When I cradled the telephone, an overwhelming sense of relief came over me. Dad was reliving experiences that had nothing to do with any of the affair I was now facing. His torment had its origin years ago and thousands of miles away. The voices were those of people he had interacted with in Vietnam who had made lasting imprints on him. He'd made no mention of a person's voice in our own language speaking to him. I was dealing with something strangely and totally different. Besides, the voice that came to me was instructive not harassing. In fact, I concluded, the outcome of its visits lately had seemed entirely to my benefit. There was a purpose for that recurring tutor to my subconscious, and I decided to welcome it and heed its advice. Could be rationalizing; it surely beat the alternative.

* * *

A solitary walk before supper seemed the best way to mull over my thoughts and sort out what was staring me down. I went to the Blue Room and put on my coat, walked out the front door and circled toward the lane in back of the Comfy. The sun was beginning its descent over the peaks to the west, which told me maybe an hour of sunlight remained. I wanted to stop by a couple of spots Carl's story and Wes's careful evasions had left hanging, see if there was more to be gained from studying them on my own.

The swimming pond waited off to the left of where the road to Pennick's Knob curled up toward the ridge. I worked my way past a crumbling fence through the tall, lifeless late fall weeds that bordered the footpath. The surface of the pond was still and blue, only the faint sound of trickling water from the mountain stream that fed it from above. I knelt down and skimmed my fingers across the water. Found it as cold and clear as the water at the springhouse.

A small metal boat sat motionless at the pond's edge, its bottom resting on solid ground. It was tethered to a wooden stake by a frayed rope. Carl had told me no one had ventured out onto the swimming pond for years. That should have sounded a loud caution somewhere in my brain, but instead I let my curiosity take over. Tried to loosen the rope's knot. It wouldn't budge. Grasped the ground stake, and tugged and waggled until it came free in my hands. Tossed the stake and rope into the boat, slid the boat into the water, stepped aboard and lifted the single splintered oar. I pushed away toward the wooden platform at the center of the swimming hole.

Drifting slowly across the calm pond, I stared down into the clear water and tried to fathom what had occurred here forty years ago. Carl had said an acquaintance of Myrtle's folks had drowned here. He had only identified her as a girl they knew from school. Wes had nothing to add other than the fact that Maxine Pride was known to be an excellent swimmer. Don't know what I expected to see from that creaky old vessel, but there was only the reflection of the boat and my eyes peering at a rocky bottom some ten or twelve feet below the surface. On an impulse I gathered a handful of small pebbles from the floor of the boat and tossed them into the water. Ripples spread and shattered my reflection.

Closed my eyes for a moment then reopened them to stare into the widening wake that swept the pond's surface. A face shimmered into view under the water, the bloated face of a young woman twisted by stark terror and desperation. I watched the open mouth move as if to shout a plea for help. A string of bubbles rose, and a dull white object spiraled up toward me. Thrust one hand toward the girl's outstretched fingers that clutched for refuge. I felt nothing, no response from the deep. For an instant I seemed to be holding something between my fingers, a stone, a piece of wood, no—a large tooth—animal more likely than human. Lifted my hand and tried to inspect it more closely; it simply vanished before my eyes. There was nothing but my empty hand, the glistening of the sun's rays dancing across the pond and my puzzled look staring back at me from below.

Slowly I returned from my hypnotic state, and I realized my left foot was wet. Then I looked down to discover water pouring through a sizable hole in the bottom of the launch through a ragged hole that looked as if it had been punched through the metal from above. I grabbed the oar and quickly changed direction, sensing this could be a race to make shore before my vessel settled to the depths of the pond. Had no desire to share the watery deep with the girl whose terrified face had pled for help. This was no day for a forced swim in near freezing water.

The boat was sinking, its stern dipping lower and the bow rising. Fully clothed and facing frigid water, I may have only seconds to reach safety. My progress toward shore was not nearly fast enough to avert disaster. I stroked harder with the oar and lunged forward in the boat as if that would get me to shore sooner.

The pond was winning this battle. I took a chance and stood up in the boat long enough to leap toward shore. Placed both feet on a cross strut and propelled myself forward. Felt my takeoff foot slip and my heart sank, but I was airborne. When I hit the ground spread-eagled, my feet plopped into the pond. I sank to thigh depth in its chill, my feet floating without touching bottom. Stretched forward as far as I could, and clawed frantically at the ground as I felt myself sliding backward. The pond had me in its clutches, pulling me down with icy fingers, and it sought to claim me for its own. A sickening fright swept over me that I may lose my grip.

Fighting, straining, I tried to move my hands away from the water's edge and dig my elbows in for leverage. There was a slight forward momentum, and my legs, now beginning to lose feeling, thumped against something, maybe the shore. Inch by careful inch I pulled myself onto the dry grass and lay very still, thinking how fortunate I was that refuge had been only twenty feet or so away when the boat faltered. Then I felt stupid for bringing on a self-inflicted predicament. What possessed me to climb into that banged up launch in the first place? I rolled over and looked back toward the water. Watched as the little vessel slowly filled, sank beneath the pond's surface and settled to the bottom. The oar bobbed up and floated away. Then I lay motionless on the hard ground for minutes, my heart fluttering, puzzling over what my mind had conjured up just before my frantic rush to shore.

I felt relieved to be on solid ground; otherwise I was feeling pretty terrible. My clothes were soaked, my limbs hurt and I was so cold my teeth were chattering. Still, I couldn't bring myself to move from the weeds.

Maxine's was the first in a series of mishaps on the Charlton farm that followed the disappearance of Myrtle's little sister. Was I making too much of it? Could it have been an unfortunate accident with no bearing on the incidents that had taken place since? Did I only imagine that for a fleeting moment I held some flotsam, a tooth-like object, in my hand? Most of all, what was I doing lying there when I could freeze to death?

I had come down to the pond fully expecting to check out the old sawmill. Needed to make some sense of the two disasters that had taken place there. But I was so shaken by my near drowning and the vision in the water that I gave up that idea. Finally got my act together and rose stiffly, streaming water behind me, to turn toward the Comfy.

Myrtle greeted me when I returned. She wore a flowered dress, a bright, frilly apron and that same warm smile I had grown to expect.

"Heavens to Betsy, Greg! Where have you been?"

"Just took a stroll down the lane, Myrtle. Had some thinking to do."

She did a double take and almost screamed at me. "You've got to be soaked clean to the bone. What in the world did you do out there? Get over here by the oven and warm up."

"Very nearly made a big mistake down at the pond, but luck was with me."

Myrtle looked perplexed by my answer, and she waited for me to say more.

"Pull off those soaked shoes. Tell me what happened." She dragged up a chair, and I sat by the open oven door.

"Well, I really didn't go down there for a swim in that icy pond, although that's what I almost had to do. It's a little embarrassing."

"I'll say. Looks like you fell in." She couldn't help but snicker.

I looked at her sheepishly. "That's close. I swamped the boat and had to fight my way out. Dumb trick."

"That pond's got to be freezing cold."

"Guess my blue lips gave you a clue." Now that the ordeal was over, I could even see the humor.

"What's for dinner, Myrtle?"

"Okay—change the subject on me." She shook her head and broke out in a big smile. "Something you're going to like. Any news from home?"

"Only that there's no news. It's a roller coaster ride every day for me—wish, hope, anticipate, then face heartbreaking disappointment. Guess I should be thankful Mom is there by her side."

"Sarah has her own Guardian Angel, and that should bring you great peace of mind," she said. "We'll all pray for her recovery soon." She took my hands in hers. "Now you just sit there and dry off. Let me get back to supper preparations while you warm up and get into some dry duds. I have to feed the inner man, you know."

Myrtle went back to her kitchen duties, but she watched me carefully out of the corner of her eye.

As for me, I was totally befuddled at this stage. Where was this twisted, convoluted chase taking me? What in the world could I possibly take away from the frightening episode at the swimming hole?

Myrtle was unaware of the soft voice that stole up behind me and whispered:

We will seek as one, and the truth will set us free.

CHAPTER 23

One more night at the Comfy then I'd be off to see my clients. Tabetha showed up late in the afternoon, and helped Myrtle prepare supper for the sparse gathering of guests. I felt so mentally worn down I'd already decided to turn in early. Wanted a fresh start on the road for Monday morning's customer visits. Then I could swing toward home and Sarah.

Outside the weather had turned noticeably colder, and a bitter wind was howling. Tomorrow could be a challenge ducking in and out of sporting goods stores as late fall threatened to turn into winter ahead of schedule. The weather forecast even hinted of an early snowfall at the upper levels of the mountain ridges. For tonight, at least, I could snuggle down into the warmth of the big comforter up in the Blue Room and ignore the raw wind.

Tabetha served my supper without a word and only a half smile. Never looked directly into my eyes. I continued to wonder why she had braved the cold and the wild animals to climb that ridge out back on Friday night. Speculated about where she could have been for most of the weekend. But then that really was none of my business.

I tested her, though. "Hope you had a nice visit, Tabetha. Didn't seem the same around here without you."

She managed to brighten a bit at my words, but I was thinking to myself that it had been unusually peaceful in my room with her out of the house. Merely a coincidence?

There you go again with that wild imagination, Bain.

After another of Myrtle's culinary triumphs, I was certain my waistline must be surging. But my drowsiness on this particular evening had to do with more than overeating. I had been driving myself relentlessly for the past two weeks, and my body was screaming for me to slow down. Had some catching up to do with my customers, so I'd best get rested for a busy trip.

Found the Roops in the parlor relaxing in front of a roaring hearth.

"Myrtle, I'm beat to a frazzle tonight. Think I'll make this an early evening, so I can catch up on my rest. Those long days and nights at the hospital with Sarah ran my nerves through the cheese grater."

She understood some of the trials I'd been through. There were others I hadn't bothered to tell her about: the trip to the saw mill, tangling with the nest of copperheads, how serious my near disaster at the swimming hole had really been. She cast a knowing smile.

"You go ahead, Greg, and have a good night's sleep. We'll talk before you leave in the morning."

"After I catch up on my client calls this week, I'll have a little breathing room. Expect to be back through for a couple more short visits with you before the month is over."

"Your room will always be ready, Greg, and remember you have to see Velma Thomas at the library and Chief John at his place tomorrow. They're both expecting you."

"No way I'd miss either one of those appointments, dear lady."

My visit to the Marlinton library would take place in the afternoon after I had seen to my morning stops. Then I wanted to visit the Shawnee shaman before the day was over, so I could move on to my business calls as early as possible on Tuesday morning.

I'd work my way across and down the Interstate and be back home on Saturday. There would be a few precious days to spend with Sarah and Mom before my return swing.

"Anything you need for the Blue Room?"

Flashed a grin at Carl then answered her. "Not a thing, Myrtle. I feel so comfortable around you. Hope Carl doesn't mind, but I think I love you, Mrs. Roop."

She replied with a shy giggle. "Greg, you're such a kidder."

* * *

I was mentally and physically spent, but there was one task left before I could turn in. Wanted to scan my notes again; think about how far my probe into Plenty's legend had brought me. Before I could get settled down to read, though, there was a gentle rap at the door.

"Come in," I called and stepped across the room. Tabetha came in carrying what looked like a pot of something for my enjoyment before bedtime. This was another of Myrtle's many loving touches, I concluded.

"Ma Roop says you should have a little treat before you turn in. Some hot cocoa to lull you to sleep, she said. Where should I put it?" I motioned toward the desk in the alcove, and followed her across the room, watching her float in that fluid motion of hers.

"I notice you call her Ma. Why, Tabetha?"

"That's what she wants me to call her. Says since she never had a daughter of her own, I'm the nearest to a child she's ever known. Makes her feel special, and I think of her as a sort of mother."

Now, wasn't that typical of Myrtle, I thought. She had a priceless knack for spreading her warmth and honest love to everyone around her. And 'Ma Roop' had already told me more than once what a sweet child she considered Tabetha to be.

"May I ask how long you've known the Roops?" I said.

"I have been here more than six years now, Mr. Bain." *That checked out with what Myrtle had told me.*

"Greg. Please. My name is Greg."

"Greg." She repeated, almost as if she wanted to see how the word felt to her mouth. She wore a bit of an amused smile now that she'd finally gotten my name right. "The Roops are like parents to me."

Tabetha set the tray down on the desk and poured a brimming cup of cocoa. Wrapped both her hands around the cup and handed it to me. For the first time I took a close look at her lovely hands, and became aware of the smooth texture, the slender fingers and pink nails. Couldn't imagine how I had overlooked that before. On one hand she wore a carved, lacquered wooden ring with a fiery red stone. Ornate carvings were boldly etched into the wood setting, and the stone gave off a glow when the lamplight played across it.

"That's a very unusual ring. May I see it?"

Taking her slight nod as a yes, I held her fingertips in my right palm and traced the smooth stone with a forefinger. She saw how intently I was staring at her hand and blushed.

"Tabetha, you have beautiful hands. Tell me about the ring."

"It is part of my heritage. We call it bloodstone. It was passed down to me through my female ancestors."

"Your heritage? Tell me, Tabetha, am I right that you're native American?"

"Shawnee."

I released her hand and turned momentarily toward the desk to take a sip of the hot cocoa.

"Did you grow up around here?" There was no answer. I looked back in her direction, and discovered that in that brief moment she had silently slipped away.

In her irritating fashion, Tabetha had simply vanished out the door before I could continue our first real conversation. Our short talk had been a breakthrough. From what I had seen so far, it must have been a new record for her to say that much at one stretch. I noted that not only was she capable of carrying on a conversation; she had a lyrical voice that fell mellow and delightful on the ear. If Myrtle thought so highly of her, my initial uncertainties about this beautiful young woman could have been too hasty and too harsh.

I dutifully downed the soothing cocoa. Sat at the desk reviewing the computer notes I had recorded earlier in the day. There may be time to organize my thoughts and review my encounters with the diary and with Myrtle and Wes. Didn't want to miss a single morsel of information that had been provided to me. I was impatient to begin my actual writing and watch the book grow. By the time I returned to Roanoke, there should be a solid beginning for the story that was crying out to be told.

That wasn't to be on this night. Within minutes an irresistible warmth swept over me in a great rush. My cheeks were aglow, my arms tingled, my hips and legs radiated a perceptible heat. Now I was certain this would be a short evening; bedtime had indeed arrived in a rush. There was barely time to struggle out of my clothes and under the comforter before night fell in the Blue Room.

CHAPTER 24

What could have been minutes or even hours later, I stirred. Slowly became aware of where I was, and fought to regain full control of my senses. I seemed to be beyond groggy, more like in a state of hypnosis. Worse, my limbs refused to move. Concentrated on raising my right arm and found it lifeless and unresponsive.

Couldn't focus my eyes, and the room revolved around me, spinning first clockwise then reversing in a dizzying fashion. There was a soft glow to the entire bedroom from moonlight streaming through the windows, but I was viewing the light as if it was passing through a prism. Couldn't fix upon objects through the swirling haze and the room's rotation around me. Every time I began to orient myself the room changed directions. A warmth well beyond comfort level clung to the length of my back and down my legs. I struggled and strained to move my body parts, but to no avail.

Then I felt the soft touch of velvety fingers circling my waist from behind me, slithering up my ribcage, caressing my chest. I willed myself to pull away, but my efforts met with no success. My inert limbs were rigid; they stubbornly refused to budge. A silken voice crooned softly, melodically into my ear, its soft tones caressing.

"You are under my power, Greg Bain, powerless to move unless I will it. You cannot resist. Feel my nearness, and know that I can lie with you for as long as I desire."

The soft pads of those smooth fingers traced a line down my back. As they made their way, the feeling returned along the entire length of my spine. I felt a female form pressing against my back, moving and flexing. Her firm flesh burned into the skin of my bare upper torso.

"What the hell . . . Are you who I think you are?" I asked. My voice sounded weak.

She skimmed her moist lips across my shoulder and up my neck. Without warning, she ground her teeth into my earlobe, and I winced with pain. A sudden warmth on my neck told me she had brought blood. Her hot breath was like a flame licking my lobe as she softly whispered again.

"I am your Night Fire, your Tabethki Scote," came the musical voice over my shoulder. "I have come to you to quench the fire that burns inside me. Tonight we will be as one."

The numbness of paralysis and the stark fear of helplessness were giving way to responses my mind fought while my body stubbornly imposed them.

She rolled me slowly toward her, and I could go only where she urged. As I relented and came face to face with her, my eyes confirmed what I already knew from the honey sweet voice. Tabetha had tossed aside the comforter and lay beside me, her lovely bare body glistening with fragrant body oils, radiating an invitation. The woman child was even lovelier and more mature than I had imagined her to be. I chided myself for the thoughts this sight prompted, and wondered if I had somehow provoked this scene by sending unintended signals. No, her actions seemed too deliberate, too perfectly choreographed to be anything less than the culmination of a well-planned act on her part. I was afraid it may be working.

"What have you done to me? Why can't I move?" Not since I lay in that hospital in Charlotte had I felt so utterly and hopelessly overwhelmed by forces beyond my command. Her only answer was a beaming smile and a penetrating stare from her infinitely deep, dark eyes that transfixed me.

This had to be a nightmare gone out of control. It simply made no sense that she had me totally under an unbreakable hypnotic spell. Somehow I had to end this now.

I struggled to move away as she reached out to caress my cheek, my lips, but the temptation was great. My wife lay silently many miles away in a deep sleep. Already it had been too long since we made love, and there was no telling how much longer it may be. This wasn't right. I couldn't let it happen. Doubted I ever wanted to stray from Sarah, but if I did, it would be at a time and place of my own choosing, not one dictated to me by some crazed woman. Had to regain the control she had somehow taken from me.

Tabetha was relentless in her offensive.

"Give me the love you withhold, my proud stallion. I have dreamed of being with you. I will be yours this night. Our bodies and our destinies will at last merge." She pressed her advantage, and I felt myself wavering before her determined advance. My will was crumbling.

Something in her voice had changed. The words were coming from Tabetha's lips, but I had the queer feeling they weren't her own. She was no longer speaking in her own soft voice. It had dropped octaves and become harsher, nearly guttural. The steely edge of that new voice alarmed me.

"Release me, whoever you are. I won't let this happen," I shouted, in a tone midway between a pronouncement and a feeble plea for help. She answered with a shrill squeal of amusement, thrust out her hands and raked her nails across my chest, leaving the skin scored and burning. Then she tasted my ravaged skin. I was hypnotized, defenseless before her offensive, wanting to withdraw but unable to stand or even turn over. She laughed aloud and the notes of her laughter were a song of delight in conquest, a confirmation of her victory over an entranced quarry.

"Now you are mine, my handsome warrior, and you will be mine always. No mortal woman can match what I can bring to you."

The enchantress held a small leather pouch up in front of my eyes, and touched it to her mouth. Then she drew it lightly in circles at my temples. A series of low, undecipherable words tumbled from her lips, and she hungrily seized me with her burning mouth full open on mine. The sensation returned abruptly to my entire body. There were involuntary responses that both excited and frightened me. As I floated, suspended between defense and acceptance of my fate, I felt her sliding closer, fitting every curve against me. Then the world of reality dissolved, and I whirled down into a dark void.

I dimly experienced sensations my mind was unable to sort out, searing pain and sensual pleasure inflicted by who or what, a vibrant woman or a distorted dream, reality or vision?

The soothing voice in my head came to encourage me.

The evil is strong, but we will prevail.

My last thought as I slipped into a silent abyss was *that's easy for you to say, voice.*

CHAPTER 25

Morning arrived in a burst of sunlight. My eyes sprang open. Tried to collect my thoughts through a murky haze filled with fragments of memories of the night. What had taken place was at once completely mystifying and deeply, peculiarly stimulating. Or had it really happened at all?

My temporary paralysis had passed. I flexed my fingers and moved my legs. The sensations in all of my limbs seemed to be normal. Turned over in bed expecting to meet Tabetha's triumphant smile. There was no one there, not even an impression on the pillow or sheets. If someone had shared my bed, she had departed without a trace.

I inhaled deeply, filled my lungs with the morning air, and sensed no remnant of the heady fragrance that had filled my head when the woman—or vision—came to me. When I raised a forearm to my nostrils, the essence of the maddening female seemed to cling to my skin like an indelible perfume. Couldn't shake the vision of her, the aroma, her glistening skin, her fierce hunger when she enveloped and claimed me. What was it she had called me, her 'proud stallion'? In my present state I felt more like a wounded gelding.

I peered down at my right arm to investigate a sharp stinging sensation. There inside the crook of my elbow was a bruise and what looked like dried blood. When I tried to clear my eyes and sit up in bed for a closer inspection, my head barely left the pillow. This stallion's energy was drained. At this moment I was having trouble raising my head, or anything else for that matter. Concentrated and focused all my will power to struggle to a sitting position, so I could look more closely at the wound on my arm. My reasoning was severely clouded; however, I derived some relief in noting that there was only a single puncture mark at the vein. That would seem to rule out vampires or even a stray copperhead from my earlier encounters on the front porch and at the saw mill. I couldn't even muster the energy to enjoy the twisted irony of this confused deduction.

Then I realized that my arm wasn't the only part of me that had suffered injury. Several angry red whelps rose on my chest and shoulders where something sharp had left long marks. The skin was broken. Those furrows had bled, and now they pulsed with a burning heat. Whatever had caused the injuries was probably the same apparition that had sent me into that wild episode I could only partially remember after the whirlpool of darkness began to close around me. The moans and squeals of delight, the frenzied thrashing of limbs, sharp points—fingernails?—piercing my skin. Weakly I told myself that if all this had really happened and it was that good for my partner, it was a shame I wasn't mentally there long enough to enjoy it as much as she had. Then I felt ashamed.

Had to shake my lethargy and get on with the important tasks of the day. There was some consolation in the fact that this ancient mansion had been retrofitted, in the Blue Room at least, with a private bath. Don't think I could have made it down a shared hallway with my head still swimming and my body drained from an overload of monumental proportions. Carefully, a little at a time, I made it to the bathroom and turned the shower on full blast.

The best I could manage was to sit in the bottom of the tub while the spray punished me all over. A semblance of life began to seep back into my wasted body.

I emerged from my wakeup dunk and unconsciously peered at the bedpost. Confirmed that my magic dream catcher was in fact still firmly perched in its assigned spot. That gave me pause. If the dream catcher's power was real—and I had enjoyed one peaceful night with it hung near me—then maybe the interlude with the frenzied woman was not a dream but brutal reality. The implications were more than I wanted to think about. It was time to shake off the dumfounding contradictions of the night. I would seek a kind word and nourishment from Myrtle's kitchen. I packed for my departure from the Comfy and plodded down the stairs to the first floor.

"So it's back on the road for you today?" Myrtle asked sadly.

"Have to sell those tennis shoes and jerseys, Ma Roop." I purposely looked at Tabetha as soon as I used that name to see if there was any reaction. Perhaps there would be a hint of her response to what I thought had happened in the big four poster upstairs. Her face remained expressionless. There wouldn't be an opportunity to confront her one on one befoe my departure, so my doubts would have to linger a little longer.

"And when can we expect you back?" Myrtle wanted to know.

"Right now I plan to return on the 21st and then again just before Halloween. Maybe we can trick or treat together."

"Oh, I always have lots of special treats baked for the children. There are so few of them left in Plenty. It's a pure joy to see their smiles when they come calling for goodies. You can dress up and help me hand out the sweets."

"I'll be sure to pack a costume, and we'll do the trick or treat honors together, Myrtle. What should I come as, Dracula or the Wolfman?" I exposed my teeth and made clawing motions with my hands.

"You just come as Greg Bain or anything that strikes your fancy. That'll be fine with me."

Tabetha hung back as usual, diverting her eyes each time she sensed I was watching her. I had the sensation that her gaze was burning holes through me every time my attention was elsewhere. In spite of wanting to put last night behind me for sanity's sake, it was impossible to look at her and not wonder whether beneath that simple housedress was the amazing body of the woman who had entranced me in the Blue Room. Was it possible that behind those innocent doe eyes lurked the cold, calculating temptress who had worked her will on me?

There was no way I could answer that question at the moment. Other guests were eating nearby, and Myrtle was ever-present and efficiently attentive to their wishes. What was I to do, hail the girl to my table and confront her?

'Excuse me, miss, if you have a moment, there's a question I need to ask. Are you the crazed nymphomaniac who crawled into my bed last night, bewitched me and pumped my brains out? Or was it all just wishful thinking and a wasted wet dream?'

The command issued by my nighttime visitor continued to rattle about in my skull, and the light of a new day did little to lessen the ache of dread it brought to me. *'You are under my power, Greg Bain . . . You cannot resist.'*

Myrtle finished her chores with the other guests and delegated their care to Tabetha so she could share a few moments with me. We spoke in near whispers, and I wondered if the other boarders found that odd. Nevertheless, we revisited some of our earlier thoughts regarding her father's diary and my plans for the coming days.

"You're leaving so soon. We haven't finished talking about Daddy's diary and your book."

"I believe I can see where this is all leading, Myrtle. Have the book framed in my mind. After work tomorrow, I'll be stopping by the Marlinton library to fill in some blanks with your friend, Velma Thomas. Then I'll swing by to see Chief John. During the next three nights on the road, I expect to get the prelude down on paper."

She was noticeably concerned about talking with her other guests nearby. She glanced about nervously then suggested we move our conversation to the parlor. Once we were alone, Myrtle began with a query.

"You didn't really answer me, Greg, about Daddy's diary."

"Ezra's diary held me spellbound, Myrtle. It was like I was there experiencing everything he wrote about in that little book. Now I want more than ever to tell the story of Plenty, the witches and the curse."

Her tone changed to one of concern, and she leaned in closer.

"I'm frightened, Greg. The more I think about this, the more I worry that we're opening doors that are best left closed."

"We've talked about this, Myrtle. I won't go forward unless you approve. You know that."

"What if we bring more evil down on us? Lord knows the Comfy has had more than its share of terrible things happen over the past fifty years. Could we be hastening the next accident?"

"As I've said before, that's exactly why I feel I have to finish what someone else has started. It's time to bring this tragic story to a conclusion, so the folks in Plenty can get on with life. With no rhyme or reason as to why it happened, I feel in my bones that if I don't personally defeat the curse, or whatever is causing these catastrophes, it will go on forever. You and Carl could be its next victims. I don't want that to happen."

The last thing I wanted to do was to cause this kind woman any undue anguish. But by now I felt a compelling urgency to either disprove my growing suspicions or meet them head on, for Myrtle's sake as well as for my own.

She looked at me with tears in her eyes, and her resistance softened. Now it was a very personal matter of us against the curse. I knew she wanted every bit as much as I did to lift this awful burden for good.

"Then do what you must, Greg. Just be careful, and stay out of harm's way. Please?"

* * *

My regularly scheduled morning call to Mom at the hospital brought an encouraging bit of news. During the middle of the night, according to her nurse, Sarah had suddenly begun to stir. When the nurse rushed to see what had brought on the change in her monitor readings, she found Sarah squirming in the bed. Twice she mumbled words that sounded like *no—mine, no—mine*. Then she lapsed back into motionless silence. That news was all the encouragement I needed to head for Roanoke.

"I need to come home now, Mom!"

"No, son. There's been no change since that one brief episode. I'll let you know immediately if she needs you here. Just keep checking in, and you'll be with her in a few more days."

As reluctant as I was to continue on the road with the faintest hope that Sarah may wake up and look for me, I knew Mom was right. She was always right. There was nothing I could do for Sarah at the moment beyond continuing to go about my work and praying for her recovery.

"If you think that's best, Mom, I'll finish my client calls. Please call me right away if anything like that happens again. When Sarah wakes up—and she will—I have to be there."

"You will be, son. Just get on with your business. I'm right here by her side."

As we finished our conversation, I began to speculate. Sarah had stirred last night, Mom said. I wondered where I was when she was calling out. Could I have been in the clutches of a bewitching vision while Tabetha, or my conjured up image of her, acted out her passion and I only weakly resisted? Perhaps Sarah somehow knew in her subconscious what was happening in the darkness of the Blue Room. Maybe she had registered her protest at the disturbing event that was taking place in my rented bed. That possibility would haunt me until I could hold her hand and explain to her that no one could ever come between us.

I hurried through three stops in nearby towns, and tried hard to stay focused on business. No matter how I tried, each time I was alone in the car the vivid image of me lying incapable of action against that strong willed nymph in my bed filled my mind. I had done nothing consciously to encourage Tabetha's aggressive passion, yet she seemed obsessed with placing me under her control. What was it about this strange village of Plenty that had sucked me into its vortex of intrigue so rapidly and so violently?

A troubled mind accompanied me on the road that day.

CHAPTER 26

My customer calls were completed for the day, and I was actually ahead of schedule. I'd made it a point to arrange my stops to allow me to hurry toward the Marlinton library as soon as possible after a quick mid-day snack. The county seat of Pocahontas County lay just ahead, so I would have most of the afternoon to peruse what the library and Velma Thomas could offer about the legend of Plenty. I was wired and ready to absorb everything.

Found the small library set back on a tree-lined plot in the middle of town and hurried inside. A gray-haired lady greeted me at the front desk. Her badge told me I had found the resident expert on county history. Velma Thomas was what I had expected from Myrtle's description, a kindly looking matron with a ready smile and a friendly word. I started to speak, but she was quicker.

"You don't have to tell me who you are; I already know. Myrtle gave me a perfect description of you, Greg. You're the special young man she sent to test my knowledge of local history." Velma gave me a wink.

Before I could even open my mouth, it was instantly apparent that she had taken charge and was ready for whatever I may throw her way. I already liked this woman.

"As advertised, Velma. I'm Greg Bain. There are so many questions, I don't know where to begin."

"At the beginning is always a good place to start. Let's take the story from the day Myrtle's poor little sister, Marietta, was spirited away. That was more than fifty years ago. It happened on a cold October day."

She led me to an alcove where a reading station stood isolated from the main library floor. Velma motioned for me to take a seat and said, "Wait here. I'll be right back."

She returned carrying a cardboard box containing a stack of papers, set it down on the table, and produced a letter size sheet from the top of the stack. It looked like a photocopy.

"This first item is a copy of a newspaper article from the Pocahontas Times about the kidnapping of the Charlton child. Tragic time. That started the whole sorry mess that's continued over the years up at the Charlton farm. There are a couple of follow-on clippings in the box that tell of the progress, or rather the lack of progress, of the search for Marietta Charlton."

"I have Myrtle's eyewitness account of that day and her father's written record of their efforts to locate Marietta. This will be helpful to put things into perspective from an outside observer's point of view."

She nodded and went back to the box to provide me with another news clipping.

"This one tells about Ezra Charlton's death. It was ruled accidental. Sheriff Westerly said he fell from a considerable height, probably the top floor of his big house, and landed head first down near the stream in back of the house. Broke his neck. Since there was no evidence to indicate someone had pushed him out the window, it had to be either a slip or an intentional jump."

"Which do you think it was, Velma?"

"I would never say this to Myrtle, but I believe he leaped. That poor man by all accounts was in constant torment over losing his wife and daughter. Certainly points to his climbing as high as he could get in that old house and jumping to his death when he couldn't stand the grieving any longer."

That brought to mind a still vivid memory of a late night visitor in the Blue Room. Chilling sight of a figure plunging from those wide open windows, A sight I would much rather forget.

I told Velma, "Myrtle said she really didn't know any more than what they told her fifty years ago, that her father fell to his death."

"I think she knows the truth, Greg, but she won't admit it to herself," Velma told me. "Myrtle's a religious woman, so it would pain her to think her daddy would commit suicide, an act so much against her beliefs. Who knows what any of us would be driven to do in his state of mind?"

I asked her, "Was there anything in the newspapers about the cabin that burned down up on Pennick's Knob? The fire happened the first night of the search for Marietta."

"Don't recall seeing any account in the papers, but I can make another search while you read. Should be something in the Times editions around the same time. They never missed reporting a fire, a hunting accident, a county fair ribbon or anything else that smacked of news. Plenty was a place that rarely saw any important events. Give me a few minutes to check."

She returned to her records files in back while I anxiously read the items her efforts had yielded for me so far. They made very interesting reading. I learned that more than fifty local and state lawmen and private citizens had searched for Marietta Charlton that icy October. They combed the entire countryside for a perimeter of several miles with no success. The searchers tromped through a couple of snowfalls, and braved cold winds on the mountain ridges. The local police brought in expert Shawnee trackers to assist. All they ever found was Marietta's locket on one of the mountain trails, and that occurred on the very first day of the search. As the call went out, more and more would-be rescuers joined the search party, and bloodhounds were brought in to help. But the massive effort ended in complete frustration for the sheriff and all his helpers. The child was not to be found. With great reluctance, they terminated the search after more than a week without results.

I picked up the next sheet of paper, and saw it was a description of the drowning death of a Maxine Pride, age 36, in a swimming pond on a local farm. She was swimming alone long after anyone should have braved the cold October pond water. The coroner concluded that she must have cramped in the chilly waters and gone under. No one was around to bring her to safety or to summon help. She hadn't been found for hours until a saw mill worker noticed her clothes at the pond's edge, checked further and made a gruesome discovery. A footnote to the news article stated that this drowning occurred on the same Charlton property where an unfortunate little child's disappearance and her father's accidental death had taken place years before. Maxine had attended the local school with Ezra and Elizabeth Charlton, deceased owners of the property. Sheriff Dillard Westerly was quoted as saying that the place was either suffering a string of bad luck or just plain had a hex on it.

Good old Wes and his big mouth. That no doubt marked the beginning of the legend surrounding the Comfy. Now the seed was planted that the incidents were connected and perhaps evil in some way. I knew from Ezra's diary that he had told the sheriff of Moni's curse. Wes didn't have the good sense to keep that fact to himself. At least the sheriff hadn't been specific about who could have placed a hex on the Charlton place.

Thought back to my scary episode at the pond when I nearly became a permanent resident of that swimming hole. The face in the water, the tooth I held for a moment in my hand. Wes investigated all of these so-called accidents. He had to have information the papers hadn't printed, or he wouldn't be so sure the events were linked to the Indian witches. Plenty's former sheriff didn't know it yet, but he had another appointment with me.

Velma returned with a single sheet of paper in her hand. It was fresh from the copier, and carried a lift from the Pocahontas Times concerning a fire in a high meadow near the summit of Pennick's Knob. The short report told of the blaze of unknown origin that had burned out of control. A small cabin was totally consumed because it was out of reach of any ready water source.

Consumed. Typical of the newspaper stories in those days. Nothing ever burned down—it was consumed by fire. No one died in Plenty—they all expired. Anyway, the firemen were forced to let the cabin blaze play out while they raked a fire line to prevent the fallout from igniting the surrounding woods. A light snow apparently helped extinguish the flames. The cabin was the home of a Shawnee woman named Blood Sky Hawk and her daughter, but only the mother's body was found after the fire. She lay on the grass near the cabin entrance where she had apparently died trying to escape. Blood Sky was already lying face up in the snow-covered grass by the time the volunteer firemen from Plenty were able to lug their equipment up the steep trail and arrive at the fire scene.

"Wes and his search party visited that cabin earlier in the day," I told Velma. "They had reason to suspect that the Charlton child was with the daughter who lived up there."

"In all my years in the valley," Velma replied, "I never heard anyone mention a connection. In fact, I was unaware until now that the fire took place. Isn't it strange that none of the other news stories picked that up?"

"Very odd, Velma. Especially since Wes and his men had such strong suspicions about Moni Hawk being the kidnapper. That was the name of the witch's daughter, Moni Hawk. See, they have me calling Blood Sky a witch, and I have no proof that she was."

"Well, you keep on reading, Greg, and come around with any questions you have. I'll be up front at the counter," she told me.

She hurried off to help a customer check out a book. Her efficient and thorough research had already advanced my efforts immeasurably. I might have been days trying to dig out a fraction of the wealth of information she'd already found.

The table where I was reading became my own private world. Tall shelves of books set me off from the rest of the library patrons and muffled all outside noise. I plunged back into the box for more prompters. I recorded my thoughts on the laptop; a soft clicking of keys was the only sound from my occluded nook. My juices were flowing now, and I wouldn't have torn myself away from that dark recess in the musty old library for any reason save one. My afternoon call to Mom was due to take place soon. Repeatedly checked my watch to be sure I wouldn't miss the appointed time.

A news article dated much later told of the untimely death of Warren Brainerd, who worked for the Charlton family on their farm and sawmill. He was a local Shawnee man, age 46, who had attended the Plenty school with Ezra and Elizabeth Charlton, and who had devoted years of faithful service to them. Warren had been found dead in the woods near the Knob. He'd been savagely mauled by wild animals. One local resident recounted hearing a mournful wail somewhere up the ridge late the previous night. That fueled speculation there was a wolf on the prowl in those woods. Another local was sure he'd seen a silver white wolf dart into the trees when he was on the ridge trail hunting squirrel several days prior to Warren's death.

Once again, neither the reporter nor the sheriff could resist mentioning prior incidents that had taken place near or on the expansive Charlton spread. Voila! The legend grew by word of mouth and innuendo.

I called Velma over to ask her about a later story of two locally prominent men who had met their deaths at the Charlton saw mill.

"That one I remember clearly, Greg. Old sawmill building had been abandoned for years. The mill operation was closed down after Warren Brainerd died and Carl Roop was injured in a tree felling accident."

"I've run across these names before, Velma. Who were they?" I pointed to the paper.

"Morton Feely owned the diner in Plenty, I believe," she said. "Jason Hatchett ran the mercantile store. They were found after the fire in the old sawmill office. There was evidence that one or more other persons may have been there, but it couldn't be confirmed. The men had been sitting at a makeshift table, and the police recovered a number of burned playing cards. Police said liquor could have contributed to the fire. Burned the mill structure to the ground. Only the old saw wheel and two charred bodies were left under a pile of rubble."

I began to see an eerie pattern beyond happenstance in these repeated mishaps near the Comfy. There was something else oddly similar in all of the accounts. But if there was a connection, it kept eluding me. By now I was nearly to the bottom of the box of papers.

Velma came to check on me and said, "We close early on Mondays since we operate on Saturday, Greg. I'm sorry, I have to lock up by three. All those materials are for you to keep."

"You've been a great help, Velma. Can't tell you how much I appreciate this. I've been through most of the materials, anyway. Just have this last article to finish."

Took the clipping from the box and looked at the title: 'Local Man Dies in Halloween Saw Mill Mishap'. The date of the paper was November 1. The victim was Bert Grace. An alarm suddenly went off in my head. Dug into the stack of papers I'd already scanned and checked their banners for dates.

"That's it! Every one of these deaths occurred around the same time of year. In fact, every one of them happened precisely on Halloween day." Velma smiled at my excitement. "Take a close look at the years, Velma. A new tragedy took place exactly every ten years."

"Myrtle says you're writing a book. The Halloween coincidence makes an interesting twist, doesn't it?"

"I'm not so sure it *was* a coincidence, Velma. Anyway, thanks again. I'd like to get back to the county's history authority later if you don't mind." She liked that title, and she nodded her willingness to talk again.

It was time to make my call home and head to my last stop of the day. Then I'd find a room for the night. If all remained well at home I would work my way to Beckley and down I-77 back to Virginia.

There was much work to be done tonight to consolidate my notes and launch into the project I had tentatively entitled *Terror at the Plenty Comfy*.

CHAPTER 27

The old man lived in a modest log home down a grass-covered lane off Route 39. The house backed up to a fast running narrow creek and a steep hillside. I could see that the wise man would have a clear view from the peak of that hill across the valley to Plenty and beyond. Parked off the lane; walked toward the house accompanied by a big, friendly yellow dog. The pooch sniffed at me. He apparently decided I presented no danger, so he wagged his tail and followed along at my heels.

We walked toward the cabin as an old man came down from the porch to meet us.

"Bear senses that you have a good spirit. He knows these things. Sit, Bear."

A dog named Bear? Perfectly logical to the man who named him, I'd wager. The important thing was that the dog had introduced me to his master as a harmless visitor, and the first impression was already made. I thrust out my hand to the ancient Shawnee wise man. He was old in years but stood straight as a totem, a warm greeting on his worn and weather beaten face. The man positively exuded a mystical charm. I hoped he could impart wisdom concerning the matters I had come to discuss with him.

"Chief John Holsclaw. You are Gregory Bain." It wasn't a question but a statement of fact. He knew. And I was not about to correct him about the use of the formal name I so disliked. If he wanted me to be Gregory, by god, I'd be Gregory! I wasn't going to displease a man who likely had powers I'd never comprehend in my lifetime.

"Sir, I have so many puzzling questions that need answers, and I believe you can help set me straight. May I have some time to ask for your help?"

He studied me as if deciding how far he wanted to pursue a conversation with a white man, a flatlander at that. I felt the Chief was looking not at me but into me, peering at my very soul and studying its contents. His intense eyes were unnerving, searching so deeply I felt stripped bare.

"Tell me the nature of your questions, Gregory. What is it you seek from me? I have been told you are troubled over stories of witchcraft in the Yew Mountains."

"Shall I call you Chief John?" He nodded agreement, and I continued. "Chief, I want to know more about the woman Blood Sky Hawk, her daughter Moni and the alleged curse on the Charlton property over in Plenty."

He rolled that around, rubbed his head crowned with receding snow-white hair and turned toward the house without a word. Assumed I was to follow, so Bear and I fell in behind him and walked up onto the porch. The aroma of food and the smell of burning wood wafted out the front door toward me. I conjured up a picture of a bracing mountain stew bubbling away in a kettle on the hearth.

He turned around long enough to say, "Wait here with Bear," and withdrew into the house.

I took another look at my surroundings. Noted how isolated his home seemed to be from any sign of neighbors. The peaks of ragged hills on three sides jutted upward to form a wooded bowl with only a single open side toward the highway. Even that view was nearly obscured by scrub pines and tall oaks that stood on either side of the lane. If he wanted seclusion, Chief John had certainly chosen the ideal place to take up residence.

In a few minutes, with Bear still standing guard over me, he returned wearing a full headdress atop his sparse pate. He carried a long, feathered spear in one hand, a blanket in the other and an ornate beaded leather pouch hung at his neck. Except that he lacked war paint, the Chief seemed to have donned his full regalia. I could visualize him marching off prepared to do battle.

Perhaps I looked a bit shocked at his transformation. He smiled and spoke.

"Do not be concerned by the spear. An old man sometimes needs extra help, and the spear makes a convenient walking stick. In a pinch it's also good for warding off snakes."

The chief beamed broadly. I interpreted his explanation as a sign that he didn't believe in unnecessary pretense. I had the overwhelming feeling that this was a genuinely powerful man with insight that had raised him to a revered station in his tribe. His manner commanded trust. What I heard from this wise man would be what he truly knew or believed, no tricks, no gimmicks.

"Where shall I begin, Chief John?"

"Not yet, Gregory. We must go to a place where I can meditate and the visions will be clear."

He turned toward the rear of his cabin, and led me across a footbridge spanning the creek. We began our trek up a rocky trail toward the hilltop. What with Carl, and now the chief, scaling these ridges like mountain goats, I felt a bit lacking. Maybe I needed one short leg so I could spiral up the hill. Myrtle delighted in repeating the old saw that all West Virginia cows were born with their legs shorter on one side so they could eat the grass on hillsides without tipping over.

We reached a rocky ledge near the summit. Below lay the open valley, and at some distance sat the village of Plenty. The late afternoon sun was commencing its long descent to dip behind the mountain ridges. A steady wind whistled across the hill's crest and stirred the dried leaves under our feet. Chief John unrolled his blanket to let it billow in the breeze. He spread the blanket out on a huge boulder worn flat by the seasons. Motioned for me to join him, and I sat facing the shaman.

"You are wondering, I know, so I will explain. My headdress is the symbol of my position among the Shawnee people. I am honored as a chief. The medicine pouch contains implements of my station, and it holds nature's offerings that permit me to see beyond the here and now. My thoughts will leave this place as we speak. You may begin."

He folded his legs, closed his eyes, and sat with both elbows bent, his hands turned upward with palms open. I admired his direct manner. Once we had reached the rock, there was no lengthy prelude, just a request for me get on with what I came to ask him.

"Chief John, I want to hear what you know about the old woman Blood Sky Hawk and her daughter, Moni."

"Ah, the evil one." His eyes opened and fixed upon me. He hadn't actually used the word witch, but his expression told me more than any words could say. Could I believe that the stories about her evil nature were true? That she actually *was* a witch?

He closed his lids and fell silent for a long time as his arms slowly rose toward the sky. Then the chief looked at me, through me, penetrating to some undefined distant point behind me, and began to speak.

"On the night the old woman was born, over one hundred years before this day, the sky burned blood red as if aflame. An omen was issued. She was given the name Blood Sky. She was a beautiful child, but evil lurked in the marrow of her bones. As her powers grew, the darkness increased and revealed itself to the tribe. Her people feared her unholy side; they banished the young woman from their midst. She went to live on a ridge high above the village of Plenty and enchanted a young Shawnee lad to mate with her. The product of their union was a lovely child she named Silver Wolf, but the child was called Moni by others. The evil woman Blood Sky Hawk held powers seldom witnessed even among my people. A look or a word from her could bring harm to one who had slighted her. She had the gift of healing, and also wielded the power to ravage one's health. I see a tormented Carter Hawk, her youthful mate, driven to leap from the high ridge to his death. Blood Sky's wickedness had pursued him and rotted his insides with corruption."

His solemn words took my breath away. I inhaled sharply and found it difficult to fill my lungs, heard my heart pounding like the drum in the Blue Room, faster, faster. It seemed that Wes had been right about his suspicions. Moni's father had been compelled to fling himself from that mountaintop by the torture of his own mate. She had heaped her scorn on him after he had fulfilled his single purpose of procreation.

"And what about the daughter Moni, Chief John, and the child she may have taken from Ezra Charlton?"

"I see a young woman who was consumed by her love for a white man. She professed this love, but he rejected her. She burned with hatred, vowed to have her revenge on Ezra and all in his family forever. I also see children who taunted the young woman daily. Each one in turn met a violent end as the young witch's powers grew to match those of her mother. Three remain to be dealt with—an old man, the son of one of those who burned her mother alive, and the white man's remaining daughter. An amulet, a ring, carries the essence of Blood Sky's powers into the hands of her descendants."

I was swept up, entranced with the impact of his pronouncements and the confirmation his words brought to all I had heard from others. These were things I couldn't imagine the chief knowing unless he truly did have insight beyond my ability to understand. As far as I knew, only Ezra and Wes were aware of the details of the curse Moni had uttered. The circumstances of Carter Hawk's death had been cloaked from the public by a finding of accidental death when he fell from Pennick's Knob.

"The kidnapping of Ezra Charlton's daughter," I said. "Do you see that?"

The shaman's eyes were distant, half a century away from our perch on the ledge. He was silent for a long interval then resumed his story.

"The young evil one, Moni Hawk, wanted Ezra to suffer after he spurned her, to feel her wrath in the most painful way. I see her sweeping down from the Knob like an icy wind to spirit away the child, the baby my friend Ezra called his Sweet Tater. She sped back to the cabin as the child struggled and fought to escape her. The baby's necklace snapped. Her locket fell onto the trail. The witch took no notice. Moni hurried on, and took the child to Blood Sky's cabin deep in the high woods."

This was no time to back off. The shaman was completely into his trance, and I wanted to press for all I could get. He must know about the fire, who had set it and who, if any, survived the flames.

"On the ridge where Blood Sky lived, Chief—can you see the cabin fire?"

"Yes, I am there in that terrible night." His face twisted and his brow furrowed.

A sinking sun hovered behind the wise man casting a corona around him. It was as if the ancient seer was emerging toward me from a raging inferno, his white hair and headdress aflame. He was an integral part of a widening burst of brilliance. From somewhere within that fire, he was inhaling visions of the past and breathing them out to me.

"Three troublemakers soaked the cabin and Blood Sky with kerosene and alcohol. Then they set the house afire. Another watched their foul deed from the shelter of the trees. He remained silent."

He proceeded to paint a vivid picture of the events as Blood Sky's cabin seared and collapsed in upon itself.

"As the cabin, was engulfed, the old witch ran screaming from the flames. She did not survive. The girl Moni fled silently into the woods before the fire played itself out. She took Ezra's child, and they went far away. The sheriff knows where they journeyed and how they became separated. Start your search with him, and look in a town called Radford."

"The curse Moni placed on the Charlton household? What can you tell me of that, Chief?"

"It continues to this day. There is a second and equally powerful curse that also endures. The revenge Blood Sky vowed against those who set fire to her house, and against their children, is yet to be finished."

"Then the accidents at the farm are linked?"

"I see Moni Mweowe, the Silver Wolf, returning time and again to wreak her vengeance. Each time her wickedness robs more of her beauty until she is a pitifully wretched old woman. It was she who dragged the girl down and held her beneath the water of the pond; she who set upon her fellow Shawnee, Warren Brainerd, with fangs and claws. Moni locked the drunken men in the saw mill after one had escaped then set it ablaze."

I asked, "Was she responsible for Bert Grace's death?"

"She returned to remain unseen over the ridge's brow beyond Pennick's Knob. She brought with her a female child. Ten years ago she drugged Bert Grace, and the two women raked him across the rusty saw mill blade until he was disemboweled. Moni lives to this day in a cave on the far side of that ridge. She is very ill, but another has been chosen to fulfill her curse and that of her mother Blood Sky."

"The child who was taken, Chief John. Is she still living?"

A long silence followed while I sat holding my breath. Then he spoke.

"My vision is fading. I can tell you no more." Chief John closed his eyes.

He abruptly returned to the present on the rocky outcropping. I knew by the look in his piercing eyes that he was no longer staring through and beyond me but directly at my astonished face. Imagined that by now I must be registering surprise, shock, a myriad of emotions, none of which were clear to me yet.

"Chief John, you're truly a great shaman, and I am in awe of your powers. I'm in your debt."

"Gregory Bain, take extreme care. You are in mortal danger from a superior force. That evil spirit knows that you, and you alone, can break its hold on the people of the valley. The spirit will seek to steal the fluids from your body to fashion potions with which you can be controlled. Once you are under the full power of a strong spell there can be no returning. The specter that you face is one that cannot be defeated by mortal hands. You must turn the evil back upon itself, and make it serve as its own destroyer."

He rose and saluted me with an outstretched palm, his signal that the session had ended.

Chief John's revelations swirled in my head. I wondered what connection they may have with my terrifying experiences in the Blue Room. Who was the phantom that had disappeared before my eyes through the windows? What, if anything, did Tabetha have to do with these events? Or did I only imagine she attacked me in the dark?

I had also confirmed from the newspaper clippings my feeling about the timing of the tragedies surrounding the Comfy. Marietta's kidnapping, Ezra's fall, Maxine's drowning, Warren's mauling, the two men burning up in the sawmill fire; all of them occurred on Halloween. Beginning with Ezra's death the incidents were precisely timed. Every ten years a new misery was being heaped on Plenty and the poor Roops.

The most recent victim was Bert Grace. The newspaper clipping said Harmon's father perished at the old saw mill on October 31st, Halloween Day.

By some combination of forces I could neither identify nor comprehend, I had been appointed to set matters straight in the community of Plenty. The weight of that realization was staggering.

Without warning, the soft, steady voice crept silently up to me and hummed.

The witch has had her fun, but now our turn has come.

CHAPTER 28

My customers were taken care of, and I was nearing home. After my most recent visit to Plenty, with the jarring encounter in the Blue Room and the eye-opening experience with Chief John, intuition told me my continued sanity could depend upon bringing my mind back to what really mattered most—Sarah.

I turned off the interstate at Roanoke and homed toward the hospital. Nearly a week had passed since I'd held her hand. I hurried to her side and bent to kiss her lips.

Mom said, "Tell me about your trip, Greg."

Couldn't tell Mom *all* about what had been happening to me. She simply wouldn't believe it. Wasn't sure *I* believed half of what I saw and heard those three days in Plenty. Most of it was better left untold until a lot of murky areas had been sorted out. It was time now for me to be at home with my two sweet ladies and to put the sinister side of my present on the back burner.

"This was a very busy trip, Mom. Caught up with the visits I missed last time out. Even saw some new people along the way. I need to go back out there again in a few days, so I'll be sleeping right here at the hospital. Missed both of you so much."

She said, "The doctor wants to try something to bring Sarah around if you agree. It's a type of shock stimulus. I'll ask him to explain it to you when he comes in."

"Whatever breaks this sleep cycle and gives me back my darling is what I want, Mom."

By now I was convinced there was a hidden coupling between the events in Plenty and Sarah's coma. This defied all logic, but I couldn't stop thinking about when her lapse into the coma had occurred and when she had seemed agitated. She was taken ill on the very night I lay in the Blue Room listening to drums and a chant while I tried to prevent the vision from leaping from the window. A few hours later Sarah slipped into a coma. Her episode of thrashing and calling out had to have taken place near the time I was in the midst of my encounter with Tabetha- or dreamed I was. The timing was too close to be merely coincidence. Somewhere in the farthest reaches of an addled and confused brain I had to find the key to bringing Sarah back. This time at home with her would give me new purpose. Now I was more determined than ever to break the spell of the witches over Plenty and, more importantly, to release Sarah from her coma.

Once I'd left the Comfy and turned my attention to clients, the days sped by. Equally encouraging was the progress I was making on the Plenty Comfy book. I had confirmed my feelings about the timing of the tragedies surrounding the Comfy having occurred precisely on Halloween and ten years apart.

Now it was time to savor the moments I could sit with my darling, tell her how much I loved her and wanted her restored to my side. She listened patiently, never interrupting, though the Lord knows I would have been overjoyed to have her do just that.

There was no question what I must do, though, and it meant leaving her again. Barring a miraculous recovery by Sarah or, heaven help us all, a turn for the worse, it was my destiny to return to the Comfy before Halloween and conclude this nasty business. I didn't yet know exactly what that meant. No clear course of action had jelled in my mind, but the quiet, reassuring voice of my invisible mentor was always just a whisper away. Together we had to defeat the evil that threatened to consume the Comfy and the Roops. Clearly, I could be involved in a race for my own survival as well. The evil forces, whoever they were, surely recognized the danger of my meddling with their grand plan for revenge.

Mom said, "I'll slip back to the house and let the two of you be alone."

I held Sarah's hands in mine and smoothed her cool fingers, stroking the little gold band that joined our hearts. She gave no sign that she was aware of my nearness. I knew, however, that she must sense my love. I talked without pause about our dates in college, our plans and dreams, the wonderful times during these past four years. I was about talked out when Doc Jameson arrived.

"Did your Mom tell you about the test I want to try, Greg?" he asked.

"She mentioned it. What is it you want to do, Doctor?"

"It's actually a series of stimulus tests devised by a specialist who's had repeated successes in bringing comatose patients back to a fully awake state. Still somewhat experimental, so only the doctor who built the tests can properly administer them. I'd have to call him in to consult."

"And you believe this can help her?"

"Yes, I do. I have to admit that at this point I'm stumped, and we need a way to get Sarah past her present condition. I don't want her coma to continue any longer than necessary from a long-term health perspective. There is a significant cost involved, Greg."

"I don't even want to discuss the cost, Doc. We still have some of my NBA bonus money left. Can't think of a better use for it. Just do it, Doc."

"I'll make the arrangements. As soon as I have a firm date, I'll let you know so you can be here when the tests are performed." He looked down at his patient.

I had every reason to believe the doctor would do only what was best for my wife. His words brought renewed hope for Sarah's recovery. But the nagging question of her important news, delayed in its delivery by this horrendous situation, ate at my subconscious. I had to know what I had missed when the storm steered me toward Plenty instead of to my tryst with Sarah.

After hours of prattling on to my sleeping wife about long ago memories, I was beginning to wind down. Mom came to provide the relief watch, and I hurried home to clean up and return for the night. All the time I was in the house, my mind wandered frantically in a search for clues. Sarah and I had always honored each other's privacy and kept our hands off each other's most private possessions. On this occasion I rationalized that I was dealing with a special situation.

Prompted myself aloud as I searched everywhere for clues. Wanted to believe that revealing her secret could help me find the way to talk her back to consciousness. For whatever hastily manufactured reason I latched onto, my search took me everywhere, into every room. Then I homed in on her desk.

"Okay, Sarah, you've hinted more than once that you were making a serious attempt to write for publication. Your tone set me to wondering if you'd brought up the subject to test me. I told you your interest in writing wasn't threatening to me. Baby, I know you could outwrite me any day of the week. Remember, I told you to go to it and make me proud."

No evidence of major works in progress. Seemed we weren't about to become a two-author family in the near term. She'd been spending a lot of time to herself the past few weeks. Maybe she had a great story mapped out in her mind, and she was saving her announcement for a homecoming surprise.

"I do see some tentative starts here, outlines of ideas. What am I doing digging in your things? Oh, baby, I want you back so much it hurts."

All the time I was invading her privacy, I marveled at the seamless beauty of her writing. If she hadn't yet attracted the attention of an astute agent or editor, it was surely only a matter of time and the right set of eyes falling on her work.

"Any recent letters that may give me a clue? Maybe big news on the teaching front? Let me see what you have here in the letter stack."

I searched her correspondence for clues to other events I may have missed. Sarah was dedicated to her work, and she was very involved in giving her teenage students the best possible language foundation for their futures. She considered a solid language arts base the most important building block for success no matter what they decided to do in life. Maybe she'd drawn special praise for her teaching, and now she wanted to share it with me.

"Nothing. Wait! A new teaching position? That would call for some discussion before you made a decision. We always make our important decisions together." No clues in that direction either.

The most frustrating dilemma in our otherwise happy marriage was the fact that we couldn't seem to conceive the child we both desperately wanted. Doc Jameson could find no organic reason, so the failure was even more disappointing. We talked about adoption and gave serious thought to checking sources that could help. Mom had told us repeatedly that we had plenty of time and shouldn't rush matters. Sarah would soon turn thirty, though, so we didn't want to wait much longer for nature to take its course.

"Adoption? You've found a promising lead to an adoption. Maybe you've even met a special child for us to nurture. You'd want to give me that news first hand."

My frustration level peaked, and I sat staring at her things neatly aligned in her work area. Ran a hand across her notes, wishing she were here to talk it out with me. Walked away in dejection.

"What am I doing, Sarah? You'll be able to tell me soon what this is all about. Honey, I have to believe you'll be all right. It's all that keeps me going."

For all my efforts I had come up dry. Returned to her side at the hospital emptier and more befuddled than when I started. Worse yet, now I felt guilty for prying into her secret preserve to satisfy my own curiosity. Said a painful apology to my sleeping beauty, and we put the subject on hold for now.

"I'll just have to be patient, Sarah. If only I'd come home on time three weeks ago. Sweetheart, I'll just have to wait and hear it from your lips."

A depressing thought suddenly hit me full force. I had automatically equated *important discussion* to *celebration*. Maybe the matter wasn't as positive as I had painted it. What if Sarah had bad news? My curiosity had been piqued by the evasiveness of the answers I was getting from both Mom and the doctor. Then the two of them had been engaged in a private conversation in the hallway that, from all indications, was timed to exclude me. What if, despite their reassurances, there was reason for them to be concerned about Sarah's prospects for recovery. Maybe they felt I wasn't yet ready to share that prognosis? On that count they would be absolutely correct. Even the mere thought of such a possibility quickened my pulse and brought tears to my eyes.

As I worked out the alternatives in my mind, I held her hand, stroked her cheek, told her of all the postponed dreams we would work on fulfilling once she was whole and healthy. I told her we would start with her sharing her secret with me. To this day I still debate whether I actually saw a flickering smile lift the corners of her mouth, or perhaps it was a delusion created by my need to know she heard my words.

The entire day on Saturday I guarded over my darling and waited for movement or word that would tell me she was clawing her way out of that dark hole back to reality. Saw no signs to lift my spirits as I talked and teased, crooned and sobbed, poured out my soul to her hour after long hour. Finally, exhausted and spent, I closed my eyes and rested my head next to her hand.

I was dimly aware of fingers touching my head. In an instant I was awake and staring at Sarah's hand. Her fingers remained outstretched, as limp and motionless as before. A split second of soaring hope was dashed as I heard Doctor Jameson speak from behind me.

"Sorry to disturb your rest, son. I know you need it. I thought you'd like to know that I've scheduled the specialist to see Sarah."

"Tell me it's soon, doctor. I need her back so badly."

"Unfortunately, Doctor Evans has had so much success that he's in great demand. The good news is that we're on his schedule, but he can't be here until Monday, November 3rd. Grit your teeth and hang in there, Greg. Who's to say she won't decide to wake up before that on her own? We'll have to keep the faith."

Another wait. It was clear there was nothing I could do to speed up the process, so I'd have to accept a few more days of agony with Sarah in that other place. It made my present plans acceptable, however. I would take my last trip to sports stores on behalf of FirstSports and a final, hopefully climactic, trip to the Comfy. That would bring me home before Doctor Evans arrived, and I would be on hand if the tests successfully awakened Sarah.

I say last trip for FirstSports because I had made an important decision. This was an answer that I had to arrive at on my own, and Sarah couldn't change my mind. I was firm on that point because it was in her best interest as well. If the offer came from Tech I was going to accept. I would give proper notice to the company then it was off to help prepare the team for the upcoming season.

Wow! Division I round ball with ten thousand screaming fans in the stands. Tournaments and young players with solid talent to mold. I was going to accept even if Sarah remained in her coma because it meant I could be home every night no matter what the future held. The commute was short, maybe forty miles each way, and I could hurry home to her each evening. Only when we had road trips would I be away from her, and at most that was three or four days at a time.

Maybe I was fooling myself and the offer wouldn't come. I had decided to change employment, anyway. There would be no more Greg Bain on the road week after week with Sarah back home. I'd flip burgers or swing a pick axe before I'd let another disaster like this one catch us unaware with me away from home. Somebody had to be looking for an athlete who was also pretty good with words. Maybe a high school had a coach/teacher opening.

Before I left her side on Sunday for my short stay in Plenty and a last swing through the client list, I told Sarah of my decision.

"You know how much I love the game, honey, and you know that I love you infinitely more. The Tech job would allow me to have both and to cling to them as never before. When you wake up we could have a whole new life ahead of us. Whatever happens, Sarah, I'm through with the road after this month. I'm going to stay near you and cherish you every minute. Just give me a few more days, and I'll be home to stay for good."

CHAPTER 29

Back on the road again. Already missing Sarah, but at least I would have a chance to get back to my writing each night in my motel room. The outline of the story was jelling, and I was cataloguing the items needed to fill in holes. Harmon Grace's version of the incidents at the Charlton place should be interesting. I also wanted another shot at Dillard Westerly. Maybe I could keep his attention long enough to delve into areas where I strongly felt he was still holding back on me. That old man may have had the answer to solving the curse all along, and either he didn't realize it, or he had other some motive for keeping quiet. Either way, he was going to open up to me if I had to squeeze him until his head popped.

Then there was the matter of pictorial background for my story. Myrtle surely must have some old photos of the Charlton farm and the mansion in their heyday. Pictures of two key players, in particular, would help my perspective as I wrote about them. Those two critically important people were Ezra and Marietta. Perhaps there were school photos or family portraits of her parents, and maybe she had an image of the baby or of the two little girls together.

For now my plan was to let Mom worry about Sarah and submerge myself in thoughts of business and glad-handing clients, of organizing and writing the fascinating story of Plenty—if that was possible. There were questions about the future to ponder in the limited amount of time available to me. Even allowed myself to speculate on how different life would be if I was given the opportunity to move over to the coaching job at Tech. Maybe Sarah could work in the time to finish her doctorate. These issues were all important to me, but my real subconscious goal was to keep busy contemplating them, so my time away from Sarah would pass more quickly.

* * *

First there was work to be done in Plenty. I pulled up to the Comfy and stepped into the foyer.

"There's my Greg come back to me," Myrtle chimed, and ran to greet me with a hug. "How is your sweetie, Greg?" she asked.

"We have new hope. She's stirred a couple of times, and a specialist is arriving soon with new methods for nudging her awake. I still believe she'll come around on her own given enough time."

"Oh, I'm so glad there are positive signs. I pray for her every day. We'll get you out of here and back to your Sarah. I want so to meet her and your Mom soon."

"You will, Myrtle. I've told Mom so much about you she feels she knows you already."

"So what do you have scheduled for your short stay in Plenty?"

"I want to talk to Dillard Westerly and Harmon Grace. Both of them should be easy enough to catch in town. Velma was very helpful, and she gave me a lot of food for thought with her news clippings."

"I knew she would. Velma's a sweet girl."

"Chief John told me things that opened my mind to new possibilities. He's truly a great man, Myrtle."

"Daddy had a special bond with him. They were close friends up to the day my Daddy . . ." Her eyes began to well up with tears.

I quickly changed the subject. "What's been happening at the Comfy since I saw you, Myrtle?"

Her normally cheerful face was clouded with concern. "I'm afraid. I don't like this creepy feeling I have." She was plainly very upset about something. "It's gone. Missing."

"What's gone, Myrtle?"

"The scoot-booger. Disappeared from the hall curio cabinet. Been there for as long as I can remember, and now I can't find it anywhere. It's not a good omen, Greg."

She put a lot of faith in that charm, and I could understand why its disappearance would leave her shaken and upset. In her mind it was the surest form of insurance against invasion by evil spirits; now that protection had been spirited away from her. Myrtle probably had visions of all manner of witches, goblins and monsters gliding in through the doors and windows of the Comfy, attacking her from every direction, bringing new tragedies to bear.

"It'll probably turn up in the least likely place, Myrtle. There has to be a logical explanation why it's not where you left it."

I hoped she was more convinced than I was. Something about my words sounded hollow in my own ears.

"Well, all I know is I'll rest much easier when I have it back in the hall cabinet where it belongs. Gives me goose bumps all over when I look at that empty shelf. I'll put it under lock and key this time."

I admitted to myself that by now I was becoming imbued with the superstitions of the hill people. Shuddered to think what the absence of that revered talisman might mean. Sometimes it's not the real truth in a belief so much as a belief in its truth that matters. My presence here was driven by an intense need to end the string of catastrophes for all time; I had yet to determine exactly how I would do that. For all my efforts and small victories along the way, the puzzle was still far from unraveling. Until I could focus on what or who was behind all the misdeeds, there couldn't be any real progress made in halting them.

The fatherly voice would surely return and guide me during these last critical days. Without the voice's advice I would be exposed, naked before the evil spirits that would surely gather around me. The scoot-booger's absence may open the floodgates for more evil than we could fend off. Then, as I despaired that I was in this fight alone and unarmed, the now welcome murmur of my gentle prompter returned.

Heed the wise man's words. Our journey is almost done.

So the voice understood the wisdom of Chief John's pronouncements. The shaman's words tumbled over and over in my mind. I played them back in slow motion trying to dissect everything he'd told me, straining to delve for clues and meanings. Exactly what had I experienced back there on that rocky ledge? What did the voice mean *'heed the wise man's words'*? Chief John had told me so much during our short time on the hilltop. Pondered that while I drove down to the village, hopeful that I could find two important players in this mystery that wouldn't quite untangle for me. Chief John said that Wes knew where Moni and the child had fled, and Wes also knew how they had been separated, whatever that meant. Old Wes had some explaining to do, and Harmon was the subject of another bit of unexpected information the chief had passed to me.

* * *

I found Wes at the diner, joking and laughing with Plenty's senior brigade as usual. He looked up as I entered and quipped, "Thought I'd seen the last of you, young man. Couldn't get enough of old Wes's stories, huh?"

"We need to talk, sheriff. Can you come with me?"

"Sure. Ain't got no pressing matters here. What am I gonna get this time—supper?" That irritating cackle followed.

"Maybe that and more, Sheriff." He looked at me; appeared puzzled over the sharp edge in my voice.

We walked to my car. I drove out of town past Harmon's, and Wes began to regard me with suspicion written all over his face. Good. I wanted him off balance when I lit into him.

"Why are we going this way, son? What's this all about?"

"You'll see soon enough."

I drove almost to State Road 39 then pulled off at a wide spot. By now my passenger was looking confused and more than a little agitated, as if he wasn't sure his getting into the car had been a good idea.

"What's your game, Bain? You're acting kind o' distant and queer like. Thought we was going up to the Comfy for some eats."

He instinctively reached for the door handle just as I locked us in. Wes turned to look at me, and he gave the outward appearance of trapped quarry. He tried to say something, but he produced no words, only a stammer.

"First I want some straight answers, Wes. Bull shit time is over, you old phony. Let's start with the drowning of Maxine Pride. What is it you're not telling me about that?"

"You know as much as I do by now. Water was cold as a polar bear's ass that time of year. Guess she took the boat and tipped over or something. Icy water got her 'fore she could recover."

"No sale, sheriff. She was known by everyone to be a strong swimmer. Should have been able to make it the short distance to shore or out to the platform, even under those frigid conditions."

I thought again about my experience on that pond and an idea struck me. *It's far fetched,* I thought, *but It's worth a try.*

"What do you know about an animal tooth at the accident scene, Wes?"

He sputtered and turned an ashen gray. "How'd you know 'bout that?"

I'd struck a chord with my random shot. Wes was flustered.

"So there *was* a tooth! Tell me, you old buzzard."

"Found a wolf's tooth in Maxine's mouth when we pulled her out of the pond. Thought it was mighty strange, but I didn't mention it. Just put the tooth in my pocket and kept it."

"Wait! The necklace in your photo of Moni. Your find made you suspect Moni had a hand in Maxine's drowning."

"Didn't really come together till ten years later," Wes said, "when Warren Brainerd was mauled by animals and I found another wolf's tooth stuck in his neck. Didn't look like a fresh tooth. Then

I saw they both had little holes drilled in them like they'd been on a string or something. Pulled out that picture of Moni, and it hit me dead on. That witch was spitting in our faces, leaving clues behind to devil us."

"Why didn't this ever come out in the investigations?" I wanted to know.

"Too late. Couldn't bring it up after Warren's mauling 'cause I'd sloughed over it when Maxine drowned. I tossed it in an old cigar box along with the first tooth and some other junk."

"Why, you old bumbler. Bet that wasn't the last one you found, was it?'

Wes hesitated. He had little choice. His tampering was already exposed. "Matter o' fact, I took a tooth that was shoved down in Jason Hatchett's ear when we pulled him out of the saw mill ashes. Bert Feeley's right eyeball was punctured with another one. Nobody saw me slip that bloody tooth in my pocket, either."

"And Bert Grace? Out with it, Wes."

He stared out the window, avoided my eyes and said, "Yeah, when Bert Grace ran afoul of that saw mill blade, there was another big ol' wolf tooth. Looked like it'd been hammered between his ribs right over his heart. Almost missed that one, what with all the blood. Damn old blade did an ugly number on Bert. Downright scary. Still got all them teeth in that box at home. Every one of 'em had holes drilled like they'd been strung together."

"So that's how you knew Moni was behind all of the so-called accidents. That they were planned killings."

"Damn witch was sitting back laughing at us. I didn't know which would give out first, the teeth on her necklace or the dwindling population of Plenty." His forced cackle was a nervous one this time. It sickened me to think he could cheapen four grisly deaths.

Wes turned in his seat, rolled down the window and let go with a stream of tobacco juice. He swiveled back to defy me with a broad grin and said, "So whatcha gonna do with that bit of outdated information, smart ass? I suggest you stuff it where the sun don't shine, and then you can drive me back down to Main Street."

"I'm not through with you yet. Now tell me about Moni and the baby girl she took from the Charltons. Where did they go, Wes?"

He tried to look genuinely surprised. "Why, whatever does that mean? I told you they disappeared without so much as a trace. Ain't nobody heard from either of 'em since." His eyes evaded me, but I could tell the old man was lying through his rotten teeth. He began to shake, and genuine fear registered on his face. "Told you all I know," he said and turned away.

"No, you haven't. Not by a damn sight, sheriff. I know you tracked her down after the search here was over. Tell me what happened between the two of you when you found Moni."

"I could have your hide for bullying me this way, you young jackleg. Where's your manners going after an old man like me? You think I ain't got friends would put you away? Lock you up good and tight, make you sorry for coming around these parts."

"Go right ahead and call them. Shout as loud as you want. It's just you and me out here, you old liar. I'll take you down the road and drop you in the woods for the bears to feed on if you don't come clean. No more playing around, Wes; you're going to spill it all. I want to know about *Radford* and what happened there."

That grabbed his attention. He was plainly struggling with a tough decision. There was no telling how much I already knew, and my steely look must have convinced him I was about to do him bodily harm. He fumbled and snorted, but finally he appeared to resign himself to speaking up to save his skin.

"I swear I'll deny this if you ever repeat it, Bain. You'll never prove a word of it."

"I don't care. You and I will know, and that's all that matters."

"Okay, I hunted that teasing little witch down. She and the child had made it out of the mountains and hot footed across the state line. Caught up to her begging for money for her and the kid over in Radford. It was New Year's Day, more than a month after she done the snatching. She nearly got away from me again. I couldn't let the bitch slip out of my grasp twice."

"Outwitted you back at the cabin and almost got away in Radford, too, huh?"

A nasty frown twisted his face. "Nah. Went back futher'n that. Snooty wench turned me down a year or so before. I'd been stalking that purty little piece for months. Told her I could make things easier for her around the valley if she was nice to me. Caught her alone one day, and decided I'd just take her my own way. Hellion bit me and scratched me 'til I had to turn her loose. Knocked her 'crost her noggin hard as I could and she ran. I'da shot her on the spot and woulda got away with it, too. Still wanted me some of that vixen, though. She may have been mean, but she was just about the purtiest female creature I ever laid eyes on."

His words disgusted me. "So when you found her after the kidnapping you already had a personal score to settle with her?"

His lecherous grin made me want to shove a fist in his face. "Damn straight I did, and now I had her over a barrel. If she didn't give me what I wanted this time, I'd take her back to stand trial for kidnapping, a damn serious charge in West Virginny."

"Where was the little girl all this time?"

"Oh, she was close by somewhere. Moni told her to be quiet while we talked. Gave her a sweet or something."

"You offered Moni a choice to get what you couldn't have otherwise."

"That's putting it kinda blunt, boy. She wanted loose from me plenty bad this time. Said she'd do whatever I wanted if I'd just turn around and go back to Plenty by myself. Didn't make the little bitch any promises; took her back in the bushes and pounded her good. She knowed she'd been had. I turned that witch every way but loose. When I walked away she was begging for more of what I give her. Fact is, she said she owed me *three times*."

The old codger actually thought Moni was complementing him on his sexual prowess. To the contrary, I believed she had cursed him to die for three insults to her. That would be his virtual rape, his earlier attack in Plenty and—what else? He smiled, and at that moment I wanted to mash his face in even if he was more than twice my age. But I needed to know more from him. His punishment would catch up with him in due time.

"So you just left her there after you used her? And what happened to the little girl? You obviously didn't bring her back to her family. Where was your sense of duty?"

"That was the most puzzling part of the whole deal. I never saw the child again. She musta wandered off and got lost while we was back there in them woods getting it on. Weren't no skin off my ass. If I took her back I'da had to answer to what happened to the Injun girl. Figured she deserved that and more for her mischief. Just wanted to be shed of that woman after she done the only thing for me I ever wanted out of the evil bitch. The Charltons never did nothing for me, so why should I worry about bringing their kid back? Screw them rich folks."

"You make me sick, Wes."

"Maybe you wouldn't talk that way if you knew the whole story. I never told another soul till today that little bitch Injun was doing all the killings in Plenty for the past fifty years. The witch was taunting us with her killings and the wolf tooth clues. I shoulda done Plenty a service and blowed her brains out when I found her and the kid, and we'd avoided all them bloody deaths later. Never seen her after that night in Radford, but I know she's done all the mischief and killings ever since."

Maybe I *would* just drive this worthless old fool down the road after all, drop him in the woods and take off. No, as much as he deserved it, that wasn't in my nature. I'd worked him over pretty hard, but I could never do physical harm to an elder, even an old reprobate like Wes. Somewhere, maybe in the after life, he'd have to stand and take the judgment he deserved. I dropped him off near the diner. Wes would probably tell his cohorts how he had dazzled and bull shitted the green kid, but we both knew better.

When Wes and I parted company, he threatened again, "I could never be accused of anything. It's your word against mine, and you're a damn outsider," he said with a wry grin and a squeaky cackle. I wanted to throw up. Then I thought about issuing him a warning that he was in grave danger. Decided he didn't even deserve that much consideration.

CHAPTER 30

Harmon Grace was nearby, and I was already fired up. This may be the best time for me to see him. Wheeled around; headed for the gas and grocery. Harmon hailed me from the back of the store.

"Finally came around, did you? Been expecting to hear from you."

"I'll only be here for a short while, Harmon. Thought we might have that talk you promised me."

"Like I told you before, the kittle's always on, and the stove's stoked up. Now's good a time as any for me." He dragged two battered old rockers up to the pot belly; motioned for me to sit. Shooed the cat away with his foot.

"Took to worrying about you, Bain, when I didn't see you for so long. Thought maybe the ghosties up at the Comfy got hold of you and scared you out of town." That odd cackle again.

"Do you believe the stories about the accidents being connected to a curse, Harmon?"

"Hell, they weren't accidents to begin with. Every one of them must have been plotted by the witches. Maxine Pride and Warren Brainerd was both schoolmates of Ezra and the young witch and they both died. Her and her momma had it in for my Daddy and his friends, too. Both of them had been throwed out of their stores more'n once for pilfering things. How you gonna explain a rusty old saw mill wheel hadn't been run for years coming on and ripping out my Daddy's insides might near ten years ago?" Harmon set his jaw, and his chin trembled with anger.

"I never did understand exactly what happened to him."

"Hell, ain't nobody else understood that one either. Least of all me, his only son. Don't even know what he was doing up at that old burned out saw mill, anyway. Wasn't nothing left but a pile o' rubble."

"My theory is, Harmon, he was drinking and playing cards with his buddies at the mill before the other two were killed ten years earlier. Must have left the mill just before the fire started."

"Mighta been. Wasn't any call to be treated the way he was, though. Took an evil mind to dream up that sorry way to get back at him for something. He never did anything to them witches except protect his things at the store from them."

It's not quite that simple, Harmon, I though to myself. *Not if I can believe what Chief John told me.*

Harmon opened the stove door, and angrily threw in a stick of firewood then stomped back to his rocking chair and sat down hard.

"I heard he fell on the mill blade, Harmon."

"More likely pushed by one of them dang witches, I'd say. That old wheel couldn't have run a lick after ten years sitting idle. Didn't even have power to that burned out place far as I know. That old rusty blade grabbed him and tore the insides clean out of him. Just don't make sense."

He pounded the rocker with his clenched fist, bitter tears in his eyes. "Wish I could get my hands on whoever did it. I'd make 'em regret it, that's for sure."

If I could believe what Chief John had said, Harmon was unaware there was a gruesomely simple explanation. Bert Grace was totally defenseless and under the influence of one of Moni's potions when she and another woman physically ripped his limp body back and forth across the teeth of that lifeless saw. The saw's teeth did the rest of the work on poor old Bert.

"What's your theory, Harmon? Who do you believe caused this series of tragedies?"

"The witches, Greg. It had to be them all along. That Moni, her maw Blood Sky and who knows how many other evil crones were a party to it."

What had me totally stumped was how Moni could come back to Plenty every ten years and wreak havoc without being seen by someone or, better yet, caught in the act. Chief John had made me feel that there were mystical events in this would I would never understand. But I wasn't ready yet to believe in spirits that materialized, killed then evaporated at will.

"Tell me what you know about the Charlton kidnapping, Harmon."

"Don't know anything except what my Daddy told me. Little girl got took away, and they looked for her high and low. Daddy went with them all over the hills, but there was no sign save the locket they found up toward Pennick's Knob. Daddy thought the young witch from up there did the snatching and her momma was in on it. Didn't make any difference 'cause they couldn't prove it. Both denied it when the search party broke in on them the first day. Heard him say more then once he shoulda strung up both of them on a tall oak when he had the chance."

"How about the cabin fire on the ridge the first day of the search?"

"Oh, yeah. He said the old witch's cabin went up in smoke that same day, and it was good riddance to the old hag. Said she must have been knocked out or something. By the time she got out of the fire it was too late for her."

"I don't understand. What do you mean she was knocked out?"

"Just repeating what he said. Anyhow, the volunteer firemen said that old woman burnt clean down to the bone right there in her own meadow. She was just a heap of bones and ashes when they found her."

"Was your father a part of the firemen's crew, too?"

"No. He'd already been up to the Knob once that day with the search party. Said one time climbing up that trail was more than enough for any human or dumb mule in a day's time."

"I know. I've been up that path with Carl. It's a long climb. Wore me out."

In my book, nothing Harmon had said let the older Grace off the hook. The shaman had told me that two of those yet to be dealt with under the curse were *an old man and the son of one of those that burned her mother.* I had a pretty good idea who both of them were, and Halloween was almost here.

"That's about all I can tell you, Greg." He went to the front of the store when a customer walked in. Sold some items from the vegetable bin, and carried a sack of flour from the back room. He returned in a few minutes to where I was sitting.

I stood and offered my hand; said, "Thanks for the information, Harmon, and watch your back. The strange happenings may not be over yet."

He settled in by the stove and seemed to want to visit for awhile longer, but I'd already gotten what I came after. Both Wes and Harmon had set me to wondering about why the incidents came every ten years and how the witches, if they were responsible, managed all that mischief undetected. Then it struck me. Caves dotted those ridges, and there must be villages on the far side of the mountains. Moni could move in and out of Plenty at times of her choosing, seek out her victims and fade back into the thick woods above Plenty. The Chief had said there was another woman who Moni had brought back with her, too.

I left Harmon sitting by the stove, and walked to my car as a ripple slipped past my ear.

Now it's you and me, boy. Turn it back till the wicked witch is dead.

"I sure hope you're with me now, voice. I need all the help I can get until this is over."

CHAPTER 31

Myrtle served up my breakfast, and she talked non-stop about her plans for Halloween. She was genuinely happy about having someone to share the evening with, and it was only a week away.

"Bless his heart, Carl does his best to make Halloween night special with the decorations and such. He just isn't much on cavorting with the kiddies and handing out the sweets. Now I'll have you to help me."

"I'll be there right beside you, providing my wife doesn't make me the happiest man on earth and open her eyes before then, Myrtle."

"Oh, that would be an automatic rain check, Greg. Sooner or later you're going to be my Halloween helper, and Sarah can join us next year."

"In fact, I've already decided how I'll dude up that night, Myrtle. I'm coming as a scarecrow: bib overalls, plaid shirt, floppy hat and straw sticking out everywhere. Tell Carl I need for him to save me some straw."

"The children will be tickled pink." Her warm brown eyes lit up, and I was sure that Myrtle derived every bit as much childlike pleasure out of the Halloween activities as did any of the little ones.

As upbeat as she was, I hesitated to inject a serious note into our chat. I genuinely cared for this woman, though, and her motherly ways. She had to be prepared for what may lie ahead. Myrtle had no way of suspecting what the evil spirits may have in mind for her when Halloween Day arrived. Chief John had told me the witches intended to fulfill their oath of revenge by dealing with three more people in Plenty. One of them was the daughter of the white man who had spurned her.

"Myrtle, I want you to listen carefully to what I'm about to tell you. The next few days could be the most important and dangerous days of your life. I can't stress enough how important it is for you to follow my instructions until Halloween has come and gone."

There was no doubt that I had her undivided attention. She sat down across the table from me, and her hands nervously fidgeted and twisted a small kitchen towel.

"You're scaring me," she said.

"I don't want you to be frightened—just alert. Chief John opened my eyes to facts that tell me the curse may be approaching its final stage. I want you and Carl as safe as possible."

"How do we go about protecting ourselves, Greg?"

"First, I think the two of you should never be out of each other's sight until Halloween night has passed."

"That seems easy enough. What else should we do?"

"I can't prove this, so you'll just have to trust my instincts for the time being. Be careful around Tabetha and watch her closely."

I had already checked to see that the girl was nowhere within earshot of our conversation. At this point, I still couldn't say with certainty that my encounter with Tabetha had been real and not merely a fevered dream. But I was taking no chances. If Tabetha's words had been more than a nightmare, the imminent danger to the Roops already lived right here in the Comfy. That was a fact they wouldn't want to accept, but they must.

"I don't understand. What could Tabby have to do with any of this? She's one of the gentlest people I've ever known, Greg."

"Sometimes we can be fooled by appearances, Myrtle. There's nothing concrete I can share with you just yet, but I want you to take extreme care whenever Tabetha is near. She may be the most serious threat to you."

"She's like my own daughter," Myrtle protested. She refused to believe that her many kindnesses to the girl would be returned with anything other than the love they deserved. If I was right, that in itself was a master stroke by the evil ones. They could have worked for years to lull Myrtle until the precise time of their choosing arrived for the final thrust of revenge.

"Do this for me, please, Myrtle. I could be wrong about Tabetha, but we can't take the chance. Please keep an eye on her and keep up your guard."

"I know your intentions are pure, Greg, so I'll take the warning to heart," she assured me.

It was time to move on to my appointments, so I would go about business and hope for the best until I could return to the Comfy.

"Have my store visits all laid out for the next few days. There's a lot of writing to do every night. By the time I return to the Comfy I should have something to show you on the story of Plenty."

"Just hurry back home to us."

"Well, I'd best make like a business man and haul my goods out of here. See you soon, dear lady."

* * *

The next three days were a blur of assorted towns and sports stores, hasty lunches and burger bags in my room at night while I hurried through my notes and put some substance on the book's framework. There were two notable events that took place in the midst of this busy schedule—a phone call and a visit. They both occurred on Thursday late in the day.

The folks at Blacksburg had several ways to reach me in the event a decision was made about the coaching position. My cell phone rang as I was about to make my last client stop of the day.

"Bain here."

"Greg, this is Bill Carter at Tech." I swallowed nervously. This could be the news I was waiting to hear. Please let it be the right answer.

"Yes, coach?" My voice probably sounded odd to him because the adrenaline was buzzing, and my mouth had instantly turned dry.

"We want you to come on board. I'd be proud to have you as an assistant. Salary and benefits would be the same as we worked out in the tentative offer."

I went completely mute. Now that the moment was finally here, I didn't know whether to shout, cry or run around in tight little circles. The words refused to come.

"Greg? Are you still there?" His question shook me back to speech.

"Just overwhelmed, coach. My answer is yes, yes! When do I report?"

"Can you be here two weeks from today? We have a lot of work to do before the season gets rolling."

"I'll be there. And, coach, can I come by to sign the contract on the morning of the 28th? I already have plans to be up that way. There's a trip to Radford I've promised myself as soon as possible."

"That's a winner," Carter said. "You can meet the team then, too. Come by my office around ten o'clock. Welcome aboard, Greg."

With all of the odd and unusual events that had surrounded me recently, this was a pleasant return to the real world. Finally I'd be able to gain some control over my life, and Sarah and I could get a fresh start. Only wished I could call her immediately to give her the wonderful news.

I was on a cloud. Had to share this with somebody *now*. Punched in Joe Dolan's number.

"Joe, you won't believe what just happened to me. I have a new job."

"Man, you sound excited. What is it, Poet?"

"I'm going to work in Blacksburg on the varsity staff as an assistant basketball coach. How's that for a kick in the old patootie?"

"Big time. Pal. I'm happy for you. Julie's gonna be tickled, too."

"How did her visit with Sarah go? Is she back home yet?"

"She came home today, and she wants to see you. Has something important to pass along. Where are you now?"

"At the moment, I'm about forty miles from Richwood and have one more stop to make today."

"Why don't you swing by here? Visit this evening and stay the night."

"Joe, there's nothing I'd like better than to see you folks. Give me directions to find you, and I'll be there by no later than six o'clock."

"Better be ready for some one on one with Jason, though. He's already a hustler, so he'll probably want to match shots with you for money. Bring a pocketful of quarters. Don't know where he gets his bad habits."

"I do. Think you still owe me a couple bucks for misses."

* * *

Seeing my old friends Joe and Julie was the best thing that had happened to me since this whole affair began on that flooded road to Plenty. Little Jason was growing fast, and he was already much like his dad with a shock of red, crew cut hair and a ruddy face. I'd swear he even had that cocky air about him that had always helped Joe succeed far beyond his innate athletic abilities.

Julie was, as I expected, the same perky little brunette who had been Sarah's best friend and a constant member of our inner circle throughout our years at Elkins. Knowing she had spent time at the hospital with Sarah was a real comfort to me.

Nearly as soon as I was in the door at the Dolans, I asked Julie, "What was your impression of Sarah?"

Julie hesitated, looked at her son then replied, "We had a wonderful visit, Greg. She didn't have to answer for me to know I was getting through to her. We've always had a special bond."

"That's for sure. Joe said you had something to tell me."

She gave a slight head nod toward Jason and said, "We can talk about that later. Let's just visit a while."

Her signal to defer further discussion of Sarah for the boy's benefit came through loud and clear. I'd wait until she chose the time to unload whatever news she had for me.

We had a grand time reminiscing about all the funky tricks we'd pulled back in school. I told them all about the visit Sarah and I had made to Blacksburg and how excited we both had been. Now, I was about to be a part of their community. They were both elated over my news. Said they'd be there the first time I appeared in Cassell Coliseum with the team. Wanted to bring Jason; let him see how basketball was played at that level.

Jason sat very quietly and gave us his full attention. Then, finally, he broke into a rare lull in the conversation and threw out a challenge.

"Dad tells me you're a pretty good shot, Mr. Bain. Want to shoot a game of horses with me?"

"Sure, big guy. And listen up. I'm Uncle Greg to you. Or Poet if you like." My godson was an impressive little fellow. Sarah was going to be tickled to see him.

Jason flashed a mouthful of gleaming white teeth to show his delight. "Poet," he muttered.

Little flash had a shortened goal pole, and he made me give him a six-foot advantage on all shots. Talk about a hustler—he'd learned his lessons well from Joe. We played until I ran out of quarters. I raised his arm and declared him the winner. When Julie called us to dinner he took my hand to lead me proudly into the dining room.

"He's not bad, Dad. Just needs a little practice." I bit my lip and kept a straight face.

Jason gave us his 'I'm the greatest' smile. Had to be genetic. Joe Dolan's own self-assurance had carried us through lots of close calls on the court, and I had to admit his enthusiasm and confidence had buoyed me many times when I was on the verge of folding. We made quite a backcourt tandem with the basics Dad had carefully coached into me and Joe's unstoppable positive attitude.

Julie trundled Jason off for a bath and bed, but he insisted on giving Uncle Poet a big goodnight hug and kiss before he went to sleep. When the three of us had once again settled down to talk, I opened the subject we had postponed earlier.

"So how *did* your visit go with Sarah?"

"I was with her for the better part of two days, Greg, and I had a strong feeling she knew the whole time that I was there. It's just an intuition thing, but Sarah and I always had an eerie way of communicating without words."

"That's one of the reasons I was happy you were going down there, Julie. There was a good chance you could get through to her. Did you see any signs of improvement?"

"She did something very strange on two occasions while I was sitting alone with her. Never opened her eyes, but she formed words. First time it sounded to me like she was saying something like *my turn*. Does that mean anything to you?

"Nothing. I'm just happy to hear that she's still having these episodes of response to her surroundings. I need her back. Now that I've taken the new job, we have so much to look forward to."

"The second time she spoke out, she mumbled some strange words, something like *lego wish*."

"Puzzles me what that could be, Julie. You can bet, though, that she knew it was you in that room, and she was trying to tell you something."

"Well, I know that girl probably better than anyone except you. She's going to whip this thing, and we'll be enjoying our Thanksgiving turkey together. That's my prediction and my promise to you, Greg."

I left the Dolans' with renewed hope. Julie was just as confident as I was that it was all going to work out. When I saw Sarah, I would explain everything to her—the job, the book, my new friends at the Comfy and, most of all, my certainty that she was coming around very soon.

Remembering now what these two friends had meant to us, I deeply regretted having shut Joe and Julie out of my life when they could have made such a difference. Sarah had continued to stay in touch with Julie after graduation. Soon my problems had so absorbed her time and thoughts that even that connection eventually disappeared.

When I finally emerged from my alcoholic fog and started acting like a human again, we had tried to reach the Dolans to be in our wedding. Somehow they had managed to move away from West Virginia without Sarah knowing how to reach them. I finally learned just tonight that was due to a series of unfortunate circumstances—missed telephone calls, a short notice move, a mailed letter that never arrived, a lost e-mail address. By the time they settled in out in Missouri and tried to reach us, Mom's new number was unlisted, and Sarah and I both were in new locations.

Well, that wasn't going to ever happen again. They had returned to West Virginia when Joe bought the store in Richwood, and Julie started a new teaching job. This time I was going to hold on for dear life to the best pals we had ever known.

All the way down the road to my motel, I concentrated on deciphering Sarah's words. *My turn* had me totally stumped. But as I stared out at the road, I could see her as clearly as if she was right there in front of me, and she was forming those other words. I watched her lips closely, and it came to me in a rush. She hadn't been saying *lego wish* at all. What she had blurted out was *let go, witch!* That confirmed the suspicion I'd been carrying that her coma and the curse were intertwined. She knew it and now so did I. The only way to rescue Sarah was to break the Plenty curse and defeat the witches. I had to put them away for good.

* * *

Arrived back in Roanoke late as the sun went down on Saturday. From Saturday night through Tuesday I poured my heart out to Sarah, and she listened silently. There was no outward sign that she comprehended, but I knew somehow I was getting through. She would know that my decision to take the new job was necessary without her agreement because it couldn't be postponed. I painted a picture of our new association with the campus crowd and how we'd enjoy the change of pace. This opened up a whole new world of options. She had worked so hard to earn her masters degree in English as a teaching credential. I encouraged her to keep moving ahead, and she had started doctorate studies, though I always wondered where she could find the time. Now I hoped she would finish her course work and dissertation, and I would have my very own Doctor Sarah.

We would have our choice of remaining in the valley or moving to the mountaintop to be close to the campus. I knew there had to be openings in Montgomery County schools for a terrific teacher like Sarah. Once she had her PhD, maybe a university position was a possibility. Mom was welcome to come along with us or stay in Roanoke where we could visit her often.

I talked on and on, telling her about the new job and my dreams for us. Then I told her as much as I knew about the Plenty Comfy, its history and the curse it was under. Self-consciously, I omitted any reference to the superheated encounter with little Miss Night Fire. Sarah didn't need to be concerned about that, particularly since I still didn't know exactly what had actually happened or how the night had ended after I blacked out. Explained to her how I hoped to break the curse, and how I would write the book that would help lift the cloud hanging over the village of Plenty. Whether or not she could hear me, I had to unload my burden to someone. Sarah was not only my closest friend and confidante, she could well be critically affected by the witches' vendetta because I had interfered with their plans. If only she would open those pretty eyes and tell me it was going to be all right. Even a terse, "Shut up, Greg. You talk too much," would have been like music to me.

* * *

Wednesday morning I made a quick trip to the hospital to see Sarah before my last business trip. From now on most of our goodbye kisses would mean *so long until I see you for supper*. That thought warmed me all over as I headed out into the chilly October mist for my drive up Christiansburg Mountain.

The formalities were over in short order, and I was officially a member of the Tech coaching staff. Coach Carter and I met briefly with the team members and staff over lunch. I was impressed with the talent he had assembled. Many of them were Virginia players whose careers were familiar to me. Our boys at the high school had competed against a couple of them, and they were top-notch prospects. Told the coach I had already called in my resignation to FirstSports and confirmed it in writing. On Thursday, November 6, I would be on board.

As soon as lunch and all the introductions were finished, I headed off, buoyed by a new purpose, toward the nearby town of Radford.

CHAPTER 32

The clerk at the Radford courthouse records room offered her assistance, and I tried to narrow our search.

"Need to see records that will tell me about any small children placed in foster homes or with adoption agencies during this period." I handed her a slip of paper listing the target months almost fifty years ago.

"Those records will be back here in this section. You'll need to come with me to review them."

She led me down a narrow hallway to a small desk, and told me to wait until she located the correct materials. The anticipation made my mouth dry. I raced ahead in my mind; projected the joy Myrtle would feel if I was successful. This could make an important piece of the puzzle fall into place for her as well as for me.

"Actually, there are two volumes you need to check for the information you want." She was carrying two heavy books. I reached out to help, but she set them down on the desk.

"Whew!"

The musty old books had both obviously been in storage for a very long time without being disturbed. Their sheer weight produced a loud thud when she released them, and a puff of dust went up my nose.

"Achoo! Sorry."

"Bless you. I'd say you're the first one who's shown interest in these particular records for ages. They go back a long way." She retrieved a cloth from a nearby shelf and wiped off the covers.

"I know," I replied. "Farther back than either of us can remember."

"This blue binder contains records of children placed by the local court in approved foster homes over a ten year period that includes the months you're interested in, Mister Bain. It also lists assignments made to organized children's homes around Virginia. The red book shows adoptions sanctioned by the court during that same period. Please let me know when you finish your research."

I set my yellow legal pad on the table top, and took a couple of pencils from my shirt pocket. Began the tedious task of wading through the books, one of which may contain the single item of information that could alter several lives. Methodically scanned the entries in the adoptions book first without success. Fearing there was a missed key entry, I double checked by making a second selective scan of its contents. There was no obvious lead to the information I wanted.

Frustrated and disappointed, I turned to the volume that listed judges' assignments of foundlings and other children to sanctioned homes. Again, there was no direct link to the keys I had in mind. A second pass through that binder likewise revealed nothing of interest. I was dashed, heartsick. This had seemed my best hope of connecting a missing child to her eventual destination, and it was a total dead end. I slumped in my chair and racked my brain.

Peered out the window toward the main street of Radford. Looked sunny outside but it had become very gloomy inside these walls. I scanned past the end of the stacks and watched patrons in the periodicals section reading magazines and newspapers. Another possibility popped into my head. I walked to the front desk and found the clerk.

"Ma'am, I'm through with these books." Plopped the massive volumes down in front of her, and offered to lug them back to their resting places.

"Thanks, but this time I'll know to use a cart. Hope you found what you're looking for."

"Sorry to say I didn't. Let me ask you a question, though. Where is the local newspaper's office?"

"That's the Radford Gazette." She gestured with one hand. "Just go left down the main street out here, and cross at the next light. You'll see their sign on the red brick building at the corner."

I hurried along to test my next source while I struggled to come up with possible alternatives, but I couldn't think of any. Either there was a lead in an old newspaper, or this was turning into an exercise in banging my head against a painfully hard wall.

When I explained what I was looking for, the Gazette receptionist turned me over to a middle aged gentleman who looked the part of the small town newspaperman. I scanned his bespectacled face, neatly trimmed beard and white shirt, his out of style tie and red suspenders. He had an unlit pipe clenched between his teeth. This could have been me if I had pursued a career in journalism as some of my classmates had done. He led me into a back room that reeked of stale tobacco and musty newsprint.

"The back issues you want to see are right here in this drawer. We used to keep all of our issues when the newspaper was a weekly. Now we have trouble storing everything for a daily paper even on film. You'll be looking at full copies, though, just as they hit the streets back in those days."

"Thanks. You can't imagine how important this is to me." He gave me a disinterested head nod.

"Now let's see. You said New Year's Day. So the news for that date would have been in the issue of . . . here it is, right on top."

I retreated to the chair he pointed out, and started on page one. By now I was getting desperate. Set out to devour every printed word until the answer surfaced.

Long minutes of frustration stretched my patience. I read about what piece of road had been patched, whose children or parents were in town for visits and whose cow had wandered off and had to be rescued. Every bit of useless information had been carefully documented and preserved for posterity except the one item that had become so vital to me. The single story that could alter my life was nowhere in print.

In hopeless resignation, I turned to the back page of the old newspaper, and scanned those items the editors had obviously felt were not newsworthy enough for more prominent placement. My eyes were glazing over by now, and I almost missed a small entry at the bottom of one column.

The account related how a young child, estimated to be about two years of age, had been found wandering near the Radford bus station. She could provide no information as to her identity except to say her name was Sweet Tater. Jackpot! My heart skipped several beats, and I found it difficult to breathe.

There was little other information given, merely a statement that the child was taken to the Baptist Children's Home in Salem to be cared for properly. I wrote down the newspaper name and date then I recreated the article verbatim on my note pad. At last I could report a solid lead to finding Myrtle's little sister. And my heart was speeding because buried in that short article was another possibility I wanted desperately to confirm.

The voice came and prompted me.

Well done. Save it 'til the witch is gone.

I took that counsel from the voice as a caution against making any hasty conclusions. His advice had proven flawless so far, so I'd keep my dangerous assumptions to myself until I could prove them.

CHAPTER 33

The afternoon was only half over. I was finally on track in my race to crack the Plenty mystery. It was time to drive toward the Comfy and the showdown that had become inevitable. Determined to press the evil forces to make the first move, I resolved to meet them head on when they showed themselves. Let me be the counterpoint to their half-century crusade to sink the town of Plenty into their morass of wickedness. One way or another, the face-off was near at hand.

Made my call to Mom from the car on the way toward Plenty.

"Sorry I'm late checking in, Mom. Had some important chores to finish today."

"Wish I could tell you there's been a change in Sarah," she said, "but there's nothing new."

"Oh, there will be. I'm convinced she's only days, maybe even hours, away from coming out of her coma. Then there could be some other wonderful news for both of you." Mom didn't respond right away, and I stopped short of spilling out what had occurred in Radford.

If my theory was correct, both the curse and Sarah's problem would find their solutions on Halloween. I was going to force a facedown with the witches that would release my wife from the grip of their powerful forces. And if my suspicions were all wrong and that didn't work, I'd still be there when the doctors put Sarah through her paces with the tests on Monday.

However, this day wasn't even close to being over yet. I planned ahead for a critically important trip and some trying hours ahead. Spotted the Comfy, and wound up the long driveway. Myrtle was on the porch before I could heft my bag out of the car. She called to me.

"Just like you promised, here's my Greg." It was nearly like being welcomed home by my own Mom.

"Wouldn't miss our Halloween outing. Came prepared," I said, holding aloft my scarecrow clothes. "Just needs a little of Carl's straw to make it complete."

She came to meet me at the top of the front stairs, and gave me a big bear hug. The way she clung to me set me to wondering if it might also indicate a note of concern.

"How's Sarah?" she asked.

"She's still holding her own. Soon, Myrtle. She'll be back to normal soon. I guarantee it."

"You come on in and get warm, and let me fix you something special for supper."

"May be a little late to the table tonight," I said. "Have something to do that's going to take awhile, maybe well past dark, I'd guess. If I'm late, pot luck will be fine."

"Pot luck, my foot. You'll have supper waiting *whenever* you finish. I'll see to that."

* * *

As the sun began its descent and twilight approached, I was compelled to make a last all-important trek. Jacket buttoned against the cold, my hiking boots laced up, I took an emergency lantern and began the climb toward Pennick's Knob. A solitary visit to that solemn cabin site was the only way I would ever know the whole truth.

The going was slow, and I was already mentally weary from my encounters with the shaman and Wes, the visits to Harmon and the back-to-back road trips. The climb was physically trying, and the mental stress of so much happening so quickly was even more draining. I knew Myrtle needed watching over, but I'd leave that task to Carl. The Knob was calling to me, and I couldn't resist its pull. There may not be another chance for me to stand alone and soak up the aura of the dreary place that was the fulcrum point for the entire riddle of the Plenty curse.

With every step, I felt eyes watching me, bearing in on me as I drew nearer to that gruesome site. The leaves had all fallen, and the bare hardwoods stood their gnarled and twisted sentinel over the winding trail. Limbs contorted to point scaly fingers upward toward my destination. Every fiber of my body told me my entry onto those miserable grounds was forbidden. Nevertheless, even if I was embarked on a treacherous one-way trip, it was impossible for me to turn around. Sounds of unseen life forms moving through the underbrush echoed back on me from both sides of the trail. Those rustles and crackles, skitters and squeals followed me up the twisting, pitching path. Kept looking to see what was out there, and stumbled along on the uneven footing.

I emerged from the woods into the deserted clearing. Once again I scanned the forlorn site of tragedy and suffering from so long ago. An eerie silence had cast its shroud over the meadow. No sound remained from the nighttime creatures that surely lurked in the dark. A lonely owl, abroad before his appointed nighttime rounds, clung to the limb of an ancient oak, and hooted his warning for me to go back. But I was committed.

I closed my eyes until I heard sounds ahead of me. Reopened them on a vision I couldn't be sure wasn't real.

An evening haze was beginning to gather. It gave the illusion that the cabin site, long since cold, was still smoldering. Then, as I watched, angry flames rose and enveloped the hovel. The pungent aroma of burning timbers filled my nostrils as surely as if the cabin still blazed before me, and I felt the flying ash settling in my hair and on my clothes. Everything in the clearing was coated with a fine gray mist carried on the moaning wind.

Then, without warning, the flames were gone.

I was standing in the quiet clearing surveying the small log cabin, restored and whole, its tin roof creaking in the wind, the glow of a hearth reflecting through a window. But I was not alone in that meadow.

Three men skulked out of the trees. They hurried toward the cabin door.

"*Be ready with that rifle, Mort. We may have to shoot the bitch if she turns on us.*"

"*If the young injun's in there, I have other plans for her, Bert.*" Mort chuckled. "*We might's well enjoy ourselves while we're at it. Right, Jason?*"

"*Let's just have this over with, and hightail it far away from that evil hag, boys.*" Jason seemed to have strong reservations about being here.

Well! This had to be three of the town's leading citizens in their earlier days—young Morton Feeley, Jason Hatchett and Bert Grace! They didn't know that in the years to come, two of them would be toasted in a sawmill fire and the other one would leave his inner self on the teeth of a big rusty blade. What were they up to?

"*What we gonna do with 'em, Bert?*" Mort asked.

"*Nobody cares what we do as long as the valley is shed of them,*" Bert replied. He didn't bother to knock; just jammed the door hard with his rifle butt, and kicked it open with one foot.

The men strode into the cabin. Blood Sky faced them defiantly.

"*Leave my house. You have twice intruded.*" She raised one hand and thrust it forward, releasing a white powder in their direction. The old woman spoke harshly in the language of the Shawnee.

"*Don't piss us off with that mumbo jumbo, hag,*" Bert Grace said. "*Where's your hussy kid and the baby she stole? We got business to conduct with her*"

Mort Feeley laughed, and he spat tobacco juice into the fireplace.

"Silver Wolf is gone and so is the baby. You and the sheriff are fools. You should have searched under the cabin floor." Her shrill cackle filled the room. "Now they have eluded you, and you will never find them."

"Told you she was the one," Mort proclaimed. "She tricked us. Scurvy bitch put one over on us. We need to have some revenge here, Bert." His smirk in Blood Sky's direction reminded me of the hunter eyeing his cornered prey, anticipating the kill.

Her voice was shrill when she screamed, "Leave my house. Give me peace from your insults."

"Yeah, we'll give you piece," Bert Grace snarled back at her. "A piece of noose around your scrawny neck" He waved a rope in front of her. "I'll hang your witch's carcass from the tallest oak I can find."

"Hell, that's too damn obvious, Bert," Mort insisted. "Let's just lock her in and torch the cabin. They'll think it was an accident. Drunken old Injun burned herself up—what a pity!"

Jason protested. "Let's us not get carried away, fellers. We scared the old bitty outta more years than she's got left in this world. Other one's already gone with the child. How 'bout we just skedaddle out of here now before we go too far?"

"Don't go weak dick on us now, Jason," Mort laughed. "Time for some fun. We gonna hold our first witch roast."

Bert seized Blood Sky by her long black hair and twisted, forcing her to sit on the floor. He wound the rope around her ankles; drew it so tightly that she winced and screamed out in pain. She pulled at the chafing rope, fought and scratched at him with her long nails. She managed to scrape Bert's forearm, and he yanked away as the blood trickled down his wrist.

"Old hag gouged me!" He hit her full in the face with his big hand, and she slumped to the floor. "That's better. Now let's get this place smoking" They bound her hands while she lay stunned and bleeding from her badly mangled mouth.

"Give me your bottle, Jason." Bert poured the booze into her open maw and dribbled it down her front. She revived and choked, tried to spit it back at him.

"Pitiful waste of good drinking whiskey, but we gotta make this look believable," Bert said.

He took a long pull on what was left and drained the bottle. Threw it down and said, "Damn. She even took our partying booze." Bert kicked Blood Sky in the ribs, and he turned away from her laughing when she spit up blood.

"It's okay, Bert. Still got the good stuff right here." Mort held aloft a quart jar of clear liquid.

He found a kerosene can in one corner, and he doused the beds, curtains and floor.

"Let's be sure we soak her bindings so they'll all burn away. That way she'll just be another unfortunate victim of demon rum." Mort roared with amusement at his own cleverness.

Bert poured out the last of the kerosene over her bindings then tipped the empty can over and left it in front of the fireplace.

Jason and Mort turned and ran, bounding down off the front porch. Bert dropped a match on the tinder box floor, and a blue kerosene flame sped toward Blood Sky's motionless form. When the flame reached her prone body, the cabin walls echoed with Blood Sky's piercing screams for help. Bert ignored her frenzied cries and sped away. Soon the entire cabin was engulfed in flames, and the trio sat in the meadow watching it roar.

"She won't be giving nobody else the evil eye. Hand that jar over here, Mort," Bert cracked. *"There's some big time celebrating to do."*

They passed the moonshine jar and drained it while they watched the fire reach its peak. The cabin roof buckled and timbers came crashing down. The men hooted and laughed their way into a drunken stupor. By now, even Jason Hatchett was caught up in the excitement of the moment, and the moonshine had dulled what little reservation he may have harbored.

"Look at her go," Mort howled. *"Maybe we shoulda brought some wienies and mushmellers to skewer."*

His partners doubled over with laughter, and they all rolled in the grass. Their liquor soaked brains belied the wickedness of what they had done. I stood helpless, knowing this was only a vision.

There was nothing I could do to help the poor soul inside. I felt the bile rise in my throat.

Their party came to an abrupt end when a figure materialized out of the flames. Blood Sky, her clothing ablaze, her long hair flaming, even her flesh on fire, charged out of the cabin door directly at her tormenters. She was no longer merely a poor human engulfed in fire; she was an apparition straight from hell. Her wailing shriek resounded through the hills and chilled my blood. *"Death to you all and to your offspring,"* she screamed, and the hideous specter rushed to attack them.

"Great gobs o' goose shit," Jason Hatchett cried as he leaped into the air and hit the ground running. The other two were not far behind. They were falling, scrambling, rolling through the underbrush in a blind charge to escape the horrific sight that was racing toward them.

The men were gone from the clearing, cut and bleeding in their headlong haste, when Blood Sky collapsed face up in the weeds covered with the first coating of a gently falling snow. The men's departure was a shame because they all deserved to witness the final horror of their misdeed and to have the vision imprinted on their souls. The witch lay there with the smoke rising from her body, and the stench of burning flesh filled the air. The wet snow sizzled on her ravaged skin. Her skull had been laid bare by the intensity of the flames. Only small, bubbling patches of skin remained to hint that she had ever been a living, breathing human.

And yet, even in this ravaged state, her eyes burned as two red hot coals staring up into the night sky.

I retched with revulsion, abhorring both the hideous corpse lying there on the ground and the despicable act that had brought her to this end. As I turned my back on the blazing hovel and the smoldering body, I perceived a hint of movement out of the corner of my eye.

A shadowy form came out of the trees, stood over what had once been the old woman and committed the final violation of her humanity by urinating on her pitiful remains.

The man's manner of dress and sidearm belied his identity, though I could not clearly see his face. Sheriff Dillard Westerly had observed the whole sorry spectacle from the woods, and he had chosen to let the good old boys have their fun. A shadowy figure across the meadow sped away through the woods.

Strike number three, Wes! Moni said she owed you three times. There were three wrongs you heaped on her and her family.

As the sheriff turned and calmly walked down the mountain trail, I forced my eyes toward the pitiful heap sizzling in the meadow. Her blackened skull slowly turned on the charred vertebra and dropped to face in the sheriff's direction. The fiery eyes pulsed and glowed. Then their light flickered, dimmed and went out.

CHAPTER 34

My descent down the treacherous trail in the gathering darkness was an adventure in nervous fright. I was afraid to look over my shoulder, convinced that by now the witch was in hot pursuit, rattling her bones and clutching at me with each step. Every furry creature or slithering serpent that moved brought flashes of stark terror. I lashed out a hundred times at unseen dangers, wrestled with tree limbs that reached to wrap their arms around me and drag me down. My feet faltered. I fell to my hands and knees time and again, scraped my palms on the stones. On the last fall, I sought to halt a headlong plunge with both hands. Dropped the emergency lamp, and it shattered against a large rock. So much for a beacon to guide me back to the Comfy.

The night closed in on all sides, and I estimated there had to be half a mile of twisting, pitching trail ahead of me.

I squinted and peered ahead trying to make out landmarks that the nightfall had concealed in its shroud of inky darkness. Remembered that the lower end of the trail wasn't well defined even in broad daylight. I couldn't depend on just walking downhill because the path I must follow back to the Comfy rose and fell as it wound snakelike down the ridge. Without the lantern to guide me, there was a strong risk of wandering off the footpath and becoming entangled in vines and brush. If I strayed down a dead end detour, deep holes waited that were large enough to swallow and conceal me. It would be too late for a rescue from the elements and the wild animals even if someone did find me. I imagined how Warren Brainerd must have felt alone and at the mercy of wolves.

My forehead and hands were clammy, and I was breathing rapidly from both the sheer effort and the pounding of my heart. Somewhere above my head toward the crest of the ridge came a moaning wail that was too savage to be that of a dog, even a wild dog. A second call was drawn out, and it sounded much nearer. The rumors of wolves on this hill were instantly confirmed in my mind. Had to quicken my pace before the animal tracked me down. I ached, my cuts and scrapes bled and burned, and I just wanted to haul myself back to civilization.

Oh, no, my foot was wet! Somehow I'd veered off the path and stepped into cold water above my ankle. Voice, friend of mine, if you *are* my benefactor, help me now. Get me out of here.

The answer came wafting in on an icy gust of wind.

Follow the flow. It will take you home, the voice crooned in my ear.

Of course! The stream bed dropped from the ridge and fed the swimming pond. I slogged through the icy stream and stepped along carefully over the slippery rocks. As long as I kept my feet wet and moved ahead and downward with the water's flow, the creek would lead me back to the Comfy. The cold stung my legs, but I moved ahead on blind faith. Had no choice now. My feet were starting to lose sensation from the cold water, yet I seemed to be sweating profusely from every pore of my shivering frame. Almost as wet from my head down as I was from my frozen feet up. Twice something wriggled by and brushed against my lower leg. Decided I really didn't want to know what else was moving with me in the icy stream. I sloshed on through the creek and downward, my shoes slipping and sliding along the rocky bottom; struggled to keep my balance.

Then I saw a light force its way through the haze, at first dim but growing brighter. The stream dipped to an open field, and I knew the lights ahead must be at the house. Then the tree line was behind me, and I was standing in calf high water coursing through a meadow. Clambered up the bank onto solid ground, dripping, shivering, with the wind making my chill even worse. I emerged onto the path near the small pond and allowed myself a hurried glance over my shoulder. All was quiet and tranquil; there was no sign of a raging fire on the ridge, and the night air was chill, but it dried and soothed my dripping brow. Now I only needed to stay alert until I could reach Myrtle's warm kitchen.

Never again, for as long as I am allotted time on this green earth, do I ever want to repeat an experience as gut-wrenching as those long terrifying minutes from the time I stood before the cabin until I reached the meadow by the pond.

I climbed the lane toward the Comfy, my feet numbing despite all efforts to keep my limbs moving. By the time I stepped onto the kitchen porch, they were like two wooden blocks devoid of feeling.

The voice came to me. *You have earned the victory. The ring and the dagger will seal her fate.*

Voice, I hope your words have meaning for me when I need them most.

* * *

"Lawsy me, you look like you fell in the creek head first," Myrtle exclaimed as I squished through the back door into the kitchen. "Where on earth have you been, Greg Bain? Surely you didn't plunge into the pond again."

Carl slapped his knee and howled. "Like to see the bear you whipped, boy. Bet he was a sight."

"It's a long story. I'm just thankful to be home." There, I'd actually used the word—home. Guess Myrtle really had domesticated me.

"I kept your supper warm, so you just sit down and eat. Looks like you've got the shivering fits. My hot beef and cabbage soup should fix that." She guided me toward the open oven door, and Carl pulled up a chair for me.

Guess that solved my worries about trailing creek dregs through her house. By the time she finished stuffing me with hot cure-alls, I'd be bone dry. After what I had just been through, it felt especially warm and cozy to be around real, live, caring people.

Sat in front of the stove with my feet as close to the open oven door as good sense would allow. Frostbite was something I knew little about, but this must be how it felt. My drenched toes had gone from an absence of feeling to the sensation of a thousand needles piercing my flesh. At least there finally *was* feeling. Myrtle brought me blankets and wrapped my toes in warm towels while I shivered and downed the bracing soup. Carl appeared with serious medicine in a pint mason jar.

"Looks to me like you need a good slug of my fix-it."

"Carl!" Myrtle shouted.

He had momentarily forgotten my confession about my troubles with alcohol. Or maybe he judged this as an allowable exception, given my present condition. But when she shrieked at him, Carl withdrew the jar with a mumbled, "I'm sorry, son."

"If it would dull the pain in my feet and warm the ice in my veins, Carl, I'd almost be tempted to tip it up. But I don't need anything tonight that could cloud my thoughts. The dread in my bones has me wide awake, and there are preparations to be made. The next forty-eight hours could be a life-or-death situation for all three of us."

They looked at me, then at each other, trying to comprehend my cryptic message.

CHAPTER 35

On Thursday morning I took my time meeting the new day. Put my legs over the side of the big bed, and gingerly placed weight on both feet. Half expected to find toes missing, or at least not properly functioning, after their thorough dousing in the spring-cold creek. It came as a pleasant surprise that the carpet felt normal, there were ten digits down there, and I could actually stand erect. Couldn't expect much more than that after my harrowing experience on Pennick's Knob.

Put away a hearty breakfast and decided to head down to the grocery to see Harmon Grace. My vision at the cabin site had convinced me that he was in eminent danger, along with Wes, the Roops and me. I had to alert him to be on guard.

"What'dja run into, boy, a mad wildcat?" Harmon asked. "You're awful dinged up."

"Tried walking one of the mountain trails after dark, Harmon. Wasn't my all-time smartest move."

"I'll say. Did you roll down that ridge or just run into a lot of trees on the way?" He rocked back in his chair, and screeched that grating cackle of his.

Harmon walked back toward the stove; lifted the coffee pot. "How 'bout some blue john to set your day right, Greg? Looks to me like you could use a little picking up."

I had misgivings about further punishing my damaged body with his high octane brew. Concluded this was no time to refuse his hospitality, though, when I was here to pump him for information. He handed me a cup, and I managed to get a few sips of the caffeine overload down.

"Harmon, I came to tell you again to watch your step until after Halloween. There's serious trouble somewhere out there, and it could be looking to find both of us."

"What is this, your trick or treat on old Harm? Trying to scare the bejabbers out of me?"

"No, I'm dead sober serious about this, friend. Have reason to believe your father had a role in the witch's death, and now the old hag's descendants are after you for revenge."

"You accusing my Daddy of a crime?" Harmon went from congenial to combative in an instant.

"Sorry. Just telling you what I believe for your own good." He rolled that around for a moment and started to say something. His thoughts were interrupted before he could answer.

A loud siren sounded outside. It was a bleating tone, jarring to the nerves. Reminded me of the air raid sirens I'd heard in old war movies. Harmon came up out of his seat like he was spring mounted, and he grabbed a set of keys from behind the counter. He shouted something at me that sounded vaguely like, "Watch the store." My startled eyes traced his path as he jumped in the rusty old ambulance outside, turned the engine over once and tore off down Main Street. The fenders flapped and the muffler roared, but the old vehicle seemed to be getting him wherever it was he had hurtled off to.

Well, I could certainly spare the time to do him a favor and play temporary storekeeper. If I could keep the cat away from the meat counter and see that the blue john didn't eat through the coffee pot, standing in for Harmon could be my good turn for today. Our conversation would obviously be delayed.

While I was waiting for him to return, I wandered around and absorbed my surroundings. I've heard of subsistence farmers, the ones that barely scratch out a living for themselves and their families on depleted land. But Harmon was the first subsistence grocer I had ever personally known. Found it difficult to believe he could get along on the meager inventory of Harmon's G&G. Picked up some of the cans from the shelves and checked their expiration dates. Most of them were well past due to be dumped. It was comforting to know that Myrtle did most of her shopping in Richwood. Let the store cat have these provisions because they surely weren't fit for human consumption. Then I chuckled to myself that if old Harmon was smart, he'd slip away to Richwood to buy the groceries for his own table.

Behind the front counter, Harmon had several pictures tacked on the wall. One of them looked like it might be Miss Farm Tractor of 1950, probably a holdover from when Bert Grace ran the store. There were a couple of fading photos of a middle-aged man that had to be the elder Grace. I say had to be because the man in the picture bore a strong resemblance to Harmon. Eerily, he was also nearly identical to the man I had seen in my vision at the cabin and pegged as Bert Grace. The fact that I so clearly saw that face, even before knowing this picture existed, gave me a creepy feeling all over.

Looked over the creaky old building, and wondered how it had withstood the ravages of West Virginia winters year in and year out. The windows were grimy and cracked. Where sections were broken, he had taped cardboard to the wooden window frames to shut out the freezing air. Overhead there were large rough-hewn timbers supporting the structure, and I could see rotting planks between the timbers and the tin roof. The wood floor underfoot was worn and splintered, and here and there small patches of tin were nailed down as stop gap repairs. Wondered how many days Harmon had sat in this virtual fire trap with the pot-belly churning out its heat and cinders up that makeshift pipe through the powder dry wood ceiling.

Less than thirty minutes later, Harmon returned to the store, his face flushed and a look of surprise still etched in his features.

"Fire emergency?" I asked.

"Afraid not. It was a call for the rescue squad. Myrtle Roop went to the springhouse and found Dillard Westerly lyin down there, cold as a fish, mouth gaping like he'd seen a ghost. We figured it was just his time finally come around. Then when we turned him over, the back of his skull was smashed in. There was no hurry, so we looked around for a weapon. Found a big old bloody rock that must have been used on him then tossed out in the pasture."

Harmon paused and scratched his head. "Damndest thing. When we pried his fist open, he was clutching what looked like an animal tooth."

All I could think was *it's not even Halloween yet, and it's already started!*

"Harmon, take care for the next two days. I have a bad feeling we could all be in danger."

"What the hell am I supposed to do?"

"I don't exactly know. Just watch your back. Some weird things could happen before Halloween passes. My advice is free, so take it or leave it."

"Yeah, probably worth every penny of the price, too," was his sarcastic reply.

I just shrugged.

*   *   *

"Oh, Greg." Myrtle began when I reached her kitchen, "It's been such a horrible day! I went to fetch . . . Land o' Goshen, boy, you sure did take a beating on that ridge last night! Your eyes look downright burnt out."

"Couldn't begin to tell you what I've been going through, physically and mentally, beginning with last night's trip up the ridge, Myrtle. What's more important, though, I want to hear you tell me you're going to be all right."

I took her hands in mine, and her eyes began to well up with tears.

"There was a time there when I wasn't so sure I'd ever be all right, Greg. Did you hear what happened at the spring house?"

"Yes. I was at the store when Harmon tore up here in the ambulance. He told me afterward that Wes had been found down in the springhouse."

She couldn't hold back the tears as she recalled the shock of that moment of discovery.

"It was terrible. I went to fetch some vegetables from the root cellar, and there he was, lying on the floor face up. His eyes were open, but they were as empty as could be. I didn't have to look twice to know his time had arrived. Just glad none of the guests saw him. That would have been awful for them." She trembled, and I hugged her to me.

"What did the rescue squad tell you, Myrtle?"

I wondered if she knew the full import of her discovery, that Wes had been brutally murdered. The rescue squad found the wound only after they started to recover his body, so maybe she thought Wes had just keeled over dead.

"Well, they shooed me right out of there," she said, "and told me they'd take him back to the firehouse. What else would there be to know? He was dead."

As much as I disliked what had to happen next, there was no avoiding it.

"I know you've been through a rough time today, Myrtle, but I have to tell you something you're not going to want to hear. Please brace yourself."

"Oh, no, Greg!" She was already racing ahead of me in her mind.

I answered her unspoken question. "Wes was murdered. Someone killed him with a rock. We have another in the long series of tragedies to deal with."

It was almost more than she could bear. She looked at me with an expression of sheer helplessness and muttered in disbelief, "Murdered? Oh, saints preserve us, Wes murdered!"

"Listen carefully to me. Where is Carl? We need him here immediately."

"I'll call him and Tabetha."

"No. I'll explain later, but Tabetha is not to hear what I have to tell the two of you. In fact, I suggest you give her something to keep her occupied, so we can talk privately. Then get Carl in here."

A few minutes later, the Roops returned to the kitchen. Myrtle was jumpy and frightened, and Carl had a look of complete puzzlement.

"All of our lives may depend on how we act during the next twenty-four hours. Where is the girl?"

"Oh, I sent her off down to Harmon's," Carl said. "Told her Myrtle needed a bag of sugar and some spices before breakfast. Harmon sometimes stays open late, so we'd just take a chance on catching him in. Couldn't call because he doesn't have a phone at the store. Says it's not worth the price when he has one across the road at home."

I hoped Harmon had taken seriously the warning I had given him. If he was down there, either at the store or his house, it may save him from a very bad fate.

"Now, I'm going to say some things that you won't believe, and I can't prove most of them. I hope you both trust me to want only what's best for you. So hear me out, please."

Carl's eyes were as big as saucers, and he gulped hard. Myrtle drew as close as she could to the man she loved.

"I haven't had a chance to relate all that's happened to me," I told them. "We have a lot to cover before Tabetha returns, so just let me spill it all out."

They listened intently. Myrtle nervously stroked Greta in her lap.

"The information Velma gathered from the library archives began to fit the puzzle pieces into place. I now know that every ten years since your sister's disappearance, just like clockwork, a terrible tragedy has occurred on or near your property. The drowning of Maxine Pride, the mauling death of Warren Brainerd, the sawmill fire and Bert Grace's death on the sawmill blade were all coldly calculated and connected events. And in each case, the old Indian woman Blood Sky and her daughter Moni had reason for revenge.

The first two were classmates who had repeatedly taunted and shunned Moni because her mother was reputed to be a witch. I couldn't connect the last three deaths until I talked to Wes. He's had evidence all along that the incidents were related."

Myrtle was staring, the shock obvious. Carl sat slack-jawed, looking like he wanted to speak, but too intent on my words to interrupt.

"Chief John told me that three troublemakers set fire to the cabin up on Pennick's Knob the first day of the search for Marietta. I now believe those three were Morton Feeley, Jason Hatchett and Bert Grace, all members of the search party. They went back to the Knob to work their mischief. Remember that they were all later victims of sawmill disasters."

Carl winced as if in pain and reached for his jar. Then he thought better of it; set it on a kitchen shelf instead. He was cold sober, and apparently he wanted to stay that way after the alert I had just issued.

"The shaman knew so many things that convince me he possesses the power to conjure up visions of the past. He told me that the sheriff knew where Moni and Marietta had gone and how they had been separated."

Myrtle took Carl's hand and squeezed it hopefully, awaiting word of her sister's fate.

"I confronted Wes. He admitted to me that he tracked them down over near Radford, Virginia. Sadly, his own cravings overshadowed his sense of duty, so he chose to satisfy his lust first. While he was violating the Shawnee girl, the child wandered off. We have to be hopeful that someone took Marietta in and protected her."

"You mean he could have brought Sweet Tater back home to us and didn't?"

"By his own admission he missed that chance in his haste to defile her kidnapper. When he was finished with the brutal rape of Moni, Marietta was nowhere in sight. So if you felt any sympathy when he was done in today, you should know he didn't deserve your pity."

"I shouldn't talk about the dead, but he must have been a wicked old man." Myrtle could only shake her head with disgust.

"At least we now have the basic information, and I've already done some checking through records in Radford. Marietta was taken to an orphanage. There has to be a trail from there to where she went. Myrtle, I promise you I'll continue to search until we find out where she went from the children's home."

The sweet lady's eyes registered a hopeful, heartfelt thank you as she touched my arm. "Bring my Sweet Tater back to me, Greg. Please."

"If it's possible, you know I will. At the moment, we have a more immediate concern. I can't prove it yet, and I know how much you feel for her, but Tabetha is somehow connected to everything that's happened. Remember that I warned you before about her."

Myrtle reacted in shocked disbelief. "That can't be. Not my sweet Tabby. She's like my own child."

"How much do you really know about her? Has she ever told either of you about her family or background?"

Carl looked at me quizzically and replied, "It just never seemed important. She showed up at the door over six years ago asking for work. We treat her like one of the family, and she's always been polite and a hard worker."

"There are two people in this house with hearts of pure gold," I said, "and I'm afraid the girl took advantage of that fact to conceal her real purpose for being here. Do either of you know that her real name is Tabethki Scote, which means Night Fire in Shawnee?"

"Carl and I always suspected she was at least part Indian from her features and skin. But that was of no consequence to us. We were always comfortable with her being in the house."

"Let me warn you now that I'll be watching her every move until Halloween night has passed. I sincerely believe that the forces that have built a cloud of suspicion around this home are ready for their final assault. Please take my word that the girl will be involved in some important way."

"I just can't believe she would wish us harm." Myrtle still doubted my conclusion, and that made her vulnerable to the cunning little witch.

"Please, for your sake, and because I pleaded with you, be on guard every moment. Lock your doors at night and keep protection near."

If Chief John's assessment of the witches' powers was correct—and so far he seemed to be on target with everything he had told me—then there probably was no real defense against their intrusion. The Roops didn't need to know that any precautions we took now could be futile. There had to remain some hope of warding off the evil sorcerers. I was working all the angles furiously in my mind. This close to a final confrontation we all had to be positive and confident that the witches could be defeated.

I was counting on the voice to point me in the right direction as the showdown rapidly approached.

"But the scoot-booger is still missing," Myrtle answered. "Our home isn't safe. If there are evil spirits about, they would have free run of the Comfy now," she despaired.

"Well, I hope they got thick skins because old Belchfire will be right by the bedstead every night," Carl told us, referring to the double-barreled shotgun he retrieved from a corner of the kitchen.

Sometime later, Carl and I were sitting in the dining room waiting for Myrtle to dish up a late supper when the girl returned from her errand. I hoped the Roops could maintain a front so they wouldn't tip her that she was suspect. To my complete surprise, they both acted as if everything was normal.

"Take a seat so we can eat, Tabetha," Carl told her, and he called out to his wife, "We're all here now."

He pulled out a chair for the young woman to sit, and Myrtle appeared from the kitchen.

"Hope you caught Harmon in, child. I need that sugar and cinnamon for my apple turnovers for breakfast."

The girl held up a brown paper bag to show her trip had been a success, and Ma Roop took it back to the kitchen.

"And how was my old friend, the storekeeper?" I asked.

She flashed that enigmatic smile and replied, "When I left the store he was just hanging around."

Something in the tone of her voice chilled me.

CHAPTER 36

The Roops apparently were more convinced by my warnings than they had let on. As soon as the kitchen was in order, Myrtle said she wanted to turn in early. There was much to be done tomorrow to prepare for the children's visits to sample her Halloween delights. She had made it a tradition to bake and decorate most of the day, so she could watch their eyes light up when she handed them their treats on Halloween night.

There seemed to be more than that behind the Roops' early trip upstairs. Both she and Carl were visibly on edge. I believe they saw their locked bedroom door as a last barrier against an invasion of bad spirits, a sort of temporary substitute for the missing scoot-booger.

In spite of the growing chill of the October nights, Myrtle always made good on their time-honored tradition. She told me that so much suspicion and speculation had built up around the Charlton place that parents warned their children never to go near the old mansion. The youngsters gave the Comfy a wide berth, not daring to venture onto the lawn, much less get near the front door. Myrtle and Carl didn't let that discourage their enthusiasm for providing the children of Plenty with Halloween treats. She always had Carl pull a covered carriage down to the Comfy's front gate on the road to town. There they set up shop sheltered from the cold winds. The antique carriage, according to Myrtle, made a perfect background prop for her decorations of pumpkins, straw bales, cornstalks and the like. She said Carl even propped a stuffed figure of a man in the driver's seat, hat, pipe, suspenders and all, and put a buggy whip and the reins in its hands.

Myrtle told me she usually dressed in a costume that was 'kind of a cross between Mother Goose and Whistler's mother'. She didn't hold with frightening the little trick-or-treaters. That was the children's department, and she was well practiced at registering fright and amazement over their costumes.

Before she retired for the night, Myrtle came over and kissed my cheek. She spoke so as not to be heard beyond where we stood.

"I know what you're going through, Greg. As much as I'd like to believe you're wrong about Tabby, I respect your judgment. Greta has acted so strange for the past several days. I think she knows there are spirits in the house that threaten us. Please be careful. I love you like a son."

As the two of them climbed the stairs to their bedroom, I reminded them in a near whisper, "Lock your door and be on guard. Don't come out of your room, no matter what you hear."

* * *

With the gruesome mishaps already beginning a day early, I couldn't be sure we wouldn't be targets as soon as tonight. It was my intent to force a confrontation on my turf, which by now the Blue Room had become.

I darkened the parlor and started my long climb to the third floor. A pair of doe eyes watched my every step from a door only slightly ajar on the second floor. Turning at the landing, I could feel those eyes as if they projected a beam of light focused on the back of my neck. She was stalking her prey. There was little doubt left that Tabetha was the key to this whole sorry mess.

Tried to pretend I was unaware of her, and continued climbing the stairs. If she didn't follow, my full intent was to go to her room and confront her. Took each step cautiously, and made the turn at the last landing on my way to the third floor. I heard a board creak; knew she was trailing behind.

Reached the Blue Room and went in. I made noises to give her the impression I was turning in. Rumpled the bed covers, flicked off the wall switch, left the desk light glowing in the alcove and moved silently to stand behind the door. A minute passed, maybe two. She opened the door cautiously and stepped inside, peered across the room at lumps in the bed that appeared to be me under the covers. She stopped long enough to step out of her moccasins, and she began to slowly and deliberately unbutton her robe. Then she continued toward the empty bed.

I sprang from my hiding place. Grasped her shoulders roughly, and spun her around to face me. She tried to retreat from my sudden advance, but I seized her upper arms and pulled her toward me. Tabetha started to speak; her words came out as startled sputters without form. I yanked her toward the open door, backed into it, slamming it shut behind us. Then I shoved her away from me, and she stumbled backward across the floor.

"Okay, let's get this out in the open, miss timid by day and man eater by night! Let's not prolong the game. Make your play, and we'll have it over right now."

Her bashful exterior dissipated, and in its place I saw behind that face a tigress ready to pounce. In the soft glow of lamplight, her piercing eyes took on the glint of winter ice. Tabetha had in an instant turned from softness to cold steel. She emitted a laugh that began as a lilting, childlike titter, as if she had been caught stealing Ma Koop's cookies. Then the laugh gradually became the shrieking cackle of an old woman. At that moment the thought crossed my mind that I could be pitted against powers I could neither understand nor defeat.

My Dad would have said, "*Greg, old boy, you may have let your mouth overload your ass this time.*"

She spoke to me, and her voice was still as soft as her own, but the words oozed with hatred and vengeance.

"You have the temerity to challenge me? To place your hands on me in anger? I own your soul, yet you challenge me face to face? You will feel my vengeance, Greg Bain."

I steeled myself for the attack I expected her to launch and defied her to act. "Only one person owns me, and she's far away from here. You know I'll break the evil hex you've put on her. If there was ever any doubt that I was going to break your curse, you made a fatal mistake when you involved my wife. You may work your magic on me, but I'll never let you harm her."

Her soft voice transformed into that rasping tone I had heard the night she slipped into my bed and pressed her assault. Now I was sure what I had experienced that night had been real.

"She will not have you, my young stallion. Her efforts to fight me have been futile. She drifts in the sleep that will become death when my purpose here is soon fulfilled. All my life has pointed toward what must be done when next the sun sets."

I stared at her in horror. Even with her spilling venomous hate at me, I couldn't help but feel drawn to her beauty. Then an overwhelming feeling of pity took hold of me. All too clearly, I saw the emptiness of a mind gone utterly mad manifesting itself behind her burning eyes. She was no longer Tabetha in her mind. She had become someone entirely different. Tragic as it was, I had to go on the offensive and end the wickedness that was driving her. The twisted mind that lurked behind those eyes would stop at nothing to impose its will with finality.

"I refuse to let you and your evil win, witch. You'll have to kill me first."

"You can not overcome a power that has grown and flourished through generations. My great grandmother Blood Sky is embedded in my soul. My grandmother Moni M'weowe has this very day breathed her last, and the soul of the White Wolf is now a part of me. I possess accumulated powers that no mortal could ever match."

"And what about your mother? Was she the only sane person in the blood line?"

"My mother was the bastard product of a white man, a wicked lawman, who took Moni M'weowe against her will. Moni despised the child of that profane act and cast her away. But by the time I was born, my grandmother's heart had softened. She returned to deliver me into the world. When my mother died soon after, Moni claimed me and took me to her bosom. Since that time she has taught me everything she knows of medicine and spells, of witchcraft and the dark arts. I am invincible, and I am her instrument of vengeance."

I reeled with the force of this unexpected news. "Dillard Westerly was your grandfather?"

"No more. I wielded the stone that took our revenge on that rotting, decrepit old man. He insulted our family three times, and my only regret is that I could not make him suffer three painful deaths."

"And now you want to make a clean sweep including me I suppose. I am next, right?"

Her voice cracked and lowered an octave, and her eyes instantly took on an incredible softness.

"No, my love. You are the one I long for. Know that I am the soul of Moni M'weowe come to you in the body of my granddaughter Tabethki Scote. I dream of sharing your love and finally belonging to you, giving you what no other ever can. Must you fight the fate that has been yours since your birth? Only you and the sweet child who was mine so briefly will survive."

"You mean Marietta, don't you? She's still alive!"

"She lives and so will you when you come with me. All others must perish. The people in this house will be no more. The foolish old shaman defied my power, and his final lesson will be a sickness unto death."

I couldn't believe my eyes. Even as she spewed out her hate, Tabetha worked her slender fingers through buttonholes, moving them down her front, opening the length of her robe. It parted, and I realized she wore nothing underneath. Her lips parted in a sly smile that told me she knew I was spellbound. She moved gracefully, so silently her movement was more insinuated than real. Her arms reached out for me, and I moved to one side.

"No, it won't work. You can't bewitch me, Tabetha." I moved with her, and we did a deadly dance, circling each other, looking for an opening for advantage.

"The one who lies in slumber will never wake," she cooed. "Tomorrow it will come to be as soon as you are all mine. But you need not wait. I can be yours now, my steed."

How could such perverse evil live in a body so beautiful and outwardly innocent? I finally understood how completely her wicked grandmother had poisoned Tabetha's mind. The girl was quite insane with Moni's own jealous rage and need for vindication. Tabetha's mind no longer existed in her own body; only the vile hatred of Blood Sky and Moni survived in a human form held hostage by their hatred.

Tabetha drew up onto her toes, stretched forward, beckoned for me to come to her. Her fingertips touched my chest. She took one step forward. With a sardonic smile twisting her lips, she raked her nails downward leaving open wounds.

"You are a mere mortal and cannot defeat the strength of my medicine. I will never die by the hand of a human. What is more, I have your blood and your seed." She stepped back and fingered a small pouch that dangled from her throat. "They will make your soul my possession." She lifted the beaded pouch with the hand that bore the bloodstone ring, its stone pulsing with intense fire. A chilling memory flashed back. I remembered the corpse's eyes.

Closed my eyes to shut out the sight of her, fighting hard to forget how her skin had felt against mine in the Blue Room, flesh burning flesh, sending my mind spinning. How far had it gone that night after I lost all sense of consciousness? I was so entranced by the raw passion she showed now that there was no sensation of pain from the fresh wounds she had inflicted. But I knew this was no time to be weak.

"I'll destroy you and all your evil ancestors," I threw out at her. "There aren't enough of you in that maddening body to overcome me."

"It is preordained, my love. One more day, then I will come for your decision tomorrow night. Consider well your choice. You can accept life with an all-powerful woman in a youthful body to make your every fantasy a reality. Your alternative is the most hideous of deaths, which I will personally administer."

"Don't count on it," I spat back, grasping her robe with one hand and the door knob with the other. Before she could fight back, I swung the door open wide and hurled her bodily into the hall, slamming the massive door behind her. She pounded and scratched, flung curses at me. Then, as I stood with my full weight pressed against the barrier between us, she emitted a last frustrated whimper and fell silent. When she retreated down the stairs, I threw the latch in case she decided to return. Then I fell onto the bed.

The battle is joined, and I am with you, son. She can not win.

You *are* still there, voice. Don't leave me now when I need you most. And bring along all the weapons you can find. The witches are ganging up on us. Situation's more desperate than I thought!

CHAPTER 37

Halloween morning broke clear and crisp, accompanied by a light dusting of snow. I had spent an uneventful night in the Blue Room after throwing Tabetha out. No visions came to haunt me, no dreams of witches or apparitions invaded my sleep. For that I was thankful and patted my dream catcher lovingly when I awoke. Then I touched the new set of welts her razor-sharp nails had inflicted down my chest. The young witch had simply granted me a night with my thoughts to consider her edict. Tonight would be the climax.

When I went down to the kitchen, Myrtle greeted me with a worried look. "Tabetha is nowhere to be found this morning. I don't know where she could have gone." Carl sat in a corner nursing his morning coffee.

"Perhaps that's for the best," I answered. "We have enough to concern us today without having to trail her every movement. She came to me last night and confirmed my worst suspicions." I opened my shirt to show them her handiwork. "Took out her rage on me. She's a witch, Myrtle."

My words took all the starch out of the Roops. Myrtle supported herself against the kitchen counter, and she sat down heavily on one of the tall stools. Carl went to her.

"Oh, no, Greg! Not my sweet little Tabetha," she wailed. "Please, no."

"If I could wish it otherwise, for your sake, I would. She's the granddaughter of Moni Hawk. Worse, she's the instrument of Moni's revenge against your father and his family."

For a long while Myrtle sat in silence, unable to grasp the full meaning of this startling revelation. Then she looked at me, and I knew she had finally, reluctantly, accepted the brutal truth.

"Tell us what to do and we'll listen," she said. Carl nodded, his eyes big as kitchen plates.

"For now we stay here, and we don't let Tabetha back in the house. She'll make her play before the night is over, and I have a plan to defeat her."

I only wished that were true, but it was all I could think of to calm Myrtle.

"I could use some help in here today, Greg. I was counting on Tabetha to work on the Halloween treats with me. Are you handy in the kitchen?"

Gratefully, I saw that Myrtle was bound to concentrate on the kiddies and their treats regardless of what personal dangers she may be facing. Now it was my turn to offer some encouragement.

"Sarah has been known to enlist me from time to time when she has a lot of baking to do. I've been told I wield a mean whisk."

Myrtle plainly needed a bit of playfulness to bring her down from a very nervous high. I expected she and Carl had spent a tense night wondering what may be lurking just outside their door. Now she at least understood why I had been so wary of impending danger. Maybe I'd come down on them a bit heavy-handed with my warnings and suppositions. But their safety was important to me.

"Let's get at it then," she said. "Break me some eggs to start with, and . . . have you ever used a separator?"

We busied ourselves with the preparations for trick or treat time. Tried small talk to avoid the other worries that were all too evident behind our chatter. I learned at least a half dozen of her secret kitchen tricks guaranteed to result in the flakiest or the lightest or the most delectable outcome for whatever we were building at the time.

Finally, I broached my work on the book. "I was wondering, Myrtle. Do you have any family pictures that may add realism and background to what I'm writing? You've never described your mother's or father's features, and I've only seen one picture of Marietta, the tiny faded one in the locket."

She brightened and held her forefinger aloft, as if to tell me to hold on for a moment, and left the kitchen.

When she returned Myrtle held out a photo to me. "It's a family picture taken not long before . . . you know. Folks said I took after my Daddy, and sister looked like Mamma."

I stared at the photo in disbelief. My mind had played so many tricks on me lately. Visions and reality had seemed to be too inexplicably melded to separate them. Couldn't be sure that what I thought I saw in the picture was actually there. Unless Myrtle showed some indication that she'd made the same discovery, I would keep my reckless thoughts to myself. I was stunned.

* * *

Mid-morning I broke from my kitchen police duties long enough to place a call to Mom at the hospital.

"Honey, I'm more hopeful than a day ago. According to her nurse, Sarah stirred again last night and moaned. She repeated those same words, "No—mine!," and moved around. Then she went back to a restful state. There's been no further activity. She's sleeping evenly again. Her vital signs are normal according to Doc Jameson."

"Did the nurse tell you when this episode happened?"

"Yes, she said it was about nine PM. The nurse had just left Sarah's side, and she had to rush back in to check on her again."

I stopped to calculate. Nine o'clock was just about when Tabetha-Moni-whoever had issued her ultimatum to me. She said my soul was her possession and that I belonged to her. Sarah had replied angrily *No—mine!* This was the second time I had been confronted by the young witch, and each time my wife had reacted strongly from miles away. There remained no doubt that if I could penetrate the witch's defense, the spell on my Sarah would be broken as well. As much as I wanted to get into my car and hurry to Sarah's side, I knew deep down that here in this place was where I belonged on her behalf. It was up to me to bring the whole sorry affair to its proper conclusion.

"Mom, I know she's going to be back with us very soon. I have to stay here for one more night. Can't explain it all to you right now, but it's important for her, for me, and also for you, that I spend one more night at the Comfy."

"Do I need to know more about this unusual place you're in, Greg? What's going on?"

"Please, Mom, trust me to do the right thing. Stay with Sarah where you can see her through the night. Will you do that for me? I have so much to tell you when this is over."

"I'll do it for both of you, son. I'll see you tomorrow. Please take care, Greg."

I was sure now, even more certain than I had been before, and I knew what must be done when the witches came to dominate me in the dark. They were not taking me, and I wouldn't forfeit Sarah to their wickedness. Old girls, you're in for the fight of your lives!

* * *

We continued our baking marathon. I told Myrtle that Sarah was beginning to show some signs of awareness that were very encouraging. She was delighted at my news. Carl sat close by checking Old Belchfire to be sure it was ready for whatever came along.

There was a rap at the kitchen door and Myrtle answered. A county policeman stood on the porch, hat in hand.

"Ma'am, I need to ask you if you saw or heard anything peculiar last evening. There's been some trouble, and we're canvassing everybody in town."

"What kind of trouble, deputy?" she asked, somewhat taken aback.

"There was a mishap down at the Harmon Gas and Grocery."

"Is Harmon all right?"

"I'm afraid not, Mrs. Roop." His tone said it all. She swooned in the doorway, and I rushed to catch her.

I hailed Carl. He saw to Myrtle while I went out onto the porch to talk to the deputy. We walked toward the front of the house, and the lawman looked me over suspiciously. "You a guest here at the Comfy?"

"Yes, I live over near Roanoke. I'm visiting the Roops for three nights."

He regarded me more closely.

"What's your name?"

"Greg Bain."

"Mister Bain, I'd like to ask that you not leave Plenty until we have this matter cleared up. Have you ever met Harmon Grace?"

"Sure have. I've spoken with him on at least three occasions. The last time was mid-afternoon yesterday down at the store."

Might as well be up front with him. I was already suspect since I was 'not from around here.' His mannerisms made that fact abundantly clear. Didn't want to add the issue of evasion to his initial doubts about me.

"Can you tell me what's happened, officer?"

"Customer walked into the store this morning and found poor old Harmon hanging from a rafter by a rope. Looked like he'd been dead at least overnight. Had a note pinned to him."

I shook my head. "Harmon seemed to be a good sort from my contacts with him. Who could have hated him that much? May I ask what the note said?"

He looked me up and down then shrugged. "It's no secret, that's for sure. Several people had read it before we got there."

Reached into his pocket and drew out a small note pad then he watched me closely. Gauging my reaction, I suppose. He'd written down the words:

> *The Curse Is Fulfilled on Halloween Night*
> *Seven have paid. One more will face her fate*
> *Then the Silver Wolf will be revenged*

"It was signed Night Fire, and there was an animal tooth taped to the note," the policeman said.

Wanted to ask him if the tooth was drilled through, but I was reasonably sure I already knew the answer. Besides, a question like that really would have made me a suspect.

I winced and hoped he hadn't noticed my guarded reaction to the note. Wondered if Wes's collection of wolf's teeth would ever be discovered now that he himself was one of the witches' victims.

Tabetha had returned sometime after eight last night from Harmon's store. I didn't know the brutal truth of the girl's words when she said that when she left him, Harmon was *just hanging around* down at the store. What a cold little vixen! And Myrtle was to be her final target.

The policeman turned away then stopped in his tracks. He spun on his heel and said as an afterthought, "You might inform Mrs. Roop that we're going door to door asking everyone to keep their kids in tonight. There have been two mysterious killings in one day, so we don't need any little ones out by themselves. We'll have patrols and investigators in Plenty until we clear up this mess. All of the Halloween functions have been cancelled. There'll be no kiddy parade in the village, no cider social at the firehouse, even trick or treat rounds are called off."

Well, they could patrol outside all they wanted, but they'd miss the real action. Right here at the Comfy is where this mess would be cleared up and where the village would regain what it's been denied for fifty years. Even if I told them I knew the identity of the murderer, it wouldn't help. First, nobody knew where Tabetha was right now. And, more importantly, no jail in this world was likely to hold the evil that filled her body to overflowing, the essence of three witches in a single form. At least they had the note and the tooth. That could be the witch's final foolish boast.

My companion, the voice, was back. *The Blue Room desk holds your weapon. Arm yourself.*

"I hear you, voice, and I'm on my way."

First I needed to call Carl out to the porch and fill him in.

"Carl, Harmon was hung in his store last night. The police are everywhere. It was Tabetha, Carl. She left a note rubbing our faces in her boldness. The girl has gone insane. Someone has to turn her in."

"Hope you're sure about this, Greg. Myrtle's mighty attached to that girl. Matter of fact, so am I."

"She admitted everything to me last night. Tried to seduce me in the bargain. She's wicked, Carl, wicked and utterly mad. As I told you this morning, she's Moni Hawk's granddaughter sent to complete the curse on the Comfy.

Dillard Westerly was her grandfather, and she's already killed him. Only you and Myrtle stand in the way of the curse being completed."

"Myrtle's pretty shook up right now, but don't you worry, we'll be on guard if Tabetha shows up." He put his big, rough hand on my shoulder and squeezed.

"We have to protect Myrtle against her at all cost, Carl. And she'd kill you in a heartbeat to get to Myrtle."

"Well, that's the only way she'll get to my Myrtle. Have to go straight through me and Belchfire."

I hurried away and took the steps as fast as my legs would pump. When I reached the landing on the third floor an eerie sound crept in through an open window. A wolf was howling somewhere out in the hills.

The voice had told me my weapon against the witches, whatever it was, was in the Blue Room desk. I searched the drawers and soon found what I was after. Underneath several old letters in the second drawer down was what looked like a hunting knife. I laid it on the desk in its leather sheath.

This was to be my weapon for the final battle.

CHAPTER 38

"Guess it'll be just the three of us again tonight, Greg," Myrtle sighed as she went about her work before supper. "Tabetha's still not back from wherever she's disappeared to. I do hope she's safe." She put her hand to her mouth when she heard her words. "I mean . . ."

"I know, Myrtle, It's hard to believe she would harm you, but you have to accept it."

Bless her heart, even knowing that the girl was a mortal threat to her, she had so much love invested in her that she clung to the hope that no harm had come to the young witch. Tabetha had killed twice during the past twenty four hours, and she fully intended to continue her destruction of everyone she and her forebears deemed a threat to their curse's fulfillment. The shaman's words and the note at Harmon's store left no doubt that Ma Roop would be her next victim. If the girl did reappear before our showdown took place, I must keep her away from Myrtle and Carl any way possible. Only I stood between the compounded evil of three powerful witches and two wonderful, innocent people.

Took Carl aside in the parlor and told him quietly, "Please watch over Myrtle today like she's the most precious treasure in the world, Carl."

"To me she is, Greg. I'm not going to let Tabetha or anybody else hurt her."

"Neither am I, Carl. Neither am I."

Myrtle stepped into the parlor and said, "What in blue blazes are you two plotting in here with work to be done? Carl, how are you coming along with our decorations out front? Is everything ready for the children?"

"Don't throw a hissy fit, Myrtle. Everything's on schedule. Brought the carriage down and lots of straw. I'm about to prop old Dan in the buggy seat. Might even give him a jug of squeezings to keep him company this year."

"Carl Roop! You do and I'll knock you on your noggin."

"Simmer down, Myrtle. I'll be done before sundown, and you can have your fun with the kids. We haven't missed a year yet, have we?"

Their exchange finally sank in. I had forgotten to pass on the policeman's words. Myrtle was going to be devastated.

"Oh, I'm terribly sorry, Myrtle. There's something important I almost forgot to tell you."

Kicked myself for what I had to tell both of them after all their hard work. "The deputy says they will be patrolling constantly and interviewing people until they solve the deaths of Wes and Harmon. They're canceling all Halloween activities. I really am sorry, Myrtle. I know how much this means to you."

She stood frozen for a moment then sat down in one of the big parlor chairs. Put her elbows on her knees; held her head in both hands. Her sobbing cut me to the quick. All of her preparation and anticipation would be wasted this year. The new troubles in town were bad enough. Now her plans for the kids were dashed. It was heaping insult on injury.

She looked up at both of us through damp eyes and asked, "What do we do with all the goodies? Poor Greg worked his fingers to the bone. Even got him into an apron to help out. We have enough to furnish all the children of Plenty with sweets for a week."

"Bet I was a cute little dickens in that frilly apron." I gave her a curtsy and did a pirouette. There was nothing to be done about the cancellation at this point, so I may as well try to lighten things up.

Myrtle wiped her tears and cast a smirk at me, then she went into fits of laughter.

"You beat all, Greg Bain. Guess I'll just have to give you a five-course supper tonight: candy apples, punkin tarts, hot sweet cider with goblin cookies, Halloween finger cakes, and more candy. That should keep your smart little mouth busy." She was in tears again, but this time they were tears with a smile.

"You made it all so it will taste like ambrosia, kind lady."

"Such a teaser. Well, I don't have many boarders to spoil with all those baked goods. As you can see, we're in the between seasons lull. Until the first natural snowfalls come, the skiers won't show up in numbers, even if the snow machines are working overtime. I'll just take it to the children myself tomorrow. Now let's eat."

We ate without speaking, a heavy note of expectancy hanging in the air around the three of us. More correctly it was apprehension about the events I had predicted for All Hallows Eve. None of us wanted to open that subject.

At length, Myrtle broke the silence.

"I just can't imagine what happened to that child. She should have been here to help with the baking. Always enjoys that part of the holiday. She's as much a child in spirit as most of the kiddies that come calling."

"You can be sure she'll be here before the night is over," I said. "I want you and Carl tucked away in your room before the real action starts. This is my battle, and I fully expect to win it!"

"Still find it hard to believe she's a witch. I know you wouldn't say so, though, it if it wasn't true, Greg."

"You saw what she did to me in a moment of anger, Myrtle. She's capable of much worse."

"All the years she's been here, and she could have done us harm whenever she chose." Myrtle shook her head. "It's so frightening to think about now, and so worrisome what may be about to happen."

"Let me do the worrying for all of us," I offered. "In a few more hours you'll be rid of the curse. Then you and everyone else in

Plenty will know the whole truth. I'm putting it all down in my book so it will be understood that you had no part in this. You've had enough harassment for most of your life. It's my task to finish the curse now."

We finished our meal then Myrtle went outside to carry the scraps away. Carl and I relaxed over our coffee, and we started to unwind from a long, troubling day. Suddenly it occurred to me that we had just committed a serious lapse of vigil. I charged onto the porch just as Myrtle screamed.

A large, shaggy animal had seized the hem of her skirt and was tugging with its menacing teeth to draw her away from the house. Terror struck me like a blow to the chest. I searched frantically for a weapon. The snow was still falling, and Carl had shoveled the back stairs before dinner. The shovel still stood by the door. I clutched it and leaped from the porch in a bound toward Myrtle and the wild animal.

Swinging the shovel as a bludgeon in overhead smashes, I struck the wolf time and again. The creature reeled, but it persisted in holding Myrtle captive. Snow flew from the beast's white coat. It snarled and held on stubbornly. With one mighty blow, I hit the intruder squarely in one eye. The wolf shook its head violently and released its hold, yelping in pain. It turned its attention to me, mounting a frenzied charge with teeth bared. I continued to swing the implement wildly, punishing the four-legged beast with blow after blow even after it turned tail. Chased the wolf, stumbling and sloshing toward the snarling animal through the deepening snow. Set it into full flight from the grounds. With one last defiant show of ugly yellow teeth, the beast turned and ran down the bank, across the meadow and toward the ridge beyond.

I looked for Myrtle and found Carl with his arms wrapped tightly around her. He was walking her back to the safety of the kitchen porch.

"I thought that horrid thing had me for sure," Myrtle gasped, and she huddled with both of us as we sought the security of the big house.

Once we were in the warmth of her kitchen, I looked Myrtle directly in the eyes and poured out the whole story. It would be unfair now to withhold anything from her after her terrifying encounter.

"I can't keep this from you any longer. The curse on the Comfy has been prolonged over the span of the past fifty years by a succession of wicked witches. Blood Sky was the first of this evil sisterhood and her daughter Moni learned well from her mother. Tabetha is the granddaughter of Moni and Dillard Westerly, who took Moni by force when he found her and Marietta together. For all her outward appearance of innocence, Tabetha is the vilest and most cunning of all because she embodies the power of all three. She's already come to me and told me that tonight will be the culmination of the witches' revenge. I can tell you that from the way Tabetha taunted and tempted me, her act of innocence is a total lie. She came to the Blue Room twice and offered herself to me. She was hell bent on having me for her own, though I'm at a total loss as to why she's chosen me."

Myrtle was shocked and puzzled. "But what does that have to do with the wolf?"

"You'll recall that in your father's diary he said that Moni M'weowe in Shawnee means Silver Wolf. The beast that assaulted you was a large wolf with a white coat, an extremely rare occurrence in nature. In her mind, Ezra wronged her, and she was exacting her revenge on you through the wolf. The shaman told me there were three more victims to be accounted for to finish the curse on the Charltons. Wes and Harmon were two of them, and you're their last target. She killed her hated grandfather, Wes then she hanged Harmon in his store. Left a note at the scene of the hanging that tells me she's coming after you next." Myrtle's eyes glazed over with sheer fright.

"Greg, how did you get so involved in this mess?" Carl asked. "Hell, you just came looking for a dry spot to lay your head down, and you ended up tangled in our problems."

"I can't tell you yet what I suspect until I know myself. My being caught up in these tragic events isn't a coincidence. Somehow it's been carefully planned and executed. I've forced a facedown tonight, and it's my task to send the witches off to hell where they belong."

"Tell us what we should do, Greg." Carl had struck me as a strong willed and self-sufficient man, but he was frozen with terror after the wolf's attack had given my warnings full credence. He was a man who wanted to protect his woman, and he was struggling with how to go about it.

"The best advice I can give you is to barricade yourself and Myrtle for the night. When the danger has passed, I'll let you know. This enchantress could be capable of deception in many forms, so don't open your door unless you hear me say something only we will recognize. You tell me what that should be."

Myrtle picked up her fur ball of a cat and weakly smiled at me. "We'll keep the door locked until you say 'Greta wants her milk.' Then we'll know it's really you come to tell us the coast is clear."

"Okay. I suggest we take our places and prepare for whatever comes. Don't venture out, no matter what you hear, unless it's me with the agreed words. I'll face my test in the Blue Room, and we'll hope that sunup tomorrow finds us all still alive."

I shook Carl's hand and kissed Myrtle's cheek, and we walked resolutely to our chambers. Putting up a brave exterior to reassure them had hopefully sent them away with a degree of confidence they would need in the dark of their room. The outward show of confidence did little for my own faith, though. I could admit to myself something I would never show the Roops. I was scared limp!

* * *

There would be no sleep tonight. I was wired for action, and no amount of effort to calm my nerves was going to work. There was only one thing to do now—position myself in the Blue Room and wait for the moment of truth to arrive on the witch's schedule.

I sat at the desk and went through the sequence of events and the players that had built and prolonged the terrifying legend surrounding the Comfy. Replayed in my mind all of the cryptic prompts my recurring visitor, the voice, had given me as we worked our way through the maze of confusion. Somewhere in his advice was the key that would spell an end to the witches' evil plan. I had perhaps only minutes to find it.

Over and over the words imparted by the voice that came back with force were *the ring and the dagger will seal her fate*. My invisible companion had carefully directed me to the place where the hunting knife was hidden. The only plausible explanation I could find for reference to a ring was the bloodstone and lacquered circle of wood on Tabetha's finger.

The shaman had also said that *the specter you must face cannot be destroyed by mere mortals*. I walked to the window and stared out at the falling snow. Fluttering flakes wafted by and settled on the windowsill. The ground below was turning white, and the snow began to increase in intensity. A curious sight caught my eye. Against all logic, I caught the hint of a glow through what had now become a blinding swirl of white. Impossibly, I was again witnessing the darting flicker of flames rising from high up toward Pennick's Knob.

I walked back over to the desk and looked at the knife. The phantom voice cautioned me in hushed tones.

Do not dull the dagger's bite with human hands.

First I pulled on my leather gloves then picked up the sheath. I slowly withdrew the blade and stared at the serrated edge and the gleaming steel shaft. Certainly a formidable weapon against any mortal challenge, but my opponent was, in Chief John's estimation at least, something far more dangerous. I knew the locations of both the ring and the dagger, the implements that would determine the fate of the sorceress. Now, in an overwhelming rush of awareness, I at last understood. The voice's latest clue had revealed to me how the witch would be overcome.

The answer had been there all along!

With renewed certainty, I stepped to the windows where my visions had begun and flung them open wide. The snow whirled around me and blinded me. I shouted my challenge into the storm.

"Here I am, you witches from hell! Come and get me if you dare."

CHAPTER 39

With jarring abruptness, the snow ceased. The wind died to calm. I stood at the open windows surrounded by a deathly silence. The quiet was so pervasive I could hear my heart beating, the pulse pounding in my ears. It was as if time had suddenly reached a standstill, and I was viewing the single frame of a celluloid world frozen in time.

But the peaceful hush was short-lived. On the distant horizon, the sky began to slowly fill with a brilliant red hue that crept forward as would a ripple in a pond. The tint spread until the sky was dyed a flaming scarlet across its entire canopy. The red flow moved relentlessly, reflecting itself in the fallen snow like the spreading of a giant bloodstain. An iridescent shower of colors from brightest pink to deepest maroon rippled across the heavens, and it cast brilliant spokes of golden light down through the trees. I recoiled from the sheer intensity of the hues that bounced off the icy needles of the evergreens.

Sparkling trails sped across the sky in a display I likened to a meteor shower. They were like balls of fire that lit their paths with glittering jewel tones until, one by one, they disappeared over the horizon. Each time I waited for the fiery dying burst that never came as the gleaming brightness merely disappeared.

Without warning an errant trail of light came rocketing through the windows. I stepped back, fell heavily to the floor and struck my head. Pinwheels of blinding light spun in front of my eyes. When I recovered my bearings, I was halfway across the Blue Room flat on my back. I shook my head and checked to see that all my parts were still attached before attempting to rise from my awkward position.

A figure in the midst of an eerie radiance loomed over me. If it was possible to merge pervasive evil and dazzling beauty, the specter that emerged from that light was the personification of such a melding. I was at once both repulsed and captivated by the wicked loveliness that stood before me. Then the vision spoke in that familiar musical lilt. My head began to spin.

"The blood sky has steered me to you, my love, and the night fire has delivered me. The time is at hand for your decision."

Tabetha stood defiantly, glowing eyes nailing me to my spot, drilling a scorching stare through me. She was dressed in fringed skins the hue of smoky silver, and her feet were clad in silver gray moccasins. Long raven tresses flowed loosely down her back. Her creamy bosom rose and fell with measured breathing. The woman was entrancingly beautiful, but she no longer retained any pretense of childlike innocence. This was a purposeful woman who felt in total command of the situation. We would soon know whether her dauntless confidence was warranted.

"You had my answer last night," I hurled at her. "Hope you didn't travel far because your trip was wasted."

She silently fumed at my impudence, and her hand tightened on the pouch at her neck. She fingered its beaded surface, and then she slowly raised it to her lips. With the tip of her tongue, Tabetha lightly brushed and moistened the nap of the sack as if she were savoring its essence.

"The blood of your vein, the seed of your loin will bend you to my wishes. It is useless to resist my spell. I own your fluids, and your soul is destined to be my possession. Those who would keep us apart will exist no more. Submit to my will!"

She extended one arm and pointed a forefinger at me as her bloodstone ring pulsed and glowed.

Tabethki Scote danced in a ceremonial circle around me, repeating the chant I had heard earlier in this same room. I moved as she did, always facing her, never leaving my back exposed to her for fear she may pounce on me on all fours. This demon woman was determined to have her way, and I knew by now that she was capable of anything to achieve her goal. Perhaps I had underestimated Tabetha's power. She may yet find the final conquest she was convinced destiny owed her. Maybe my resistance *was* futile.

I withheld my answer, and she grew impatient. The chant rose in pitch, became more insistent as her nimble limbs moved more rapidly. She circled while I turned to keep her constantly in my view. The dizzying whirl of our motions coupled as though twin gears had meshed and joined us. Our circular path confused and disoriented me. The pace she set and her heady fragrance addled my brain. The pace of her dance made her a blur, and her long limbs and swirling hair turned her dance into a frenzy of motion.

"Tell me we're going to kick her witch's ass, voice. Speak to me. You are there, aren't you?"

The ring and the dagger are her downfall. Turn them back on her, son.

Maybe I wasn't outnumbered after all. The voice was prompting me if I could only trust my instincts. By now there seemed to be a dozen gorgeous nymphs scampering and dipping nearer and nearer to me, their eyes burning into my skin, their coal black tresses flying with the dance.

"Don't desert me now, voice." I begged.

Tabetha commanded, "Your answer must be given now. I offer you the ecstasy of unending delights as my mate. Choose to answer no and you will endure a painful and lingering death at my hand."

I beamed at the beautiful woman who offered all she had to me in a final triumph of unbridled passion. Her eyes cooled to liquid brown pools of alluring innocence. They were drawing me ever nearer to her warm embrace. She sensed the tide was turning and glided slowly toward me. I took her beautiful hands in mine and felt her stroking my palms with her slender fingers. Slowly I drew closer and brushed her moist lips with mine. She pressed against me; the heat of her body surged through my veins. The lovely Tabetha began to smile, basking in the glow of the triumph she now saw within her grasp.

Before she could react, I violently snatched the ring from her finger and hurled it forcefully through the open window over her head. She sputtered and hissed, trying to regain control with her most revered talisman gone.

"Ring around the rosy, you wicked witch! Your end is near. Strike now. Let me end this affair and destroy you, your wicked grandmother and her mother before her. You all disgust me."

I lunged for the unsheathed knife that glinted on the desktop. She followed my eyes and blocked my way. Her hand shot forward to snatch the dagger from the desk before I could reach it.

Good, she was right on cue. Following the script to the letter.

"Blasphemous white man, you dishonor my elders and insult me. Die now by my hand!"

Tabetha lunged toward me, vicious vengeance surging and the jagged blade held high above her head to plunge downward into my heart. There would be only one chance for me, and it was now. I charged to meet her rush. We collided head on. The force of our impact sent the witch reeling backward. She fought to regain her balance, then visibly stumbled on some unseen obstacle and fell back toward the window. I grasped her right hand with both of mine and thrust the knife downward in a powerful arc. Her own hand drove it deep into her bosom until only the hilt was visible.

Her flaming eyes opened wide with panic and disbelief. The shocking realization crept into her wicked brain that she had been tricked into wielding the instrument of her own destruction. What no mortal could achieve she had accomplished with one fatal stroke. I leaned in and brushed her lips with mine and twisted her hand. The knife she held tightly ground through flesh and membrane. Then I ripped the beaded pouch from her neck and crushed it under my heel.

"That's the Poet Bain version of the kiss of death, you insufferable piece of corruption. A fond farewell to all of you miserable girls on your journey to hell."

Her pitiful eyes pulsed once again with a dull pink flicker, and a crimson rivulet coursed from her lips. The beautiful young face transformed into that of an evil crone with one bloodshot eye and a huge, ugly bruise covering her cheek. Moni the Silver Wolf was finally passing from this place to her just desserts. The worn face withered into the countenance of an old and horridly ugly hag. I had finally seen with my own eyes the face of the wretched Blood Sky Hawk.

A blood chilling cackle gurgled up from her throat then became a terrifying shriek. The wail of her death song echoed long after she tumbled through the open window and plunged screaming to the ground far below. It was at last ended.

I looked to the floor and retrieved an object lying where the witch's tumble had begun.

There it lay in all its mystic majesty—the elusive scoot-booger! Myrtle's steadfast trust had been confirmed. It had, at the critical moment of need, served as our last line of defense.

CHAPTER 40

I don't know how long I stood at the window stroking the feathers of that charm. All concept of time left me. A tremendous weight had been lifted. People I dearly loved would now be safe from the witches' insane revenge. I felt empty of all sensation beyond one of pure relief.

Eventually, I gathered the strength to look over the windowsill to the ground below. The warm glow of a full moon had replaced the fiery chaos of the bloody sky. The red cast in the snow had receded and died, leaving only the pure whiteness of the first snowfall. Two motionless figures were illuminated by the moon's glow. Tabetha lay near the creek bed in a strangely peaceful repose in death. Her hand still grasped the jagged knife that had pierced her heart, but even from this distance I could see that a sweet, innocent smile lit her face. Perhaps she had found sanity at last in those final moments when her life was ebbing away.

Beside her, its limbs askew, one paw clawing at the snow-covered grass to reach toward Tabetha's silent form, was the silver wolf. A widening redness stained the snow beneath its body.

As I stared at the wolf, the face of evil unmasked, I suddenly experienced a strong sense of another presence in the Blue Room. Scanned the space around me, hoping there were no more spirits to be vanquished. I had already been reduced to a flaccid pool of humanity by my first deadly encounter.

Slowly, almost as a photo developing before my unbelieving eyes, an apparition shimmered and formed to face me. That vision's face was turned in my direction and for the first time I saw it plainly. It was exactly as I had suspected. We stood there fixing each other in our lines of vision like two people on opposite sides of a mirror. The vision no longer wore a beard or mustache as it had in the worn photograph. He was clean-shaven and smiling and he was . . . me!

"You're Ezra Charlton, aren't you?"

His answer was unnecessary, but I needed to hear him say the words.

"Yes, son, I'm Ezra. And you are my grandson."

"Why did you never reveal yourself until now?"

"This was a task you had to perform on your own because you wanted it, not because you felt an obligation. I could prod and prompt, but only you could make it happen."

"It was you who stood at the window and relived your final leap to death half a century ago."

"Oh, no. I was your vision, but on that other terrible night it wasn't a jump that caused my death."

"Your diary said you were being drawn to the Blue Room."

"And I wrote the truth. I wanted the solace I thought my fevered mind could find in that room with memories of Lizbeth. But the witch Moni couldn't bear to admit her defeat. She stole into the house and placed me under her trance. She led me to the Blue Room and told me our love bond would be sealed there."

"Then you didn't purposely climb those stairs to put an end to your misery?"

"No. I was powerless under her spell. She had once offered me true friendship; Moni now demanded my body and my soul for her taking. She boasted about her victory after years of waiting and how she had seen to it that my wife could no longer stand in her way. Even in my bewitched state, I couldn't allow such a profane act to take place in that room."

"Because it was a special place for you and Lizbeth."

"I would not permit her to desecrate the memory of your grandmother and insult all that Lizbeth and I had shared in that room. I struggled with the witch and stumbled through the windows. Tonight Moni has ironically plunged through those same windows and met her fate."

"Not a jump. It was a tragic accident." I could sense Myrtle's relief when she learned the truth of her father's tragic death. And to hear him refer to his wife as my grandmother gave new depth to the emotion I was feeling.

"Yes, son. My fall was an accident. The last sight I experienced alive on this earth was Moni frantically clutching, trying to stop my fall. Then I heard her scream in grief."

"Now I understand Tabetha's obsession with me when I did nothing to encourage her. It was her grandmother Moni M'weowe looking out through Tabetha's eyes and seeing you, the one person who she had truly loved."

"Yes, Greg. To the girl's confused mind, you *were* me."

"And what about you and me now, Ezra? There's so much I want to know. You can tell me about my family. I want to know you as my grandfather, an ancestor I didn't even know existed until tonight."

"That's not to be, son. I was granted the time to resolve my long years of anguish. Now my quest here is ended, thanks to you. I can go to my peace after all my torment and unrest."

"Wait. Tell me more. You can't just leave me. Not after what we've been through together."

"No, Greg. My stay here is at an end. You are the son I always wanted, and I am proud of all that you are. Cling to your wife and your mother who love you above all others. You surely have many happy years ahead."

"Please. Now that I've discovered you, stay with me, Ezra. Don't deny me the grandfather I'm just now beginning to know."

"It's not my choice to make, Greg. My work is done. I will always love my Lizbeth, my Punkin and my Sweet Tater. And now I've seen the fine young man who will carry on for me. Tell my daughters my love is forever. You are now my legacy in this world."

Before I could answer, the image faded and disappeared from view. I was once again alone in the silent room.

CHAPTER 41

I had the most wonderful news for Myrtle. Couldn't wait to tell her. Off to the second floor I dashed and hurled myself downward, scarcely touching the stairs on the way. When I stood outside their room, my heart was bursting with joy and unbridled relief.

"It's me. Greg. Open up."

No answer. I pictured Myrtle and Carl cowering in that bedroom, frightened by the strange sounds and horrific scream they must have heard. Imagined them huddled together in shock and agony behind that locked door, awaiting their fate. They didn't know if they would hear me coming to tell them we were safe, or would be greeted by a vengeful witch.

I pounded on the door and called out. "You can come out now. It's Greg." Still no reply.

Oh, god, I thought, please let them be alive. Could Tabetha have come to this room first? What if she had carried out the curse and slaughtered those dear people even before she descended on me?

Then I realized my mistake. The victory over the witches had so buoyed me that I had forgotten my own explicit instructions to the Roops. They were to lie low and open the door to no one but me. Even then, they would respond only if

I repeated the code. What had she told me to say when I came to their door?

Something warm rubbed against my leg, and I almost jumped out of my skin. I prepared to face another opponent. It was only Greta looking for attention. I lifted her into my arms.

Of course! That's it.

"Greta wants her milk," I intoned carefully for the gentle souls I prayed were alive and listening.

"G-g-greg?" Myrtle stammered. "Is it really you?"

"Yes, and Greta really does want her milk. She's right here with me." I patted the cat's furry head.

Heard heavy footsteps, and a relieved Carl Roop opened the door a tiny bit then swung it wide for me to come in.

"It's over, folks. The curse is lifted, and we can help Plenty return to normal."

Myrtle came running and folded me in her arms. "I'm so happy you're safe. I was terrified for you."

"Let's go down and put on the coffee pot," I said. "Have some very important news for you. I want you wide awake when you hear what I have to say."

I walked toward the kitchen with the Roops following close behind. Carl and I sat impatiently while Myrtle set to brewing our wakeup coffee.

Carl looked perplexed. "From the sound of things up there, I'd say the Blue Room is a mess. What or who are we going to find in there?"

"Actually it was a very clean exorcism, Carl. The Blue Room is as good as new. Maybe even better."

"What in hell were you doing one of them for? You a doctor? I know you're not a rabbi."

Myrtle scowled at him and said, "No, Carl. *Exorcism.*" She let go all her pent up tension, and the three of us shared our first light moment since my smart-mouthed crack about me in an apron. Carl laughed so hard he held his stomach.

When we had all finally regained our composure, I said to Myrtle, "I brought something back to you that you'll be happy to see." The scoot-booger was standing out of her view by one leg of my chair. I reached down and retrieved it; held it out for her to take.

Myrtle grasped the charm, and she clutched it to her breast. "Where did you find it?"

"The witch found it for me at a most inopportune time for her. She stumbled over it in the Blue Room while we were struggling for control of the knife that took her life."

Myrtle gasped at the picture my words must have evoked. Then she brightened. "It will *always* have a place of honor in my home." She stroked the treasured talisman.

"The spiritual embodiment of two ancestors who possessed the body of Tabetha lies out there on the lawn near the creek. It's the white wolf that attacked Myrtle. With it dead, both Blood Sky and Moni are gone forever. Unfortunately, Tabetha's body is out there, too."

Myrtle raised her hand to her mouth and clamped down hard.

Carl had become so attached to carrying his shotgun around for protection that he had unconsciously brought it down to the kitchen with him. He snatched it up and started for the kitchen door.

"This time I'm gonna blast that beast clear to hell with old Belchfire. I'm taking no chances there's a hint of life left in that shaggy sumbitch."

"Wait, Carl. We don't want to attract the lawmen up here. A shotgun blast would have them on us in a wink." He heard my warning and hesitated then set the gun down beside the door.

"Don't need this. Got something that'll do the job just as well."

Carl stepped out onto the porch. I watched him take the firewood ax from its block, pick up a shovel and head off toward the creek. He paused to look briefly at the girl's still form. Then he slid the shovel under the wolf's carcass and dragged it far away from her. Carl grasped the ax with both hands, swung it high above his head and began to vent his frustration and anger on the symbol of his torment. He chopped and diced, pounded and cursed, then shoveled the animal's remains down the slope. I didn't have the stomach to go any closer than the porch, but I was very sure there wasn't enough of the carcass left to recover for evidence. More importantly, I didn't want to see Tabetha up close ever again.

When at last his rage had subsided, Carl turned toward Tabetha, shucked his coat, bent down and placed it over her as if to protect her from the elements. Clearly the love remained for the child she had been to him until her madness had completely consumed her.

Carl returned to the kitchen, and I told the Roops what had transpired in the Blue Room. At first, I could sense that they were reliving every terrifying moment with me, and I felt guilty for putting them through that. But to ever be totally cleansed of the grime of the long-standing curse, they had to know everything. Not since I first arrived at the Comfy had they both shown the contentment their relieved expressions beamed when I had finished my story.

"I've saved the best news for last, Myrtle. My grandfather was in that room tonight."

"Whatever would your grandfather be doing here?" Myrtle asked.

"This was once his home. He revealed my own past to me tonight."

I smiled and waited for her to absorb my words. She looked puzzled then stared at Carl in utter disbelief. Finally, she ran to me. I lifted her off the floor and swung her round and round. When I set her down she spluttered, and her words came spilling out.

"Now I know why I felt the way I did about you, Greg. From the minute you stood dripping on my foyer carpet, I knew there was something special about you. Why, put some whiskers on your cheeks and lip and you're my Daddy all over again!"

"The likeness *is* amazing," I agreed.

"But . . . but that means. Oh, bless us all, that means . . ."

She swallowed me up in the circle of her arms. I glanced in Carl's direction, and his smile was positively radiant. He reached out and rubbed my head much as one might greet a youthful nephew.

"Yes, my dear Aunt Myrtle. My Mom is your Marietta, and she's alive and well."

"I have to see her. Let me go to her, Carl. Oh, take me to my Sweet Tater, please."

"You go with Greg. I'll look after the place," Carl said.

"We can't leave here in the middle of the night," I told her, "or I'd bundle up and go right now."

I knew we had to exercise extreme care after the tragic events Plenty had been through over the past twenty four hours. The patrolling policemen would be alert to any suspicious movements.

"Why can't we go now?" Myrtle asked.

"Because the police are going to want to know why anyone would leave town at this unusual hour. We'll have to wait until sunup and take your car. You drive, and I'll lie in the trunk until we're well down the road. They're not about to let a stranger get away before they wrap up their case against the girl."

"What do I tell them when they stop us?" she wanted to know.

"People have to eat, and Harmon had the only grocery store in the village. You're headed to Richwood for groceries to cook today's meals for your guests at the Comfy. How could they deny you that necessity? Carl should retrieve his coat and wait for the police to find Tabetha lying by the creek bank when they patrol this morning."

Carl asked, "What do I tell them when they come knocking and I'm the only one here?"

"You say that Myrtle and I went to Roanoke on an emergency, and you hand over the contact numbers I'll write down for you. They have their guilty party, a troubled young woman who committed at least two murders and then plunged the knife into her own heart in a final fit of madness and recrimination. Tell them her Shawnee name, Tabethki Scote, means Night Fire. She was the one who left the note at Harmon's and signed it with the name Night Fire. Tell them I'm not trying to elude them. Have no qualms about talking to the police; just can't stick around here and wait for them to let me go with my wife waiting in the hospital."

"Okay, it's settled then," Myrtle said. "We'll get up with the sun and have breakfast. As soon as we eat, we'll drive away. That would put us in Richwood when the farmers' market opens up, if that was where we were going."

* * *

Myrtle looked totally exhausted, and the day was just beginning. She had worked feverishly most of yesterday to prepare a mountain of Halloween goodies that now would go unused. Then the mental stress of her near miss with the wolf and the long tense evening locked in her bedroom had worn her down.

She told Carl, "If I'm going to be myself when I see Marietta, I have to get some sleep. She'll take one look at me and think I'm some crazy old shrew, not her sister." Myrtle sounded nervous, apprehensive, downright frightened now that the long-awaited reunion was so close. She had an inner glow, however, that filled the room.

"Mom's going to be thrilled, Myrtle. I'm excited for both of you."

"Well, I'm going back to bed until the sun comes up. Carl, don't you let me oversleep. Wake me at first light. I've waited all my life for this day to arrive." She trundled off to bed, and Carl and I went to the parlor.

"Counting on you to keep Myrtle together today, Greg. I swear, she's giddy as a teenager over your news. Does my heart good to see her so happy. Don't know what brought you to us, son, but it's wiped out five decades of grief for her. Thank God."

"Ezra Charlton deserves our thanks too, Uncle Carl."

He smiled, obviously liking his new title. But the furrowed brow that followed showed he was somewhat puzzled about my reference to Ezra. Well, the role my grandfather had played from the beginning was something only two people would ever understand, and one of those two had returned to the afterworld.

Carl yawned and rubbed his eyes. "May try for a couple winks myself. Myrtle's gonna have enough trouble sleeping as nervous as she is, so I'll just curl up over there on the couch. You stir me when it's time for me to wake Myrtle. She said first light."

As for me, there was no use trying to sleep in my pumped condition. I sat in the parlor with my laptop and a mug of coffee. Wrote about last night's climactic events. Worked through the quiet hours before dawn while both the stark terror and the jubilant triumph were both fresh in my mind. Even Carl's robust snoring couldn't distract me. Typed as fast as my fingers could track my racing mind. The words flew onto the computer screen.

Morning sun had barely peeked over Plenty's ridges when the parlor telephone rang. I immediately snatched it from its cradle.

"You had to be awake to answer that quickly," Doctor Jameson said.

"What's happened? This has to be about Sarah." I was petrified.

"Calm down, Greg. It's good news, my boy. The best. She's awake!"

Suddenly I was too choked up to speak. Sarah had fought her way back to me at last. My darling had returned, just as my intuition had told me she would, when the battle against the witches was over.

"Greg, are you there?" The doctor waited for my answer.

Tears were streaming down my face. I couldn't help myself. The dam had burst, and I wanted to wash away all the hurt, all the uncertainty. Before the day was over Sarah would be in my arms.

Finally I regained control, cleared my throat and replied.

"I'm here, doctor, but you can be sure I'll be *there* as soon as it's humanly possible."

"Good, I'm calling your Mom now. And someone wants to speak to you, Greg."

There was a moment of silence then my prayers were answered.

"Hi there, you big lug. Told you I'd be here for you and, sure enough, I'm back." Her voice was weak but it was the sweetest sound in the universe.

"I love you, Sarah. More than anything I want to be there with you. We're leaving right after sunup, so I'll see you very soon. Just behave, listen to the doctor and take it slow and easy, baby."

"I'll be waiting right here, Poet man. Remember we have something important to talk about."

Carl, awakened by the phone ringing, had apparently been listening to my side of the conversation. He sat up on the couch and asked, "Good news?"

"Couldn't be better, Carl. She's awake! I talked to Sarah, and she sounds great."

At that moment I could have run all the way to Roanoke under my own power, over mountains, through policemen, rainstorms and witches.

CHAPTER 42

Myrtle, Carl and I sat in the kitchen over a hasty light breakfast. Probably the first time in years Myrtle had spent so little time preparing a meal. We ate quietly. Guess everything we needed to say to each other had been said during the frantic minutes before dawn.

While Carl and I were finishing our coffee, Myrtle busied herself tidying the kitchen. Carl assured her she didn't need to worry about any guests that may show up while she was away. He'd learned a trick or two watching her in the kitchen, so he could keep them fed for the couple days she was gone. Wouldn't be on the level of Chef Roop's cooking, but they'd manage.

She put away the last plate and stowed the frying pan. "When I get back, Carl," she told him, "I'll bring Sweet Tater for you to meet. After all these years I'll have my two most special people together with me." Tears welled up again. Myrtle began to sniff.

Carl went to her and held her in the circle of his big arms. "Now don't you start that, Myrtle. You'll get us both going, and you don't want Greg to have to watch a grown man cry."

She broke into a nervous giggle and touched his cheek.

"That's better," he told her. "This is a special, happy day. I want to see you smile."

I felt renewed with the curse broken and Sarah awake and waiting for me. Couldn't fathom what may be going through Carl's mind, but I knew exactly where Myrtle's thoughts had to be this sunny morning. She was totally immersed in putting fifty years of frustration and disappointment behind her. In a matter of hours she would see her beloved little sister. When that moment arrived, I was going to be overjoyed to see my Mom and her adoring big sister reunited.

While Myrtle finished packing and gave her last minute instructions to Carl, I brought her car around to the side of the house toward the kitchen to shield it from view. Transferred my bags and waited for Myrtle to appear in the kitchen doorway. There was no sign of the roving policemen, but this was no time to take a chance. I was perfectly happy for them to have all the information they needed from Carl, when they asked, to find me in Roanoke. However, no one, including the law, was going to keep me from my beautiful Sarah now that she was awake.

Carl and Myrtle walked toward the car, and we all carefully avoided looking in the direction of the covered body near the stream bed.

I did offer a reminder to Carl. "Don't forget your coat." He nodded.

As we had agreed, Myrtle was prepared to cast this as a routine shopping run for groceries in Richwood. She carefully draped towels over the top of a box and deposited it on the floor in the rear. Smiled at me and said, "Family mementos and photographs to share with Sweet Tater." Despite her attempt to stay calm, I could tell she was as nervous as a kitten about her upcoming reunion with Mom. Could only guess how thrilling it would be for them, but I knew how excited I was for two of the sweetest people in my life to be rediscovering each other.

"Remember we have an important stop to make on Route 39," I cautioned. "Let me ride in the trunk until then."

"Leave it to me," Myrtle replied. "I'll try not to jostle you too much." She smiled and followed me to the rear of her car.

"See you shortly, aunt of mine. Don't let me freeze back here."

I popped the lid. Stared at what would quickly become a small, dark space inside. Reflected that it was a good thing for me Carl had an older sedan with a big trunk. Those suitcases and I were going to be a snug fit as it was.

I took one last look at the Comfy before settling into the trunk. There had been some long and troubling nights for me in that big old mansion. Now, in the light of a new day, it no longer looked foreboding. This was the home of my grandfather, and I wanted to know everything about that kind and tragic man. The two of us had shared an adventure no other living human could ever appreciate; one that I was still working hard to comprehend.

"Time for me to do my disappearing act," I told Carl and began to fold my frame into the car's trunk.

Made me feel akin to Clark Kent dashing into his telephone booth. Except for the cloak and x-ray vision, I hoped to emerge as Sarah's Superman rushing to reclaim her from her terrifying life suspension.

Carl closed the trunk lid, and I suddenly felt very confined and terribly alone.

Heard Myrtle reassure Carl as he saw her into the front seat. "We'll be down the road in a jiffy, and I'll get him out of there. I brought along a thermos of coffee and lots of goodies to warm him up."

"Just turn on your charm, Myrtle, with the policemen," he told her, "and you'll be fine."

I hunkered down and resigned myself to a cramped, bumpy ride. Now if she could pull off our exit without tipping the deputies, we'd be on our way. That part worried me due to the extreme case of nerves she'd shown ever since the sun came up.

* * *

"Morning, ma'am. Mrs. Roop, is it?" the policeman asked when he stopped the car.

"That's right. From up there on the hill. The Comfy Bed and Breakfast."

"Can I ask where you're going this morning?"

"Well, with Harmon Grace's place shut down, I'm a little strapped for some necessities for my kitchen. Could be some starving people up there if I don't lay in supplies. I don't remember your face, officer. Have you ever had one of my suppers at the Comfy?"

She was doing fine for openers. I crossed my fingers and rooted for her to maintain her cool.

"No, ma'am, but I understand you do have quite a reputation for your cooking. Maybe I'll get up there soon."

"I'd love to have you. Nothing I like better than feeding newcomers. Right now I have to hurry on down to the Richwood markets and restock the larder. Can't have any guests drop in and go hungry at my place. Reputations have to be constantly re-earned to last, you know."

"How many guests there today, Mrs. Roop? We don't want to miss talking to anyone."

"Just a few. You already met one of them at the house. A charming young man. We expect a new crowd to show up any time now from the snow slopes."

"Okay, Mrs. Roop, go ahead. I'd appreciate it if you didn't discuss what's going on down here with anyone from out of town. The situation is under control. We'll have everything taken care of real soon. Last thing we need is gawkers and the curious cluttering up Plenty."

"I wouldn't breathe a word, officer. Lord knows, we like our privacy. You have a nice day."

I nearly laughed out loud. Caught myself and stifled in time. Sure, they were in control! I had given Carl the information to hand them Wes and Harmon's killer, and they had her note confessing to other killings that could be traced back to the common clue—a wolf's tooth. The contents of Dillard Westerly's old cigar box would attest to that. There wasn't anybody to arrest for either of the most recent crimes with Tabetha dead unless they wanted to jail a very badly mangled wolf carcass. Considering the truth behind these murders, I couldn't imagine the sheriff coming to the proper conclusion for fear of being considered a bit off center. The headline would read something like "Pocahontas County Sheriff Says Killings in Plenty Responsibility of Witches". Right. After that he could find himself another occupation before the next election. Once the investigation was over, they would no doubt portray the multiple murders as the tragic results of a long vendetta by a wretched old woman and her insane granddaughter. They would avoid mentioning the word witch. Come to think of it, that may be all there was to the story, anyway. There was still the strong possibility that my own vivid imagination had manufactured the rest. The legend of Plenty would finally be laid to rest along with Tabetha and the silver wolf.

Step one passed with honors, Aunt Myrtle. Now please, please hurry and get me out of this dark, cold trunk and pour some hot coffee in me.

We headed out toward the main road. Myrtle hummed to herself, probably as a hedge against nerves. The melody was that same old hymn I'd whistled what seemed like a lifetime ago.

Just keep it together, I pled silently. *We're in good shape now.*

CHAPTER 43

A few minutes later I felt the car slow and turn. She had found the lane off Route 39. At last, with my legs beginning to ache for stretching room, she slowed to a stop and released the trunk lid. We were in the lane between the rows of pines, and it was time for me to unfold. I carefully crawled out of my space, stood stiffly and tested my legs. Myrtle poured from the thermos; greeted me with a steaming cup of brew and a warm smile.

"Drink this down, Greg. You must feel like an icicle by now."

"Myrtle, you are amazing. Charmed that cop like a professional con artist." I eagerly took the cup and warmed my hands and insides.

Bear met us as we started toward the cabin. Wagged his tail in greeting to an old friend, and sniffed the air near Myrtle. Apparently satisfied that we came in peace, he nudged my leg and panted. I patted his side as I reached out to take Myrtle's hand. We followed the big dog down the path toward Chief John's cabin. I was growing a bit concerned that the chief hadn't come out by now to greet us. My main purpose in stopping was to be sure no harm had come to him for giving me information for my defiance of the witches.

I hurried along worrying for his safety. Tabetha, at the height of her dizzying dance in the Blue Room, had made a chilling prediction. She said his reward for defying her would be *a sickness unto death.* I said a silent prayer that she was wrong, that I had defeated her in time.

Just as I was about to reach for the cabin door, Bear ran past the house in the direction of the creek. I circled around the cabin and saw Chief John, in full regalia, crossing the footbridge toward home. The blanket and spear told me he had likely just descended from a session on the hilltop rock. He thrust one hand high into the air to acknowledge our presence then proceeded at a measured pace toward us.

The chief took one look at Myrtle and said, "Greetings, daughter of my friend Ezra. I see our young warrior has told you his news." He smiled at her with pearly white teeth; invited us in and poured tea. Bear sat with his nose against the old man's foot, waiting, as we were, for his counsel.

"The young witch is dead, Chief John."

"I know, Gregory. Much has happened since last we met. I saw the mortal conflict you bravely faced and won. There was much power aligned against you, but it is now no more. Night Fire no longer breathes her hatred and deceit, the Silver Wolf is vanquished and Blood Sky has returned to the depths from which she came. You are a brave, steadfast warrior, Gregory Bain."

If he only knew how terrified I had been last night, he would have used a different term. Concern for my wife was my driving force to overcome the intense fear. Pure stubbornness fueled my actions because I refused to let the witches win. But Greg Bain could never be accused of being a brave warrior!

"Tabetha told me she would do you harm, Chief. I had to know you were well."

"The witches hated me for defying their evil power, son. They sought to sweep aside all who would stand in their way. A sudden illness came over me before the last sunset, and I wondered if somehow my food had been poisoned. My strength waned; my own medicine was severely tested by three powerful spirits who set themselves against me as one. I somehow made my way to the top of the hill, and my mind's eye saw you when you claimed your final victory over the evil ones. A great peace descended over me, my fever broke and I remained on the rock until now in a deep, restful slumber."

Myrtle stood transfixed as if overcome by the aura of strength and wisdom the chief radiated.

I told Chief John, "Tabetha said that Blood Sky and Moni had passed away, and that they had willed their wickedness into Tabetha's body. She was strong and determined, felt invincible with their spirits to bolster her."

"I know, Gregory. You fought valiantly. You lifted my sickness by overcoming her witchcraft. I am grateful to you for my life." He pushed his upraised arm toward me, palm out, and again issued the open hand salute.

"With your wise counsel I succeeded, Chief John."

The chief continued. "My old friend Ezra Charlton appeared in my visions; I know it was he who guided you through your troubled times. We were childhood friends with a special bond between us." He looked at Myrtle and smiled.

"Then you know I'm his grandson." I said.

"There could be no doubt. I saw him in you when we met. You are a fitting legacy for a kind man who suffered at the hands of those evil women. They shamed the proud traditions of my fellow Shawnee with their vile medicine, and we are well rid of them."

Bear got up on his haunches and scooted over to rest his nose on my foot. I scratched his ear. Bear licked my shoe. Chief John looked at him and grinned with amusement

"You've shown me the answers to so many questions, Chief John. Solve one more mystery for me." I looked down at the dog and chuckled. "How in the world did he ever get the name Bear?"

"I called him simply dog until he proved his bravery. That yellow dog is a warrior. He found a man in the woods being mauled by a black bear and attacked the beast. He bit and ripped at the bear's heels until it released the man and ran away. I gave him the name Bear Chaser that day and have called him Bear ever since."

"Did the man survive?"

"You met him. It was Dillard Westerly. He stayed in my cabin for many days and nights raving and telling tales while I treated him with my medicines. At length he overcame his injuries and his fever."

That could answer a number of my unasked questions, but I decided to leave the subject and the questions alone for the present. Only one important matter remained.

"Can we be sure the witches are gone for good and that the curse is broken, chief?"

"It is finished. They are done; the cloud is forever lifted." He rose and saw us to the door.

* * *

Soon I had taken over the driving duties for Myrtle, and we were well down the road toward Roanoke. She was becoming more excited by the minute knowing that her all-important reunion was drawing nearer. We talked almost non-stop while we munched on the sandwiches and Halloween goodies she had brought along. She didn't want any food stops to delay her first glimpse in fifty years of the little sister she so adored. I did finally persuade her that a rest stop for gas and my full bladder may be in our best interest. I'm convinced she agreed strictly for my health benefit because she was so hyped at this stage she probably could have pushed the car to Roanoke, fuel or no fuel. Myrtle was like a little kid on Christmas Eve. Soon she would receive the best present she had ever been given.

After a long silence she asked me, "Did you even suspect there was a family connection before Daddy appeared and told you, Greg?"

"There were lots of little things I kept picking up on, but it wouldn't quite come together. The chinquapins and gooseberry pie took me back to a jump rope ditty my sister knew."

"I know the one. Chinkypins, crabapples . . ." Myrtle sang.

"That's it. Beth couldn't remember where she learned it. She thought Mom may have taught her."

"It was Marietta's favorite. She tried so hard to skip rope with her short little legs. Just had to imitate the bigger girls."

"Mom had a nickname for me when I was small, Myrtle, and she still uses it at times. Tater. Sound familiar?"

"Why didn't you say something to me sooner, Greg?"

"Because my mind was in overload with so much else going on. Most of all, I didn't want to hold out any false hopes until I was certain. Then when you showed me the family photo the truth was obvious. I could have been Ezra in that picture; I remember when Mom looked exactly like Grandma. My search over in Radford confirmed that a little girl had been found on New Years Day. Wes admitted he caught up with Moni and Marietta, but the child had disappeared. The newspaper account confirmed that she had been sent to live at the Baptist Children's Home in Salem. Mom never kept it secret from Beth and me that the Adamses had adopted her as a young girl. They were the only parents she could remember. Gramps had later told me how they fell in love with a beautiful child at the Baptist Home where she had been sent as a foundling. The Adamses adopted that little girl, and she grew up to be my Mom. The clincher was Ezra telling me I'm his grandson and his legacy. His words were too real to be just my imagination."

It sounded strange to think of Elizabeth Charlton as my grandmother, but I no longer had difficulty accepting that I was lucky enough to have been granted three sets of grandparents.

"Myrtle, you need to know that Ezra told me something else about his last trip to the Blue Room. He didn't take his own life."

Her eyes instantly sparkled when my words sank in. It was as if the last dark cloud had been lifted.

"Oh, I want so desperately to believe that, Greg. He was such a good man. All these years I've despaired that his soul was lost when he took his life that Halloween night."

"He told me how Moni entranced him and led him up those stairs. She wanted to have her way in your mother's own room in defiance of her memory. Ezra fought to defend the sanctity of Lizbeth's love, but he stumbled and fell through the window. His death was accidental."

She stared out into the glare of the morning sun, and a tear rolled down her cheek.

"Thank you, my dear Greg. Now you've given me back both my Marietta *and* my Daddy. I love you for that."

For the longest while we didn't speak at all. Myrtle was lost in her thoughts and her memories. Once I heard her again humming that old familiar hymn *farther along we'll understand why.*

At length she turned to me and said, "Daddy would have been proud of you, Greg."

"He told me he was proud, and that made it all worthwhile. He also said he was grateful to me for bringing him the peace that had eluded him for so long. Ezra Charlton saved my hide when the chips were down. I want to know more about him, Myrtle."

That was an invitation to talk about one of her favorite subjects, the father she had always idolized. I was transported by her words back to her childhood and the happiness the Charltons had enjoyed before Moni launched her vendetta. The picture Myrtle painted was one of care and devotion by loving parents. It also told me why fragments of those memories were forever imprinted in the thoughts of that two-year old baby who grew up to be my Mom.

CHAPTER 44

My long journey was almost over. I had traveled full circle by way of the Comfy Bed and Breakfast and a half-century of history. Twice in the past hour I had made quick stops at Myrtle's insistence that she needed 'the little girls' room'. She was a bundle of nerves. At last we drove into the parking lot at Roanoke Memorial Hospital.

"Let's hurry up and get inside, Greg. I need to make a stop."

Her excitement and anticipation would soon end, and she and Mom could have the rest of their lives to recapture those early years. I hoped they would salvage some of the missed memories they could have shared. And my sweet Sarah was up there waiting for me. Myrtle certainly wasn't the only one with a case of the nervous jitters.

When I rushed into her room, Sarah was sitting up in bed looking her beautiful self once more. All of the machines and tubes were gone, and she was smiling at me as if she had just finished a refreshing nap. I don't remember walking across the room—maybe I just levitated. I do remember most vividly the instant we were wrapped in each other's arms and I was kissing her.

"There's my Poet. *I could hardly wait for you to be here, honey.*"

Her words from my dream echoed once again, but this time it was real. Oh, you bet it was real!

"Twinkle Toes, you had us so worried. Just talk to me, and let me hear your voice."

"Your Mom has been here with me every minute since I woke up until about two minutes ago. She's been such a comfort to me."

"Don't tell me she's left. I have a huge surprise for her."

"Oh, she's just down the hall. Should be back any second."

As she finished her statement, I saw Mom round the corner and come through the door. Myrtle had been hanging back to allow Sarah and me a moment alone. Now she stepped forward. Mom turned to face her. I've never seen such instant joy and love on any face as Myrtle showed when she looked directly into Mom's eyes.

Mom stared at her then at me. She was puzzled, but something was getting through, some long forgotten connection was seeping back into her head.

Myrtle was the first to speak. "Marietta. Sweet Tater. It's Myrtle, honey. It's Punkin."

I could almost feel the bits of times remembered reassembling and the sights and sounds, no longer suppressed, rushing back. Mom emerged from her frozen shock. The walls of time crumbled under the sheer force of sister love.

"P-punkin? Yes, my Punkin!"

She flew into Myrtle's arms, and they were lost in erasing fifty years of denial of the strong bond they had always shared. Sarah stared at me like she was wondering what she had missed. When their tears of joy had subsided, Mom and Myrtle clung to each other and beamed. I took both of them by the hand to bring them to Sarah's side.

"Sweetie, I want you to meet my aunt, Myrtle Roop. She owns the Plenty Comfy Bed and Breakfast. She's Mom's big sister. Mom's given name was Marietta Charlton."

Sarah motioned for both of them to let her hug them, and she whispered to Mom, "Marietta. What a beautiful name."

The doctor had slipped quietly into the room during the reunion.

"I see our girl is doing wonderfully well. As soon as we get a couple of normal meals in her, I'm going to let you take her home. This whole episode is still baffling to me, but, with all our medical knowledge, some things are just beyond us."

"Doc," I said, "I know exactly what was wrong with her, and I know how she was cured. It defies all the medical science you know, and I couldn't explain it to you, or to myself, in a hundred years. Just accept it, and please accept my thanks for your vigil when Sarah needed you."

Doctor Jameson shook my hand. He turned to leave. He looked directly at Sarah, and I felt a silent signal pass between them. Mom gave him a head nod then stepped closer to the bed.

"Sis and I have a lifetime of catching up to do, Greg, and you two need some time alone. We'll be at my house." They walked hand in hand into the hallway where Mom introduced Myrtle to the doctor as her big sister and shared her jubilation with him.

Sarah patted the bed for me to sit by her side. She assumed an alarmingly serious look as she took my hand. There was something going on here that I didn't understand, and I was uneasy about it. Sarah, Mom and the doctor had been sharing a private matter, but I wasn't yet a party to their secret.

I began fearfully, "Before I blew my return in that rain storm, Sarah, you told me we had a serious matter to discuss. It's been driving me up the wall ever since. Can we talk about it now?"

She broke into a positively radiant beam that melted away the fear I was feeling.

"Greg, honey, I have the most wonderful news. I'm going to have a baby."

Her amused expression told me I must have totally disassembled when her words sank in. All I could hear was a voice faintly resembling my own saying something like, "Ba—*glurp*—*baby?*"

"I found out soon after you left on your trip. I wanted so to tell you, but it had to be face to face. Then my coma ruined my plans for a celebration."

"I love you, Sarah, and I love our baby." I leaned over and kissed her where our child was growing.

"The day I came to the hospital, I swore Mom and the doctor to secrecy," she said. "Under no circumstances were they to tell you I was pregnant. We didn't know yet what had caused my sudden fever, and I didn't want you worrying about the extra complication of my pregnancy. Then I sank into that frightening coma. The only other person I told was Julie. At least I tried to tell her when she sat by my side. She had her beautiful little Jason, and I told her that now it was *my turn*."

That's what Julie heard. Sarah wanted her to know she was having a baby!

"So you knew Julie was here."

"I've known all along that you and your Mom were standing by me, too. Tried so hard to talk to you, to get through the wall that witch had built."

"Then you were aware the witch was behind your coma?"

"I only knew that something sinister was holding me against my will. After you sat with me and told me about the strange circumstances in Plenty, I imagined all sorts of demons pursuing the man I love. I felt helpless to rescue you. Fought them so hard, Greg. There was a horrid witch in my nightmares who was pulling you away from me. I told her over and over that you were *mine, mine* and she couldn't have you. Screamed at her to let go of you, but she just answered me with an insane laugh."

I took her into my arms and held her until she calmed.

"Shush. It's all over now, and I have you back. Sarah, tell me the baby is all right."

"Doc says there was never any danger to our baby."

That sounded so fantastic—our baby.

"This gives me another important reason to be close to you and not on the road. Haven't told you about the job."

"When you were talking to me, I heard you trying to explain about a job, but it wasn't clear. You didn't quit your job, did you?"

"Not until I had a new one. You remember when we went to Blacksburg, and I interviewed for the coaching position? Coach Carter called me with a job offer. Sarah, honey, I accepted. Now I'll be at home every night if you can stand that much togetherness."

"Oh, I can stand it. Welcome home, honey. Now tell me about your adventures in West Virginia."

"That can wait. We have lots of time to hash out the crazy things I've been going through. I wanted you to be the editor and critic for my book that explains everything. As much as I've poured my heart and soul into that book, though, it may never be finished. May be best to let sleeping dogs lie—or wolves, in this case."

"But you've been so intent on telling this story. If there were two things that came through clearly on all those days and nights when you stayed by me and talked, they were your love for me and your excitement over writing a first novel. Why stop now?"

"The authorities have a perfectly logical explanation for everything that happened in Plenty over the past fifty years, Sarah. Two insane women used their knowledge of spells and drugs to carry out their wretched curse, and they're both dead. Maybe it's best I leave it at that. I know there are powers at work that we can't begin to understand. The Shawnee shaman Chief John has abilities one can only believe by listening and observing him. He may have learned important facts from Wes while the sheriff was in his cabin feverishly raving after the bear attack. But his visions seemed too real, too vivid and prophetic to be a guess or a ruse. The timing of your coma also seems entirely too convenient to be coincidental. Somehow my grandfather, Ezra Charlton, communicated with me so we could defeat the witches."

My words were coming so fast and so disjointed that Sarah lay there overwhelmed. I could see she was wondering what in blazes I was jabbering about, but I had to get it all out. We'd make sense of it later.

"Sarah, I would swear to anyone that the sky turned fiery red on Halloween night, and the snow went from white to scarlet. Even that could have been my confused mind playing tricks on me. Whether *any* of this was real or only my imagination doesn't matter now. What *does* matter is that the ordeal is over for both of us. I'll be glad to tell the sheriff most of what I've put together about the deaths in Plenty, but no one except Ezra and I need to know what led up to the showdown in the Blue Room on Halloween night."

She put her arms around my neck and held on. Then she spoke softly.

"We have a lifetime to sort it all out, Greg. In time, you'll understand. Let me make a request."

"Anything your heart desires, Sarah."

"If our baby is a girl, I have the perfect name for her. Your Mom has been such an influence in my life and so much support to me, I'd love to give our daughter both of her names—Marietta Ruth."

"Nothing would make me happier, but what if the baby is a boy?"

"Then we'll just keep trying for a little sister—every night!"

I held her close to me and gave thanks that I was home, and my days of dread and breakfast were over.

BVG